LETHAL VENGEANCE

STELLA BRIE

COPYRIGHT

Cover Design: JV Arts (Just Venture Arts)

Editing: Kaye Kemp Book Polishing

❀ Created with Vellum

Playlist

"In My Blood" - The Score

"Dangerous" - Royal Deluxe

"Fire to the Night" - Native 51

"Even If It Hurts" - Sam Tinnesz

"Speak of the Strong" - The Score and

Magic Whatever

"Shadow" - Icon for Hire

"One Last Breath" - Tommee Profitt

"All I Feel Is You" - The Broken View

"Nothing Left To Say" - Imagine Dragons

"Lover. Fighter." - SRVCINA

"From The Ashes" - ILLENIUM & Skylar Grey

"Whataya Want From Me' (Remix)" - Adam Lambert

& PINK

Playlists for all my books can be found on youtube

@authorstellabrie

AUTHOR'S NOTE

This book is a Why Choose romance, which means the heroine does not have to choose between male interests. The book is a spin-off from The Savages Series but can be read as a standalone.

Please note—this book contains references to human trafficking that may be difficult for some readers. It also contains death, sex, graphic violence, and cursing. Please take care of yourself and read at your own discretion. Recommended for 18+ due to mature content.

VENGEANCE

Become the darkness to find your strength.
Embrace it. Wield it. Own it.
Make peace with it.
It's yours, forever.

VENGEANCE IS
THE NAME YOUR SOUL SCREAMS
WHEN IT SHATTERS

1

QUINN

The sparkling blue water of the lake laps gently onto the shore, lending a peaceful, rhythmic sound to the still air. Only to be shattered a second later by the infectious sound of children screaming and laughing on the swings behind me. I sigh and shift restlessly on the hard bench. It's a beautiful place for two killers to meet.

Lifting my face toward the warm sun, my eyelids drift to half-mast while I covertly survey the people around me knowing he won't be alone. Sifting through the potential options, I quickly dismiss most of them. Two men stand out. The nervous-looking one standing by the edge of the lake who glances in my direction every two minutes on the dot, and the jogger who's been stretching his hamstring three benches down from mine for the last fifteen minutes. A prickling sensation on the back of my neck tells me there is a third behind me, but I don't turn around.

Noon brings an influx of people desperate to take advantage of the cooler April temps. Workers from nearby office buildings plop down at picnic tables to eat their lunch. Their chatter and laughter automatically shift the atmosphere in the park from serene to lively.

Mimicking those around me, I pull a sandwich from the brown bag on my lap, unwrap it, and pretend to take a small bite. My mouth moves in a chewing motion while I discreetly pinch off a piece and drop it on the ground. A simple charade to blend in with the crowd.

I glance at my watch. Five minutes.

It's our first in-person meeting. For the last year, job details have been delivered via a series of messages and men. Small at first, they progressively scaled in both difficulty and risk until I proved myself capable of handling anything and everything—all for a chance to get closer to him.

My body quivers, and a tiny jerk escapes. Coiled like a spring, my muscles tense in anticipation of being inches away from him. All the options for a quick strike and kill run through my mind like an action flick. My fingers flex. My breathing picks up. The sun gets hotter. My jaw locks rebelliously. Head and body war with each other for a few precious seconds while I try to shove the murderous need down into the deepest part of me.

A quick death isn't the answer. Sophia is counting on you to give her peace, I remind myself.

A bead of sweat rolls down my face. But when I reach up to swipe it away, the past collides with the present.

I raise my hand to wipe the wetness from my cheek, but the Texas air is thick and dry, stealing the tears before they can fall very far. My black dress clings to the sweat on my body, but for me, the heat is a distant thing. Ice coats my insides until I'm almost numb.

The white casket in front of me, draped with a bounty of yellow roses, contains my beautiful mother. Sixteen, and both my parents are dead. I'm officially an orphan. I glance at my stepfather, Roberto, the man crying beside me, and wonder when God will decide to take him, too.

Tiny fingers grip mine, and I look down at my favorite person in the whole world… my sister, Sophia.

"Who's going to take care of me, Quinn?" she asks, her bottom lip quivering.

"Me. And your dad," I state firmly.

"Promise?" Her dark brown eyes search mine for reassurance.

"I'll always take care of you. Promise," I reply, holding my pinky out for her to hook with hers.

The memory fades to nothing, like a broken promise.

I breathe in for a few seconds, then slowly exhale to the same count. Inhale. Exhale. False moves will only scare my prey away. A mutilated body swims up from the depths of my memory, and I smile in satisfaction. That's the fate my enemy deserves—the same brutal death I gave to his brother.

A glint catches my eye, and I swiftly turn my head to the right to search for the source, but I don't see anything. Tensing, I scan the people on the path. Another quick flash, and I zero in on it… and breathe a huge sigh of relief. It's not a gun or a knife aimed at me, but a watch glinting in the sun.

A man in a white suit is leisurely strolling down the park path, licking an ice cream cone. Every time he raises his arm to his mouth, the sun catches on the gold watch circling his wrist.

Tall, dark, and handsome. Wealthy too, judging by the custom-tailored cut of his spring suit. The epitome of casual elegance. He pauses to flash a brilliant smile at the beautiful woman walking past him. She slows in response. Admiration crinkles the corners of his eyes, but he doesn't stop. His long legs continue to eat up the distance between us. A charade. One he's perfected for years.

His tongue darts out and licks the ice cream cone in his hand, bringing my gaze to his handsome face. Close enough to see his eyes, I watch their dark depths flick toward me. He murmurs something to the man next to him, then moves to take the seat beside me.

Armando Morales waves a hand toward the water. "Such a beautiful spot, is it not?"

I lift my hand and take a bite of my neglected sandwich, which lost its flavor hours ago. "Beautiful." The flat tone of my voice gives little away.

The slight stiffening of his body is the only indication of his irritation. "Quinn Jones. Or is it Quinn Smith this week? Who needs last names, right?" He chuckles. "I'd heard you were all business. While it's a sentiment I echo most of the time, I implore you to think of how much more you can accomplish with some manners." His voice is hard when he delivers his warning.

I say nothing. It's all I can do to keep myself contained during this first meeting.

He gives a strained chuckle and studies me for a minute. "My men provided me with pictures and detailed reports on you. Beautiful, but cold. Hard. Business focused, with little personal life. Intelligent with an ability to think fast on your feet. I'm happy to see it's all true." He pauses. "What they failed to mention is the fire inside you. Even now, I feel the edge of its burn. Maybe they didn't notice. Is it ambition? I hope so, but I guess time will tell."

More perceptive than his brother.

Thinking fast, I decide to go with the ambitious thread and give him a firm nod. "The organization funnels quite a lot of business through this area, and I want to establish myself as a major player. With my extensive contacts and resources north of the border, I'm able to provide what others can't. Which means the potential profit margin is astronomical." I wait to see if that solves the concern I hear in his voice.

He gives a satisfied smile. "For the last year, you've successfully delivered on every job I've given you and exhibited remarkable discretion. Both are traits I need for the next job. It's more... delicate. If you succeed, I'll help you get established as a trusted partner for the organization. If you fail, I'll give you to Rodrigo." His right-hand man and the ultimate threat.

Lean brown fingers casually brush a crumb off his trousers.

I almost smile in satisfaction. This is it—the moment I've been waiting for—an opportunity to get closer to him and his operations.

"I'm listening," I murmur, unwilling to give him the slightest indication of interest. I lift my drink and take a sip while I wait to hear the details of the sins I must commit to stay in the good graces of hell.

"My twin brother, Julio, God rest his soul, expanded our business a few years ago," he begins. "Until that time, we'd been exclusive suppliers of general laborers—individuals necessary for farms and other large operations. At an organizational meeting, he realized the real money was in a more specialized laborer. Unfortunately, it's an incredibly competitive market, and nobody was willing to share their knowledge." He sighs.

After another lick of his cone, he continues. "My brother, eager to prove we could compete in this space, didn't realize how much due diligence is necessary to make sure we obtain the *right* merchandise. As a result, mistakes were made. Big ones. I took care of one mistake a couple of years ago, but I just learned we have another potentially explosive situation on our hands."

My breath stutters and stops. *Mistake*, I silently repeat, rage filling every crevice of my mind. My fingers tighten on the cup in my hand, and I carefully set it down beside the bench before I crush it in my anger. Grinding my teeth, I stare desperately at the water, trying to find the calm to continue this conversation without killing him, but it does nothing. Furious, I slam all the doors in my mind shut until every emotional thought is blocked.

Thankfully, he takes my silence in stride. "We picked up the sister of a Chicago *family* by mistake, a close-knit Sicilian family, and her friend, who happens to be the heir to a wealthy developer out of Miami. If you could help me get them back to their families, I'll be in your debt. There are a few catches, of course."

Relief brings back the calm I'd been desperately searching for the last couple of minutes. He wants me to *save* them.

Practical options and scenarios swim in my brain. "Of course," I finally get out. "What are the terms?"

He raises a finger. "Absolutely no one can know. You'll be on your own. If you're caught, I'll deny everything," he states firmly before raising a second finger. "No law enforcement. I know you have contacts on both sides, but it needs to be an off-books type of rescue. And third, only those two girls. Do not attempt to rescue any others. I've removed them from the general population and assigned them a caregiver. Most of my men think they were sold."

"What about Rodrigo?" I ask about his right-hand man, a psycho with torturous tendencies. Pot. Kettle, I guess, but whatever. He's a strong adversary.

"He cannot know about this," he emphasizes. "Rodrigo's loyalty is to the organization first. Always. They would likely send him to eliminate me and the girls. Mistakes aren't tolerated. You should remember that rule."

I dip my chin in acknowledgement of his warning.

He taps the bench. "I'll either arrange to meet you here or will tape a note to the bottom. Check it every Sunday. I usually come here on Wednesdays and Saturdays."

"This sounds like a headache," I say dismissively.

He chuckles. "It will be, but you'll be well compensated. I'll pay all expenses and triple your current fee, and if you're up for it, I'll put you in charge of procurement for our more specialized operations." He flashes me a smug smile, knowing the true carrot is the extremely lucrative job of finding girls for his sex trafficking operations.

In my wildest dreams, I couldn't have asked for a better reward. I smile.

The job might have been presented as a request, but declining isn't an option. "I'll reach out to a few contacts and find a team for the extraction," I inform him, indicating my agreement of the terms. "I'll need information on the location, guard rotations, security systems, and so forth. It's Wednesday, but I should be able to get a good start on this by Saturday. Same place and time?" I throw my partially eaten sandwich into the paper bag and pick up the cup. When he nods his agreement, I leave him there licking his ice cream cone.

BY SATURDAY, I'VE MADE A MILLION PLANS, BUT HE ONLY NEEDS TO know a few details. When I get to the park, he's sitting on the bench waiting for me. The running shorts and a sleeveless shirt throw me for a second. In all my surveillance, I'd rarely caught him in anything but a suit.

Sliding onto the seat beside him, I set my large bag on the bench between us. "Good morning." After the last meeting, I was able to gain a little perspective and equilibrium. Obviously, manners are important to him and using them benefits me.

He tilts his head and smiles at the words. "Good morning." Dark brown eyes flick over my attire and bag, then narrow with suspicion. "Yoga class?"

I shrug. "I needed an excuse to come to this side of town on a regular basis. There's a yoga studio across from the park's entrance. You're looking at its newest member."

He relaxes. "Update?"

Picking up my phone, I scroll mindlessly through social media while I relay the information. "They'll touch down in two weeks. Once here, they can assess the situation and determine a timeframe for removal, but likely within a week or two."

A dramatic, disappointed sigh fills the air. "Too long. Find someone else," he orders.

I shake my head. "Not too many are keen to take on a rescue of this nature. If something goes wrong, it's their neck on the line with the families. Most of the groups I approached demanded to meet with you as added insurance."

His silence and anger are expected, but it's tough holding on to my patience. "The Santos Foundation is one of the best. Recommended by all my contacts. They understand the need for secrecy, and their only requirement is the victim's innocence." I shrug. "But they're on another job right now. It's either them or you need to find your own team."

I hold my breath while he contemplates my words. Out of all the references my contacts sent me, this is the only group I trust to accomplish the task successfully. Every report I received on them reinforced my opinion of their competency and underlying integrity. Good guys or bad guys, it doesn't matter, only their code matters, and reports state it's solid.

He dips his chin in a sharp nod. "I'll move the girls to a different facility and give them new identities, which will buy us some time. I want to know when they land." With a subtle shift, he straightens and drops a flash drive into my purse.

I rush into my other news before he can leave. "When I left Wednesday, I saw Rodrigo at the entrance to the park. He recognized me. Maybe you should assign another job to me and ask him to deliver the details. A distraction. I won't be successful if he starts following me around all the time."

He stands and studies my face. Reaching back, he grabs his foot to stretch his quadriceps. Dropping it, he lifts the other.

I stare at the muscular leg in front of me. Cut, with hard lines and a smattering of dark hair. I'm sure many women would find his legs attractive. But I'm only interested in the smooth spot near the top of his thigh. My fingers caress the knife in the side pocket of my leggings while I stare at it.

It would only take one deep stab to puncture the femoral artery, and in that particular spot, it's too high up for a tourniquet to be effective. The image of him bleeding out on the ground in front of me makes me smile. The whole thing would take five minutes.

He clears his throat and I glance up to find a smirk on his mouth. "I'll arrange it. Rodrigo will reach out to you soon. Is there anything else I can do for you?" he asks suggestively.

My fingers slide over the knife one more time. I sigh, knowing it's not time. "No, I'm good."

He winks, circles his hand, and the jogger sitting on a nearby bench rises. They both take off running on the path around the lake.

Soon, I whisper to the darkness in my soul.

2

QUINN

A dark, almost empty dive bar outside of the tourist area, Cantina Iguana was probably popular a good twenty years ago. Now, the worn red and yellow booths are ripped, and the air is musty and full of stale cigarettes. For me, it's perfect. Both a reflection of my soul and the perfect ambiance for planning my next move.

"Gracias," I tell Lupe when she sets my usual beer down in front of me. The young woman is the only bartender I've seen working here in the last year.

A familiar smell hits my nose when someone takes the seat next to me. Eternity by Calvin Klein—the smell of my boyfriend, Mario, in middle school. My mouth twists, knowing the memory is ruined forever by the psycho wearing it now. I dart a glance at the mirror behind the bar. Rodrigo, Armando's right-hand man, sits to my left.

Rodrigo smiles at me when I glance his way. "Surprise!" His

tone is almost gleeful, which makes me wonder who he killed today.

I dip my chin to acknowledge him and lift my glass.

"Negro Modelo." He orders Lupe.

She pales but immediately grabs a glass from a cooler and pulls a draft of beer. After setting it down, she waits until he nods, then scurries away.

Irritated at this show of power, I swivel until I'm facing him. "Do you have information on my next job?" I arch an eyebrow purely to piss him off.

His black eyes dart to my forehead and tighten. "Don't you want to know how I found you?" He retorts with a smirk.

"Was I lost?" I counter with a shrug.

Cocking my head to the side, I contemplate the devil in front of me. With thinning brown hair and a dark complexion, there isn't anything remarkable about him. At around five feet seven, he's a couple of inches taller than me and lean like the stray dogs that fight for scraps in the street. Anyone who thinks he's not much of a threat only has to look into his eyes—dark, almost pitch black, and empty. In their depths, there's no light or glimmer of conscience, only death—the worst he can deliver to you.

He's the cartel's designated man for torture and murder. And if there's one thing he excels at in this world, it's death. He's a master. I should know; I studied his techniques. Copying some of his more creative ways meant my work carried the same psychotic flavor as his. An effective way to establish my reputation and instill a sense of fear.

Torture aside, I've rarely had to deal with him in person. Most of the time, one of his lackeys delivers the information. Probably a good thing, or I might have been tempted to kill him sooner. When I do decide to take him off the board, I'll be doing the world a huge favor. But I won't torture him. A bullet to the back of the head—execution style—will work perfectly. Plus, it has the added bonus of looking like a hit instead of something personal.

His lips curve into a facsimile of a smile before he takes a drink of his beer. "Not lost, but you're certainly hiding… something. Although I do have to commend you. It's been a while since I've spied such clever prey. I thought you might be undercover police for a while, but I ruled that out long ago. The crimes you've committed go far beyond the boundaries of law enforcement."

My eyes dart around the restaurant before coming back to rest on him. "I'm just a visitor to Monterrey, Mexico. No crimes here." I look at him pointedly, ignoring the prey comment for now.

He laughs. "Nobody would dare listen in on my conversations."

I guess I won't admit to listening to him on a regular basis. "Some of us are not so fortunate. Do you have the information or not? I'm tired and want to get some sleep."

"Not so fast, mi amiga. I want to have a chat with you about your park visits with Armando Morales. It's my job to protect him and make sure he doesn't get himself into trouble like his brother," Rodrigo explains. "The organization was very upset when Julio died."

"I heard. Qué pena que haya muerto, toda la familia lo va a extrañar mucho," I murmur the expected platitude. The image of Julio's tortured body splayed out in the desert with my knife in his chest flashes in my mind. It really is a pity you can only kill someone once.

He makes the sign of the cross. "Some blamed me. So, you see, I can't fail the organization a second time."

I narrow my eyes, contemplating what version of the truth to tell him. I can't lie. He'd spot it instantly. "He wanted to meet me. I've successfully been doing jobs for him and the organization for over a year now, and he was curious about me. He asked a lot of questions, including what I envision for my future. I want to be a major player in his organization." I lean forward to impart my exciting news. "Basically, if I keep up the good work, he might have an opportunity to bring me on in a bigger role."

Dark eyes stare into mine while he sifts through my words in his mind. After a minute or two, he slides his hand in mine to pass over the drive. "Usual password. Quick job. Must be done in the next couple of days."

"Product or labor?" I ask, pulling my hand from his smooth palm.

"Product," he replies with a smirk.

Bastard knows I hate his touch, but I imagine most women do. He thinks it's the burns on his hands, but it's not. His skin is saturated with the deaths of his victims. You can feel the evil inside when you touch him.

I finish my drink and slide off the barstool. "Good chat, Rodrigo, but I need some beauty sleep. Good night."

Deliberately turning my back to him, I walk to the end of the bar and hand Lupe, the bartender, a hefty tip. There's no way he'll leave her one. I just hope he's not in the mood to stay long. I like this little cantina.

A lean hand and a cold beer in the bar mirror catch my eye. I freeze. It's rare for me not to notice someone sitting so close. The bar was empty when I sat down. Did he come in with Rodrigo or after?

Adjusting my purse, I slip my phone into my hand and tap the camera icon. As I leave, I snap a few pics on my way out the door. After a couple of blocks, I stop to flip through the images.

A good-looking man with chin-length, blondish-brown hair, and intense brown eyes, stares back at me, his lips pressed flat with emotion, as if he's pissed off or something. Until I get to the last two frames, when a raised eyebrow and a half-smile show up.

I chuckle. He must have figured out I took his picture.

Obviously not a tourist, I muse, tapping save.

Fifteen minutes later, on a more secure network, I send the

picture to one of my contacts. This particular person is buried deep in the dark web with access to almost any information. She charges a ton, but it's worth it.

While I wait for her to get back to me, I plug in the drive. Quickly reading through the information, I note the time and date of the rendezvous, but the rest of the details are sparse. Tomorrow night, five products will be waiting for me across the border. Specific coordinates will be given to me when I get there. My job is to transport the contents safely to the next location. Usually I transport the goods myself, but it looks like I'll be transporting drug mules tomorrow.

I bite the inside of my cheek, thinking of the danger they face transporting packets in their body. The only time Armando transports drugs in humans is when it's a particularly valuable, specialized product, because the transport cost is high. Unlike other drug lords, his mules are typically high-end individuals who happen to be desperate for money. The payout is astronomical because the success rate is extremely high—few law enforcement agencies will stop someone who is well-dressed with a bored expression on their face. I shudder.

With a sigh, I prepare several injections and stow them in my bag. It's easier to make shipments disappear at various checkpoints, but mules require a different strategy.

After dinner, I walk over to my computer to shut it down and find a message waiting.

Who did you piss off? His name is Cruz, used to be CIA's "ghost," sent to eliminate potential problems. Highly skilled and dangerous. Lethal. Unknown kill count but estimated to be high. Rumored to be private sector now. No known sightings in the last six years until you. Sorry for the bad news. It's been nice knowing you. Payment due upon receipt.

Sliding into the chair, I instantly send my thanks along with the payment. I chew the inside of my cheek while I try to figure out this latest twist. Did one of my contacts spill their secrets? Very few people know I'm alive, much less where I'm living.

For hours, I try to figure out his angle, but I finally give up and drop into sleep. If he wants to kill me, he'll have to wait. Tomorrow will be here before I know it, and these jobs take every bit of my focus.

3

QUINN

odrigo is a lying, mother fucking asshole and if he was here right now, I'd put a bullet in his brain. No, I'd cut off his balls, shove them down his throat, and blow his head off. I blink a few times, praying the image in front of me will disappear, but it doesn't. Five beautiful unconscious young girls lie side-by-side in the back of a windowless van. The product I have to transport. No wonder Rodrigo was smirking last night.

My breath stutters while I stand there helplessly trying to swallow the lump in my throat. I turn burning eyes toward the man beside me, who's leering at them. He reaches for one of the girls. A split second later, my gun is pointed at his head.

"If you lay one finger on that girl, it will be the last thing you do," I inform him, my voice full of rage. "Now, why don't you do your job and give me the fucking coordinates? Time is ticking." My finger twitches, desperate to pull the trigger.

Hate-filled eyes turn toward me, but whatever he sees in my

face quickly convinces him to do what he was paid to do. He hands me a piece of paper.

"Coordinates. Keys are in the ignition. They will wake in about three hours. Give them the water and it will knock them out the rest of the way." His eyes dart to the gun in my hand. "You have what you need."

After a few seconds, I pull out my phone with my other hand and tap the camera icon. When I raise it, he puts a hand in front of his face.

"What are you doing?" He spits out.

I lower the gun and push the nozzle into his chest. "Taking your picture. I don't know you, but I assume Rodrigo does." When he finally drops his hand, I snap a pic and text it to Rodrigo to confirm.

"Friend" is the reply I get back.

"Looks like you passed," I laughingly inform the man sweating profusely in front of me while I put my gun away. Rodrigo's name generates fear. It's a useful tool, especially when dealing with scum like him.

He sighs in relief and quickly backs away from me.

I guess we're not going to be friends. What a shame. I shut the back doors and head to the front. Once in, I toss my bag into the passenger seat, take a deep breath, and jam my foot on the pedal.

Did Rodrigo set this job up or Armando?

Does it matter? My inner voice mocks me.

Like all the others, it's a test that I need to pass to get to the final phase. For three years, I've been hunting my prey. I caught his brother, Julio, a little over a year ago, but Armando has proved to be more elusive. Maybe he's smarter than his twin, or more paranoid, but he's almost impossible to catch. I've thought about shooting him a million times, but every time I do, the image of my sister, Sophia, splayed out naked in the middle of the desert, food for the vultures, flashes through my mind, and I can't do it. It's not enough. Especially now that I know Armando killed her.

The van swerves into the shoulder, and I yank it back to the road. My thoughts linger on the girls in the back. It's almost time to stop and give them some water.

What do I do? Is this the fate Sophia faced? If so, how did she end up with Julio? Torturing Julio didn't give me all the information I needed. He just kept repeating her name until the reaper finally claimed him.

Death wasn't the future Sophia envisioned when she went to college. These girls have dreams, too. By transporting them, I am essentially stealing every hope they might have for their future.

The headache pounding at the base of my skull makes it tough to think. Maybe food will help. I unzip the bag in the passenger seat to grab a power bar, and a long, thin case catches my eye.

My foot slips off the pedal, and the van slows.

Would it work? What if they scanned them?

I stop the van and shoot off a text to my tech contact.

A minute later, she replies. *If they scan them, they will find it. Add a decoy.*

I dig through the bag and find the container with the extra microchips. One, two, three,… five. Ok. Now I just need to find a way to stick them to their bodies.

Bringing up Google maps on my phone, I type in a few keywords. Bingo. An hour from the drop-off point in Ciudad Victoria is a Walmart.

Shuffling noises come from the back of the van. Surprised, I glance at my watch and see it's been three hours. My eyes scan the horizon, finding nothing but stubby trees, brush, and the nearby mountains. Bringing up maps again, I zoom in until I can see the area around us. There's a small turnoff two miles ahead.

Minutes later, the van is parked between a group of trees and I'm heading to the back. When I open the doors, terror-filled eyes meet mine. The girls try to move away from me, but it's impossible. Their feet are tied, and they're handcuffed to the bed of the van.

Dark brown eyes, so similar to Sophia's, draw my attention. She's about the same size as her too. They could have been sisters. The thought is like a shard of glass in my heart.

I leave her feet tied together but release the handcuff and motion for her to get out. When she's standing beside me, I shut the doors and flick a hand behind us.

Her bewildered gaze takes in the unfamiliar surroundings. "Where am I?"

"Mexico," I tell her. "Go to the bathroom." I point to the nearest tree. "Don't try anything or I'll shoot you. Trust me, this isn't the place you want to die."

Tears roll down her cheeks when she looks around the desolate area, but she finally shuffles over and squats down. When she's finished, I can see her mind catching up with her new reality.

"Here. Drink some water. It will flush the drug out of your system," I tell her. My hand holds out the bottle of water, but she just shakes her head.

Smart girl. "Suit yourself," I reply with a shrug. Taking off the cap, I raise the bottle and pretend to drink. "We've got a few hours to go." With a twirl of the gun, I motion for her to head back to the van.

She sways several times. Her eyes dart uncertainly to the water in my hand. For a few minutes, she weighs the two options. Drink or don't drink. A few minutes later, a shaking hand reaches out to take the water from me. She takes one sip and lowers the bottle. When nothing happens, she gulps down the rest.

I open the rear doors, make her lie down and cuff her to the floor again. One down, four to go. I motion to the blond next to her.

Thirty minutes later, we're back on the road.

When I pull into the Walmart parking lot, they're asleep.

Hurrying into the store, I grab a pack of clear adhesive dots and checkout. Once back in the van, I toss the pack into the passenger seat and get back to the route. This delivery is on a schedule, and missing the deadline is not an option.

We're thirty minutes from the private airstrip when I pull into a gas station. After filling up, I realize this is my last opportunity to turn around. I look at each of the girls, but I don't see their unique, beautiful features.

I see her. Sophia. My beautiful, sweet sister. Bruises all over her body. A long scar across her stomach. Raped. Naked. Splayed out in the desert sand like some sort of sacrifice. Her mahogany brown eyes staring at the midday sun.

Swallowing the bile rising in the back of my throat, I slip into the back of the van and inject each of them with a tracker. With a flick of my wrist, I sweep back their hair and stick the decoy tracker behind their ear. If they scan them, I'm hoping they will stop searching after finding the latter.

Such beautiful, innocent faces. I snap a picture of each of them and vow to find a way to save them. Even if I'm dead, I'll find a way.

Today's price is steep, but vengeance is a demanding bastard. Payment must be paid. A chunk of my soul withers and dies.

4

QUINN

With carefully measured steps, I make my way to the polished black bar and slide onto a plush velvet stool with a relieved sigh. Between the shots of tequila and the high heels, walking here was like navigating an obstacle course blind.

My fingers stroke the soft nubby texture on my seat while I scan the restaurant. I've passed by this place many times, but never entered, preferring Cantina Iguana where I could comfortably sit and plot my vengeance without anyone noticing me.

This place is the polar opposite of my favorite dive bar, with its dark, musty interior. Here, the ambiance is inviting, with luxurious furnishings and soft, subtle lighting. It's popular and packed with gorgeous people, their laughter light and infectious, as if they have few cares in the world.

It's the perfect escape from the sordidness of my life.

A good-looking, dark-haired man two stools down catches my eye.

Hmm, maybe it has more to offer than I thought, I muse.

A beautiful blond woman strides up to the barstool beside him and kisses his cheek. "Sorry, I'm late, darling."

A wry smile slides across my lips.

Luck doesn't favor the wicked.

My smile fades, and my throat burns for another shot.

I chose to embrace this life full of dark deeds, each one worse than the last. And somewhere along the way, I made a strange temporary peace with myself by promising the end would be worth it. But now, I'm not sure it will. The last job splintered my soul into the tiniest of pieces, and I doubt I'll ever find them all, much less be able to glue them back together.

The trackers are not foolproof, but they were the best I could do under the circumstances. I immediately alerted my contacts at the FBI, but I can only hope they get to them before too much damage is done.

The entire drive home, I couldn't help but wonder how they transported Sophia. Snatched from the San Antonio River Walk when she was nineteen years old, did they toss her into a van with several other girls? We scoured every inch of the River Walk's fifteen miles and watched hours and hours of video. Nothing. Not one clue or shred of evidence.

If we had seen a van, we would've noticed it, right?

To my intense frustration, I couldn't remember.

Minutes after returning to Monterrey, I was online combing through all my files and notes. It took several hours, but I confirmed it—no van.

"Would you like something to drink?"

A handsome young bartender stands behind the bar waiting for an answer.

"Casamigos Blanco, chilled." The world sways a bit. "A water and a menu, please."

Moments later, the drinks sit in front of me.

With a trembling hand, I down the glass of water, then the

shot. I'd intended to save the tequila until I got some food, but the thoughts and images swirling in my brain won't stop.

My original plan was to drink myself to sleep tonight, but my ghosts refused to leave me alone. Desperate to escape, I dressed up and fled here. A place with zero memories.

My gaze swings around to the individuals seated around the bar. Most of them are couples out for a night on the town or single men. I skip over the man I smiled at earlier and continue down the bar.

An incredibly handsome and superbly dressed man catches my eye. Blond hair, artfully styled, a strong, square jawline, and a gorgeous, full-blown smile is all I can make out from this distance. I let my gaze drift away, so he doesn't catch me staring, but continue to watch him from the corner of my eye.

Someone sits beside him, and a resigned sigh escapes. I casually swivel around to check out his companion and find the man from the cantina. The CIA's ghost. A chill runs down my spine.

A coincidence? Doubtful. I jerk my head toward the empty shot glass sitting in front of me and stare at it while I contemplate what to do next.

My contact said he went into the private sector. He's not US government. While he could be part of the cartel, it doesn't feel like it fits either, especially with his blond friend. Could this be about the money and drugs I stole? It's been a couple of years, though. Why come after me now? Or did I piss off someone else?

Before I can decide, the bartender comes back with a refill of water and another shot. My eyes settle on the cute young man in front of me. His expression changes from pleasant to impatient while he waits for me to order.

Make a decision, I urge.

He's obviously following me. I assume his friend is in on it, too. Two against one. It would be crazy to stay. Or would it? A feeling of recklessness washes over me. Maybe I'll watch them for a while.

Their faces blur. I need food. Knowing I need something in my stomach and wanting to eat are two very different things, but I force myself to order.

"I'll take the chicken flautas from the appetizer menu," I tell the bartender.

Laughter comes from the end of the bar, and I steal a quick glance at the two men. The handsome, gregarious man I saw earlier is laughing and slapping the ghost on the back.

Their friendship seems unlikely. One polished and sophisticated with a confident laugh, and the other casual and reserved, his smile rare and brief. But their gestures are relaxed, not forced, and even though I can't hear their words, the banter feels easy, like they've been friends for a long time. Colleagues or friends? Maybe both.

I know I need to stop staring, but I can't.

Damn tequila.

All my fucking common sense is gone.

Might as well go all in tonight. I down the shot sitting in front of me and ask for another.

Thankfully, my dinner comes, and I get enough food down to counteract the tequila. Not enough to kill the lovely haze surrounding me, but enough to feel steadier.

About thirty minutes after I finish my meal, the bar begins to thin out, and panic hits me. I need to get out of here. Raising a finger, I capture the bartender's attention and request my bill. While I'm waiting, a flash of light shines briefly, and I turn to see the two men staring down at their phone. I frown. Did they snap a picture of me?

Warning flares in my gut. Uneasy, I glance around the restaurant, but nothing stands out. I swivel back to them. *Shit!* The polished blond is gone. The ghost remains.

The bartender returns, and I hand him a hundred. He can have the change. Something isn't right. Sliding from the stool, I sling my purse across my body and head toward the door. When I hear footsteps closing in behind me, I dart around the group in front of me to put distance between the person following me. The front door is close, but at the last minute, I dart into coat check to hide.

Barely breathing, I listen for anyone who might have followed me in here. My heart thumps wildly while I count off the seconds. Ten minutes go by. Several women come in to get a jacket, but nobody notices me standing in the corner. It's been long enough. I need to move.

The black silk wrap hanging nearby becomes my newest possession. Draping it across my shoulders, I steadily move to the doorway, and when the coast is clear, I move farther into the restaurant.

The back entrance shares an alley with a nightclub. If I go out this one and into the other, I'll be able to hide there for an hour before I call a taxi.

When I pass by the bar, it's empty. Does that mean they're waiting outside? I quicken my steps, wincing at how loudly my heels strike against the tile floor. I'm tempted to stop and take them off, but I don't dare slow down.

Using the wrap to hide my actions, I reach into my purse and pull out my gun. Feeling considerably better with a weapon in my hand, I steadily make my way down the dimly lit hall to the kitchen. I'm five feet from the door when the airs stirs behind me.

Turning, I raise my hand, but I'm too late. Disarmed in record time, he pushes me face first against the wall and holds me there, his hard body pressed into mine. I throw an elbow back. It misses, but my heel doesn't, and I hear him inhale sharply. The weight pressing against me never moves.

Shoving against the wall, I create a bit of space and reach for the knife strapped to my thigh. My fingers grab the handle, but his comes down on top of mine, trapping it in place.

"What do you want?" I grind out, still pushing against the hard body behind me.

"Rodrigo is following you." A low voice with a slight Southern accent states quietly in my ear.

Rodrigo? I still. "Who?" I ask in a slightly bewildered tone. I can't afford to admit knowing that psycho.

"Your boss' right-hand man, Rodrigo. What happened? Did you mess up your last job?" the voice taunts behind me. This time it's filled with a tinge of anger.

Is it a ploy to get me to admit I work for Armando? "I am the boss. If you're telling the truth about someone following me, prove it."

I shove backwards, but he doesn't budge.

The hand moves from my thigh.

Taking advantage of the freedom, I whip my knife out of its sheath and thrust backward. It slides into muscle. I yank it out to do it again.

A harsh breath whistles through his teeth, but not a single word or scream escapes him. A shiver runs up my spine. Who takes a knife to the thigh without even a whimper?

Before I can think of the answer, he moves like lightning. Clamping down on my fist with his hand, he brings my arm up, spins me around, and slams me back against the wall.

"Look," he orders, holding a phone up to my face.

I stare into his intense brown eyes for a second before lowering them to the phone. It's him and the blond man he was sitting with earlier. They're taking a selfie. For a second, I'm captivated by the image of the two handsome men.

Puzzled, I stare up at him.

"In the background," he replies impatiently.

Startled, I study the picture but shift my focus to the people behind Cruz and his friend. Ten feet behind the bar, sitting at a table, is Rodrigo. He's staring intently at something in front of him. Given the direction, I'd say it's me.

"Shit," I mutter. Of all nights to be out drinking tequila, Rodrigo wants to have a chat.

"He's been following you for a couple of weeks," he informs me.

Since the meeting at the park.

Damn it.

"Thanks for the warning. Now that I know who it is, I can handle the situation myself," I state confidently.

He grips my chin. "He's hunting you, you fool. Trust me. I recognize the signs. Whatever you think will stop him won't work tonight. Unless you're prepared to put a bullet in him?"

Soon.

"Not yet," I reply. Wait a minute. "The only way you could know he's been following me is if you've been doing the same. Who are you?" I grip the knife tighter.

"Cruz," he murmurs, eyes darting around the corridor. "Where were you headed?"

I shake my head. "Uh uh. Answers first. Why have you been following me, and where is your friend?"

He cocks his head to the side. "Damn it. Rodrigo is heading back into the restaurant. You need to get out of here. Now." He yanks me off the wall and shoves me in the direction of the kitchen door. "Go."

"What about you?" I ask, walking backward.

He holds up a finger. "Wait. Sterling, repeat." With two steps, he grabs my wrist and scans the hall. "He's coming fast. We need to hide."

My heart pounds while my fuzzy brain tries to play catch up. I point to the door on the right. "Try that one."

He rushes over and finds it unlocked. Motioning to me, he stands in the doorway waiting for me to join him.

I step forward, then stop. What am I doing? I don't even know this guy and suddenly I trust him? With a shake of my head, I turn to run in the opposite direction, but I don't get far before an arm sweeps around my stomach and pulls me off my feet. We stumble sideways into a door, and it swings open from the force.

As soon as we're inside, he lets go. I frantically glance around for an exit but realize we're in the restroom. We're trapped. I try to dart past him, but he shuts the door.

"It's too late," he whispers harshly. "Sterling says he's in the hall." His eyes dart around the room before coming back to rest on me. "Maybe we can spin this another way. Unbutton your dress." He grabs the neck of his t-shirt and pulls it off.

"I…" My voice fades when I hear Rodrigo singing in the hall. I shudder. Moving quickly, I slide the knife back into its holder. My fingers try to quickly push buttons through holes, but they've shrunk. "Shit."

His hands sweep mine away. Grabbing a hold of each side, he rips the dress until it's open to my waist. Intense brown eyes stare down at me. "Ready?"

Not trusting my voice, I nod.

He backs me into the cool wall behind me and lifts me into his arms.

Instinctively, I wrap my legs tightly around him and thread my fingers through his hair the exact same way I would if this was real. When he pushes his body into mine, I gasp.

"Your leg," I remind him.

"It's fine," he replies dismissively.

Someone knocks.

I stiffen.

Brown eyes hold mine. He calls out, "Someone's in here."

We hear Rodrigo's singing move farther down the hall.

"Tell me why," I rasp, waiting for him to answer. The tequila and adrenaline are pumping through my veins in full force, heightening everything around me, including the tension rising between us.

I should be scrambling to get out of here, but all I want is answers. While I'm studying the strong, determined face in front of me, his tongue darts out to lick his bottom lip, making me silently groan. This man looks like he knows how to kiss.

"Surveillance," he murmurs, his mouth moving slowly towards mine.

My legs instinctively tighten. "For whom?" The air stills around us.

Instead of moving in for a kiss, his head slips to the side and he whispers, "Santos Foundation."

Relief washes over me. "Thank—"

A faint scratching noise fills the room, and his head jerks up.

Seconds later, firm lips crash down on mine, and words disappear from my brain. His strong tongue sweeps inside in an intimate takeover, demanding I concede to him. Swept up in the kiss I'd been craving only moments ago, I surrender without a second thought. My breath escapes in a sigh. I need this. It's been too long since I've felt anything but rage and hate. Fire roars to life, and I throw myself into kissing him back.

The kiss becomes wilder.

All the guilt I've been carrying this week is buried under the onslaught of desire. I tighten my fingers in his hair in an attempt to hold on to this temporary reprieve from the darkness surrounding me.

A cool draft of air hits me.

With a jerk, he rips his lips from mine and shoves my face into his shoulder. "Get out!" he orders.

"My, oh my," Rodrigo sings. "What a delightful surprise. Can I watch?"

Cruz pulls a gun from the waistband of his pants and points it at Rodrigo. "Get out." This time, his voice is almost a whisper.

Rodrigo freezes with his hands in the air. "I'm tempted to see if you're serious, but Armando doesn't like it when I make messes. Don't worry, I'm going. Quinn, I'll see you later." The promise in his voice is filled with anger at being thwarted.

Cruz waits silently until Rodrigo is gone. "Let's go."

The abrupt change from passion to cold focus is like a punch in the gut. "He could be waiting for us outside," I reply, slowly untangling myself from him.

"He's not," he assures me, tapping his ear. "Sterling is covering us."

"Where are we going?" I snap back in frustration, placing my hands on my hips.

Fingers reach out to start buttoning my dress. "We've got a place not far from here." As he nears my waist, he realizes a few buttons are missing and frowns.

I sigh and drape the black wrap over the ruined dress. My eyes drift from his face to the lean, cut abs he has on display. Silvery lines catch my attention and I reach out to glide my fingers across the scars crisscrossing his torso. Shutters come down, and he immediately steps back to pull on his shirt.

Humph, I understand now. "I'm surprised you trust me enough to bring me back to your place."

"The meeting you set up via email is scheduled for tomorrow morning. I'm only moving the timetable up a few hours," he returns, running a hand through his hair. "Are you ready?"

"I was hoping we could continue our… delightful encounter, but I'm guessing you don't feel the same way?" I ask lightly, not wanting to seem desperate, even if my body is shouting obscenities at me right now.

He hesitates for a brief second. "We need to get going."

I swallow hard but force my lips to curve into what I hope resembles a smile. "I'm not going anywhere without my gun." Two can play this game.

He pulls out the one in his waistband and hands it to me. "Here."

The fact that he pulled my gun on Rodrigo turns my fake smile into something more genuine. I gesture to the door and follow him out. When we get to the hall, I raise the gun and point it at him. "Hand me the earpiece."

A tic jumps in his jaw, but something in my eyes convinces him. He removes it and holds it out for me to take.

Leaning over, I pluck it from his fingers. "Thank you for saving me from that psycho. I do appreciate it, as well as your offer of a… safe… haven. But I'm good. If you are who you say, I already have the address and I'll see you tomorrow. If you're not, I'll make it a point to find you. Now, if you'll excuse me, I'm going to find someone to finish what you started."

Fists clench tightly by his side, but he doesn't move. I back slowly down the hallway to follow the plan I'd mapped out earlier. I've got plenty of safe houses in this city. One of them happens to be in the same building as our meeting tomorrow.

5

CRUZ

Silently following her through the kitchen to the back alley, I wait for her to turn toward the street. Instead, she crosses the alley to another door—La Vaquita. Based on the music blaring, it's a club, and a good place for her to hide for a while.

I stand in the shadows with her words ringing in my ear. Thoughts of her *finishing* with someone else makes me want to plow my fist through the brick wall behind me. I lit that fire. Me.

For the past two weeks, I've watched her every move, listened to most of her conversations, and I still can't figure her out. Her operation is comprised of nothing but sheer will and contacts. She's completely independent, without any back-up, and in an extremely vulnerable position. Is it her goal to work for the cartel, or is there a bigger agenda?

At first, I thought she might be agency, but my contacts have never heard of her. And her jobs come from one source—Armando Morales.

She's in deep, taking everything he throws at her, but to what purpose? I listened to the spiel she gave Armando about becoming a major player, but I'm not convinced. She spends too much time alone in dive bars, shunning the very life she's building here.

Her face and eyes reveal little, but the darkness clinging to her is achingly familiar. I'd recognize those shadows anywhere, and I bet the others will too, especially Raider. Something is driving her to the edge, over and over, but stopping isn't even a choice in her mind. I shake my head. She'll either achieve her goal or be consumed by the darkness. Maybe both.

Those thoughts fill me with anger. If you'd asked me a week ago, I'd have shrugged and left her chances to fate, but I saw the devastation on her face when she returned from this last job. The obsessive need to search for answers. The tequila consumed to forget. It's the reason I couldn't finish what we'd started earlier.

My hand brushes against my thigh, and I wince.

Damn hellcat.

Peripheral movement makes me slide deeper into the shadows. Sterling strolls down the center between the two buildings and stops right in front of me.

A blond eyebrow is raised high on his head. A sure sign of his irritation. "Care to explain to me why you haven't answered?" Posture ramrod straight, he shifts lightly on his feet, never taking his eyes off me.

"I don't have my earpiece," I mumble.

A line appears between his brows. "Did it fall out? I thought we tested them."

"I took it out," I drawl. He's going to push until I give him all the answers, but hell if I'm going to make it easy on him.

"Why? I heard Rodrigo singing in the hallway, but the feed cut out. Did the earpiece quit working?"

"It didn't quit. I turned it off and took it out," I bite out.

"You turned it off," he repeats quietly, eyes narrowed on me. "Where is it now?"

"She has it," I reply, pushing off the wall. "I need to get back and dress this wound. Are you coming?"

I face him, waiting for his big brain to catch up. It only takes a second.

He whistles. "Did she stab you before you kissed her or after?"

Scowling, I start walking without answering.

"Real or charade?" he asks, his voice carefully neutral.

"Charade," I reply, watching him frown. "And real. Hell, I don't know. She's… complicated. I thought I had her pegged the first week. Cold, calculated, smart. Successful. A tool for the cartel. The only thing intriguing was her independence, but I thought it was only a matter of time until she joined them."

"So, what changed?" Sterling presses. "I'm surprised anyone could interest you, given your recent infatuation with Henley."

"First, Henley is happy and where she's meant to be. Second, I'm not interested in Quinn," I retort, ignoring the sharp protest from my body. "It's just… cracks are appearing. Inconsistencies in her actions and responses. I don't want to say more and influence you or the others." I rake the hair back from my face into a short ponytail. "She tugs some thread in me that I don't understand and can't explain."

After one final glance around us, we reach our temporary base of operations and enter through a side door. When I raise my foot to take the stairs, fresh blood seeps through the hole in my jeans and drops to the floor.

Sterling eyes the blood and motions for me to keep moving. "I'll come back down and clean it up. Let's patch the wound first."

An hour later, Zane and Raider return, their hard expressions telling me they didn't like what they found. While

Sterling and I took the easy job of watching Quinn tonight, they went into the bowels of the city to get information on Armando and his business dealings.

Zane halts when he sees the bandage around my leg. "What happened?"

"I ran into a knife. It's fine," I tell him.

"She stabbed him," Sterling cheerfully pipes up.

Zane's brows lower like thunder clouds. Raider cocks his head to the side, waiting to hear how she got the drop on me.

I quickly explain.

Raider's cold blue eyes flicker with interest. "Let me get this straight. She stabbed you, kissed you, pulled a gun on you, and stole your comms? She's… interesting."

I level a look at him. "I kissed her, but the rest is… accurate. It was a last ditch effort to dissuade Rodrigo, but it backfired. He's more obsessed and pissed than ever. He's going to be a huge problem."

Zane paces around the room. "Rodrigo is her problem. She dealt with him before we got here. She can damn well figure out how to maneuver around him now."

"He's hunting her," I bite out. "For some reason, his leash has slipped. The cartel is likely the only thing keeping him in check, but it won't for long."

Zane stops, his face set in stone. "She needs to deal with Rodrigo. End of discussion." He waits for me to agree, but I can't.

He sighs. "Based on what we found out tonight, we're going to have a hard enough time getting those girls out. There are three facilities, and all of them are heavily guarded. Huge buildings filled to the brim with laborers and girls destined for their trafficking operations. Unless she has a magic key, I'm not sure how we're going to pull this off. Blowing up a facility would be easier than getting two girls out."

"She'll have a plan," I confidently state. "Believe me. Her

planning skills rival yours. In fact, it's going to be interesting to see who leads this mission."

Zane laughs heartily, unable to picture anyone leading but him. Plus, he's only seen pictures of her. Dark brown hair, light green eyes, petite, athletic build. She doesn't look like a power-house, but she's managed to successfully work with the cartel for over a year, and they haven't killed her. That's a significant accomplishment.

6

—————

<u>CRUZ</u>

The knock on the door the next morning startles us. Zane looks sharply at Sterling, who is typing rapidly on the keyboard in front of him and speaking into his headpiece.

"Raider hasn't seen anyone enter the building in the last thirty-five minutes," he relays, still typing. An image comes up on the screen. Quinn is standing in front of our door with a box in her hands.

Sterling's eyes widen. He informs Raider of her arrival.

With gun in hand, I cross over and open the door.

Quinn enters slowly, taking in the three of us, before setting the pink box down on the coffee table. "You should tell the man on the roof across the street to come in and grab some breakfast before it's gone." She flips the lid open and waves a hand over the assorted pastries inside.

Zane steps forward, his eyes scanning her from head to toe. "Weapons?"

She tilts her head to the side. "As a show of good faith, I only brought two weapons with me—a gun and a knife. I'll keep them both, if you don't mind."

Zane nods uneasily. "As a precaution, Cruz will keep his weapon out."

"That works for me," she coolly informs him. "Does anyone want a pastry?"

When we don't move, she picks up the box and carries it over to me. When her eyes meet mine, I notice the softness from last night is gone. She's all business today.

"It would be counterproductive for me to poison them. It's a simple gift. My mother taught me to bring one when visiting. And with the amount of tequila I consumed last night, bread was the only choice this morning." She states matter-of-factly, then folds the lid back. "Choose one for me to eat. I'm not picky." Her light green eyes flash with a challenge I can't resist.

Picking up the chocolate croissant, I hold it to her pink lips until she takes a bite. When she reaches for it, I pass the box to Sterling. He sets the box down on his desk.

While she eats, Zane begins. "Quinn, err... Smith, is it? I'm Zane Boseman. I run operations for the Santos Foundation, among other things."

"Quinn is fine," she replies, walking over to shake Zane's hand. "I've heard good things about you and your team, particularly the success you've had with rescue missions. I'm sorry to hear about your friend, Marcos."

At five feet, four inches, she looks tiny standing in front of Zane, who's a foot taller, and yet, her stance is wide and full of confidence.

Zane stills, studying her with new interest. Very few people know about Marcos. Her network is good, damn good. As an opening remark, it was stellar.

She waits patiently for him to make the next move.

"Why did you pick us for this mission?" Zane asks, his voice gruff with suspicion.

"I could state your success rate, but there are other successful outfits out there," she answers coolly. "Only two groups offered the key ingredient… integrity. Most of the groups do it solely for the money. You'll do it for them: the girls we're rescuing. The innocents."

"Sounds altruistic," Raider sneers from the doorway. He strides confidently into the room, his eyes riveted on her.

She swivels to face him, an empty laugh filling the air. "On the contrary. It's for purely selfish reasons. Individuals who are interested in saving innocents aren't likely to shoot me in the back. This mission is going to be tough. The last thing I need to worry about is whether you're going to turn on me."

"Maybe we should be worrying about your intentions," Raider taunts, glancing at my leg.

Her face turns delightfully pink. "Purely self-defense."

Zane points to Sterling. "Slick, show her what we've discovered." He turns back to her. "Unless you have a magic key, the mission isn't going to be successful. We're a small group. It will take more soldiers than we have at our disposal to break into a facility as heavily guarded as these to extract two individuals."

Sterling types a few things on his keyboard. Three facilities appear in 3D on top of the dining table. Tiny dots move rapidly in all directions, like a swarm of ants protecting a hill, showing people and guards everywhere.

Instead of studying the projection, she's staring at Sterling. "You must be Sterling. I saw you at the restaurant last night. Thanks for helping me escape Rodrigo."

He leans forward and clasps her hand. "I am, and it was my pleasure. You can repay me by recounting the best moments—stabbing Cruz, holding a gun on him, etc. Oh, by the way, do you have my earpiece? We only brought a few of them with us."

Her head tilts. "British, huh? That's an unexpected delight." She pauses for a second. "I don't have it anymore. Sorry. How about I give you another gift to show my appreciation?"

When she pulls her hand back, Sterling is holding a flash drive. "What's this?"

"A magic key," she states flatly. Her eyes dart to Zane. "Isn't that what you called it?"

Raider moves to my side and flashes a look at me. I nod subtly. She's prepared for every answer, maybe too prepared. Could this be a trap?

She points to one of the buildings and asks Sterling to delete the other two. "The two girls are in the annex adjacent to this building. Getting to them will be tough, but not impossible for a crew of five. There are two guards who rotate shifts. One leaves twice a day to get food. He's usually gone for about forty-five minutes, which gives us the best window for a rescue."

Silence falls on the room when she finishes.

"Is this information based on your own surveillance or another source?" Zane asks, brows lowered while he assesses her.

"The information came directly from Armando Morales," she admits. "But I fully intend to complete my own reconnaissance to make sure the information is accurate. He's been known to leave out a few pertinent details." Her green eyes dart nervously from Zane to the rest of us.

"The only reason he would give you the information is because he wants to handle this outside the organization," Zane states softly. "Is that correct?"

"Yes," she answers. "If we're caught, he'll deny all knowledge of the mission."

"So, we're to do his dirty work?" Raider interjects. "I vote no. Let him clean up his own messes."

I nod, agreeing with Raider on this one.

Zane doesn't say anything, but I can tell he's debating the wisdom of moving forward.

Sterling is locked on the schematics, surveying the building from different angles and measuring the distances between two points. "It's doable. The annex is isolated and less secure than the rest of the building. We might even be able to tap into nearby tunnels built for the sewage system. I'll have to check and see how far they run." He relays the information quietly, but we know this means he's in favor of the mission.

Quinn stills. "You don't want Armando to clean up his own mess," she states firmly. "Mistakes are eliminated. Period. If you can't continue with the mission, I understand. I'll hire another group." She takes a deep breath and raises her chin.

"Why are you doing this job?" Zane questions, watching every expression on her face.

"He asked me to do the job and promised me a very lucrative and important position as a reward," she replies, all emotion suddenly wiped from her voice. "After the death of his brother, he became reclusive. It's been hard to get noticed. For a year, I've taken every job he offered, hoping for this result. I'll do this job, with or without you."

There it is... the darkness I've witnessed more than a few times during the two weeks I've had her under surveillance. Eyes flat, voice hollow, it's like she's wearing a mask, but underneath it, the darkness churns.

Her adamant reply is revealing. This is a pivotal moment for her. Whatever event or demon has driven her to this point has her firmly in its grip. Quitting isn't an option.

My eyes dart to the others. We've all been there, so we understand the risk she poses. It's an incredibly dangerous time to be around her. Do we take the chance things will go smoothly and she won't sell us out to reach her goals?

"We need a couple of hours to weigh the pros and cons based on the additional information," Zane informs her, striding to the door. "Why don't you come back around noon, and we'll have an answer for you?"

She gives a firm nod, as if she knew this would happen, and leaves.

WHEN THE DOOR CLICKS SHUT, ZANE RUBS A HAND OVER HIS shaved head and heaves a big sigh. Usually, he's quick to call the shots, but with so many pieces of the puzzle missing, and the surrounding circumstances, he's spinning.

"She's determined to complete this job. And whether we do it or not, I don't believe she'll let those girls die," I say. The throbbing in my leg pushes me to grab a seat on the couch. "I'm not sure we should get involved. It's personal for her, which means it's dangerous for us. Beyond the usual mission surprises, we face her turning against us to achieve her goals."

"When is it not dangerous?" Raider interjects, to my surprise. "Could you really leave her to face this on her own?"

I hunch my shoulders, knowing he isn't talking about the rescue, but the path of destruction she's chosen. "A second ago, you were against the mission."

"That was before," he replies softly. When he turns to me, the past is in his eyes—full of battles, hard fought, barely won, and not easily forgotten. "I had my brother to help me. She doesn't seem to have anyone."

Mine had been fought alone. And he's right… I'd have done anything to have one person by my side. Unwilling to admit it, I turn to Zane and Sterling.

"I had my stepfather," Sterling reminds me. "And later, Zane. Is this really any more dangerous than trusting other strangers on a mission? We do what we've always done—put the rescue first and figure out the rest along the way. From what I can tell, she's being more honest than I would expect, given the circumstances." His analytical mind distills it down to the facts rather neatly, but emotion is a factor, whether he likes it or not.

"Slick's right," he mutters, calling Sterling by the nickname he gave him when they met. "We don't always know the motives behind the rescues. We've been here before. If we follow the usual protocol, our priority is rescuing the girls. Once that's done, we can reevaluate Quinn and our position. Fair?"

We all nod our agreement, but the uneasiness is apparent in the tight set of our shoulders.

7

QUINN

My fist slams down on the couch, but the muffled response is less than satisfying. Sheer frustration drives me to do it again anyway.

I didn't intend to reveal as much as I did, especially Armando's involvement, but once I met them, it felt like the only fair thing to do.

Fair. I snort, angry at myself. I lied. I don't have another team confirmed. If they don't do it, I'll have to ask Armando for more time, which is the equivalent of admitting failure. And if that happens, it could set my plans back months.

My head flops back onto the pillow so I can stare at the plaster ceiling. They're two floors above me, close enough to listen in on their conversation, but somehow I stop myself.

Which ones will vote for the mission and which ones against?

Sterling ignored most of the conversation. His focus remained on the schematics while he tried to figure out whether the logistics would work. Analytical nature, I conclude. If he thinks it can work, he's likely to vote for the mission.

Cruz is against. I snort softly. It makes sense. He's been watching me for the last two weeks, and I'm clearly not the poster child for innocence. Although I'm not in the organization, I take jobs from an important player in the cartel, and I'm only doing this mission for the promised reward. All that kind of blows trust out the window.

Raider is an unknown. Based on the few words he did say, he's cynical and adamantly opposed to doing Armando's dirty work. I can't tell which way he'd vote.

Zane is their leader and protector. He's concerned for two things—his men and the girls. It's what I'd expect from someone in his position. He could lean either way, but my bet is he'll be in favor of the mission. Could he trust the rescue to another team knowing their motives would be driven by money?

Two for the mission. One against. One unknown. It could go either way.

Maybe I should go ahead and put out feelers to my second choice. It's better to be safe than sorry. If Zane's group doesn't move forward, I'll need to present an alternative to Armando. I shoot off a text to ask for their availability.

Zane and his team aren't what I expected. Well, Cruz is, but only because I've had two encounters with him. Raider spoke very little, but he doesn't seem the type to follow anyone. Dressed in a pressed button down shirt and sharply creased slacks, Sterling looks like he'd be more at ease in a chic London row house than a slightly worn apartment in northern Mexico. Zane is exactly the type I'd expect for a rescue operation. Military background with a keen eye for trouble. He wanted to show me to the door sooner, but he cares too much for the world.

Standing in the middle of the room was intimidating. Not one of them is shorter than six feet, and I bet all of them are well-versed in martial arts. Intimidating, but protective too. It felt like a towering wall of strength around me, or maybe that's wishful thinking. Regardless, it was comforting. Probably why I couldn't stop giving them information.

I pick up my phone. Almost eleven. One hour to go. Enough time for a nap. I pull the blanket from the back of the couch and snuggle into it. After staying at the club for a couple of hours, it was early morning when I got here. My sluggish brain is screaming for a nap. After setting the alarm on my phone, I let my eyelids drift close.

WHEN I KNOCK, RAIDER OPENS THE DOOR. I WAIT FOR HIM TO INVITE me in, but instead he stands and stares, intently searching for something.

He's dangerously beautiful. Dark-haired and complected, with strong, masculine features, he's almost model perfect. Even his height and build, tall and lean, fit the specifics, but I don't think he could play the role even if he wanted to. It's not in him.

His gorgeous eyes give it away. A clear sign to anyone who gazes into them. A piercing light blue, they're almost hypnotic; the danger in them is so extremely enticing. A killer hides behind his pretty facade.

A thousand lifetimes ago, he would have scared the shit out of me. From the time I was born, I surrounded myself with rules and plans. The more people I lost, the worse I became—mapping out every step to reach my goals and eliminating anything in my way. Raider would have been deemed a threat and avoided at all costs.

He's dangerous, but there's something recognizable in his darkness. It calls to me like a beacon in this insane world I've constructed.

He steps back, and I blink.

What the hell am I doing?

I pass through the doorway, slowing only for a second to

breathe him in when I pass. Even the spicy scent surrounding him is entirely masculine. Butterflies caress my lower stomach, making me inhale sharply.

Needing to create distance between Raider and me, I rapidly cross the room to Zane. Stopping before him, I take another deep breath to replace the smell lingering in my nose. I look up at Zane, but he says nothing. The tension in the air is heavy, like a wet blanket. I'm guessing the vote wasn't unanimous.

Zane's eyes dart from me to Raider and back. Then, to Cruz. A pained expression crosses his face before he returns his gaze to me. "We'll stay and rescue those girls. We know there are gaps in your story. Heed my warning. If you put my team in danger, or if your agenda deviates from mine, I'll do whatever is necessary to get my team and the girls out safely. I'll leave you hanging. Do you understand me?" The formidable scowl on his face has me automatically agreeing. This is a man I don't want to piss off.

"I understand," I reiterate. I'd originally intended to lead the mission, but clearly that's not happening. This is his domain, and he's really, really good at it. I remind myself I chose them for a reason.

A weight falls off my shoulders, making me roll them in relief. It's kind of nice to have someone else take the lead. I clasp my hands together in the most innocent pose I can think of and wait for him to continue.

A gleam enters his eyes, but when I tilt my head to consider what it means, it's gone. Maybe he's anticipating the mission.

"We've studied the information on your flash drive. While it gives us a decent amount of intel, it's not enough to accomplish the task." He confirms what I initially thought. "Sterling is going to map the water and sewage tunnels beneath the city. From this street to the facility." He points to the map in front of him. "Since you're familiar with the area, you'll go with him to help guide and translate."

When I look surprised, he waves a hand. "His Spanish is rusty."

"It's significantly better than you think," Sterling retorts with a laugh. "But I'm always happy to have the company of a beautiful woman instead of one of these Neanderthals." He gestures to Raider and Cruz.

"Good, that's settled," Zane says absentmindedly. "Raider, I want eyes on all three facilities. It's just a precaution, but I want to know how much they interact. Also, pick up a shift or two at our target facility. We need intel."

Raider nods.

"He's just going to walk in and start working at the facility?" I jokingly question.

"Exactly," Zane confirms. "He's a chameleon. A damn good one." He eyes me for a second while I digest his response. Lines crinkle at the corners when he sees the doubt. "I'll make you a bet. If he works a shift tonight, you'll buy dinner tomorrow night. If he doesn't, I'll treat."

Damn, that's confidence, I muse. "Deal," I reply, unable to resist the taunt.

He gives a satisfied nod. "Cruz, confirm if the guards' movements match our schematics. See if anything's changed recently. Also, slip in and confirm there are two girls in the annex." Zane waits for me to say something.

"Good call. I haven't had time to check Armando's information," I admit quietly.

Remembering the CIA's moniker for Cruz and his ability to sneak up on me, I have complete faith in his ability to slip into the facility undetected. The guards won't even realize he's there. Even in a room with few people, he recedes into the background. My eyes meet his brown ones, but they're blank, allowing none of his thoughts to show. I turn back to Zane.

"And you?" I challenge the big man in front of me. He's good. Confident in his team. Concise. It makes me wonder how long he's been leading this group.

His eyes narrow. "I'll set everything up for our exit. We have a network in place, but it needs coordination. This will go down fast. Staying in Monterrey would be the equivalent of suicide."

"True," I reflect, although leaving isn't an option for me. "I do need to meet with Armando and give him an update. Also, I need him to distract Rodrigo, or the mission will fail."

Cruz grunts in protest behind me, but Zane's eyes gleam with approval. I can't help flushing when I see it. Until three years ago, my whole life was geared toward gaining recognition for my achievements from the important people in my life. I didn't think I'd ever see it again.

I glance at my watch. "It's almost two p.m.," I state, looking at Sterling. "What time do you want to leave?"

"Can you be ready in fifteen minutes?"

I turn and head to the door. "Fifteen minutes. I'm two floors down in apartment 313." Turning the handle, I catch Raider's smirk from the corner of my eye. He didn't miss my entrance this morning. I was already here.

8

QUINN

"The tunnels are used by one of the local street gangs to escape the police, run drugs, and other business. If we enter at Paloma Street, we'll avoid the lookouts and it will put us a bit farther outside their 'jurisdiction'," I inform Sterling, slightly breathless from the sight of the good-looking man beside me.

Gone is the carefully styled hair and tailored clothing. When he showed up at my door wearing black fatigues, a matching ball cap, and a solemn expression, I almost took him for Cruz. The ultra-confident, but strangely geeky, man I met earlier is almost unrecognizable. For a solid minute, I stood in the doorway trying to reconcile this lethal-looking version with the handsome analytical one, with little success.

Until he smiled. Sterling's smile has no rivals. It's brilliant and wide, full of confidence, and it warms a person from the inside out. I want to bask in it for days.

His attention shifts from the rooftops to me, and he slows his stride.

My head swivels around, but I don't see anybody. "What is it? Is there somebody following us?"

He lifts a shoulder. "I just realized you're taking two strides to my one, and I'm adjusting the pace."

With an exasperated sigh, I lean in close to him. "Get a move on. I don't want to be down in those tunnels after dark." With a few strides, I return to the previous pace. "Besides, I'm used to it. Most people are taller than me."

We get to the four-way stop but must wait for the light to change to cross. A couple of older ladies out doing their Sunday shopping stand to our right. One lady nudges the other, and I watch her tilt her head toward the street in front of us. Following her line of sight, I watch three men cross the street to speak to two others. Nothing out of the ordinary until you notice the large roman numeral tattoos on their forearms indicating their allegiance to the local gang.

The ladies make the decision to go farther up the street before crossing over, and I grab Sterling's hand to follow.

One woman glances nervously at me.

I smile and utter a few words of reassurance. "Sometimes it's better to go the long route." My eyes dart to the other street and back.

She turns back around and pats her friend's arm. "Si, mas segura."

"I wish we could escort them home," Sterling murmurs by my side, his lips pressed tightly together in frustration.

"Me too," I state softly, but we both know we'd be putting them in more danger if someone stopped us. There's no way either of us would be able to pass as a local. At best, they might assume we were tourists—until they found our weapons.

At the next corner, the ladies turn left to cross, but I continue our current path. "One more block should put some distance between us."

When we finally cross, we're closer to the entrance than expected. The tunnels are dark and damp, so I pull us into a nearby alley to grab the gear we'll need. Dropping his hand, I slide on a headband with a light embedded in it, which allows me to keep my hands free, then add my shoulder harness and a lightweight jacket. Lastly, I slip my gun from my ankle holster to my side.

Sterling slips a similar headband over his ball cap and adds a dark jacket. He bends down to clip a circular object onto the lacings of his boot. Sliding his arms through the pack, he adds his pistol to a shoulder harness, then grabs the crowbar with the extended hook on the end.

He turns to me. "Ready?"

I point to the item on his boot. "Is that a tracker?"

He nods. "I make everyone wear one when we leave our base of operations. It's come in handy a few times."

With a quick glance around the corner, he makes sure the path to the entrance is clear. Motioning for me to follow, he quickly strides to the center of the street and hooks the opening of the utility access hole with the crowbar. Once it's lying quietly to the side, he motions for me to start down the shaft.

The metal bars are cold and wet, making fast movements a challenge, so I carefully step down each rung until I'm about three feet from the bottom, then hook my boots on the outside and slide the rest of the way.

"Down."

Sterling's boots enter first. After taking a few steps, he squeezes his broad shoulders into the hole. Once the cover is back in place, he mimics my move and slides the rest of the way.

"Hello, gorgeous. Fancy meeting you here."

Even in this dimly lit, humid-as-hell place, his smile glows. Rolling my eyes, I yank my pack forward to grab the map I stashed in the side pocket.

He pushes his sleeve up and shines a penlight on his forearm. Bluish white lines glow in response.

"Did you use UV ink to draw a map on your arm? Such a geek," I ask, wishing I'd thought of it.

He winks. "We head straight for about half a kilometer, then turn right. I'll take point. Keep an eye on our rear."

Of course, my eyes drift down when he turns.

He chuckles. "You should watch where you're going." Silently, he takes off, his boots barely making a sound, even in the echoing chamber of the tunnel.

Smartass.

We make good time. It takes fifty minutes to reach our chosen exit. It's not the one closest to the annex, but this hill gives us the best overall view of the facility. Blinking against the sun's rays, I follow him up and out of the shaft.

In an army crawl, he moves to the hill in front of us and pulls a pair of binoculars out of his pack to survey the facility. Whispered numbers fall from his lips.

My watch flashes, and I tap it. Without saying a word, I scoot back until I'm out of the facility's sight. Standing in a semi-crouch, I quietly move through the brush, mapping the best route to the annex. Along the way, I take pictures of the good spots for cover. When I'm fifty yards from the side gate, I pause and wait.

Two minutes later, a guard hurries out the gate into a waiting jeep, and I tap my watch again when he's in the driver's seat. Three minutes, six seconds to get around to the gate, and another forty seconds for the guard to get to the jeep. I add a twenty-second buffer. Four minutes, six seconds. Forty seconds to reach the door of the building. Our route time is four minutes, forty-six seconds. I'll have to ask Cruz or Raider to map our time from the door to the girls' cells.

A twig snaps, and a hand wraps around my mouth. "Hmm, Cruz told me you were fast, but I'm still impressed. Mind sliding the tip to the right?"

Raider's not as quiet as Cruz, but close. Still, it's not nice to sneak up on a woman with a knife. I angle the tip in the other direction, and a sharp inhale comes from behind me.

"Your other right, mon petit oiseau," the strained voice instructs.

The smooth words coming from his lips are a surprise. French isn't what I expected. With a muffled chuckle, I slide the knife back into the special pocket in my pants.

He moves to my right, his icy blue eyes sparkling with amusement. "You need to get back to Sterling."

"I've got eleven seconds," I say, tilting my watch face toward him. "Can you time the inside from point-of-entry and back? I've tracked everything else." Without waiting for him to nod, I slide back into the brush. "Guard should be back in thirty-nine minutes."

There's no answer, of course.

The return is quicker than I anticipated, but I decide any extra is just buffer. When I come out of the brush, Sterling is crouched by the entrance to the tunnels, looking at his watch.

Green eyes assess me from head to toe. "Did you get the intel?"

"Most of it. Raider's going to time the interior," I confirm, stepping down into the shaft. After clicking on the headlamp, I wait.

"Raider?" he asks a minute later when he joins me.

"He arrived a few seconds before I left," I tell him. "Didn't you see him?"

"Hmm," he says noncommittally, taking off down the tunnel.

The scene with Raider plays in my mind. I didn't expect the amusement. Not between us. "Do you know what mon petit oiseau means?" I murmur to Sterling.

He stops abruptly, shutting off his light.

I do the same. Barely breathing, I listen. A flood of swearing echoes loudly in the tunnel ahead of us.

Hard lips press against my ear. "I'm going to try to get us past them on the right, but I can't be sure of their exact location. Keep your headlamp off. If I've counted correctly, we should take a slight right into a parallel tunnel in about a hundred paces." He grabs my hand. "I've got you."

Paces? Military? Quietly, I follow him. My eyes slowly adjust to the dark, but not enough to move quickly. I can't help but worry it's taking us too long. Every few feet, we pause to listen again, then move forward.

The voices are getting louder.

We're close to making the turn when a long, loud whistle comes from the shadows on my right. A young man steps out of a small alcove and shines a flashlight on us. A lookout. And by the sound of rushing feet, his buddies heard his warning.

Sterling shoves the guy hard into the wall, and we take off running toward the others. Lights bounce against the walls in front of us. I start to slow, but he quickly grabs my hand and turns right into the other tunnel.

We run for about a quarter mile. By my calculations, we should be close to the entrance. Maybe forty feet? I try to think of how long the first tunnel was, but I can't remember. I'd been distracted by the sight in front of me.

Shouts come from behind, and I turn to see they're close. Doubling down to run harder, I swivel back around and run right into Sterling, who's come to a dead stop.

He rocks hard on his feet but remains standing.

I peer around him and find three men blocking our exit.

"Fuck," I whisper. I dart a glance behind me. "Two more. Six o'clock."

"No guns unless you have no choice," he orders softly. "The entrance isn't far, and we don't want to bring anyone else down here to investigate. We can handle five." A bright white smile flashes. "Have a little faith."

Confidence in spades. With a deep breath, I squeeze his hand and pull my knife out. Shrugging my shoulders, I let the straps of my backpack fall to one elbow and wait.

A bright light shines in my face, followed by a stream of Spanish. I shrug my shoulders and smile. Taking off my headband, I let it drop to the ground. If I can't use the light, the strap becomes a weapon for them to use against me.

"Hola, no hablo Español," I say, then pause. "A local told us about some catacombs, but we couldn't find them. If you could point out the exit, we'll head back to our tour." Straws based in truth. This is a popular scam to isolate tourists. Maybe if they think someone is waiting for us, they'll let us pass.

"Black fatigues. Headlamps. I don't think so," a deep voice replies with a chuckle. "Tourists or not, the boss doesn't like strangers in his backyard. He pays us to make sure nobody gets out of here alive."

The boss, that's… interesting.

Is Armando trying to keep people from the facility, or is he using the tunnels for something else? I don't have time to think about it because the man in front of me reaches toward my face.

"Don't touch me," I warn him, letting the backpack slide off.

I catch it with my left hand and swing it into the face of the guy next to him. At the same time, my knife slashes forward to slice the first guy's hand. He bellows in anger and drops his flashlight on the ground.

Air moves behind me, indicating Sterling is also in play. Taking advantage of the dark, I crouch down and shuffle slightly to the left. When the guy I hit with the backpack rushes forward, I come up on his right. Using all my force, I slam the knife into his stomach, twist, then yank it out. Screaming in pain, he bends over and grabs his stomach. In seconds, the knife is gliding smoothly across his throat, silencing his screams.

He drops to the floor.

A Mack truck drives me into the tunnel wall. Pain radiates up my spine, but he doesn't even pause.

A bloody hand wraps around my throat while the other grabs for my knife.

Desperate to keep hold of it, I move my hand wildly in every direction.

When he can't capture my hand, his meaty fingers wrap around my wrist, squeezing hard.

Pain shoots up my right arm, but I continue to grip the knife tightly. Just a few more seconds.

He puts additional pressure on my throat, cutting off my oxygen.

Fuck, where the hell is it?

Darkness threatens. My fingers glide around the edges of my belt. A protruding ridge. There. Using my fingernails, I grasp the tip and pull the long, thin weapon from my belt loop.

With a deep breath, I drop the knife and gasp, letting my body go limp.

He waits. Thirty seconds go by. He shakes me hard.

My head lolls. Sounds from the other fight filter to me.

Come on, I know you want to join the other fight.

Finally, he releases me, dropping me into a crumpled heap on the ground.

My body lands with a thud, with the left side taking the brunt of my weight. Tears spring to my eyes, but I lock my jaw and ignore the pain.

For several long seconds, he stands above me.

My throat burns with the need to breathe or cough, but I use all my willpower to hold it in.

He bends down and picks up my knife and wipes it on his pants. His booted feet make little sound as he moves toward the fight.

I let him get a few feet, then rise. With the wooden ends in each hand, I jump on the big guy's back and sling the wire over his head. It loops around his neck, but instead of sawing right to left, I drop and hang off his back. The weight of my body easily pulls the wire through bone, muscle, and his carotid artery.

He drops to his knees, hands at his throat to staunch the blood, but he can't. The move tore halfway through his neck.

Alternating between coughing and breathing, I move around to face him.

Even in the darkening light, his coal-black eyes mutely convey pure hatred at the death I delivered to him. He's gone a second later.

After stuffing the garrote in my pocket, I bend and pluck my knife off the ground. A deep grunt catches my attention.

Sterling is fiercely fighting two men. The third is already on the ground.

He's good, very, very good. Sharp, forceful hits. Specialized training. More than the usual military standard. He's lightning fast, too. Arms and feet fly. Very little sound escapes him. A silent, golden menace. Who would have thought?

His boot kicks out, smashing the knee of the man on his right.

Agony flashes across his enemy's face. Yelling and cursing wildly, he goes down.

Sterling moves, drawing his other opponent deeper into the tunnel, away from his buddies.

I move steadily toward the guy on the ground.

He's slithering across the wet tunnel floor, trying to reach his buddy lying five feet away. He must think he has a weapon he can use. When he sees me coming, he pushes himself to move faster.

Unfortunately for him, I make it to him first. Big hands grab for the knife, making it hard to get too close. So, I yank his head up, and stab straight down into his neck, then rip it out. Blood streams from the gaping hole, silently flowing down his neck, like a black river in the near dark.

I let him fall, then check to make sure his buddy is dead too.

"Hurry up," I call out softly, turning my phone on. There is half a dozen missed calls from Zane… and seven texts. I flash the light across the ground to locate our stuff. There. I slide my backpack on and search for the rest. Sterling's pack is a couple feet away. Beside it is my headband with the light, and I slip it on.

Footsteps pound to my left. I draw my gun. Screw the noise. If that bastard defeated Sterling, I'm going to be pissed.

Sterling's broad smile gleams in the light.

Relieved, I slide my gun back in its holster and take a deep breath.

He strides forward, immediately wrapping his long arms tightly around me. "Quinn." His chest is heaving from the fight. The adrenaline is pumping so hard, it takes several deep breaths for him to settle.

After moving the headband out of the way, I grip him tightly, spreading my hands across his hard back to hold him to me. My head drops to his broad chest. Blood and sweat fill my nostrils, but I can't tell if it's from him or me, and honestly, I don't care. It's been a long time since someone gave me comfort, especially after a fight.

"Zane is blowing up my phone," I murmur, loath to break the moment but knowing we need to leave.

He pulls my head back and swipes a piece of hair off my face. "You're one hell of a fighter to have at one's back, beautiful."

The air is still and quiet. I study him closely. A myriad of emotions crosses his face, but it's the admiration in his eyes that finally pierces my walls. Rising on my tiptoes, I stretch up and clasp the back of his neck. He bends to meet me halfway, and my lips capture his.

Long and slow, I stroke my tongue along his, tasting everything he is and isn't. Breathing in the same air as him. I take my time, languishing in the heat of the kiss for several minutes. He understands this is my kiss. Not once does he push for more or take over.

He shifts, pulling me in closer. Taller by almost a foot, he wraps his body around mine, holding me safe from the world around us.

The thought sobers me, forcing my lips from his. With my heart thundering in my chest and ears, I stand in his embrace for a second or two more, savoring this moment. *Damn.*

My tongue swipes along my lips for one last taste. I could kiss this man for days. Easy as breathing, it is, but twice as hard to stop. And we must stop. It isn't fair to him.

He doesn't know me. Or what I've done. The girls I transported the other day. The men I've tortured and killed, and the ones still on my list. The vow of vengeance I made to hunt them all down.

I pull out of his arms and answer my phone. "Hi, Zane. Yes, we ran into some trouble, but we're heading back now. Fifteen or twenty minutes."

When I hang up, I toe the nearest body. "We should hide them."

He exhales. "I stashed the other one in an alcove a few feet back. We can add these guys to the pile."

In only a couple of minutes, we've hidden the rest of the bodies.

Sterling guides me to the entrance. When we emerge, the cooler air swipes across my wet jacket, making me grimace. Who knows how much blood is on it? But I can't take it off. At least with the dark clothing, the gruesome splatters aren't visible.

Sterling took a few hard hits, and a couple of the cuts on his face are still bleeding. I motion for him to bend down. Peeling back the cuff of my jacket, I use my t-shirt sleeve to wipe off the blood. With a quick tug, I pull his hat down low on his face to hide the rest.

Green eyes study me for a second. With a nod of thanks, he turns. Keeping a fast pace on the way back, he says nothing, but he's thinking hard. So hard I can almost hear his thoughts.

Before we enter the side door, he pulls me to a halt. Tense, I stare up at him, waiting.

He leans over. "That was one hell of a kiss, beautiful. Next time, it's my turn." The door opens, and he motions me forward.

9

ZANE

"Local gang jumped us in the tunnels on the way back. It sounds like they're being paid to patrol," Sterling bites out, his face full of exhaustion and a hint of pain. He drops the backpack on the table, then peels off his hat and jacket. Blond hair, drenched in sweat and dirt, springs free from its confinement.

Besides the damage to his face, his knuckles are swollen and red. I'm sure there's a few hidden wounds, too. With a grunt, I reach for the first aid kit and slide it across to him.

Turning my attention to her, I assess her petite frame. No red splotches on her jeans. Upper body took most of the hits. Right wrist is a dark, mottled red. Surprisingly, they spared her face. My eyes catch on the angry ring around her neck, where the red is slowly becoming a defined handprint. My fist clenches, but I walk away before she sees my response. Too many members of my team are already interested in her. Someone needs to keep a clear head. Striding to the freezer, I pull out a couple of gel ice packs and hand them to her.

She nods gratefully and places them on her body. "I can't tell if Armando's just paranoid or if he's using the tunnels for transport." She rolls her neck. "Overall, the rest of the recon went well. The timing is good. Whether we use the tunnels to get there or not, we have solid intel for the mission. Two or three more days, and we should be a go."

"Dress those cuts and get a shower," I order Sterling. "What about you?" I eye Quinn's apparel, noting the wet areas of her jacket. "Is that your blood or someone else's?"

She grimaces. "Probably a bit of both. It's fine," she replies with a wave of her hand. "I'm going to grab a shower and some hot food." She turns toward the door, her movements slow and stiff.

I frown. "Get a shower but come back here. Cruz and Raider will return soon. We'll order some food and regroup."

Her eyes narrow on me, but I keep my face locked in a scowl.

"Did Raider complete a shift?" she asks, her eyebrow raised high.

I fight the urge to smile. "He did. I guess that means you're buying."

She pulls out a credit card. "Do you need a list of good places, too?"

I snort. "I'll figure it out. For fifteen years, I've been leading men and not one of them has died of starvation."

Now both her eyebrows are up. "Fifteen years? How old are you?"

Sterling laughs.

My scowl becomes real. "Old enough. Do you want food or not?"

Her fingers lift to her lips to mimic a zipper closing. With a wink, she slowly turns and makes her way out the door.

Sterling and I watch her on the monitors until she safely reaches her apartment.

Once she's inside, I swivel to him. "How many?"

He lifts a shoulder. "Five. Big and mean. Gang fighters. If we hadn't had more extensive training, it would have gone down differently."

I lean back and rub the scruff on my chin, hating the fact I didn't shave today. "How much training?"

"Hard to tell. Formal training. Her fight techniques are a mix of training and street," he admits. "Have you noticed the changes in her language? I can't tell if she's a chameleon like Raider, picking up our vocabulary, or if her background is showing. My bet is the latter."

"I agree. Did you get anything back on her prints?"

Sterling stands and stretches. "They were too smudged. Maybe she's sanding them or wearing an extra layer. I didn't feel anything when I held her hand today, but I'm not sure I could tell, especially if she paid for the premium covers."

My eyebrows lower. "You held her hand?"

A devilish light gleams in his eyes. "Was it before I kissed her or after? Oh, wait, she kissed me. That's right. It was before our kiss. To be fair, she held my hand first, but I did hold hers when I guided her through a dark tunnel with enemies on our ass." His mouth lifts in a half smirk.

I snort. "You're a grown man, I get it. Still, two out of four is unusual for our group. Although, I seem to recall both you and Cruz drooling over a pink-haired woman not too long ago." Bending down, I yank open the mini fridge and grab a beer.

"Bold, unique women are always interesting," Sterling replies with a shrug. His serious green eyes meet mine. "Quinn's kiss. Her taste. The sharp edges glazed with passion. It's… more than I expected." He strolls out the door without another word, but his expression tells me he's in deep thought.

I sigh, wondering where all this is going to go. There's not an ounce of me that doesn't see Quinn's appeal. Young and beautiful, with dark hair and green eyes and a trim, athletic figure; a man would be a fool not to want her. But every time I look at her,

I see the cold determination reflected in her eyes. She's only working with us to achieve a goal. We can't lose sight of that fact.

AFTER GETTING A FEW BITES DOWN, STERLING RECAPS THEIR findings. "We may be able to use the tunnels for an emergency escape, but it won't work as our way in. The good news is we can use the spot on the hill to survey the facility first. Then we can easily move to the annex. Shouldn't take us long, right Quinn?"

Quinn grabs the container of pad kee mao and dumps some on her plate. "Four minutes, forty-six seconds. Buffer of twenty to twenty-five seconds. I forwarded Zane some pictures of good ground cover on the route. Did you get a chance to time the rest?" she questions Raider.

Raider tilts his head to the side, eyes darting to mine with a silent message. "If guards are down ahead of time, two minutes, sixteen seconds. Four minutes, if we need to take them out."

"There's a lot of chatter about something big happening in a week. We need to rescue the girls and evacuate before that happens," Cruz informs us, his eyes never leaving Quinn.

She freezes. "Did you get any additional details?"

"Speculation is rampant, possibly a visit from one of the cartel leaders. Looks like Armando is looking to move up in the world." His keen eyes watch her face harden when he delivers the news.

"You're right. We need to move the timetable up. Do we have enough surveillance, or are there holes?" She directs her question to me.

I lift the bottle to my lips and take a deep drink of my beer while I consider her question. "We're close. I'd be more comfortable with at least one more day. If the guard rotation and numbers stay the same, we can move. Although, I'd like video footage of the path inside." Several heads nod in agreement.

Raider stands with his empty paper plate in his hand. "I'll get the video tomorrow." After dropping it in the trash, he leaves the room.

"Cruz, I need you to get intel on the security cameras and guard rotations. I've got most of them, but there are a few blank spots I'm not comfortable with right now," Sterling announces, which is followed by a yawn. "I'll send them to you after we finish here."

"I need to regroup with Armando tomorrow and give him a deb... an update," Quinn states, almost tripping over her correction.

"You were going to say 'debrief,' weren't you?" I challenge her. "It almost sounds like you served." My hand flies up to stop her from lying. "I'm not asking you to share your secrets. We all have pasts. But you're meeting with him tomorrow, and you need to be aware of your language. You don't want to slip up."

Her eyes widen with surprise. She opens her mouth to speak but is stopped again when Raider places a jar on the table beside her. Her eyes dart to his in question.

He lightly taps her wrist. "Put it on the bruises, especially the ones on your neck and arm. Rub it in and let it sit all night. It will help with the pain."

Her hand slowly reaches out and picks up the jar. "Thank you, Raider."

He returns to his seat beside me, his eyes never leaving hers.

She stares at the jar in her hand.

Without looking up, she addresses my comment. "A long time ago, when I was somebody else, I believed a world existed where justice prevailed over evil. I was absolutely sure if I fought hard enough, followed all the rules, and stayed on the right side of the path, I would make a difference. And I did. For a long time. Until the very thing I was protecting was taken from me, murdered, and dumped like trash in the desert."

Her laugh is hollow and dry. "Turns out, nobody speaks to the law-abiding ones seeking answers, but they sure as hell speak to those seeking vengeance. Thank you for dinner. If you'll excuse me, I'm tired." Shoulders back, head held high, she stands and walks out the door.

10

QUINN

I t's pure magic. The concoction in the jar eased the worst of the pain. My neck and wrists are still sore but functioning considerably better than I expected. I rub my chest. If only it worked on the wounds inside. Last night's discussion hurt. Maybe because I haven't thought about my old self in a long time. When you're alone, you don't have to remember.

Rules. Law enforcement. Following in my dad's footsteps. The pillars of my foundation growing up. I couldn't imagine anything derailing me from the path of straight and narrow. Not once did I ever imagine I'd abandon everything I was to become the person standing in front of the mirror right now. The one preparing for a meeting with a member of the cartel, not to take them down or arrest them, but to earn their favor.

Dressed in leggings and a tank top for "yoga," I frown at the bruises in my reflection. Turning back to the closet, I grab a light-weight jacket with a short, standup collar and slip it on. No bruises. Perfect. With my colorful neck covered, and my knife in its hidden pocket, I head out the door.

The park is packed with people and animals, all of them reveling in the sunshine on this beautiful Saturday. I escape their happy faces to sit beside him on our bench.

Our bench. I silently snort. Maybe after all this is done, I'll rip the bench from its bolts and throw it in the damn lake. If I survive, of course.

His expensive cologne makes my nose twitch. "Good morning," I murmur, remembering to show my manners.

"It is, isn't it?" he says warmly. "Tell me you're not going to ruin my good mood."

"We'll get the girls out in the next couple of days. We're just finishing up some last-minute details," I inform him, relieved to be able to pass on the news. "We originally thought to use the tunnels, but they're full of gang members." I casually throw in the info, wondering what he'll say. "We came up with an alternative plan."

Tension fills the brief space between us. "It's probably for the best. The gang is notoriously brutal. I've tried speaking to them, but they do as they wish, running rampant in certain areas of the city."

"Yes, my source said the same. It's fine. There are many ways to get to our destination," I state briskly, dropping the conversation. He's using the tunnels.

He looks away. "Is there anything else?"

"Rodrigo. If you don't find somewhere else for him to go the next few days, we won't be able to complete the rescue. Apparently, I'm his newest obsession. And with his ties to the… group, I doubt you want me to get rid of him," I state, my voice cold.

"If only we could," he murmurs.

"I can," I state, emphasizing my independence from him and the organization. "Normally, I'd have already taken care of the situation, but I respect your loyalty to him. Take note. Respect only goes so far. I won't tolerate him stalking me."

Dark eyes narrow in anger. "Watch yourself. The organization has spies everywhere. It would be a shame for you to leave this earth before you finish the job." He waves a hand. "I'll give him something to do, at least for the next few days."

Hmm, sounds like his control of Rodrigo is limited. His pet has more clout in the organization than I thought. Not that it matters. He's on the list.

"Thank you," I grit out, barely able to form the words.

Without another word, he gets up and strolls off.

I guess the meeting is over.

THE SKIN ON THE BACK OF MY NECK TIGHTENS. I TAKE AN IMMEDIATE right at the next corner, then jaywalk straight across the middle of the street, stopping cars left and right to get to the other side. Horns blare, and curses fill the air, but I don't care. The maneuver gives me a head start. I swivel around to see who is following me.

Zane's scowling at me from the other side of the street. His large hand swipes across his shaved head in frustration.

I wonder what it feels like—is it smooth or prickly like scruff?

He cocks his head to the side and pulls a black phone out of his pocket.

I answer on the first ring.

"Do you always walk into traffic?" he bites out, apparently pissed at my actions.

"I do when I sense someone following me," I fire back. "What do you want?"

"I'm not the only one tailing you today," he reveals. "Don't worry. I didn't take him out. Rodrigo is sleeping peacefully in the park."

Fuck. I hadn't even sensed Rodrigo or Zane this morning, too busy letting the past get its hooks into me. "I don't need you to take care of me. Why are you following me?"

Silence. "I thought you might need back-up."

Back-up. Another word from the past. Something dark beats hard in my chest and the need to escape becomes overwhelming. "I've got an appointment. I'll be back soon." I hang up.

He slowly lowers the phone from his ear. The scowl on his face changes to something more contemplative.

Wanting to avoid any deep discussions on my background, I join a group of people passing by. Laughing and chatting, they don't even notice I'm there. After a couple blocks, I break away and head to my favorite cantina.

The faded green iguana greets me at the door like an old friend welcoming guests into his humble abode. The worn, dated look isn't inviting to most people, but for me, the relative obscurity of this place makes it perfect. With a sigh, I pull open the door and enter the dim interior, pausing only a second to allow my eyes to adjust, before moving forward to slide onto my favorite ripped leather barstool.

A quick scan of the bar confirms it's empty, but the thought doesn't generate the same satisfaction it usually does. Instead, a shiver runs up my spine, along with a sense of uneasiness. I frown. This is my escape hole, the place I come to hide from the world. The cantina is perfect because it has few visitors. I've plotted every single step of my plan at this bar and in this very seat.

A hand slaps the bar. "Qué quieres?" a woman asks, her voice rough like sandpaper.

Startled, I blink. An old woman glares at me from behind the bar. My frown deepens. I scan the area around her, searching for Lupe, the girl who's waited on me every single time for over a year. She's not here.

"Where's Lupe?"

Her eyes narrow. "Muerta."

Dead. "How?" I demand.

Her eyes fill with fear, and she shakes her head in refusal.

Very few people generate that much fear. A few come to mind, but my gut says it's the psychotic one. The one who was in here just a few days ago.

Rodrigo.

She props one hand on her hip and waves the other in the air. "Apúrate!"

I take a deep breath to order, but the thick smell of stale cigarettes clings to the back of my throat, choking the words before they can form. Stumbling off the stool, I ignore the muttering coming from the woman in front of me and head toward the door. Once outside, I lean against the rough brick, breathing in and out.

Sadness, rage, grief… it's all piling up inside me. Every time I think I've got nothing left to lose, the world shows me differently.

Was I close to Lupe? No. Will I take her death as a debt? Yes. Intentionally or not, I brought that animal here.

The only reason Lupe took this job was to be near her father who had lost his sight and lived nearby. From here, she could easily check on him throughout the day. I wonder who's taking care of him now. I'll call back later and try to get some information. It's the least I can do since it's my fault his daughter is dead.

Nausea rises, and I stumble to the corner of the building to throw up. It's not much. Once breakfast is gone, there's nothing left except dry heaves. Bent over, with my hands on my knees, I wait for them to pass.

"Quinn," a deep, familiar voice calls my name.

I turn my head toward Zane, needing to share my questions with someone who can help. "Lupe is dead. Who's going to take care of her father?"

When he frowns in confusion, I shake my head and wave him away. He can't help me. Nobody can. Nobody helped Lupe, either.

God, I pray he didn't torture her.

"Torture who? Lupe? Who's Lupe?"

Oops, guess I said it out loud.

Zane moves closer and holds out a bottle of water.

I grab the bottle and jerk my thumb over my shoulder toward the cantina. "Bartender." Opening the bottle, I take a mouthful of water, swish it around, then spit it out. "She waited on me for a year. Her life was good. Until I led Rodrigo here." My voice cracks under the pressure of that statement.

A large, muscular arm pulls me into his side. "Let's go. This isn't the best of neighborhoods."

My head bobs back and forth like it's barely attached. "It's perfect." I cringe. "It was perfect." A disturbing thought occurs to me, and I shift to the right to get a good look at Zane's face. "Did Rodrigo see you today?"

He snorts. "It might surprise you, but I can be stealthy. He didn't see me."

My eyes skim over his tall, muscular body in disbelief. Unlike the other three, Zane is big. His size kind of reminds me of The Rock. Well, that and the shaved head. Add in the scar on his face, and the hardness in his grey eyes, and I can't imagine someone not noticing him.

"You're not inconspicuous," I state dryly. "Are you sure?"

The corners of his mouth twitch. "He didn't see me. I didn't have to track him because I knew where you were going. I passed him in a crowd crossing the street."

My brow furrows. "How did you put him asleep?"

He reaches into his pocket and pulls out a small silver box. He opens it with a flick of his thumb and shows me a tiny scrap of fabric inside. "A friend of mine at the CIA asked me to test it for him. It's doused with a sleep-inducing chemical. You swipe it on someone's skin, and within five to seven minutes, they're asleep. It's not as efficient as a chokehold, but it works when you don't want to get too close." He snaps the box shut. A look of disappointment flashes across his face. "It doesn't work long, though. Rodrigo woke up right after you left the park."

Nervously, I turn my head to scan the street around us.

"Cruz said he went to meet Armando," Zane reassures me.

"I thought Cruz was completing surveillance at the facility today," I interject, unsettled by the thought of the two of them following me. Technically, Cruz has had me under surveillance for a couple of weeks, but I thought he'd stopped. Maybe they wanted to be sure I didn't give Armando too much info, or they wanted to hear the conversation for themselves.

Zane scrutinizes my face. "You would have done the same."

His confidence irks me, but he's right. Unwilling to concede his point, I announce my intention to leave. "I'm going to get food. And a drink." Maybe sit under a dark cloud and let it rain on my head until it washes away my sins.

The arm around my shoulders tightens. "A friend recommended a place near the apartment. He said they have the best burgers in town. Mind some company?"

He's not going to go away. With a huff, I give in, but secretly, I'm relieved to share this burden today.

"You're obviously determined to spend time with me." My eyes meet his grey ones. "On one condition. Find out what happened to Lupe for me."

With a dip of his chin, he strides inside the cantina.

11

ZANE

Before I walk out of Cantina Iguana, I take a deep breath and school my features into something neutral. Her condition for dinner... information on Lupe and her father. She mumbled something about my size and fluency in Spanish, but honestly, she couldn't face going back in there. Although she would never admit it.

Quinn's hunch was right. It was Rodrigo. A cook taking out the trash saw him grab Lupe when she left work. The same cook found her the next day in the alley dumpster, barely recognizable except for the sun tattoo on her wrist. Words of hate and death had been carved into her face and body until you could barely see the girl underneath.

Is the fucker just a psycho who does this to every woman he meets? Or did he do this to get to Quinn? Cruz said he was *hunting* her, and he would know. Is this part of the hunt—to terrify his future victims until he catches them? He had to know she would find out about Lupe.

This is why she was worried he'd seen me. A dry laugh escapes. My fist clenches. If only he would come after me, or any of us. He would learn how sheltered he's been in his little kingdom of power. The real world is a lot tougher.

Quinn's pacing the sidewalk when I reach her side. She takes one look at my face and immediately blanches. "Fuck."

Surprised, I stare back at her. I know my poker face is good.

"The lack of expression gave it away, and the anger in your eyes confirmed it," she says dully. "Tell me."

I assure myself she can handle it. After all, she's been working for a ruthless man and his psycho lackey for over a year, but it's like beating a stray dog with a stick. I can't do it.

"It was Rodrigo."

"Details, Zane," she orders, her eyes narrowed in anger.

An idea springs to mind. "Do you want the information on Lupe's death or her father? You pick, but you can't have both," I offer, gambling she'll make the right choice.

Indecision wars on her face for several minutes, making me question myself, but she finally concedes.

"The father," she spits out, anger coloring her voice. But her eyes are filled with relief, too.

Relieved myself, I yank her into my side and start moving away from the cantina and the sad, faded iguana on the door. The details of Lupe's death would only haunt her.

"Lupe's brother, Bruno, lives in Saltillo. If the father's willing to go, we can move him to his son's house," I tell her. "I'll even drive him over myself."

Her shoulders soften, and she leans into me. "Armando promised to keep Rodrigo busy for a couple of days, which gives me a small window. I'll visit him tomorrow."

She's tough, but today was a punch in the gut. I rub my hand up and down her arm, trying to soothe the sting.

I'm glad she made me go in and get the information. Knowing she'd designated the cantina her "haven" gave me a glimpse into the despair and darkness she's been living in since she arrived, and what she'll likely return to when we leave. It hits a chord in me I hadn't expected.

"I used to frequent dives like the cantina." The words pop out of my mouth like a jack-in-the-box.

She looks up, her green eyes urging me to continue.

Shit.

"My team and I were part of a multi-country, multi-unit task force under orders to hunt down an international terrorist. It took two years, but we finally located the bastard in Cabo Delgado, Mozambique. Our intel and the surveillance were solid, but we didn't want to rush into it and potentially tip him off. We did our due diligence. A week after we arrived, we moved in to capture him," I tell her, my voice gruff with memories. I draw her in closer.

She wraps her free arm around my waist.

"They were waiting for us. When we realized it was an ambush, we tried to retreat, but we were miles from safety. It was a bloodbath. Twelve of us made it out. Out of fifty-seven men." I pause to get my anger under control. Even after all these years, the rage is like acid in my veins.

I heave a sigh. "When we returned, they disbanded the force and sent us home. I tried to resign from the Army, but my CO refused to accept it. He sent me on extended leave."

She looks up at me hesitantly. "Is that because of your father?"

Someone did their research. "So, you know about him?"

"Retired Admiral John Boseman, West Point star athlete, decorated war hero, shining example of our military's finest?" she says with derision. "And Senator of the great state of Texas, of course. I'm not a fan of his politics."

I stumble but quickly recover. "Sorry, crack in the sidewalk."

She looks at me warily. "Is this when you slummed it in dive bars?"

"My father's extreme," I admit, my mind reeling with possibilities. "And yes. I probably frequented every dive bar in Texas during those six months, drowning in drink, cloaking myself in their seediness. I'd probably still be there if it weren't for Marcos." I study her face intently, satisfied when I see her flinch at the word Texas.

"Marcos showed me a picture of two men being held hostage. A lieutenant from the US and a squadron sergeant major from the UK. Men captured during our retreat. I didn't even know," I admit to her, my voice low with anguish. Guilt never goes away. With time, it dulls like a tarnished penny, but it never leaves.

The sign for the burger place shines brightly just a few feet ahead. With relief, I pick up the pace and hurry us inside.

At the table, I grab the menu, studiously avoiding her gaze. "The jalapeno bacon avocado burger sounds delicious. Do you know what you're going to have?"

Her hand captures mine, and she forces me to lower the barrier between us. "Zane, I appreciate what you're trying to do, but not at the expense of yourself." Troubled eyes look back at me.

Frustrated, I lean forward. She needs to know it's possible to get through the dark and find something meaningful again. If my crap ass story is going to help her, I can damn well buck up and tell it.

"A high-ranking official covered up the hostage situation. When I confronted the man responsible, my father stepped in and defended him." I rub the scar along my cheek in memory. "They blacklisted me, kicked me out of the Army, and threatened me with prison. But I didn't fall into a black hole this time. Marcos ordered me to rescue those men, so I did."

Although sometimes I almost wish they had died in the ambush. Tortured every day for a year, their minds and bodies were fractured. Even the love of their families couldn't save them, and they committed suicide within weeks of returning home.

"Marcos also gave me the evidence to clear my name. When

it went through, I immediately resigned, and went to work with him, rescuing others," I finish, desperate for her to see that she can find another path besides the one she's on now.

The server comes over and takes our order.

Quinn avoids my eyes to stare out the window. "If it was covered up, how did Marcos get the information?"

"A young hacker intercepted the ransom demand," I say softly.

Her eyes leave the window to stare at me for several long minutes. "Is that how you and Sterling met?"

"Yes," I answer, hesitantly. "But any more info will have to come from him."

She nods and bites into her burger. "Your friend is right. This is delicious."

Those are the last words she says for the rest of the meal. I want to believe she's digesting the information, but the air is thick with undercurrents.

When I return from the restroom, she's waiting for me by the front door. "I paid the bill, and I'm ready to go back to my apartment. Would you mind texting me the address for Lupe's father?"

"I'll send it," I reassure her. Hesitantly, I lay my hand on her shoulder. "I didn't mean to upset you."

"You're a very good man, Zane," she replies, tapping my chest. "Marcos, the people you rescue, your current team—they're lucky to have you on their side."

"I can be on your side, too—if you let me," I state firmly, offering her the same friendship and support I give to my team.

She smiles but says nothing in return.

We walk back to the apartment side-by-side, but miles apart.

OUR TEMPORARY HEADQUARTERS IS EMPTY WHEN I RETURN. RAIDER and Cruz are at the facility gathering intel, and Sterling is mapping different routes in and out of the city to give us exit options. I grab a beer and sit down on the couch.

My conversation with Quinn repeats over and over in my mind. I can't figure out what I said to cause the distance between us, and it's driving me crazy.

I'm still brooding when Raider walks through the door.

"Why are you sitting in the dark?" he cautiously asks, taking the seat across from me.

Reluctant to disclose my confusing night with Quinn, I shrug and take a sip of the very warm beer in my hand. I grimace and set it down. "Did you find anything new?"

Raider gets up and grabs two beers. He hands one to me and sits. "Nothing. Spill."

It couldn't hurt. Raider's got an uncanny sense about people. It's probably why he's such a good chameleon. I blurt it all out. His expression is blank while he listens, except for the times I mention Rodrigo. That's when Raider gets what I call his "killer face" … an unemotional mask of death. I tilt my beer toward him and nod in agreement. Rodrigo's days are numbered.

Ten minutes later, I wrap up. "Tell me, oh wise one, what the hell did I do wrong?"

"Nothing. She told you why she was withdrawing, but I don't think you heard her. Not a surprise. You get tunnel vision when you're trying to help others," he says coolly, taking the last sip of his beer. "You and Sterling are good men. Not once in your lives have you abandoned your principles."

I shake my head. "We've killed people, hacked systems, bribed officials, and a hell of a lot more. I don't understand."

"You did those things to protect others, to fight for what's right, or to do the right thing. It's admirable, and it's why I joined your team. I needed something to good to balance the bad," he explains, then leans forward, his eyes locked on mine.

"Quinn is seeking vengeance; the opposite of doing what's right."

His light blue eyes gleam with memory. "Vengeance is the name your soul screams when it shatters. It's a call into the darkness, a promise to Death himself, to abandon the light until death is served to those who wronged you. Quinn is fighting for death, not life."

He hesitates for a brief second. "The guards at the facility whisper about Armando's twin brother, Julio. Almost two years ago, he was brutally tortured, and killed, along with every single one of his men." He pulls up a picture on his phone. "My brother sent these to me."

Rearing back from the image on his phone, I swipe through the rest of them, full of disbelief. "You think Quinn did this to them?" My mind stutters, trying to reconcile the fierce, petite woman with the brutality of those deaths. But if Raider's brother sent it, the picture is authentic. "I'm not a fan of digging into someone's past, but maybe we need to know more about Quinn."

"I agree, but not for the same reasons," Raider slowly admits. "Your priority is to protect our team, but I've been in her shoes. She needs someone to make sure *she* comes out of this alive."

After Mozambique, I swore to do everything in my power to protect my men. I look at Raider. I also swore to never leave a man behind. Quinn's face flashes in my mind. Fuck me.

12

QUINN

Zane paired me with Cruz this morning and sent us to the facility to map the guard routes on the inside. Most of the routes have been fairly predictable, except this one. Now we're stuck in a closet, trying to figure out when the next guard will make his rounds.

Standing chest to chest with Cruz in the incredibly tight space, I can barely draw a breath. I strain to hear the slightest noise beyond the door.

Silence.

Exhaling slowly, I shuffle back a half a step to alleviate the friction of our bodies rubbing lightly against each other.

The stifling heat in the closet is causing sweat to drip down my face, but the cool metal shelves against my back are helping to alleviate the worst of it.

Cruz bends forward to whisper in my ear. "Tell me, Quinn. Did you find someone to help you finish?" His finger traces a path down my neck.

Hmph, someone's ego is dented.

I snort. "Does it matter?"

"Yes," he flatly states, lifting his head to stare down at me, eyes boring into mine, while he waits for an answer.

Good. I press my lips together and stare at his chest. The subtle scent of soap and man drifts up to my nose. Cruz. The smell is barely there, but it makes me want to dive into his skin until it surrounds me.

He shifts closer until the space between us disappears. The palm of his hand cups my neck and jaw, holding me in place. Hard lips brush mine, but they don't settle. Instead, they journey to the other side of my neck and begin nibbling and kissing up and down its length.

I gasp, and his hand immediately moves to cover my mouth.

He lifts his head to listen, but when only silence reigns, he drops those devastating lips to the juncture between my neck and shoulder.

Instead of shoving him back, I turn my head and arch up to give him greater access. My hands grasp his hips tightly, the need to pull him closer like a drum beating in my blood, but I lock my arms and resist its call.

Tongue joins lips, flicking lightly against a sensitive spot, and I barely hold back my words.

"Tell me," he orders softly in my ear. The pad of his thumb slides across my lips. "Let's start with something easier. Did you kiss another?"

My shoulder lifts, unwilling to give him an answer.

The slight movement is like waving a red cape. Hard lips capture mine in a demanding kiss, but unlike our first one, this one has a possessive edge to it. Every stroke of his tongue is intent on owning my lips, until the thought and feel of another's kiss is nothing but smoke.

Booted footsteps filter through the closed door. They stop. Start again.

Cruz' lips refuse to release mine. My heart beats faster.

A radio crackles. The guard stops, but after a second, he takes three more steps. The handle jiggles. He curses. Keys jingle.

Cruz pulls his mouth from mine and reaches behind his back for his gun.

I shift to give him room for the shot.

Another voice calls out.

The guard in front of our closet answers, but the words are muffled.

Keys jingle again, but this time, he moves away from the door.

We listen for a minute, but he doesn't return.

Eager to get out of the closet, I reach for the handle.

An arm locks around my body, pulling me back. His breath caresses the shell of my ear. "Quinn."

Hearing the need in his voice makes me smile with satisfaction. "I went home and finished myself."

"Always twisting the knife, aren't you?" he asks, with a low chuckle.

With his own quick twist, he unlocks the door and turns the handle.

Light from the hallway filters into the dark closet.

I pull up my phone. "Unlike the last one, this guard was exactly on time. There are two more patrolling on the east side of the building. Once we confirm their movements, we'll be done. Let's go."

WE FINISH MAPPING THE TIMING AND ROUTE OF THE GUARDS. CRUZ moves toward our exit, a side door near the back of the building. Suddenly, the sound of feet pounding the ground outside has us scrambling for cover.

Cruz' head swivels and stops. He points up and cups his hands.

After a brief glance, I take a few steps back to get momentum, step into the cradle, and spring up. I grab the steel beam and haul my body on top of it.

Once he's sure I'm secure, he runs up the side wall and catches the same beam I used and lifts himself up. He quickly scans our surroundings until he finds a corner with more cover. One long, elegant finger motions for me to move.

With arms held straight out, I carefully stand. Looking across to the next beam, I realize they're farther apart than I can comfortably step. I'll have to jump. Taking a half step back until my toes are the only thing on the back of the twelve inch beam, I spring off the back, hit the front with the other foot, and quickly launch myself across each one until I get to the corner. Using the ceiling for balance, I turn and face Cruz, an exhilarated smile on my face.

Intense brown eyes flicker with heat. He stands and steps forward, long legs easily reaching the next beam.

The exit door below me flies opens, and I press my back into the corner, praying the guard doesn't look up.

Cruz freezes.

The radio in the guard's hand squawks several times, but I only catch a few words before he disappears down the hall. Girl. Missing.

My eyes dart to Cruz. *Fuck*. I hope it's not one of our girls.

One minute, he's standing in front of me, the next, he's gone. Silently disappearing like a mirage in the middle of the desert.

The door swings open, and two more guards rush in, quickly following the first. Neither of them looks up.

I let my head drop back to rest on the concrete wall. This is as good a place to hide as any. Once it's dark, I'll make my way out of the facility. Hopefully, the guards will soon return to their normal routines.

STANDING IN ONE SPOT FOR TWO HOURS IS BRUTAL. WHY HAVE I never realized that fact? Maybe because I never could be still. My mother used to laugh and tell me I skipped crawling and walking and went straight to running, because I was in a hurry from the minute I was born.

My mouth twists at the memory. It's been so long since I thought of her. With a laid back personality, her green eyes constantly sparkled with life and laughter, and her zest for fun infected everyone around her until we had no choice but to join in on her shenanigans.

An ultra-serious child, I would roll my eyes in protest, but even I wasn't impervious to her charms. She once told me it was her job to make sure I spent time laughing and playing, so I would look back on my childhood with no regrets.

She was right. I treasure those moments more than anything.

Sometimes when I dream, I see her in heaven with my father and stepfather, their arms around each other, laughing. It hurts more than I can describe to know I won't ever be there with them.

Sophia is never with them, either. She's here, waiting for me to avenge her death and give her peace. When I'm done, she'll be able to move on and join them.

A soft whistle jerks me out of my dark thoughts, and I look down to find Cruz below me with his arms outstretched. He came back for me.

Blinking, I scramble to maneuver around until my body hangs off the beam, then I let go. Strong arms catch my waist, and he lowers me to the ground.

He holds a finger to his lips. Moving fast, he heads for the door.

Following tightly behind him, I watch the fluid way he moves, his body weightless against the gravity that pulls me down. Pure stealth.

A clumsy step to my right, and a sharp sound punctures the

silence. *Damn it.* We can't stop, though. With my lip between my teeth, I focus on making the next step quieter.

The open gate at the corner finally appears.

"How far to the car?" I murmur, swiping at the sweat on my face.

"Three miles," his low voice answers.

"How did you learn to move so quietly?" I ask, curious about the training one must go through to become a ghost.

He says nothing for a minute. "When I was a kid growing up in North Carolina, a man came to visit once a month. He would train me—how to walk silently, hide in plain sight, use weapons, take a hit without sound. After he left, I'd practice every day until he returned to teach me something new. By the time I was an adult, it was ingrained in me."

His voice is full of undercurrents. I tilt my head. "Did your parents hire him?"

"No. He'd show up, my mother would kiss me on the forehead, then send me with him. He stopped coming when I went off to college," he states, his tone matter-of-fact.

His mother. "He was your father."

"Yes."

Silence.

A lot of muddy water under that bridge.

"Did you ever see him again?" I tentatively ask, wondering if he'll answer.

"When I graduated from college, he offered me a job with the CIA," he reveals nonchalantly, but I can't help but shiver.

If it quacks like a duck...

"He trained you all your life so he could offer you a job with the CIA? He was a spy, too?" I press, knowing the answer but wanting him to confirm it.

"Yes. We're almost to the car. Another half mile," he informs me.

"I'm guessing you're not close?"

He looks back at me with a wry smile. "We were never close.

I spent years trying to figure him out. He was the best ghost in the business, but the only thing he cared about more than his country was leaving a legacy."

Legacy. Growing up, all I wanted was to follow in my dad's footsteps. All his dad wanted was his son to follow his. And yet, the two are vastly different in nature.

"I'm sorry," I reply softly.

He looks startled. "Why are you sorry?"

"As someone lucky enough to have two fathers growing up, I can't imagine what it was like to know he would never be the person you wanted him to be," I explain.

He's silent for a second. "Two fathers?"

"My father died when I was eight. Line of duty. My mother married a wonderful man when I was ten. He cared for me like I was his own child. Both men taught me a lot. Practical things, like how to shoot a gun and change a tire, how to defend myself, and how to get back up after getting knocked down." My voice dies when I realize this is the second time I've thought of my family tonight.

He steps in front of me.

Even in the dark, I can feel his eyes sweeping over me.

"I was a weapon. They would point me in a direction, and I would kill, no questions asked." His voice is neutral, but I can't help feeling like this is a test.

"You served your country," I say, without looking at him. "There's the car." I point to the left and turn toward it.

A harsh laugh escapes him. "That's what everyone says. What would they say if they knew the government wasn't so noble? What would you say if I told you how much I enjoyed planning and executing my duty?"

It stops me in my tracks. "Did you?" I ask, studying his face for the truth.

He jerks his chin down. "Yes. It was both challenging and a thrill. To see a target die by my hand and know they didn't even see it coming."

My eyes drop briefly to his right hand. "Why did you stop?"

He looks up at the stars in the sky. "One day, I woke up empty. There was nothing left inside. The thrill, the satisfaction, the ambition to be the best… it was gone. Nothing I did brought it back. I tried to explain it to them, but the CIA didn't care. Weapons are meant to be used. They kept sending me out on missions."

He runs a hand through his hair before tucking it behind his ears. "Until I screwed up. Accidentally killed a family. Mom, dad, and two kids." His breath comes in short bursts, but he manages to get it out. "It almost destroyed me. The CIA classified me as a liability and recalled me. Once I was grounded, I looked for a way forward. Something that allowed me to breathe again. With help from Marcos and Zane, I extricated myself from the CIA and went to work for them—rescuing people and protecting my team."

"When you look back, are you proud or ashamed?" I ask, desperate to know if the conflict raging inside me will ever be resolved.

"Both." His answer is short, but the impact is like a shot to the gut.

Now I know. I'll never be whole again.

13

QUINN

Before Zane and his team arrived in Monterrey, my thoughts were consumed with killing Armando and his men. It's all I did. Plot, plan, and dream of it.

Now, the past is knocking on the door of my mind, teasing me with good memories and reminding me of the person I used to be. It's bittersweet—seeing them but knowing I'll never be that person again.

Both Zane and Cruz found a way forward, and I know they're trying to help me, too. But I don't give a damn about later. I can't. Sophia deserves to rest in peace, and I'm the only one left to give it to her.

"Why did you tell me?" I ask Cruz. "Is this a conspiracy to get me to give up my plans to come rescue with you?"

"If I thought it would work, yes," he replies, his voice low. "The real answer… honesty. I don't want my past standing between us." There's a raw note in his voice that makes me believe him. "I won't apologize for who I am. The deaths are mine to own—both the good and bad—those in the past and those yet to come. It took a long time for me to step out of the darkness, but I can't live fully in the light either. I'm not wired that way. Does that bother you?"

Relief rushes through me, and my knees go weak. I don't have to pretend I'm anyone but who I am with him. Flawed, broken, strong, cold. It doesn't matter.

"I knew your past before we kissed," I admit softly, wanting him to know it didn't matter to me either. "I didn't give it one ounce of thought except to wonder who I'd pissed off."

He chuckles. "My past is buried deep. You must have one hell of a network," he murmurs. His eyes drop to my lips, and he takes a step closer. "Before we kissed?"

Would he stay with me tonight? Or would he reject me again? I bite my lip, trying to decide if I should ask him.

Fuck it.

"Are you going to leave me to finish by myself tonight?" I taunt him. "If so, I need to get back and charge the batteries."

Brown eyes narrow. "Maybe, but I want to watch," he says with a husky laugh, but I see the fire flare in his eyes.

Frustrated, I lift a shoulder. "Maybe I'll let you." A laugh escapes. "Or maybe I'll decide to invite someone else in to finish what you started… someone real."

Without a whisper of noise, he pounces, sweeping me up in his arms and carrying me the last few feet to the car. "Don't make me kill someone tonight."

But before he can open the door, I point to the hood. "The sky's lit up. There's no one for miles around. I want you. Here. Now."

He sets me down on the hood and steps between my legs. Lean hands reach up and cup my jaw. "Are you sure?"

Within five seconds, I'm naked from the waist up and tossing my clothes behind me. The night air lightly caresses my skin, adding a sensual note to my decision.

"Yes." I reach for him.

He catches my hands and pulls them behind my back. "The thought of you letting someone else put out the fire I started has driven me crazy for days." His mouth descends until it's a whisper above mine. "Not tonight. You're going to feel me on every inch of you when I'm done."

The leash snaps, and his lips descend, landing on mine in a ruthlessly carnal kiss. The fire he lit days ago, barely tempered by the finish I gave myself, flares into a roar. My mouth meets his demands with my own, building the flames into an inferno.

I tug on my arms, needing to touch and feel him beneath my fingers, wanting his hardness in the palm of my hand.

"No," he murmurs, tightening his grip.

Instead of returning to my mouth, his lips and tongue blaze a trail to my neck. Licking and sucking, searching out the most sensitive spots to tease them repeatedly.

I breathe out and surrender. My body arches into his every touch, wanting more, demanding he live up to his promise.

His mouth finishes torturing my neck and shoulders and finally moves down to my aching breasts. A warm, wet mouth latches on to my nipple, sucking and flicking, while his cool hand does the same to the other one. The dual sensation makes my breath catch.

Moaning softly, I plead for more.

Fingers walk themselves down my stomach to the snap in my jeans.

I inhale sharply.

He stops.

"No, no, no. Don't stop," I moan.

"I'm going to lay you back with your arms above your head. You're not to move them. If you do, I'll stop and make you wait until we get back," he threatens softly. "Do you understand?"

Instead of replying, I lie back and pull my arms over my head. "Give me your shirt."

A curious glint enters his eyes, and he pulls his t-shirt off and hands it to me.

The curves and valleys on his lean but muscular chest are sexier than hell in the moonlight. Shadows and light play upon the muscles that make me clench with need. With a groan, I grip his t-shirt, knowing I'll need something in my hands, or I'll forget and move them.

With me lying across the hood, his fingers start back at the top of my shoulders and travel a leisurely path down to my waist. "You look beautiful lying there in the moonlight, the curves of your body on display for me and only me. Everything I've touched and tasted has only left me craving more."

He unsnaps my jeans and pulls them off me. "So beautiful." Fingers trail softly around the edges of my underwear. When they get to the back, he turns my body to the side and runs his hand over my cheeks.

I arch up and back, picturing myself on all fours, and a moan escapes.

His breath stutters, and I smile.

Easing me down on my back, he rips off my underwear, and his mouth descends on the center of my desire, devouring me, bringing me to the edge, only to stop. Over and over.

Spread wide, I look down and meet his intense eyes. "Are you going to finish what you started?" I pant, barely able to get the words out. I'm so close.

"Hold on," he says with a growl.

His mouth drops to my nub and sucks hard, but it's only the beginning. His wicked tongue flicks rapidly back and forth for several minutes. It changes one more time to a soft suck. My moans tell him which I like better, and he focuses on that one move.

When the edge appears, I find his eyes and let myself fall, my body clenching tightly with heat and desire. He's curved protectively above me, framed by the stars in the night sky.

His brown eyes are practically obsidian, his own passion riding him hard. Yet he continues to watch me.

"I want you. Now," I tell him as soon as I can speak again. "But I want to touch you, too."

"Not yet," he returns, his voice harsh. "I'm on the edge. One touch from you and it will all be over." He pulls a condom from his back pocket and shoves the denim down his lean hips.

I raise my head to watch him roll the condom on. Within seconds, he's pushing into me, inch by inch.

Hands slide under my back, and he pulls me up to face him. "It's not going to be slow," he warns me.

I wrap my legs around him tightly. "Hallelujah. I thought I was going to have to beg you to fuck me."

"Maybe another time," he retorts, his cock sliding in and out. Hard and fast. His breathing becomes ragged, but he doesn't slow.

My body tightens, and I moan at the feel of his body in mine. "It feels so good. Keep going, just a little more." I reach down and bring myself over the edge again.

As soon as my body clenches, he comes, too.

Locked together tightly while our bodies come back down, I take a second to enjoy the feel of him, not moving but still a part of me.

Cool hands rub lightly down my back, soothing me with each stroke.

Once our breathing is under control, he pulls back and gives me one of his usual dominating kisses, like he needs to imprint himself on me.

"That was so much better than me or my toys," I say with a sigh. It has been too damn long since the last time I had sex. So long, I don't even remember it.

"We're not done," he coolly informs me. "I said, 'every inch,' and I've only touched the top half." His hand rubs across my butt. "And I heard your breathless moan when I turned you over. It took every ounce of will I have to stop myself from putting you on your hands and knees. I won't be so lenient again."

I push him back and slide off the hood. With a couple of hops and jumps, it only takes a minute to get dressed. When I look over, he's wearing an amused expression on his face.

"Let's go."

14

RAIDER

Cruz strolls in the next morning and sets his tracker on the charger. While he pours himself a cup of coffee, I study him, intrigued by the undercurrent of mood I sense. He's almost *relaxed*.

"Did you hear the weird situation with the girl yesterday?" I ask, puzzled by the incident.

He leans against the counter, mug in hand, and thinks about it for a second. "They thought a girl was missing, but in fact, she had been there the whole time. Somebody miscounted, I guess."

"A girl went to the showers. An hour later, they conducted their counts, and she was missing. They sounded the alarm. Guards searched but didn't find her. They lined everyone up again and did a recount. She was there. Said she had been there the whole time," I briefly recount the incident. When he nods, I smirk. It's not like him to miss the details. "I find it interesting that the girl who went into the showers isn't the same girl who showed up for the recount, don't you?"

He lowers the mug. "Where's the first girl?"

I frown. "Even I didn't see where she went."

"How did you realize they were different girls?"

I shake my head in disbelief. "One was considerably taller than the other." With a shrug, I take my mug over to the sink. "One or two of the guards were paid extra last night."

He nods in agreement. "It's good to know they can be bribed."

Sterling and Zane stride into the room.

"What's the plan for today?" I ask Zane, tamping down the restlessness stirring inside me. Unlike Cruz, I need constant movement. It helps me rein in the darkness that's constantly searching for its next target.

Zane's grey eyes flash me a knowing look. "I want you, Cruz, and Sterling to walk through the plans for tomorrow. Make sure there are no holes, or we'll have an army coming down on top of us. Check each other. Quinn and I will be back around noon."

I raise an eyebrow. "Where are you going?"

Both Cruz and Sterling turn to Zane, waiting for him to answer.

He scowls irritably. "You're like a bunch of children with a favorite toy. We're moving Lupe's father to Saltillo. Satisfied?"

"If you're concerned about the planning, I can take them and you can stay here," I offer, knowing his obsessive need to walk through every detail again and again.

Not a flicker of indecision crosses his face. "No. I told her I'd drive him over." His eyes dart to the coffee pot and back to his watch. "She should be here in a minute."

I jerk my head toward the coffee. "Not everyone is as punctual as you. Grab some coffee."

He glances at his watch a second time but gives into his caffeine addiction. "Sterling, I want you to investigate Quinn. See what you can find on her background. The preliminary one we did isn't enough."

Sterling nods reluctantly. "Is there a reason why we're

digging deeper?" Green eyes narrow, looking at each of us, before focusing in on Zane and me. "Raider? Zane?"

That's one of the things I like most about Sterling. He's damn good at reading people.

Zane crosses his arms in defense. "I want to do our due diligence prior to the mission. It's hard to predict someone's actions when we don't know their motivations." He waits for Sterling to agree, which he reluctantly does. "We know a few things about her that can help. A past in law enforcement. Probably from Texas… She apparently doesn't care for my father's politics."

"Her father died in the line of duty when she was eight. Mother remarried," Cruz adds, without looking up from his coffee cup.

"Somebody she loved was found dead in the desert," I remind them. "There might be a newspaper article."

The roads we take when others destroy our lives have no rhyme or reason, only the pain driving us to change course. Hearing her story, even vaguely, hit me hard, and I'll do everything I can to help her. I've been there. The road she's on will destroy her if there isn't someone to help her out of the darkness.

"That's quite a lot more than I expected," Sterling admits with a sigh. "I'll also run facial recognition, but not through our usual channels. Maybe Henley can assist. I'm sure she's probably bored getting a legitimate company up and running." He winks at Cruz, who chuckles.

Zane sighs impatiently, his eyes fixed on his watch.

"Why don't I go check on her? You get the car and pull it around," I tell him. Zane can be a grumpy bastard when someone is running late. Too much military in the man.

Cruz tosses Zane the keys to the car. "Here." His eyes shift to me, and he lifts his chin toward the door.

I disappear without another word.

When I get to the third floor, Quinn is leaning against the door to her apartment, staring at Rodrigo.

"Make sure you don't go anywhere while I'm gone," Rodrigo

warns her. "I've been working on a few surprises I know you're going to love." He laughs. "I can't wait to see your face."

In a flash, she's standing toe to toe with him. "I know what you did to Lupe," she snarls. "Make sure you come back, because I'll be here waiting for you."

She pushes the nuzzle of her gun into his cheek. "You've been on my list for a long time. I originally thought about shooting you. Execution style. Done in an instant. After all, you're just a lapdog for the cartel, no real power." With a flick of her hand, she shoves the gun into the holster on her side. "Congratulations. You've moved up on the list. Shooting is too good for you, too quick. I can't wait to see your face when I carve you up like a pig."

Enraged, he grabs her by the throat.

Outside noises disappear, and the world stills around me. My attention narrows to a pinprick with Rodrigo at the center. I stride forward, but before I get there, he's releasing her and backing away.

"You'd better go before Armando pulls on your chain," she advises him, her voice devoid of all emotion.

Rodrigo gives an excited, high-pitched laugh. "You're absolutely perfect. Soon, we'll be able to spend some time together. I've got a special place picked out."

He passes me in the hall and heads for the stairs.

Quinn's face turns to me, death lingering in her eyes.

With careful movements, I lean on the wall beside her. "If Rodrigo knows you're here, we should move you up to our place."

She flips the knife in her hand over and over.

The darkness inside lifts its head to watch her, intrigued by someone who seems to match with it. But my body instinctively tightens to defend itself against the predator it senses nearby.

"Why?" she asks with a frown. "After the mission, you'll be gone. I'd rather be on my home turf when he comes calling. He doesn't know it, but I've got plans of my own for him." Her head tilts. "I've got to go. Zane is waiting for me."

Is she back to normal? "Look at me," I order her.

Empty green eyes turn toward me.

Zane won't take her anywhere if she shows up in this state. "That's what I thought," I murmur. "You know I'm not going to hurt you, right?" When she lifts a shoulder, I decide to take that as a yes. "Put the knife away."

Her fingers caress the blade, like she's saying goodbye to an old friend, before she slides it into the side pocket.

"You should really switch up where you hide it on your body. Being predictable gets you killed," I admonish her. "Zane is waiting downstairs in the car."

She takes a step to leave, but I grab her wrist.

Her body tenses.

"I want a kiss," I state firmly, hoping to shock her mind out of its current state. "I've been wanting to taste those killer lips of yours for a while. I bet you've already kissed Cruz, Sterling, and Zane."

"Not Zane," she interjects, but there's an intrigued note to her voice.

Interesting. "It's the age thing, isn't it? Zane never gets the girl," I state with a chuckle. "All the women fall for Lord Sterling. Handsome, rich bastard. Or for Cruz' brooding."

She eyes me curiously, and I'm relieved to see full awareness in them again. "My guess is you get all the girls, but you're too picky to want them back."

Amused by her reply, I shake my head. "No, I never get the girl either."

Her eyes travel from my head to my toes and back. She snorts.

"They don't like me because I scare them. When they see a killer looking back at them, they run and hide," I whisper, purposely allowing myself to turn colder. "Want to see?"

Her eyes meet mine, but instead of the usual fear, she's

entranced. Slim hands cup each side of my jaw, then she turns my head from side to side. A sigh escapes her pink mouth, and a second later, she pulls me down for a kiss.

Soft, pouty lips cling to the outside, while her tongue sweeps inside to taste and sweetly suck on mine. Sensual and unhurried, she kisses me like she's got forever in the palm of her hand.

It makes me want to consume her. Tamping down the beast inside, I continue to let her lead this kiss.

A horn honks several times, each one angrier than the last.

With regret, I pull back and place a sweet kiss goodbye on her lips. "Go, Zane is waiting."

She tilts her head, assessing me in a new light, but I keep my expression neutral. "I get... lost... sometimes. Thank you for bringing me back."

When she's gone, I stare at the empty space in front of me, wondering what the hell just happened.

15

———

<u>ZANE</u>

T he second she buckles the seatbelt, I stomp on the gas. "We're going to be late picking up Eduardo." Maybe I can shave off a few minutes. "Did you oversleep?" Although the dark circles under her eyes indicates lack of sleep. The street sign catches my eye and I automatically jerk the wheel to the right, sending us careening around the corner a little faster than normal.

She flicks her eyes at the speedometer and raises an eyebrow. "Rodrigo's leaving town for a couple of days. Wanted to say bye." The whole time she's talking, her thumbs never stop moving.

"Are you texting Armando to let him know?"

She stops for a second. "No, I'm texting a contact. Rodrigo's planning something. Since he stopped by my place on his way out of town, I can't help but think his trip is about me." After a second of deep thought, she continues texting.

"One minute out," I inform her. "How much have you let slip?"

Her brow furrows. "Absolutely nothing," she spits out. "Why would you think I had?"

I slam on the brakes and look at my watch. "Two minutes late," I state, satisfied with the three minutes I'd made up. "Let's go."

Her mouth opens, but something in the side mirror catches her eye, and it snaps shut. The door slams behind her.

I chuckle when I get out and follow her to the man standing in the doorway of a shop.

Quinn is holding his wrinkled hand in the crook of her arm. "Eduardo, this is Zane, my… friend. He's going to drive us to Saltillo this morning."

Eduardo releases Quinn and holds out his hand. Dark eyebrows shoot up when I place my hand in his. "Zane. Mucho gusto." He leans into Quinn and whispers something that makes her laugh.

She squints up at me. "He's definitely big. About six foot, three inches, muscles everywhere, legs like tree trunks, shaved head, tan complexion, scar on his cheek." Her lips twitch with laughter. "Are you ready to go see your son?"

"Si," he replies, taking her elbow again. They walk past, and he throws a thumb over his shoulder.

Wily old goat. "I'll get the bags," I call out, laughing. It dies when I see the three small bags sitting in the corner. That's not much for the long life he's led. I pick them up and carefully stow them in the trunk.

Quinn puts Eduardo in the front passenger seat. It reminds me of what you would do for an elderly relative and makes me smile.

On the hour drive to Saltillo, Eduardo regales us with stories from his life with his children and wife in Monterrey. The sadness in his voice when he speaks of Lupe is heartbreaking. It's apparent how much he's going to miss her and his home.

"Take a right here," Quinn instructs from the back seat. "It's the third house on the left."

I turn into the driveway and shut off the car. "It's a nice house. White and tan. Modern. A bike is lying in the front yard. A family neighborhood. It looks safe." I don't specifically address Eduardo, but if I were blind and moving to a new place, I'd want a little reassurance.

"Gracias," he replies softly. Wrinkled hands glide over the side of the door until he finds the handle. He gets out and stands by the side of the car.

Quinn pats my shoulder and steps out to help Eduardo.

"I'll get the bags," I call out, making the old man chuckle.

The front door opens, and a young boy runs out of the house. "Abuelo." His thin arms wrap around Eduardo's waist.

Eduardo hugs him tightly. "Hola, Antonio."

A man and woman walk out of the house. After greetings and introductions, we hand them Eduardo's belongings.

I take a quick second to shoot off a text to Raider.

Eduardo grabs Quinn's arms when she gives him a hug goodbye, his face serious, and says something that puts a look of fierce determination on hers.

In response, she takes his hand and places his palm on her cheek. "I promise."

Satisfied, he pats her cheek and says goodbye.

On the way back to Monterrey, she turns to face me. "Why would you think I would let something slip to Rodrigo?"

My mouth compresses. "We've all picked up on things the last few days. If Rodrigo has enough pieces, he'll find your past."

"I admit," she begins, almost haltingly. "Being around all of you is affecting me. For over two years, all my thoughts have centered around what I need to do. Isolating made it easier to stay focused."

She nervously hooks a strand of hair behind her ear. "It's been me and only me for a long time. Suddenly, you four are here, plucking at invisible strings I didn't know were there. The comradery of a team, having back-up, and being comforted…" Her gaze turns to the outside. "The memories of my family, and the reminder I'm more than a machine." Her voice trails off for a second.

"You're right. It's made me careless," she admits defensively. "But not around Rodrigo. Prior to getting this rescue assignment, I've only seen him a dozen times. We exchanged flash drives, not words. It wasn't until Armando and I met in person that things changed."

Sterling and I were the first to team up on a rescue. We clicked immediately, bringing the same sense of freedom, and understanding, so I understand why she is more relaxed with us, but it still doesn't explain why Rodrigo is hunting her.

I grab her hand. "Maybe you were meant to find something beyond this… task you've set for yourself. Finding us might be fate giving you what you need." Knowing she doesn't want to hear these things and stopping myself from saying them are two different beasts, but when she doesn't respond, I let it drop. "Obsessions don't start overnight. Something must have triggered Rodrigo."

Her slim shoulders rise and fall. "I don't know, but I'll deal with him when he returns. I'm done playing cat-and-mouse. And I promised Eduardo I'd get the man responsible for Lupe's death."

Conflicted, I shift restlessly. The idea of her dealing with that psycho on her own makes me a little crazy.

"Have you run another background check on me?" The question explodes into the silence. "It's what I would do with more info."

My eyes leave the road to study her face for a second. Green eyes steadily hold mine.

"It's in progress," I confirm.

A wry smile graces her lips. "Good to know. I hate surprises."

"I don't like them, either. Never have. They rarely turn out the way you expect," I gruffly admit.

She chuckles. "What's on the agenda for today? Are we still a go for tomorrow night?"

I nod. "I've got Sterling, Raider, and Cruz running through the mission now. We'll grab some lunch and catch up when we get back." My stomach tightens. "You know, we'll have to alert the officials when we return and tell them about the facilities. Someone needs to rescue the rest of them."

She looks down at her hands. "I'm counting on it."

But where will she be?

THE 3D MODEL OF THE BUILDING IS DISPLAYED ON THE TABLE WHEN we return. I toss the pizzas on the kitchen counters and walk back to review their progress.

Red lines show the paths we've chosen for entry and exit, along with times posted for each leg. Yellow lines are the alternatives. Guard rotations are noted with times, especially for the two in the annex.

Quinn stands at my side, studying each piece of the mission. "What time are we going in?"

Sterling finishes a slice and wipes off his fingers. He points to the time in the upper right corner. "Two a.m. We considered the idea of going in when the other guard leaves to get food, but both times occur in broad daylight. The cover of night is still better." He winks at her.

A pink blush washes over her cheeks.

Cruz takes over. "Once we have the girls, we'll split up. Sterling and I will take one girl and Raider and Zane will take the other. We'll regroup at our new base of operations."

Her eyes dart to each of us. She turns to me and crosses her arms. "Zane?"

Seeing the determined look on her face, I sigh. "I originally thought to limit the mission to the four of us. We've been working together for a long time and can anticipate each other's moves. Plus, we trust each other."

She flinches at the word. "And now?"

"Without trust, we need leverage. Something you can give us that we can use against you if you turn on us." My voice is firm when I give her my condition for joining the mission. I like her, but my men come first.

Fingers tap lightly on her arm. "How about my real name?"

"Is that something Armando would find interesting?" I counter.

She thinks about it. "No, my name wouldn't mean anything to him." Her eyes linger on each of us. "Won't you have my background back soon?"

All three give me a look of approval. Deception doesn't sit well with them. Any of us, really. "We don't know when the information will get back to us, but I have a feeling you planned for that contingency. We need something concrete now."

Small hands clench into fists. "My sister's name is... was Sophia Lopez."

Raider steps closer.

None of us say a word. The devastation on her face tells us how hard this is for her.

"Armando... he... killed her," she finishes, her whole body shaking. "It was personal."

Raider's eyes turn wild, but this time, he shifts back a few steps.

Ah, hell.

Cruz reaches out and places a hand on Raider's shoulder to stop him.

Quinn watches everything with wide eyes.

"Sophia is a beautiful name, love," Sterling states softly, his voice soothing in the tense atmosphere. "I think we all need a break, don't you?" When she nods, he motions to Cruz. "Why don't you go with Cruz and pack your stuff up? We'll take it over with ours in the morning."

She drags her eyes from Raider to Cruz and nods.

Cruz laces his fingers with hers and pulls her out the door.

Raider explodes into movement the second the door shuts.

I place my body in front of his, but I don't touch him. "Stop. Two girls are counting on us to get them out of that hellhole tomorrow. After they are safe, we can figure out what to do for Quinn and the rest of the people in the facilities."

Raider stops laying weapons on the table. Blank icy blue eyes drill into me.

"Personally, I think we should ask Quinn what she has planned for that bloody bastard," Sterling interjects. "If you take her vengeance, will she find peace?" Green eyes meet blue, and a shared understanding passes between them.

Raider's body shudders, and he gives a negative shake. "No, she won't." He kicks the chair from the table. "Merda!"

"They're on their way back," Sterling says, getting to his feet. "Try to act civilized." His tone is snobby, upper crust English and dripping with disdain.

A spate of French spills from Raider's mouth.

They both laugh, and I sigh with relief. The last thing we need before a mission is for Raider to go on a killing spree.

16

QUINN

The last time I said her name aloud, I was carving Julio's body into pieces—while he was alive, of course. He was blubbering on about his brother and someone named Gabriel. And love. Like I would believe he'd *loved* my sister. Not all the bruises and breaks on her body were caused by her death.

When it was all done, I dragged his carcass outside and walked away. Leaving the bodies for the carrion and wild animals roaming the desert. Like they did to Sophia.

My eyes burn, but the tears dried up long ago. I stand in the middle of the room trying to remember the reason I'm standing in the middle of this room.

His intense eyes search mine, but thankfully, he doesn't ask if I'm okay. What a bland, insipid word. Okay. Like anything can ever be okay again. But he knows. It's why he doesn't ask.

After a deep breath, I head to the bedroom and pack my clothes. Two drawers. Each safe place has the same clothes. It's all I've allowed myself. I stash them in my duffle and grab my backpack with my laptop, listening gear, and a few other electronics that have come in handy. At the last minute, I stuff the pot of Raider's cream into the bag. I can't believe how well the stuff worked to get rid of my bruises.

"Ready."

An eyebrow rises, and he turns slowly around the room. "What about the pictures or the rest of the stuff?"

"It's not mine. I rent the apartments fully furnished. And under the table. My name is never on the rental agreement," I relay with a shrug, dropping the keys on the table.

He walks over to me and swings my duffle over his shoulder. The tip of his finger traces the furrow between my brows, down the center of my nose, to my lips. "I never did get to tell you thank you for last night."

I grab his hand and place a kiss in the center of his palm. "It was a wonderful moment out of time." The memories of the hours spent in this man's arms tumble through my mind, making me yearn for something impossible—more than one night.

With determination, I deliberately replace the tempting images with Sophia's face. Nothing can deter me from my goal. "But I can't look beyond here and now. Not until it's done. All of it." And if I don't survive, it's a moot point, anyway.

His mouth firms, but he doesn't argue. Lips find mine in a brief kiss.

I'd ask him about Raider, but I doubt he'd tell me. They guard each other's pasts with dedication and loyalty. And honestly, I'm not sure I can handle hearing about the brutal death of another sister right now, even if it's not my own.

I take Cruz' outstretched hand and walk out the door.

RAIDER'S ICE-BLUE EYES LOCK ON ME THE SECOND I ENTER THEIR place, but neither of us takes a step toward the other. It's better we stay separated until the mission is over, or Armando's world will burn to the ground.

"I'll go with Sterling and Cruz tomorrow night when we split," I inform them.

Zane scrutinizes my face but relaxes when he doesn't find anything disturbing.

He shouldn't. I've had plenty of practice.

He points across the room. "Raider, I want you to complete one last day shift tomorrow to make sure there's nothing new or suspicious. Sterling and Cruz, get us moved to our new base. Quinn, I'll need your help to finalize the plan to get the girls home. My contact in Miami is ready, but the one in Chicago isn't going to work."

A large palm smooths over his head in frustration. "He's familiar with the Luciano family, and he believes they'll shoot on sight. Apparently, they're a little overprotective of their sister, and this situation isn't going to help matters."

"We need a woman," I tell him. "I'll pull up a list tonight."

I spin around, grab my duffle from Cruz, and drop it beside the couch.

Sterling immediately stands, but I shake my head. "I'll be more comfortable out here."

His face is thunderous. "I can't sleep knowing you're on the bloody couch," he angrily informs me in his posh British accent.

There's something about a man who cusses in a British accent. Who am I kidding? He could probably read me a recipe in that accent, and I'd want to hear more.

"I prefer to sleep in a room with an exit," I say exasperatedly, plopping down on the couch. The only bed I've used in the last couple of years was last night, but we weren't exactly sleeping.

Zane, Cruz, and Raider snort a couple of times, but finally give up and start laughing.

Sterling's wearing an incredulous look on his face. "Not

another one." He throws his hands up and storms out of the room. A second later, he returns with a mattress. He leaves again but soon comes back with the bedding. "I guess we're all sleeping in this room together. It will be like fucking boarding school." His green eyes shift to me. "At least the view is a thousand times better. I'm going to grab a shower."

He stops in front of the couch. "You're welcome to join me. I'll even wash your back, gorgeous."

The laughter in the room dies.

Pure temptation in a warm, golden package. Not trusting my voice to say no to his outrageous flirting, I shake my head.

"All right, beautiful. Next time," he says with a blinding smile and walks off.

Beautiful, gorgeous—he's an outrageous flirt, but the words sound so good coming out of his mouth.

17

Light is barely filtering through the clouds when I wake. Movement draws my eye, and I roll to my left side. Quinn's slipping on a pair of trainers—running shoes. My brain constantly switches back and forth between the two English styles, although in America I often find myself using their version instead of the one I grew up speaking.

"Would you mind some company? I run in the mornings… Although not usually quite this early," I state wryly, silently groaning at the time. But you do what you must when you want to spend a few minutes with an interesting woman.

She taps her phone. "I'll give you five minutes."

Throwing the covers off, I stand and stretch the kinks out. Sleeping on the ground is brutal. It's one thing to do it for the British Army, but quite another for a woman.

When I look at Quinn, her eyes are fixed on the morning wood that's tenting my jogging bottoms.

"Ahem," I politely clear my throat, praying silently to the

supreme being above as she slowly drags her eyes up to mine. "How about ten minutes?" Even harder now than when I awoke, the extra minutes are necessary.

"Sure," she replies, her voice strained. "I need some water." She scrambles to her feet and walks over to the kitchen.

The view of her from behind in those form fitting leggings almost puts me on the ground. I dart a glance at the other three, who are wide awake and watching the whole thing, an amused expressions on their faces.

"Oh, sod off, will you," I say irritably, striding across the room to the shower.

Eleven minutes later, I walk out to find Quinn gone.

Zane taps on his watch. "One minute late."

Cruz smirks. "She said to tell you she's heading east, if you want to join her."

I bring up a mental map of the area to find the best place to intersect her and take off running.

Four minutes later, I exit the alley right after she passes. My eyes automatically drop to take in the incredible view, but it's not the sight I most want to see. Pushing forward, I come up alongside her.

She pulls out her earbud. "Took you long enough. I usually run five to six miles each morning. Are you up for it?"

It was dim in the loft this morning, so I wasn't able to get a really good look at her, but now I can clearly see the toll of last night's events. There are dark circles under her eyes, and a world of thinking behind them.

My body settles into its stride, ready to take on a few miles, and I nod. "Sounds good."

Running clears the clutter from my mind. The best ideas and solutions come when my feet are pounding the pavement and my mind is free to wander. It's my favorite part of running.

About a mile in, an idea hits me. I glance at her face. It's still drawn, her thoughts weighing her down, and I can't stand it.

God, I hope this works or I'm going to look like a bloody fool.

"Tag, you're it," I tap her on the shoulder and take off. When I look back, her mouth is wide open in astonishment. I laugh and lift my hands, egging her on.

She shakes her head at my antics, but a second later, her eyes narrow and a look of determination settles on her face. I'm about a half a block ahead when she disappears down an alley.

The map in mind tells me there are four possible routes she could take and more than a two dozen exits. Game on.

For the first exit, I keep people between me and the cross street. When nothing happens, I decide to take a stealthier approach at the next intersect point. Entering a shop, I exit out the back into the alley, hoping to catch her off guard, but she's not there.

The third option is a huge intersection. The light is red, and a dozen people are waiting to cross. I jog in place beside them. It's almost impossible to keep track of all the people here. I smile. This is the place I'd choose. My eyes dart from face to face, up and down the block, but I don't see her. Unable to relax, I run across the street the second the light changes. There's still no sign of her.

A peddler on the street hands me a flyer. Not willing to throw it on the street, I look for the nearest rubbish bin and spot one almost three doors down by the chemist. Jogging toward it, I start to slide the flyer into the trash when I see the bright red letters: *Tag, You're It!*

I stop. My head swivels back to the peddler on the corner. The old man is looking directly at me and laughing.

Playing dirty, huh? I pull out my phone and find the app I'm using to track everyone's phone. I assigned each person their own color. The green dot tells me she's about a mile ahead and to the right. With a burst of speed, I take off, phone in hand, tracking her down.

Twenty yards, I'm close. My eyes bounce from one dark-haired woman to the next. A swinging ponytail catches my eye. Laughing silently, I slide up from behind and tap her on the shoulder.

"Tag! You're it!"

But the woman who turns around isn't Quinn. Confused, I look down at the app on my phone. The green dot is right here.

The lady laughs and hands me the phone in her hand. "She said to tell you. 'Double tag, you're out.' She'll wait for you at the pastry shop around the corner from the apartment." Her eyes skim me from head to toe. "Lucky woman."

Stunned to find I'd lost, I stand in the middle of the sidewalk, letting pedestrians flow around me. It suddenly hits me. I haven't had this much fun in ages. With a quick pivot, I start the run back with a huge smile on my face.

She's sitting at one of the café tables out front, sipping a frothy concoction, and eating a chocolate croissant when I arrive. The clouds from this morning have gone. A smile lingers on her face. Maybe I didn't lose after all.

"Good morning, minx. Well played," I congratulate her and bow.

She waves a hand to the seat in front of her with all the elegance of a British lady inviting someone to tea. "Please join me. Our server will be right out."

I place her phone on the table. "I've never heard of the double tag rule."

She chuckles. "Tag was my sister's favorite game, and we played it all the time. The age difference didn't matter. We were both stubborn and competitive... and utterly unwilling to concede to the other. My stepfather got tired of us running around the house, so he made up the double tag rule. If your opponent tagged you twice in a row, you were out and couldn't go back in for twenty-four hours. His ingenuity earned him a few hours of peace."

My brow furrows. "I didn't know it would remind you of her. My intent was the opposite."

Her strong fingers clasp mine. "Thank you. The good memories are hard to recall unless something triggers them. This is the first time in a long time I've felt her close, and it means a lot."

My fingers curl around hers, lightly playing with them. "How long has she been gone?"

"Three years. Yesterday. A lifetime. Time is a funny thing," she replies.

The server comes up and I order black coffee, a butter croissant, and a bowl of fruit. "It is." I tilt my head. "Zane told you about rescuing the men from Africa, right?"

She nods.

The server returns with my order, and I take a much needed sip of the dark brew.

"One of those men was my… father. Technically, my stepfather, but I've never thought of him in those terms." I stumble around the words a bit, but it's been a long time since I willingly explained my past to someone.

"I'm sorry," she inserts, rubbing her thumb over the back of my hand. "I know what it's like to lose both a father and stepfather. It's like this huge rock is removed from the center of your life, and suddenly, you're adrift in a strong current with no way to get back to shore."

I think about it for a second. "Exactly. I've felt that way twice, though. When my biological father found out about me, he forced my mother to send me to boarding school. One day, I was home, enjoying life with my family, and the next, I was alone in a world radically different from the one I'd left. It was a bit screwed up for a while. The dust finally settled, and I got to spend time with the man I considered my father. But for a few years, it felt like I'd lost him. Later, I did lose him when he died."

She props her chin in her hand. "Zane told me a hacker intercepted a communication from the terrorist with a ransom demand?"

Picking up the strawberry from my plate, I place it on hers. My mouth twitches. She's been staring at it for a while. "When they told me he died, I didn't believe it. He'd been larger than life and tough. They didn't find a body, and I couldn't rest until I knew for sure. By day, I was Lord Northbrook's proper British heir, but at night, I hacked into everything looking for some clue that they were wrong. I found one."

"You and Zane rescued him," she surmises, taking a bite of the strawberry. Juice runs across her bottom lip, and her tongue swipes across to catch it.

Transfixed by the sight, I stare at those lips, surprised by how much I want to kiss her. Instead, I just nod. My mouth opens to say more, but I close it.

"A lord, huh? You *are* insufferably posh," she decrees with a snicker, waving her hand at my jogging attire. "Makes the rest of us look so utterly common."

My mouth twitches. "Not impressed by the title, huh?"

"Oh, I'm impressed," she drawls. "By how graciously you accepted your defeat today. Manners are the hallmark of a true gentleman. And a lord, apparently." She laughs.

The darkness has receded, which means it's time to go. Handing the server money for the bill, I pull her up from the table.

"That's enough laziness for today. We've got a lot to get done."

My eyes follow the woman pacing back and forth across the living room floor. She's been on the phone calling contacts for the Chicago transport, but without luck so far. With her distracted, I call Zane and Cruz over, and hand them the folder with her background information that came in about a half hour ago.

Zoe Fairchild, born in Texas. Grew up mostly in Coppell. Father was David Quinn Fairchild, Texas Ranger, died in a shootout when she was eight.

There's a picture of a little girl at a funeral surrounded by men wearing the badge with the large trademark star.

School reports are excellent.

Mother, Victoria Fairchild, married Roberto Lopez when she was ten. Had a daughter, Sophia Lopez, a year later. Mother died in car accident when she was sixteen and Sophia five. Bachelor's degree from Texas A&M in Criminal Justice. Became a police officer at the age of twenty while she was finishing her degree. Became a Texas Ranger at the age of twenty-eight.

They sift through the papers. Commendations for service and excellence.

Nineteen-year-old sister abducted from River Walk in San Antonio. No leads. Found eleven months later in the desert. Victim of trafficking.

The rest of the information is a detailed account of Quinn's spiral, starting with her accusations against members of her department on charges of bribery and colluding with traffickers. She was written up for insubordination multiple times. Drugs and money went missing from evidence, and she became the prime suspect. Suspended while they investigated. Death certificate for Zoe Fairchild. Car bombing.

Her voice comes softly from Zane's side. "Zoe was my name. I took my dad's middle name when I started down this path." She's staring at the picture of her at her father's funeral. "It's true. All of it. Several of my superiors were guilty of looking the other way when girls were kidnapped and trafficked, but I couldn't prove it. They made it look like I was losing my mind."

She laughs. "Maybe I was. Right before I was suspended, a huge raid netted a fortune in drugs and money. I took it all, and it paved my way here."

She hands Zane a piece of paper. "There's your contact for

the transfer. She's somebody I helped a couple of years back. You can trust her, but she does require payment." Her eyes rest on the picture of her father's funeral. "The only thing missing from the file seems to be my stepfather's death. Heart attack. Last year."

She looks at her watch. "While you're taking our stuff to the new place, I'm going to take a walk to clear my head."

18

QUINN

"Quinn, wait," Zane returns, hurrying after me.

Halfway between one step and the next, I stop. "I need to walk." I don't want to hear whatever he has to say right now. Escaping is the only thing I need.

He gestures down the stairs. "Let's go."

I pause, trying to read his face, but it's almost impossible. With a shrug, I step down and keep going. When I hit the outer door, I don't stop, just turn, and continue walking.

It's not like I didn't know they were running a deeper background check. Zane has been completely transparent with me. And honestly, I'd have done the same thing if the tables were turned. We live in a dangerous world. Trust is a high value commodity and tough to come by.

I understand. I do. But I'm still spinning. For some reason, I didn't think it would matter. It does, but why? Is it because I've gotten closer to them? Maybe. Possibly. I'm angry they know. They didn't tell me their secrets.

That's not fair or true. I sigh. They did tell me some of their personal secrets, and they didn't need to do so.

It's not just anger, either. Other emotions are swirling around and around. Embarrassment. Sadness. Grief. Even relief.

Maybe it's the method of delivery. It's brutal to see your life described in such stark terms with no context or color to fill in the blank spaces. There's so much missing—good and bad.

Zane keeps pace but says nothing.

Irrationally, it makes me crazy. "Why aren't you saying anything?" I yell, stopping in the middle of the street. "Forget it. Just leave. I'll be back in time for the mission."

Grey eyes blankly assess me. "Are you ready to talk?"

A horn blares, and I throw up my hand. "Go around." It's not like the street isn't wide enough for two people and a damn car.

The driver throws open the door and storms toward me. Zane steps in front of him. The guy takes one look at Zane's big body and scrambles to return to the car. Cursing and waving his hands, he drives around us.

Zane holds out his large hand, palm up. "Come on. We'll have plenty of time to talk on the long walk back."

Confused, I look around at the street signs. My eyes widen. We're at least a couple miles north of the apartment. In a part of town I'd only been to once.

I place my hand in his.

"I probably know some of what you're feeling," he states wryly. "When they stripped me of my military career, everything I'd ever done, good and bad, was dragged out in court and printed in the newspapers. Commendations. Men who'd died under my watch. Successful missions. Failures. It was my life, and those were my actions, but none of it had any meaning behind it."

The breath I'd been holding comes out like one big sigh. "Exactly. I didn't think I would care, but some part of me hated it. Maybe it's pride. My whole life I was proud of who I was—too proud, I think."

"What about the person you are now?" Zane probes.

I stare at the colorful houses on this street, admiring their boldness. "I've been thinking about that question a lot lately," I reflect softly. "I'm not sure I know the answer. I'm proud of how strong I've become. The old me would be ashamed of the horrible, almost unforgiveable acts I've committed, but the new me accepts them. I only truly regret one thing. Is that enough? It's a tough call. I don't think a person can ever really know what's inside until they're put to the test. My test is coming."

Zane looks out into the night. "There are some things you can't come back from, and I don't want that for you. Sometimes, it's okay to put yourself first."

I give a half-laugh. "That's rich coming from you. When do you ever put yourself first?" He looks surprised by my words. "Maybe you should try it and let me know how it goes."

The door to the apartment building is just a few feet ahead. I tug him to a stop.

"Sophia won't be able to find peace until they're dead. All of them. I know this with every fiber of my shattered soul. It's why I'm here," I say, trying to put into words why this is so important to me.

"Kill them and give her peace. It can be done in a day. Why do you need to torture them?" he bellows, his voice loud in the night air.

Ahh, Julio. "Do they all know?"

"We don't keep secrets from each other," he rasps, looking conflicted. "Why? Help me understand."

All my secrets are out there. Good. "I'm not torturing them." His eyes are full of disbelief. "I'm reminding them. Every single thing I do to them, they did to her first. It wasn't enough for them to steal her life. They beat her, raped her, forced her to have a baby, and stole her organs. And the icing on the cake: they left her in the desert for the vultures to feed off," I spit out, my teeth bared in fury. "Now that I think about it, they're getting the better end of the deal. I should really find a way to up my game."

His eyes close, and when they open, I see a glimmer of understanding and deep, deep sorrow. "I'm sorry. So, so sorry." Broad shoulders bend under the knowledge I've been carrying around for three years.

I'm done talking. Spinning around, I turn to open the door and see the other three standing on the sidewalk behind us, anger pouring off them. I tense, but their eyes are on the man behind me. I leave them to deal with each other.

Five flights of stairs give me time to cool and gain some perspective. It would be so easy to be furious with Zane, but I can't. I understand him too well. I used to be him. Always doing what's right and good.

Now that I think about it, I was worse than him. I had zero empathy for those who took the law into their own hands. It was wrong. Period. I would have viewed Zane with contempt and seen him as nothing but a man willing to bend the law to fit his purpose, even if that purpose was to rescue others.

Surprisingly, I don't feel contempt coming from him. Worry, frustration, a need to understand why I'm set on this path, but overall, I think he doesn't want me to cross the line of no return.

Zane is fine with breaking the law, even killing someone, but in his mind, torture is a tool used by only the worst of the worst —the terrorists, drug lords, and other predators. Those without a conscience.

For me, there is no line I won't cross for Sophia. I raised her. She was mine to love and protect. Now, all I can do is make sure she finds peace so she can go to heaven like the rest of my family.

Weary, I stumble over to the couch and lie down. I close my eyes, needing to truly escape the world for a while. If I'm lucky, I'll catch a couple of hours of sleep before the mission tonight.

19

QUINN

The low murmur of voices wakes me. All four men, dressed in black fatigues and combat boots, are loading and strapping weapons to their bodies. The 3D model is live on the table giving them a visual reference to check.

I sit up and stretch. Grabbing my backpack, I head to the bathroom to clean up and get changed. Not one of them says a word when I pass.

The mirror has plenty to say. My hair is windblown and wild, and my face is stained with dirt, but all that is fixable. The lines of sadness and grief on my face are a different story. I'm thirty-three going on fifty according to this mirror.

Averting my eyes, I concentrate on getting mission ready. Unlike the guys, I'm only wearing the black camouflage pants. The jacket is too bulky and hinders my ability to fight. Pairing it with a skimming long sleeve bodysuit gives me the room I need to move. Lastly, I add black boots. I swiftly French braid my hair and tuck the end into my shirt to keep it out of the way.

Next, I pack my body with weapons and supplies, add the tracker to my boot strap, and put my phone into an inside zip pocket.

The mirror reflects a competent, combat-ready woman. A badass. I grin and stride out, full of confidence.

They've already taken the rest of my stuff to the new place. "Here's my pack. Is it okay to leave it in the car, or should I leave it here?" I ask Sterling.

His sharp green eyes search mine. "If there's anything identifiable, leave it here."

"There's nothing. I'll leave it in the car," I inform him, glancing at the watch on my wrist. It's one of the few times I wear it. "What time does everyone have?"

"One forty-seven," Cruz returns. "You don't have to go, you know."

"Yes, I do, but I'm good," I assure him with a small smile. Bending my head, I set each of the times on my watch and change it to vibrate.

"Did you get a tracker?" Zane asks, his voice gruff with an undercurrent of emotion.

I've been avoiding him, but now I look up. His grey eyes are dark with remorse and guilt, but I can't acknowledge it. Not right now. "It's on my boot."

Zane's hands move rapidly, checking and rechecking the items on his body. "Maintain silence unless it's urgent." He taps the piece on his neck. "Use your comms to speak." He points to the map. "We changed things up a bit. I'll be here. The four of you will go in and retrieve the packages. Sterling and Cruz will take one, Raider and Quinn the other. I'll cover your exit. We'll rendezvous at the new base of operations. Everybody clear?"

Everything else is pretty much the same, except I'm now paired with Raider. My guess is the change is due to what happened between Zane and me earlier today.

My eyes dart to Raider's across the table, and I nod. "Clear."

"Let's roll," Zane commands, leading the way out.

THE FACILITY IS QUIET. GUARDS AND ROTATIONS ARE UNCHANGED. The five of us move to the other side of the building where the annex is located. My watch vibrates with an alert for checkpoint one. We're on time.

Zane sets up position in the brush, and the rest of us proceed to the building.

My phone vibrates with checkpoint two a few seconds after we enter. Ahead of schedule.

The hallway lights have been dimmed for the night. One guard is asleep. We hold him down and inject him with a sedative to make sure he doesn't wake for several more hours.

The other guard is in the restroom. Cruz waits outside the door. He's down in seconds and given a sedative to keep him asleep.

We make our way to the two cells, but when we reach ours, it's empty. Startled, I glance at Raider, who signals to Cruz.

He points to his cell and motions for us to come closer.

We move forward, and I peer between the bars. Two girls, about the same age Sophia was when she was taken. One dark-haired and dark complected, sitting tall, her scrubs pressed neatly. The other fair, hiding slightly behind the first girl, wearing similar scrubs, but hers are too big and hang off her thin body. Both girls cling to each other in solidarity.

The brunette stares at the four of us, searching for an indication of our intent. Her mahogany brown eyes remind me so much of Sophia's that I need to blink a few times to assure myself it isn't her.

"We're here to get you out," I inform her.

She doesn't move. "Where will you send us?"

"We're sending you home to Chicago," I announce. "And we're sending her to Miami."

The blond lifts her head and opens her mouth, but the dark-haired girl whispers something urgent to her. They argue back and forth for a few minutes until the girl reluctantly nods.

"What is it?" I ask, uneasy with the exchange.

"She wants to go home with me, but I told her my brothers wouldn't like it. They're going to want reparation for my kidnapping… in blood. It's best if she comes to visit after it's all over," the dark-haired girl states, her voice matter of fact.

Ah, yes, the Sicilian mafia princess. What was her name? Aria Luciano. Well, I guess if I don't succeed in killing Armando, the Luciano family will take care of it for me.

"Aria, right? You'll go with these two men," I inform her, pointing at Sterling and Cruz. "And Margot, you'll come with us."

Aria studies all four of us like she's memorizing our faces, then nods.

My watch vibrates. "We need to go now. Our window is closing."

The two girls hug.

Sterling takes the lead, Aria falls in behind him, and Cruz takes the rear. They head out first.

I motion for Margot to come closer. She eyes me nervously and shuffles half a step closer.

"Your hair is too bright," I explain tersely. "Turn around and I'll braid it." My eyes dart to Raider, who's watching my fingers move. "Find a dark cloth. Something thin enough to tie into a headpiece."

He disappears into their cell, reappearing seconds later with a piece of the dark grey lining from the mattress.

"Perfect, thank you," I murmur, finishing the braid. Grabbing the extra hair tie I always carry on my wrist, I tie it off. The lining folds easily into a triangle. I place it over her head and tie it in the back to keep it in place. "There. Let's go."

I head out, taking the lead, and Margot slides in behind me. Raider brings up the rear.

We leave out the same door but turn left instead of right. A few seconds later, Zane soundlessly slides in a few feet behind Raider.

Margot pauses when she sees the old car waiting for us.

"It will get us where we need to go," I assure her, opening the back door for her to get in.

Raider takes the front passenger seat, and I slide in the backseat behind Zane, who's driving.

Fifteen minutes later, Zane parks the car in front of an older house and leads us on foot for the last mile. Expecting to see a house or apartment, I'm surprised when he opens the door to a shop in a rundown strip mall.

A very dirty tailor's shop. Dust, at least an inch thick, coats everything. It's obviously been closed for several years. I can't imagine how Sterling even found this place, much less got a key.

My nose twitches, and I pinch the end, trying hard not to sneeze. It does little good. "Achoo!"

Margot immediately coughs. "Sorry."

"I doubt anyone is up at this hour," I say dryly. Maybe I should have offered one of my safe spaces.

Zane's tall head is easy to follow, even in the dark. At the back of the shop, he takes a sharp right. "Careful, we're heading upstairs."

It's not until I round the corner that I can see the steps. I turn around to let Margot know and notice Raider's no longer behind her. I motion for her to follow Zane. When she starts up, I fall in to protect the rear.

A couple of steps from the top, a hand pulls me to a stop. I turn. The difference in steps brings his face almost even with mine.

Light blue eyes roam over me.

"What?" I ask.

"Trying to figure out how you're doing. You look fine, but I know how easy it is for you to hide behind that mask of yours," Raider comments, trailing his fingers down my face. "If I ask, will you tell me the truth?"

This man unnerves me with how much he sees. Is it because he went through something similar when his sister died? Or is it because the same shadow of death lives in us both? I'm not sure it really matters why. It just is. Like us.

Regardless, I don't feel the need to hide myself from him. "Yes."

His hand drops to my hip, and he pulls me closer. "I need to know."

"Right now?" I murmur, dropping my hand to his shoulder to prevent myself from falling forward, even if it's exactly what I want to do.

He nods.

It's not the darkness that rises in me, but shame and anger. The shame burrows into the deepest parts of me, leaving the anger simmering on the surface. It's easy to be angry.

"Resentful," I whisper, ashamed to even say it out loud. "Rescuing people is supposed to make you feel good, right? I can barely stand to look at those girls. All this hate rises and boils inside me, and all I can think about is why didn't someone rescue Sophia? Why am I rescuing these girls when I couldn't even rescue my own sister? Because Armando deemed them worthy to save is not good enough."

I search his eyes for any hint of disappointment or condemnation, but there isn't any. Only acceptance and understanding.

His palm comes up and rests on my chest. "When I first came on board, I swore I'd never rescue any young girls. Zane worked around it. Until one day, he needed someone who could seamlessly join the staff and get inside." He grunts. "He conveniently left out the part where I would be driving a ten-year-old girl back and forth to school every day for a week. I hated it."

Riveted, I stare at Raider. "What happened?"

"The mission was successful. We rescued her and her mother from a very bad situation, and it was good work, but I didn't care. I threatened to quit if Zane ever put me in a similar situation," he says solemnly. "He asked me one question."

My brow furrows.

"If I knew the only person who could rescue her was me, would I do it all over again?" He chuckles. "It took me a long time to see their individual faces, and even longer to care. Then, one day, something remarkable happened. One of the girls we were rescuing laughed, and it sounded exactly like Camila, my sister. For a split second, she was alive and in the room with me. It stole my breath. That first time and every time since."

He leans forward. "Be resentful. Hate them if you want. But listen and watch too. You never know when Sophia will come alive for you."

My mind turns his words over, wanting to dismiss them, but even the game of tag with Sterling brought the memory of Sophia alive.

Raider makes people uneasy because they only see the killer in him. The surface. There are so many layers to this man... For the briefest of seconds, all I want in life is time to dive in and discover them all.

Instead, I lean forward and place a lingering kiss on his lips. "Thank you."

"Are you two coming? We have a lot of things to do to get these girls home safely," Zane's voice bellows behind me.

"Coming," I reply. With a quick pivot, I take the last two steps and enter a large and decently clean room. It's a studio apartment with a large bed in the corner, a couch, some chairs scattered around, and a tiny kitchen in the corner.

"How in the world did you find this place?" I ask Sterling.

"Eduardo," Zane interjects. "He offered it to me. Told me he'd converted it years ago but lost his sight before he could live in it."

Secretive old man, I convey silently to Zane. We both laugh... and it feels good to shake off some of the tension between us.

I look over at Aria and Margot. "We'll spend the night here. Tomorrow, you'll split up. One to Chicago, and one to Miami. They're long trips, so get some rest."

Margot shakes off Aria's hand and steps forward.

"I'm not Margot," she announces.

20

I hate surprises. "Wait, what?" I question her. "You're not Margot?" Tension builds at the base of my neck. This is what they were arguing about in the cell. "Fuck!"

Zane folds his arms and stares down at the young girl. "Care to explain?"

The words tumble out of her mouth in a rush. "I'm a diabetic, and without good nutrition and medicine, I was getting sick. Margot tried to get them to move me in with her and Aria because their food was better, but they wouldn't do it. I'm not valuable to them. She—Margot—insisted we switch places. We only intended it to be for a few days."

Cruz and Raider exchange glances.

"We knew two girls switched places, but we didn't see their faces, or we would have been able to head this off," Raider stiffly reveals. "I should have followed up on it. I'm sorry."

Phone in hand, I peer at the photos Armando provided to us. They both have blond, slender, delicate features. "The photos aren't the best, but the two look incredibly similar." I hold it up to the unknown girl's face. "Who the hell are you?"

She reaches back and grabs Aria's hand. "Samantha Baston," she replies in a low voice. "Nobody is going to pay a ransom for me."

I put the name in my phone and take a picture of her. "How did you get here, Samantha Baston?"

"My father… was a border patrol agent. My mother got cancer. The money dried up. To keep paying for her treatments, he started looking the other way." Her eyes flash in anger. "One night, he came home in a panic and told me he'd screwed up. He insisted I didn't have to go, but he was the only who could keep paying for my mother's treatment. When the men came for me, I went."

Aria makes a rude gesture, and I shake my head in agreement. "Aria's right. Your dad's an asshole playing on your mother's cancer. There are always other options."

Zane swivels around to give me a pointed look, but I ignore him.

"I'll meet with Armando and inform him of the error tomorrow," I calmly tell her, even though I want to scream and rage at her. This is so fucked up. Maybe I can turn this around and play up the incompetency of his soldiers.

Her blue eyes fill with tears. "Will he make you take me back?"

"Nobody is going to take you back," Aria adamantly states, her dark eyes staring me down. "If they do, they'll have to answer to my brothers." She throws it out there like she's used the threat a million times to get what she wants.

I laugh. "Threats don't work on a ghost, mafia princess. Sometimes there are consequences to your actions. You've put me in a very tough spot. Armando and I had an agreement, and I broke it. Unintentionally, but I doubt he'll see it that way. This puts me in the wrong. I'm sure your brothers would see it the same way if I broke an agreement with them."

She whitens. A deal is a deal. Growing up in her family, I'm sure she's seen what happens to those who don't fulfill their end of the bargain. Smoothing her face, she grabs Samantha's hand and pulls her over to the bed.

"Let's get some sleep. I'm exhausted."

"Good idea," I state, heading to the stairs. "I need some air."

When I get to the bottom, I take a right instead of a left. Propping the back door open, I stand behind the little strip mall and raise my head to the stars above. This little favor for Armando is exploding the careful life I've built here. More has gone wrong in two weeks than right—Rodrigo's obsessed, I transported five girls, my background is exposed, Lupe's dead, and I screwed up the one assignment that could bring me closer to Armando.

The door creaks open. Cruz, Sterling, and Zane step out.

And I have four men stirring everything up inside me. One minute, I'm bleeding from memories of the past, and the next moment, I'm kissing one of them. My head is spinning.

"What's the plan?" Zane asks gruffly.

My shoulders drop. "Soldier incompetency and dim lighting is all I've got at the moment, but I'm going to have to own up to my own failure in order to sell it. After all, I could have pulled better pictures of the *right* two girls before the mission. Or asked them to confirm their names instead of assuming they were Aria and Margot."

"Could you really leave an innocent girl behind?" Sterling asks quietly.

To his shock, I nod my head yes. "When you live in this world, you realize you can't save every single person. I'm leaving hundreds of girls behind. My original plan was to stop Armando permanently, then, if I was still alive, alert the authorities. Now, my hope is you'll find a way to get the rest of them out and shut down the facilities."

"You don't think you're coming out of this alive," Cruz interjects into the quiet night air. Angry brown eyes pin me to the wall.

"I don't know, but I'd be stupid not to be prepared for it," I concede. The odds of Armando or Rodrigo not killing me are astronomical. Maybe I should buy a lottery ticket.

Zane brings the topic back around to the task at hand. "I'm responsible for this fuck-up, too. What if I go with you?"

I sift through the possibilities, but it comes down to one thing. Armando has zero trust of strangers. It took me over a year to meet him in person.

The wind picks up and a few loose strands slide across my face. A strong hand reaches out and tucks them behind my ear. Before he can pull his hand back, I grab it.

"Thank you for offering. You can't come with me to the meeting, but I'd love some back-up," I tell him.

Admitting I could use someone feels like I'm opening another door, but it would be worse if something happened because I was too proud to ask.

ARMANDO'S STUDYING ME LIKE I'M A BUG UNDER THE MICROSCOPE. "You're nervous. I don't like it when people are nervous. It means I'm not going to hear good news."

"There's good news and bad news," I begin, and he narrows his eyes even further. "We rescued two girls from the annex, but one of them is not Margot Rutherford from Miami. Apparently, Margot bribed your guards to look the other way and switched places with another. The two girls look similar—blond, with blue eyes, slender. Her name is Samantha Baston."

Recognition flares briefly in his eyes. "You're telling me you failed. Is that correct?"

"Yes. We sent Aria back to her family this morning. I'm sure the Luciano brothers will be incredibly grateful for the return of their sister. We're prepared to go back in and retrieve Margot," I tell him, emphasizing the positive.

I hold his dark, serpent-like gaze with my own and wait for him to decide how this is going to play out.

Lean brown fingers tap his thigh. "Rodrigo called and gave me bad news this morning, too. I'm so disappointed in both of you. My best people are letting me down." He flashes me a shark's smile, all hungry teeth. "Fortunately for you, I'm in a tough position, so I'm willing to extend you some leniency. VIPs are arriving in three days. The girl must be gone tomorrow. No later."

He leans in to emphasize his point, and it takes all my willpower to hold my ground. "The counts have already been given to the higher ups, and there can be no margin of error. There must be a hundred and seventeen girls in that facility. Understand?"

One hundred and seventeen. Got it.

I don't tell him Samantha Baston is heading to Chicago with Aria. Luckily, Sterling was able to immediately acquire an ID and documentation for her from his friend Henley.

Armando raises an eyebrow.

"Yes," I answer. "I sent the bill to you last week. Once it's paid, we'll go back in and finish the job." Zane never mentioned the bill, but I don't trust Armando to pay it without some leverage.

"Good. Failure is not tolerated. You already have one punishment awaiting you. Don't make it worse," he cautions me. He picks up his phone and opens an app.

Rage eclipses the nervousness. Unable to speak, I nod and look down at the notification on my phone. Payment made.

"Don't worry. I know you will complete this job. And after my visitors leave, we're going to celebrate with you as my honored guest. It's time you met my top men and, of course, my family," he divulges, unaware of the bomb he just dropped on me.

My intel said the twins were orphans. Where the hell did he get more family?

21

ZANE

"Listen up! Here's the plan." I turn the 3D building around until we're facing the side door closest to the rear. "This is our entry and exit point. Once we're in, Quinn will masquerade as one of the girls and make her way to Margot."

"The two will slip out to the restroom, where they will change from the scrubs into guard uniforms. From there, they will take this route to the corner of the facility where Sterling will be waiting for them. Raider and Cruz will post themselves here and here to cut off any potential threats," I instruct them, jabbing a finger at various areas of the building while I scan their faces to make sure everyone is on the same page. "It should take one hour. Max. If we can cut it shorter without jeopardizing the mission, let's do so."

Cruz and Quinn's eyes meet, and something heated flashes between them. She licks her lips, almost like it's involuntary, and my train of thought vanishes.

"Ahem," Sterling murmurs next to me.

Scowling at the two of them, I finish the orders. "Right. Does everybody understand?"

Nods all around the table.

"Good. I'll take point outside to cover everyone. Comms and trackers required. If something doesn't go according to plan, I'll hear it and be ready. We leave in two hours."

Quinn strides over to her bag by the window, with Cruz following silently behind her. His hands slide around Quinn's hips and pull her back against him. She inhales sharply and pushes further into him. My eyes are drawn to the lack of space between them, and my body pulses with the thought of it being me instead of him.

Where the hell did that thought come from?

"How long do you think that's been going on?" I ask Sterling, who's also watching the two of them.

"A few days," he murmurs, a hint of longing in his voice. "Are we still planning to leave tomorrow?"

My shoulders drop. Rescuing people is what I do, but for the first time, I want to hand off the responsibility to someone else. "We need to take Margot home."

Sterling's eyes flick to Quinn. "I'll go with you, but I'm not staying in Miami."

My eyes dart around the room. Every single one of us has one eye on the woman in the corner. "Neither am I."

"Movement ahead." Sterling's clipped voice comes in quietly over comms.

"Where's Quinn?"

Murmuring in the background.

"Bloody hell," Sterling cusses. "Let's go. Z, on our way. Package of one. I repeat, package of one."

Where is Quinn?

Looking through the scope at the rear door, I wait for them to appear. "Copy." A few seconds later, two "guards" exit the door and head to the gate in the corner of the facility.

"Cruz, check in," I command.

"All clear. Heading out now," Cruz replies.

Through the scope, I see a shadow slip by the rear door and head toward the gate. Two down. Two to go.

"Quinn, report," I order her.

"Staying here to keep the count," she murmurs quietly into the comms. "Will get myself out in a couple of days."

The shadow pauses at the gate.

"Don't do anything rash. I'll be back to cover you when the package is safe," Cruz informs Quinn, his voice hard.

Why the hell didn't I see this coming? I assume Armando ordered her to bring back Samantha, and this was Quinn's solution. One she didn't feel comfortable sharing with us... me. A sharp sting pierces my chest, but I shove it away with anger.

Sterling and a tall, blond girl slip in beside me.

"Raider, check in," I tell him.

A flood of Spanish comes over the comms. "Merda. Go."

Heaving to my feet, I quickly pack up the sniper's rifle and stow it in its case. Pulling out my pistol, I wave them forward. "Move out."

Sterling takes lead, we position Margot in the middle, and I cover us from the rear.

"Cruz, double back. Get a status," I order him. "Rendezvous base."

"Copy," he replies.

The night is quiet on the way back to our base of operations. When we get there, Sterling helps Margot get settled while I pace a rut in the floor.

Thirty minutes later, Cruz walks in the door.

"Status," I rap out impatiently.

"Guards were given Raider's picture tonight. Not sure where

it originated. He's being held in one of the annex cells," Cruz reveals. "Quinn pulled off her neck comms, but she tapped her ear when I went by." His lips quirk in memory. "She must be wearing the earpiece I had from the first night."

Sterling breathes out a sigh of relief. "Her comms went dark a few seconds before you walked in, and I'd feared the worst." He walks over to take our neck comms from us. "Unfortunately, the range of our earpieces is roughly two miles, and the battery lasts six hours on average. We'll have to keep switching them out."

I slam my fist on the table. "That bastard! This whole situation stinks of Armando. But why? For failing to get the right girl out?"

Sterling nods. "Possibly. Something he said convinced Quinn there would be dire consequences if the count wasn't right."

"Three of the cartel's top dogs are arriving tomorrow," the girl interjects. "If he gave them counts, the numbers would include Samantha." She looks around expectantly. "I assume you decided not to send her back?" Her deep blue eyes are watching us closely.

Tomorrow. It's too soon to get either of them out. I rub a hand over my face while I think of our options. "We sent her to Chicago with Aria."

"Good," Margot says firmly. "She isn't a fighter, so it's best she stays out of the way. What's the plan?"

My eyes dart to the confident girl standing on my left. "We won't be able to get them out tomorrow. I'll take you to Miami, then return." I glance at Sterling and Cruz. "You two will stay here. Find out more information. Start working on a plan to get them out. Quinn will be easy once the cartel leaves. Raider is likely only staying because of Quinn."

"No, I mean—what is your plan to rescue everyone and shut down this entire operation?" she demands, arms crossed with a defiant look on her face.

"We intend to deal with that after you're home and our

people are out," I state slowly, trying to force some level of patience into my voice.

She scowls. "First, I'm not going home. Second, if you wait, it will be too late. Everyone is getting shipped out in a week," she smugly informs me. "The cartel is moving Armando and his trafficking operations closer to their headquarters."

And the fucking hits keep on coming.

22

___

ZANE

Sterling drops into the chair across from me and immediately pulls his computer closer. A few keys later, he brings up the cams I had Raider install the first day. A few guards are walking the perimeter, but there's not a soul inside.

I narrow my eyes at her. "How did you know?"

"The captain of the guard is very fond of money, and Armando doesn't pay well," she returns with a delicate shrug. "It's too late to save them. The captain told me they took them out through the tunnels and loaded them into trucks a week ago." The weight of this knowledge makes her shoulders droop.

"That's what the gangs were doing in the tunnels," Sterling murmurs.

But why? Secret exit through the tunnel. Timing of the cartel. The counts. The pieces swirl round in my head. The one facility is getting him moved up in the ranks giving him more power. That only leaves… money.

"He lined his own pockets first." Greedy bastard.

Cruz and Sterling nod in agreement.

"We need a plan to get everyone out in less than a week." Her eyes dart to Cruz and Sterling. "Please tell me you have more than five people here."

"Four actually," I say dryly. "Quinn is our contact. Look, we don't have enough soldiers here. Our specialty is small extractions, not large-scale war. The best we can do is inform our government contacts and get them to move on it."

Head tilted, she studies me for a few minutes. "Former military, right? If I get you more men, can you lead the attack?"

"Can and will are two different things," I retort. "Not only would we have to hit the facility—we'd have to simultaneously attack Armando's place, too. It would require an army and a hell of a lot more time than we have at our disposal."

"One facility and Armando's," Sterling points out. "To take the facility, we'd need roughly seventy-five men?" He pulls his laptop over and brings up the facility.

Knowing it would be futile to interrupt him, I quickly calculate. "Seems about right. Maybe a few more to guard the transports for the victims." A week to pull off an operation of this magnitude. Normally, I'd say it's impossible, but we've spent the last week and a half studying this facility. We have the intel. And we have two people on the inside.

Shit.

My eyes meet Cruz' and he frowns, immediately picking up on my train of thought. "With the tight timing, it would be best if Quinn and Raider stayed in the facility. Quinn can use the earpiece to give us information during the attack while Raider disrupts their operations with a little chaos." I stare steadily at Sterling, waiting for the explosion.

Sterling stands. Eyes dart to mine, a mutinous look in their depths. "No. If something happens, they could be trapped in there. We need to get them out." Green eyes glare at me while his super intelligent brain starts turning over the new information.

I want to agree, but I can't. It takes everything in me to say the next words. "If they're inside, it gives us an advantage," I insert calmly.

"NO!" he roars, his arm sweeping everything off the table in front of him. "We are not leaving them in there." Chest heaving, he leans forward and jabs a finger into my chest. Memories of the past strain his voice until he can barely get another sentence out. "There has to be a solution."

I clamp my hands down on his shoulders to ground him. "It's their choice. I'll send in Cruz to ask them." I pause to let him digest that information. "And he'll make sure they have a way to escape, if needed."

Sterling shrugs off my hold. "I don't like it." He squats down and picks up his computer. "There are too many variables to safely predict the outcome." Carefully placing it back on the table, he examines the damage. "If they say no, they come out." His green eyes drill into Cruz, then slide to me, looking for our agreement.

Cruz and I give him our word.

The girl steps forward. "I need to call my father to let him know I'm out. And to ask for some men. How many do we need?"

"For the facility attack, we'll need roughly eighty men," I tell her. "More if we're going to hit Armando's home at the same time. Do you have any intel on his place?"

She thinks about it for a second. "No."

Sterling taps a few keys. "I'll start working on the location of his residence."

I hand Margot my phone. "Here. We'll likely need a hundred men to do what we need, but I can work with eighty, if they're trained. See how many you can get, and we'll work on finding the rest." I study the strong-minded girl in front of me. The determination lining her face reminds me so much of Quinn. "Won't your father want you to go home where it's safe?"

She takes the phone and walks over to the window. "My

father has been providing me with money this entire time. The only reason he hasn't attacked is because I asked him to wait." Her eyes gleam under her blond lashes. "People like me can always find a way out. Money, power." She snorts. "A ruthless, corrupt father. We have almost limitless resources. The people left in that facility have nothing. Why not save them and get my revenge at the same time?"

Her matter-of-fact tone sends a chill down my spine. From what I hear about her father, he's a take-no-prisoners type, and she's a chip off the block. Glad she's on our side. I leave her to make her call in private.

Cruz is setting the earpieces on the chargers when I walk over to him.

"You okay?"

He flashes me a look I can't read.

"Of course. Why wouldn't I be? Raider's been in tighter spots than this one," he murmurs.

Interesting statement. "And Quinn? You two seem to be… close. Are you truly okay with leaving her inside?" The last thing I need is for Cruz to go rogue.

He twirls the earpiece between his restless fingers, and I tense. Cruz is never restless. Still. Stealthy. Those are his hallmarks.

"Yes," he replies. With careful precision, he places the last earpiece on the charger. "She won't leave until she's done—with everything. I don't like it, but it's her decision. Whatever this is between the two of us, it's separate and sits outside her vengeance. Whether it survives remains to be seen. But it doesn't matter; it's secondary." He faces me, dark eyes filled with resolution. "I've seen the good in her. The conflict she feels. And I refuse to let the darkness have her."

The magnitude of his declaration hits me like a ton of bricks. Raider said something similar a few days ago, but I'm not sure I fully comprehended it.

My fault entirely. What did Raider call it? Tunnel vision. He's right. This whole time I've been trying to get her to walk away from vengeance and return with us to Miami. And I really thought the closeness she was developing with us meant she was considering it. Stupid, stupid, stupid.

Cruz and Raider plan to save her *after* she gets her vengeance. They know she won't abandon the path she's on. Is it even possible? Will there be enough of her to save? If there isn't, will it destroy us?

23

ZANE

Before I fall into the dark rabbit hole of speculation, I pull myself back to the present. It does no good to dwell on a future that may not even happen if we don't survive the attack. I look at the plans Sterling's already detailing out, my eyes quickly finding the strengths and weaknesses in each step. This is what I can do to help Quinn and everyone else. It's my expertise, and I'm damn good at it.

Margot ends her call with a smile. "Good news. My father can have roughly thirty men here tomorrow, and another twenty in two days."

A quick tally brings us up to our new total. "Fifty. Good." Who can I call? Thiago, a friend in Miami, has men, but they're busy protecting his family and Henley right now. We could contact Raider's brother, but he's more of a last resort. I put him on the bottom of my list.

There's a small group of mercenaries we've worked with on rescues in the past. Trustworthy men. I pick up the phone.

Ten minutes later, I hang up. "They have twelve men right now. That puts us at sixty-two."

"Aria!" Margot exclaims. "Let me have your phone."

I give it to her while I run through the massive list of contacts in my head. Most of them are military, or ex-military, and would be willing to take on something this important but pulling them together with such short notice might not be possible.

"I'm going to grab coffee. And breakfast. Anybody want anything?"

Arms full, I return twenty minutes later to a whirlwind of activity.

"What happened?" I set everything down on the small kitchen counter.

"The Luciano family is very grateful for the return of their sister," Sterling states with a broad grin.

"And very interested in sending a message to Armando and the cartel," Cruz adds dryly.

I raise an eyebrow. "How many?"

Margot's practically dancing on her toes. "Fifty men of their own, including the two brothers and their... underboss? I think that's what Aria called him."

A grim smile stretches across my face. We have the numbers. "Get some coffee. We're going to need it."

It takes all day to figure out the details.

Margot coordinates the arrival of our "army," finding places for them to stay, along with food and necessities. The money at her disposal goes a long way to getting us what we need without the usual wait. It's impressive to watch her in action. She's only nineteen. In another five years, she'll be running her father's empire.

Cruz and I work on planning the attack. We determine the

best time to be two days after the cartel visit—approximately four days from now—at dawn. It gives the guards time to settle back into their usual routine. We'll go in from two directions. The rear and the annex.

Sterling sources weapons and other military supplies. He also digs into the captain's past to see if we can bribe him into unlocking Raider's cell for us. Taking small bribes from Margot for equally small favors is one thing, but we need him to turn traitor.

"He's lived in Monterrey his entire life and has a lot of family here," Sterling reports. "Income is modest. Married. Kids. Used to be on the state police force until he went to work for Armando. He could go either way."

He swivels the computer around to show me the list on the screen. "Armando owns property throughout the city. All but two are residential. I can't tell which one is his. I bet the captain would know."

My phone buzzes, and I pull it out of my pocket. Thiago. "Is everything okay?" I don't waste time with preliminaries when it comes to him. A billionaire CEO, Thiago has little patience for small talk.

"We got Henley's stalker. A few days ago. Dead," he informs me, the hard edge of satisfaction apparent in his voice. "Diego killed him."

A dead man killed her stalker. I snort. "That's convenient. Your idea?"

He chuckles. "Thomas' actually. Surprised me."

I'm not. "Thomas is even keeled until you kill his men, then all bets are off. How's Henley?"

Thiago's silent for a second. "Good, very good. She sends her love to everyone, but don't tell them. I don't want them to get any ideas. She's very, very happy with us, and we intend to keep her that way."

The possessive tone in his voice makes me chuckle. Marcos would be ecstatic. "Good. I'm glad. Although things have changed a bit around here, so I don't think you need to worry on that account."

"Good. How is everything?"

"Complicated," I reply with a heavy sigh. Signaling to the others, I let them know I'm stepping outside. Once I'm away from prying ears, I bring Thiago up to speed on everything that's happened over the last couple of weeks. "If we succeed, we'll need a place to bring these people. Can you set something up? We'll also need Henley's assistance to create proper documentation and IDs."

There's some rustling in the background. "I'll get it done. I'm going to send Thomas to you, too. He could use a few days away, and you could use his expertise."

I could use another commander to lead the second attack. "Good idea."

"Done," Thiago confirms. "I'll text you when they're on their way. Henley and I will get everything set up for the rescues. Call if you need anything." He hangs up.

With a flick of my wrist, I slide the phone back into my pocket. It's amazing how much of an impact Henley has had on Thiago. Mateo and Grayson, too. I wasn't sure they'd ever let anyone else into their family. Instead of Marcos, she's the center of their universe now, bringing them all together.

I thought Quinn was pulling us in opposite directions, but maybe it's been me all along. If we all make it through, could she be the one for all of us?

24

QUINN

The facility is eerily silent. Grasping the brim, I tug the guard's hat lower until I can barely see under it. Dawn should be breaking soon. Based on our earlier surveillance, there should only be four guards patrolling the hall at this hour. I try to channel Cruz' stealth, but when a squeak emits from my boot hitting the linoleum, I realize it's never going to happen.

It feels like forever, but I finally reach the annex. This is where it becomes tricky. Will the two guards be in the same spot they were the last time? When I enter the area, it's empty, allowing me to slide up to the cells and peer inside. I breathe a sigh of relief. He's here.

I tap lightly on the bar with my nail, and the man on the cot shifts in my direction. Raider's light blue eyes meet mine, and his usual cold stare evaporates.

He moves to sit beside the bars. "Mon petit oiseau. What are you doing up so early?"

I scan him for any bruises, but don't see any.

"Before I removed my comms, I heard them grab you. What does mon petit oiseau mean?"

His eyes crinkle at the corners, but he says nothing.

I'll have to look it up later. "Your accent is slight, but it's not French. South American, maybe. Where did you grow up?"

Ice-blue eyes study me intently. "Brazil."

"Was it just you and Camila, or do you have other brothers and sisters?" I ask, curious about the man who can so easily blend in with the world.

A lazy smile stretches across his face. "In my house, it was just my mother and me. In my father's house, it was him, his wife, and son."

A mistress? "Was your father powerful?"

He sighs. "He thought so. But he thought wrong." His strong hand reaches through the bars to grasp mine. "Did you really get up early to ask me about my family?"

My eyes narrow. "What are you still doing here?"

He tilts his head to the side. "I'm curious as to who wants to hold me here and why. Someone went to a lot of trouble to capture me. When I have the answers, maybe I will leave." Fingers slide through mine. "Or maybe I'll stay until you decide to leave."

A noise comes from the hallway.

"Go, get some sleep. If I'm lucky, you'll dream about kissing me again," he says with a chuckle.

I roll my eyes, but the guard is closing in on us, so I can't say anything in return.

Making it back to my hard cot isn't difficult. Neither is falling asleep. Dreaming about something pleasant is nearly impossible. Nightmares invade until it's better to wake and find the sun.

The other girls eye me with curiosity, but none approach. The guards shepherd us into the showers, and on to breakfast. We move like sheep in the direction they wish us to go, rarely speaking a word to each other.

At the end of the first day, a girl around twenty approaches me. "We don't know who you are or where Margot went, but we hope you're not here to cause trouble. The cartel's visiting tomorrow, and if we step out of line, Armando has promised to kill us on sight." She twists her hands nervously. "Please do not do anything to upset him or ruin the visit. We beg you. Things can get really bad around here if he's not happy. No food. No blankets. No leash on the guards." Her voice drops to a whisper with the last phrase.

I blink. Part of me wants to reach out and slap her until she fights back, but the other half understands her need to keep the little safety and comfort she's been given. "I'll be on my best behavior."

She squints at me, as if my answer makes her nervous, but bobs her head and disappears. Whispers from the corner of the room reach me, but I don't turn to look.

My presence is the one thing guaranteed to make the visit go smoothly but explaining to anyone that my stay is both voluntary and temporary is moot. And I doubt Armando will punish them when I "disappear" because he'll be too busy dealing with me. My stomach tightens with the thought, not in fear, but in anticipation. I need to see the monster inside him. The one he shows to everyone but me—the face Sophia saw when he killed her.

Soon, I whisper to her, but it's so hard to believe. It's been almost three years since her death. One way or another, I need to finish. She needs closure.

When everyone is asleep, I get up to use the restroom. Standing in the stall, I listen for any footfalls. Nothing. I stretch up toward the ceiling and pull open the vent to get my guard uniform and earpiece.

The annex is quiet when I enter, but something feels different, causing the hair on the back of my neck to stand up. Instead of heading directly to the cells, I slip into the small bathroom and wait. Boots stride by. Quiet Spanish drifts into the air, but I can't make out the words. Keys jingle. Grunts. The cell door slams shut.

Armando's voice is clear when he states his intent to wash his hands and orders the guard to stand by the door. Panicking, I look around. The shower beckons. I keep looking. At the last second, I open another door and slip inside.

Fluorescent light floods the crack. Water turns on full blast and runs for several minutes. I'm beginning to think he's never going to finish washing his hands when it shuts off. There's a rustling noise, a pause, and the light blinks out. I don't move. Boots stride away, but in the opposite direction—toward the side entrance—the same one we used that night to rescue Aria and Samantha. Whoever it is just left the facility. I pray it was Armando.

I open the door a crack to listen. It's quiet, and the unsettling feeling is gone, too. With a huge sigh of relief, I crawl out of the tiny linen closet, my body cracking and protesting the cramped position I forced it to hold. With a twist, I crack my back one way, then the other.

I'm starting to think I should have chosen the shower to hide in, but when I look over at it, the curtain is open. A chill runs down my spine. It had been closed when I entered the closet.

Thank you, I murmur to Sophia, firmly believing it was her guidance that led me to a better hiding place.

It doesn't take long to reach Raider's cell, but when I see him lying on the floor, I rush the final few feet. Shirtless, his back is covered with dark splotches that will almost certainly turn to ugly bruises in the next couple of days. I curse silently, adding this grievance to Armando's long list. Why, though?

"Raider," I whisper loudly. He doesn't stir.

"Raider," I murmur. Nothing. Damn it.

I eye the lock on the cell door. Could I pick it? It's not my best skill, but it couldn't hurt to try. With a quick swivel, I run back to the restroom and search through the linen closet until I find several options—a metal nail file, bobby pins, and tweezers—then rush back.

An hour later, I throw down the tweezers in frustration. It's useless. I'm useless. A noise down the hall startles me.

Shit.

With a mad dash, I scramble for the tools on the ground. Tweezers. Where are the tweezers? My eyes scan every inch of the ground, but nothing pointy jumps out. Giving up, I run back to the restroom and my little linen closet. My heart's beating out of my chest when I crouch under the bottom shelf, and pull the door shut.

Someone comes into pee. I clamp my hands over my ears, not wanting to hear it. Unlike Armando, they wash their hands quickly, and leave.

I wait until it's all quiet before making my way back to the cells. As I near them, the light catches on a glint of metal near the adjoining cell. It's the tweezers. I grab them and put them in my pocket. Like the night of the rescue, this cell is empty. I pivot to return to the other one when I see it. A key in the lock. I yank it out and rush over to Raider's cell. It slides in with ease and with a quick turn, the door opens.

I slide to the cold floor to get a good look at his face. His eyes are closed. One lid is swollen almost shut, and blood is seeping from his nose and a cut on his bottom lip. He looks rough.

Biting my lip, I contemplate the best way to wake him. With a man like Raider, distance is probably best. I reach out and tap him on the hand. He doesn't move. I repeat it a few more times. Nothing.

Stretching a bit farther, I tap him on the shoulder. Not one twitch of muscle. I shake him a couple of times. He's out. I sigh and flop down.

The cold concrete seeps through my clothing until I'm shivering. If I leave him on the floor, he'll be in worse shape come morning. There's only one thing to try. I push myself up from the floor and leave the cell.

Returning, I stand there trying to figure out the best way to do it, but I'm not sure there is a good way. And time is running out. It's now or never.

Tipping the plastic cup over his head, the water pours out in one big wave.

My head hits the floor with a bang. Mother freaking trucker!

I squint through the pain to find Raider hovering over me. The warmth I'm used to is gone. His light blue eyes stare icily into mine. I'm not concerned until I register the hand wrapped tightly around my throat to hold me down.

"Raider," I rasp. "It's me. Quinn. Raider." The hand eases. "Remember me? Quinn." That day in my hallway. "Kiss me."

When he doesn't move, I strain against the hand holding me down and arch up until my lips are brushing his. My kiss is barely there, but it's enough to break the hold on him. He shudders and jerks his hand away.

"Mon Dieu," he whispers. Fingers trace the lines of my neck softly. "I'm sorry, so sorry, Quinn." Pushing himself up, he groans. "If you weren't already intent on killing him, I'd happily do it for you. Bastard."

I roll over to my hands and knees, get my feet under me and straighten. The world sways, and I hold still until it stops. My fingers gingerly probe the back of my head and discover a small knot. Ouch. When I see him frowning at me, I drop my hand.

"Lie down. I'll get a wet cloth."

When I return, he's half sitting, half lying on the bed, and even with the blood and darkening areas, my eyes greedily take in every inch of him. Tattoos grace one shoulder and pec. Camilla's name appears close to his heart. The rest of the tattoos are a mix of Portuguese words and symbols.

I scan the rest of his body. His abdomen is dark from the punches he must have taken, but it doesn't detract from the sight of his lean waist and defined abs. A small trail of dark hair disappears into his pants.

He grunts. "Tonight's going to be a bit uncomfortable."

Silently reprimanding myself, I pick up the washcloth and gently clean the blood from his face. "What the hell does he want from you?"

He chuckles. "He wants us to leave town. Not you. Me, Zane, and the rest. The only reason he pinpointed me was because he noticed me on the security cameras and knew I wasn't one of his men."

Why do I never seem to learn this lesson? I ask myself. Instead, I let myself get close to someone and they get hurt, or worse, killed.

I jerk a thumb over my shoulder. "The door is open, Raider, and I want you to use it. Go back to them. Tonight. I'll be fine." He jerks when the washcloth touches the cut on his lip. "Please. For me."

Light blue eyes narrow. "If I leave, I'll kill him. But if I do, you'll hate me for stealing your vengeance." He shakes his head. "It's better if I stay here and let you patch me up. Every time you look at my bruises, you'll hate him more. That's a better plan, don't you think?" A satisfied grin flashes across his face, along with a wince.

Unable to meet his eyes, I stand and toss him the washcloth. "The key's on the table."

25

QUINN

"**A**ttention!" the voice loudly orders. "Line up along the walls. Don't say a word to each other or the visitors. Stare straight ahead. Everyone understand?"

"Yes, captain!" we reply in unison.

The other women quickly scramble to find a place in the middle of the wall. Nobody wants to be on the outside edges where it would be easy to be picked off.

I saunter over and find a spot in the corner that allows me to see the entire room in one glance. The women beside me stand staring straight ahead, hands clenched into fists or twisted in the fabric of their scrubs, lips tucked into teeth, and shoulders bowed in submission.

Four people enter the room, followed by a group of guards. Two men, one good-looking with dark hair and the coldest of dark eyes, and the second, paunchy, balding, almost grandfatherly looking except for the leer plastered on his face. Surprisingly, the third is a woman. Statuesque and beautiful, with gleaming, almost black hair, mahogany skin, and almost black eyes. She reminds me of an Amazonian warrior I saw in a book once, right down to the calculating gleam in her eyes. It almost makes me feel like she's tallying up the worth of each one of us. All three are led by Armando.

"We have a hundred and seventeen women here. A good number to seed our operations. It took me a little over a year to obtain all of them, but every single one is healthy and free of diseases," he proudly states, his arm sweeping out to encompass all of us.

Smiling eyes land on me and instantly change. Rage sweeps across his features for the briefest of seconds until he smooths his expression. Dark eyes flick toward me, a promise highlighted in their depths.

The girl next to me whimpers and shuffles closer to her other neighbor.

"He's not looking at you, but at me," I whisper, trying to assure her.

Stalking forward, Armando grabs my arm and shoves me toward a guard. "I explicitly said 'no talking.' Take her to the cells."

"It's always good to deal with rebellions quickly," the woman says approvingly.

Bald man nods emphatically, agreeing with her.

Armando preens under their attention, smoothing his suit and hair a couple of times before he continues with his tour.

The guard squeezes my arm as he drags me out the door and to the annex.

I completely ignore him and the pain he's inflicting. He's not worth an ounce of effort. We pass Raider's cell to get to the adjoining one, and the guard slams me against the bars, holding me there with one hand in the middle of my back.

With little expression, Raider watches the guard's actions.

When the guard doesn't find the key, he calls out, until another guard comes running.

"Where the hell is the key?" he snarls at the younger man.

The new guard blanches and stutters out some explanation of being new.

Cursing floods the air. "Do you have any keys?"

He shakily points to Raider's cell. "I have a key to his."

The guard holding me grimaces. "Fine. Open it." When the door opens, he shoves me into Raider's waiting arms.

Corded muscles lock around me.

Raider waits until the guards are gone, then spins me around to face him. "Still angry with me?" His mouth twitches while he waits for me to answer.

I narrow my eyes. "That depends on how entertaining you can be. We're going to be spending a lot of time together, and I'm pissy when I'm bored."

His finger trails softly along the red area on my arm. "Hmm. I don't like it when someone hurts you. It pisses me off." His eyes flicker between cold and warm. "Entertaining, huh? I'm not much of a storyteller, but I'll swap my stories for yours." He stares at me intently.

This might be worth the pain coming later. "Deal."

I slide around him to sit down on the cot, then scoot backward until my back hits the wall. "Tell me about your first fight."

Moving slowly, he follows my lead until we're sitting side by side. A small smile plays with the corners of his full lips. "It's certainly memorable. There was a playground near my house where I'd go after school and swing. My favorite thing to do was to pump my legs until it reached the highest point and jump off. It was thrilling." He chuckles.

Strong fingers tap against each other while he recounts the story. "One day, an arrogant boy, a couple of years older than me, got out of the backseat of a car, the type we rarely saw in our neighborhood. He stood there in his expensive clothes, watching me swing for at least thirty minutes. The longer he stood there, the angrier he became, until he just exploded. He stalked over to the swings, and when I jumped off, he threw his arm back and punched me."

He rubs his nose in memory. "Stunned, I lay on the ground looking up at him until he yelled at me to get up. When I did, I tackled him. We exchanged hits equally until his driver came over and separated us. He handed the boy a phone, and he stood there with it pressed to his ear for a couple of minutes. After hanging up, he walked away, a sneer on his face."

Fascinated by both the story and his amused tone, I can't help but ask for more. "Did he ever say anything to you?"

"Not that time, or all the other times that followed. Every week, he showed up at the park to fight. After the call, he would leave," he reveals to my astonishment.

"How long did this go on?"

"For almost a year."

"What happened then?" I murmur.

"Our father decided to show up in person to end the fights," he returns with a flash of anger. "When he arrived that day, Paulo watched his every move. When he saw how our father completely ignored me, it soothed the wound festering inside him. It was two years before I saw my brother again."

These memories must have taken place almost thirty years ago, and yet the hurt is still prevalent. I slide my hand into his.

"Your father sucks. Come to think of it, Cruz' and Zane's fathers suck, too. And I think Sterling got a good and bad one, right? It's a terrible thing to have in common."

He squeezes my hand. "I never really thought about it, but I guess we do."

I reach over his body and grab the pillow to place it behind our backs and make us more comfortable. Laying my head on his broad shoulder, I tuck myself in tight and wait.

"Tell me a story about a good father," he urges, thumb stroking back and forth across my hand.

"I was lucky enough to get two good fathers, although I didn't think so at the time," I chuckle, remembering the moment my mother told me she was marrying Roberto. "I'd always been a daddy's girl. When I lost my father, I was devastated. About a year after he died, my mother started dating Roberto. Angry at this massive betrayal, and convinced she was just lonely, I drafted a master plan to chase him away."

"You do seem to be a very focused individual," he comments, laughter in his voice. "What was in this master plan?"

I fake cough. "You haven't seen anything yet," I return with a smile. "Every good plan begins with research. I went to the library and read every book they had on pranks and made a list of the most effective ones. I drew my battle lines and waged war with the tools at my disposal. I replaced his sugar with salt, let the air out of his tires, wiped my sticky sucker on all the handles in his bathroom, toilet papered his car, dug up worms to put in his bed…"

When I get to the worms, laughter bursts out of me until I can barely breathe. Tears flow from the corner of my eyes. Every time I try to speak, I see the earthworms crawling across the sheets.

After several minutes, I manage to get a hold of myself. "Long story short, he put up with every single prank I pulled on him and even managed to get a few over me, too. After six months of war, I gave up. My mother married him the next month. He was a remarkable man and a great father to me and Sophia."

It's been a long time since I told that story, and I can't keep the grin off my face. When I look over, Raider's staring at me with an utterly fascinated look on his face.

"What?"

"I want to kiss you so badly right now," he says gruffly. "While the laughter still lingers on your lips and in your eyes."

Swiping my tongue across my lips in anticipation, I lean forward.

His lips meet mine. Expecting to be consumed by his kiss, I'm surprised by the tenor of it. It's a reflection of this moment—

playfully light one second and serious the next. It's a memory in the making, reminiscent of both the past and an unknown future. Unhurried, but firm, it makes me want to delve into the secrets that make up the man behind the kiss.

His lips leave mine, and all I want is more. So much more I can't breathe. Does he feel the same, or is it just me? Wordlessly, I stare up at him. He's infinitely more dangerous than I thought.

"Now, you know," he says firmly.

26

QUINN

The clanging of the door slamming against the bars wakes me. My eyes flick to the opening and find Armando practically foaming at the mouth. I slowly get to my feet.

"What is she doing in the cell with him?" he asks softly, his dark eyes darting to the soldier beside him.

The young man stammers out a reply, informing him about the missing key.

Armando frowns. "Strip him of his uniform and put him in with the laborers. Maybe some time spent working in the coca fields will teach him some discipline," he orders the other man behind him. "Come." His hand motions me forward.

The wood cot cracks where Raider grips the edge, but he doesn't move. We spoke about this earlier. It needs to happen. Armando must believe he calls all the shots. Raider's ice-blue eyes hold mine, anger and promise in their depths. I nod and walk out of the cell behind Armando.

The room we enter isn't on Sterling's 3D rendering is the first thought I have walking into the space. I'll have to let him know so he can update it.

Dark grey tiles line the walls and floor, and a big drain sits in the center. Lovely. This is the fun room.

"You stipulated the requirements. One hundred and seventeen women must be accounted for in this facility. I met your terms," I recite unemotionally, turning to face the man at my back.

His backhand knocks me off my feet.

From the cold tile floor, I peer up at him. A calm and collected Armando stands above me. Disappointed, I push myself to my feet only to get knocked down with the same move.

Unoriginal bastard, I muse.

"Fortunately for you, I have to be at a dinner tonight," he announces, satisfaction in his voice. "Things are progressing quite nicely. And since you did play a part in my success, I won't let Hugo rough you up too much. After all, we're celebrating with a party in two nights. As my guest of honor, it's imperative you attend." He snaps his fingers.

Two men appear from the shadows. One grabs my wrists, while the other loops a rope over them and pulls it tight. A machine in the corner starts up, and I'm yanked backward and upward until I'm hanging from the ceiling.

My shoulders scream at the weight of my body, but I simply flash Hugo a bored grin.

A maniacal gleam enters Armando's eyes. "Three minutes. No more. I'll be watching. Light work. And not the face. I don't want to scare Gabriel." He turns to the door, calling out over his shoulder. "I'll text you the invitation. Don't disappoint me again, Quinn."

The bastard leaves. Damn it. A fist plows into my stomach, and the air in my lungs releases in a rush. The next few minutes are going to be brutal.

Something Armando said echoes repeatedly in my mind, but I'm too distracted by the fists pounding my body to focus on it. Staring down at the floor, I recite police codes in my head to distract me from the pain. Tears and snot roll down my face, but I refuse to let one sound escape.

A loud beep interrupts my train of thought.

"Time's up." A tall, rough-looking man bends down to peer into my face. "I'm impressed. You took that better than most men. Cut her down and take her back to the cell for tonight. She can leave tomorrow." His big black boots disappear from my line of sight.

My body tumbles to the ground, and I cry out.

They drag me back to the cell and drop me on the floor.

Raider scoops me up and gently places me on the cot. The cold cloth glides along the side of my face as he wipes off the evidence of my tears. He pulls up my shirt and curses.

Without a word, he leaves, returning several minutes later with a couple of cold washcloths from the nearby bathroom. He gingerly places them on my face and body.

"I'm sorry," I blurt out, trying to ease the tension between us.

"I know," he says, finally looking at me. Fierce anger blazes from his eyes. "I hated every fucking minute you were gone." His mouth compresses while he stares at the damage to my body. "And a part of me hates you—for letting them do this to you and for making me stand down. It goes against everything I am." His blue eyes burn with fire, not a trace of cold in sight.

His words. Those words. *Fuck, that hurt worse than I expected.*

Tears slip down my cheeks, and the lump in my throat grows until I can barely swallow. "I know. I hated all of it. And myself, too. For asking you to do it. But I don't matter and neither do you. Only she matters." Her haunted brown eyes flash in my mind.

He shakes his head. "You're wrong. You matter… but I know you can't see it right now. That's okay. You'll get there," he replies, a promise in his voice.

"Tell me a story," I plead, needing to escape for a while.

Lean fingers sweep the hair back from my face. "I will only tell you this story once, so you need to stay awake and listen." He stares down at me, but it's obvious his eyes are only seeing the past. "When I was nine, I lost my mother to cancer. She didn't have any relatives, so my father moved me in with his family. It was a disaster. We all hated each other." He shrugs, but I can see the hurt that lingers in his eyes. "But his house was big, so we could easily avoid seeing anyone. That same year, Camila was born. My half-sister, Paulo's sister. It didn't matter. From the moment she arrived, we both loved her."

He smiles. "Camila was truly beautiful, inside and out. Her laugh was infectious, bringing the best out of everyone, including my father. He absolutely doted on her." His eyes focus on me. "Camila hated when we fought, so we declared a tentative truce, and for the next nine years, life became easier."

His voice drops. "My father was a drug lord, leader of a cartel in Brazil. In a grab for more power, he accidentally killed the son of our enemy. In retaliation, they went to war with us."

He rubs a hand over his face. "Their leader was smart, and he made some good moves. They were winning. My father became increasingly worried. He knew he needed to end the war before they wiped us out. So, he went to them and made a secret deal. They took Camila on the way to school the next day. Months later, she came back in a box. She didn't even look the same. Her body…"

Tears roll down his strong face. I reach up and wipe them away, then do the same to my own.

"They could have given her an easy death, but they chose not to. We were devastated and furious. When we found out about the deal, Paulo and I took down every single one of them, starting with our father. The worst of deaths was what we promised and what we delivered," he reveals, his voice grim with memory. "When it was done, we clawed our way out of the darkness together."

His hand grips mine. "I understand vengeance more than anyone, and I'll do everything in my power to help you." He puts his face directly in front of mine. "But don't ever ask me to sit quietly on the sidelines while someone beats you again. It's a hard line."

His blue eyes reflect the fury and helplessness he felt tonight.

"I won't. I promise," I vow, taking our joined hands and placing them on my heart. "Never again."

27

———

RAIDER

Cruz' low voice comes through clearly on the earpiece. "Quinn? Are you there?"

The worry in his voice makes me smile with satisfaction. "Raider here. Quinn's with me in the cell. We're both a little broken and need your assistance to get out."

A sharp inhale is the only response I get.

Cruz slides quietly around the corner ten minutes later. "What happened?" His eyes sweep over Quinn and land on me.

"Armando's punishment," I spit out, fury coating my voice.

"Did you kill him?" His voice is a whisper filled with the promise of death.

Grinding my teeth, I manage to grunt out a reply. "She made me promise to stay here."

He winces. "And you?"

"A little warning from the man himself to all of us. Get out of town," I state with a snort. "If you can carry her, I'm ready to get out of this hellhole."

Cruz holds up a hand to stop me. "We're attacking the facility in a few days." He taps his ear. "You have the option of staying here to feed us intel from the inside or getting out now."

"He's getting out now," Quinn states firmly beside me. Her eyes pleading with me to agree. "You're already hurt. If Armando comes back, who knows what he'll do?"

I cock my head to the side and raise an eyebrow. "Even in our short time together, I believe you know me better than that, mon petit oiseau. I can be of more help here."

Her jaw locks. Fierce green eyes wage a silent battle against me. My mouth twitches, but I press my lips firmly together to hold back my smile. Besides, her protectiveness feels good. It means there is something between us besides a kiss. Or two.

She sighs. "Fine. We all have jobs to do." Her words are clipped, but from worry, not anger. She darts a glance at Cruz. "Did you happen to bring my backpack and some clothes?"

He nods and disappears, only to return a few minutes later with the requested items.

She takes the backpack from him and digs around inside it. With a triumphant smile, she pulls out the cream I gave her the night of the fight.

"I don't know what's in this, but it's a miracle in a jar. The soreness and bruises on my neck and wrist disappeared a million times quicker than anything I've ever used. Thank you." She hands it to me.

Her fingers pull the bottom of her shirt to expose the bruises on her abdomen and back. "If you wouldn't mind putting it on me, I can leave the rest here with you."

Danger makes the hairs on the back of my neck rise. I quickly glance toward the hallway, but it's empty. With a frown, I look up at Cruz to ask him to check, but the words die in my throat. The threat is coming from him.

Observant eyes catalog every bruise on Quinn's body as if locking them into his memory. "How the hell did you do it?" he softly questions me.

"Not sure. But it's never happening again," I retort, a firm promise in my statement.

He assesses the look in my eyes and sucks in a huge breath. "I'm going to sweep nearby. The guards will finish their rotation in six minutes, which gives us a small exit window." With one last glare at Quinn's injuries, he disappears.

I turn my attention back to Quinn.

Should I tell her they each have a jar?

The thought makes me shake my head. Even though I promised her I wouldn't intervene, these bruises are on me. I need to do this. "Lie back. I'll do your front first."

She eases down onto the hard cot. Her beautiful eyes flick up to watch me.

With careful precision, I smooth the cream into her body, making sure to get every single spot. Her skin feels soft and luxurious beneath my fingers, and the desire to touch her every-where thrums in my veins. Thankfully, the clock ticking in the back of my mind helps me rein it in.

Slim fingers entwine with mine, and my eyes dart to hers. "Would you mind helping me up?" Her husky voice and flushed cheeks makes me groan.

Quickly coughing to cover it up, I help her stand, then finish putting the cream on her back.

"How much time?" she asks suddenly.

"Two minutes."

She twirls around and scoops some cream into her hand. "Turn around. Let me put this on your back before I leave."

I stare down at the petite woman in front of me. There are so few people I would turn my back to in this world, but I don't hesitate to give her mine. Cool hands lightly spread the cream over my sore body. Pain threatens the moment, but I push it aside to concentrate on the hypnotic glide of her fingers across my body.

"I'm done," she murmurs.

Too soon.

I turn around and pick up her hands. "Thank you." With a devilish grin, I place her palms on my chest. "Aren't you going to do the front?"

An answering gleam meets my challenge. Her hands slide lightly down the front of my body until they reach my abdomen. Fingers spread out to cover more of me except for her thumb. It sweeps across the hair in the center of my body, following it down to my waist.

The soft pad reaches my pants, briefly dips inside, coming dangerously close to my hard cock, and stops. Sucking in a breath, I tip my head, conceding the win to her.

"Maybe another time," she replies with a smirk.

A low whistle interrupts our game, seconds before Cruz steps into the hallway in front of us.

It's time.

I grip her chin and pull it up. "We have more stories to swap. I'll see you soon." Pressing my lips to hers, I can't help thinking this is the best beating I've ever gotten.

She stares steadily back at me but says nothing. I'm not surprised. She refuses to give hope where she believes there is none. Her eyes, though, tell me everything I need to know. I smile.

"Take care of her," I order Cruz, needing him to know she's important to me, too.

In reply, he flips up a single finger, then a fist. One day until the attack, not several like he stated earlier. You never know who's listening, so it pays to be cautious. I breathe a sigh of relief and nod.

After she's gone, I apply the cream onto the bruises on my chest. The callouses in my hand rub harshly against my skin, and I can't help wishing she was here to help. I close my eyes and picture her hands on me.

A whisper of movement wakes me. Several men are in the cell. Too many to count. I spring up, taking down the two closest, but more enter to replace them. A bag is dropped over my head from behind and a prick stings my right arm.

Fuck.

Heaviness seeps into my muscles until I can't move. The last thing I hear is Armando giving his men orders to take me to the ranch.

28

QUINN

Completely preoccupied, Cruz barely answered any of my questions on the way back. I thought he might be upset with me, but he held my hand tightly the entire way.

The small studio above the tailor's shop is a hive of activity when I arrive. Zane's in the middle of the room, outlining an attack plan using Sterling's 3D model with a sea of strangers surrounding him.

Where did all these people come from?

Zane's eyes dart to me the second I walk in the room, and he stops mid-sentence. "Let's pause here for a moment. Review the plan, and I'll answer any questions in a second."

They follow his gaze and part like the Red Sea, allowing him to head directly toward me.

I tense.

"Easy, she's injured," Cruz states softly.

Zane's large arms wrap carefully around my shoulders and

pull me in for a hug. Surprised, I freeze. The last time we were together, things were strained between us. I look up and meet his grey eyes. Instead of frustration and anger, they're filled with… understanding.

A relieved sigh escapes. It's enough.

The protectiveness and strength of his embrace beckons me, and I allow myself to melt into his arms. The tightness in my chest eases. My hands slide up and around, fingers gripping him tightly, like an anchor, and I close my eyes to savor the feeling.

When I'm around him, the darkness eases, giving me a break from the burden of this path I've chosen. But it scares me, too. I can't afford to walk in the light too long.

After a few minutes, he pulls back a few inches.

I reluctantly open my eyes and drop my head back to meet his grey stare.

"Whether you like it or not, you're a part of this team. We don't hide things from each other. If you're going to deviate from the mission plan, it's your responsibility to inform the lead. That's me, in case you're wondering. You should have told me you were staying," he says gruffly.

When I say nothing, he sighs. "I know I've been a pushy asshole. It's a bad trait, but you'll get used to it. Eventually. Our team works because we respect each other. Got it?" His grey eyes are like flint, hard and unyielding, but his hands stroke softly down my back.

"You're not the only one on this team who has gone off alone to take care of something. It seems to be a pre-requisite for us," he adds with a chuckle, looking pointedly at Cruz.

The thought of being a part of them is so tempting, I can't breathe. I can't…

Large hands wrap around my arms to hold me away from him. "Did you hear me? You *are* a part of this team. Do whatever you need to do. Leave the rest to us. We'll help you find your way." His deep voice is steady and reassuring. "Just don't shut us out. Deal?"

Do I take him up on his offer? "What if you don't like what I have to say? Or the things I do?"

This is already eating my soul. I can't afford to let someone chip away at the rest of me.

A wry smile appears. "We'll talk about it. All of us, not just me. In the end, we all choose to stay. Nobody makes us."

Unconditional acceptance? Is there such a thing? Besides my family, I've never felt it from others. My entire life, I fought so hard to be the best and make everyone proud of me. But when I needed my friends and colleagues the most, they abandoned me. I search his grey eyes. Will they do the same?

His eyes drop down to my abdomen and harden. "How badly are you hurt?"

My face warms. "Sore, but bearable, especially after applying Raider's miracle cream. Where does he get that stuff, anyway?"

He lifts a shoulder. "A shop in Africa, I believe." His hands slide up my shoulders to cup my jaw, and he bends down to stare directly into my eyes. "Concentrate on what you need to do. Be transparent. Trust us to have your back. That's it." Grey eyes search my face, filling with relief when I slowly nod.

"Okay. We'll start with transparency and see how it goes," I concede, unwilling to commit a hundred percent without proof, especially from him.

He straightens. "We're planning tomorrow's attack. Grab something to eat and don't forget to say hi to Sterling. He's been very worried about you and Raider," he orders softly. Placing a kiss on my temple, he points me toward the corner, then strides back to the group.

When I glance in that direction, I find Sterling seated in front of a computer with a blond woman bent over his shoulder, looking at the screen. My stomach twists, making me frown. Wondering who she might be, I walk over to the fair couple.

She turns.

"Margot? What are you doing here? Did something happen?" I ask, surprised to see the young woman still here.

She smiles. "Saving the others, getting revenge, and other stuff. The usual." Her eyes narrow as she studies me. "Why did you stay?"

Her confidence comes across in spades. Even Aria didn't have this level of command. "Samantha Baston, vengeance, and stuff," I reply with a shrug. "Those people, the women… they're lucky to have you on their side." I mean it, too. The fierce determination shining on her face tells me how far she'll go to save them. Someone needs to care, and it can't be me.

I reach around her to tap Sterling on the shoulder.

He slides the headset off one ear. "What is it? Do you see a gap?"

"There's a room missing from your model. Right here," I tell him, pointing to an area in the back. "Roughly ten by ten, tiled…"

Mmph.

Like he did in the tunnels, he wraps his entire body around mine. I wince, but when I see the pinched look in his eyes, I hold back the grunt of pain. The past has been riding him hard.

"Hello, gorgeous," I tease him with his own words. "Does this mean you missed me?"

His finger sweeps a lock of hair behind my ear. "I was ready to storm the castle to get you out." Worried green eyes stare down at me. "Are you okay?"

I give him a half-smile. "So, so. A few bruises."

He holds me out in front of him and scans my body. When he doesn't find anything, he reaches for the hem of my shirt.

I grab his hand. "Later," I tell him, tilting my head toward the room full of people. The image on the screen catches my eye. "There is a room missing. Not sure it matters, though. There is only one entrance and exit."

He doesn't even glance at the screen. "Forget the bloody room," he orders in a hoarse voice.

Bending down, his warm lips meet mine in a scorching kiss full of feelings. He pours them into me one at a time until my heart aches for him. Gone is the cheerful, happy-go-lucky Brit. In its place is a man wrecked by reliving the past. His emotions are dark and full of sadness, but there's an undercurrent of hope in there, too. And heat. The kind that burns you up from the inside.

His arms tighten around me, and this time, I grunt in pain.

Jerking back, he raises his head and stares down at me. "It's worse than a few bruises. Tell me."

"Three minutes dangling from a rope," I reply. "Could have been worse. It was worse for Raider."

He frowns fiercely, and he swivels around to look across the room. "Where is he?"

"Stayed inside to help."

He jerks away and spears his fingers through his golden locks, pulling the strands in frustration. "Damn him."

"Sterling, where's the update?" Zane asks loudly.

Indecision wars in Sterling's eyes.

"Go back to work," I urge him. "Raider's choices are his own."

I blink at the words. It's obvious these men don't like the fact that Raider chose to stay, but they accept it's his decision. Just like they accepted mine to stay in Samantha's place.

"I can't wait for this mission to be over," he rasps. Dropping a kiss on my lips, he sinks into his chair. "I should be done with this soon. Go rest. I'll find you."

Margot drifts over to stand behind him, but with a glance at me, she stands a little farther away.

I look around the room, feeling a little lost and left out. Angry at the thought, I stalk over to the kitchen and open the refrigerator. Pizza boxes are stacked inside. I pull one out, heat up a few slices, and scarf them down. Samantha was right about the food in the facility. I wouldn't feed it to a dog.

"Got any extras?" a gravelly voice asks behind me.

I turn and find a dark-haired man behind me.

He flashes a charming smile, but it does nothing for me.

Without a word, I grab another plate, add a few slices, and pop it in the microwave. When it dings, I turn to hand it to him.

"Thank you. We traveled down early this morning from Chicago and didn't get time to eat. Too many preparations," he explains with a shrug.

I tilt my head. "Chicago? What's your name?"

"Dante Luciano." He takes a large bite of the pizza.

My eyebrow rises sky high. "Aria's brother? She made it home? What about Samantha? Is she there, too?"

He stills. "You must be Quinn." Eyes that shined with friendliness a moment ago turn to suspicion. "Aria informed me you saved her, at the request of Armando, of course." Sinister light gleams in his eye.

"That's correct."

Two men walk over and stand beside him. I eye the younger one. This must be the other brother Aria mentioned. He looks remarkably like her. His smile disappears when he sees the look on his brother's face.

The last man is older, hardened compared to the other two. He looks like he could fight his way out of a dark alley with his hands tied behind his back. The muscle, I'm guessing.

"This is my brother, Leonardo. And our right-hand man, Giovanni," he says, introducing each of the men beside him. "This is Quinn." Teeth gleam in their pseudo smiles, but I can see the predators behind the façade.

"Nice to meet you," I state flatly. "There's more pizza in the fridge." I pivot to my left to walk away, but a large hand grabs my elbow.

Furious, I glare at Dante, knowing he's their leader. "Tell him to let me go, or I'll cut off his balls."

He laughs, but it dies quickly when Giovanni darts a glance down to his crotch where my knife is resting against him. I'd grabbed it from the facility before we left.

Leonardo moves in closer but stops when a knife presses against his throat. Cruz stands behind him, eyes fixed on Dante.

Giovanni instantly releases me.

I sigh. "Look. It may not look like it, but we want the same thing. In the end, if you decide the punishment isn't enough, we can settle up. Deal?"

Dante narrows his eyes. "What is it you think I want?"

"The kind of death that sends a brutal message ringing across the cartel," I say simply.

"And you're going to deliver this warning?" He scoffs with a glance at my petite frame. "Why should I believe you?"

Tired and sore, I scowl and jerk my phone out of my pocket. Swiping quickly through the pics, I land on one of my favorites. "This is why. His brother: Julio." The body lies spread-eagle in the desert with a gaping hole in his chest. A mirror image of the knife in my hand is staked through the center.

The younger man blanches, but the other two nod in satisfaction.

Cruz retracts the knife at Leonardo's throat.

"Deal," Dante returns.

29

———

QUINN

The casual way the Luciano family deals with death is refreshing, I muse.

One minute the space behind me is empty, and the next, it's filled. There's no sound, no smell, just him.

Moving my head to the right, I murmur, "Thank you." It's nice to have back-up again.

Cruz' finger glides lightly down the center of my spine, making me arch my back. "Hmm, you could have handled them, but it's better if your focus is on your target."

Target. Such a mediocre word for Armando. It reduces him down to nothing but six letters. I smile. I like it.

The phone in my pocket buzzes, and I pull it out. "Looks like the target is calling," I inform Cruz.

When he goes to move away, I grab his hand. Time to test a little of Zane's transparency.

After a deep breath to pull my emotions back, I answer. "Hello."

"You took your punishment well. Not one scream or cry of pain escaped those beautiful lips of yours. You continue to impress me," he praises. "Tomorrow's celebration begins at seven p.m. sharp. Formal attire. No weapons, and your new friends are not invited. I'll text you an address."

"I'll require a car and driver," I interject quickly. "Driving in four-inch heels and a formal dress is near impossible."

Silence. "Granted. One person." He hangs up.

A text comes through a second later with an address and directions.

My phone pings, notifying me of a second text. This one includes a video attachment.

I tap play.

"Fuck!" I exclaim, my eyes riveted to the sight of a man standing outside, shirtless, with his tattoos on display and a bag over his head. Familiar tattoos. Raider.

Cruz leans over my shoulder, then lets out a loud whistle.

Everything stops.

"What is it?" Zane practically growls, his body tense while he waits for us to answer.

"He took Raider," Cruz calls out. "There's a video. I don't recognize the location."

Zane stalks over with Sterling on his heels. "Let me see." He holds out his hand and I place the phone in it.

The three of them watch it several times. I can't bear to see it more than once. Damn it. I knew something like this was going to happen. How the hell do we find him before tomorrow?

Zane hands the phone to Sterling. "Run a location trace on the message and video. Maybe we'll get lucky." He turns to the rest of the room. "We have good news and bad news."

"First, the bad. Our inside man has been taken. We need to figure out a retrieval plan," he informs them. When they start shouting questions, he holds up his hand. "Second, the good news. Quinn has been invited to a celebration at Armando's home tomorrow. With his full attention on the party, it gives us the perfect opportunity to attack. We're pushing everything back a day and shifting the timeline a bit."

A short, stocky man steps forward. "What time?"

"Event starts at…" Zane pauses to look at the phone. "Seven p.m."

The man writes it down. "I'll get started on revising the timeline. You concentrate on finding Raider."

"Thanks, Thomas," Zane replies, anger making his voice harsh. "Options." He looks at Cruz and me.

Trading myself wouldn't do any good. For some reason, Armando is obsessed with this event.

"We could pick up Rodrigo or Hugo, see if they know where the video was taken," I suggest. "Although I'm not sure where either of them live, I have Rodrigo's number and could arrange a meeting."

Zane and Cruz grimace. "We have a small window. I'm not sure Rodrigo would break quickly enough. What do you know about Hugo?"

"The man can punch," I state dryly, rubbing my stomach. "Other than that, nothing."

Zane scowls and shares a look with Cruz, who nods.

Running a hand across his shaved head, Zane scans the room. "Margot, do you have a second?"

The young woman nods and walks over.

"Do you have any information on one of Armando's men named Hugo?" he asks her.

"No, but I might be able to get the info. Just a sec," she replies, holding up her phone. She dials a number.

"Hello, Captain. Do you miss me?" Her mouth twitches as she listens to him. "Of course, I need something. A piece of information. A thousand. What do you know about Hugo?"

She listens quietly for a minute. "You expect me to believe you only know his name? Weren't you a first sergeant on the police force?" A golden eyebrow raises. "I see. I'll call one of my other contacts. I'm sure they want the money."

With a tap, she hangs up. "One, two, three…"

The phone rings. "Hello? Captain. That's wonderful. Same account? I'll pay once the information is verified. Always a pleasure doing business."

She quickly types something into her phone, then holds it up. "His name and address. It's all I could get out of the captain. This man, Hugo, must be high in the ranks and bad news."

Cruz snaps a picture. "Sterling, address coming your way. Need some intel."

"Thank you," Zane says. He motions for us to follow him over to Sterling's computer.

I grab Margot's hand when we pass. "Come on. I know you're dying to know whether it's accurate or not."

A surprised expression crosses her face, but it's gone in a microsecond. "Thank you." With her chin raised, she follows.

"Address is a house in Monterrey. Nice neighborhood. Owned by Hugo Ramirez. Bought it ten years ago. Let's see if we get any hits on him," Sterling says, pulling up a new screen and entering the info.

A few articles pop up with his name. Most of them are focused on Armando, but they mention his friend, a local businessman named Hugo Ramirez. Sterling zooms in on the pic.

My stomach tightens. "That's him."

While he scans the articles, Margot picks up the phone. "One thousand. Same account." She hangs up.

"Lived here all his life. Has a wife and kids," Sterling spits out nuggets from the articles. "Reported income of fifty thousand a year." He snorts. "Someone isn't reporting all their income."

Cruz zooms in and snaps a picture of Hugo with his phone. "I'll head over to his house. Text me any additional information you find." He grabs his backpack and leaves.

Sterling absentmindedly nods and points to the screen where numerous dots are now displayed. "The video traced back to a phone. It matches Armando's number."

He clicks on a cluster. "He was everywhere last night. All over the city." A single outlying dot lies east, close to the city. "Now that we have his address—his home." With a slide of his mouse, he circles two dots about an inch apart. "The facility, where they grabbed Raider, and a second location, where they must have made the video."

"So, we know where he is?" I ask.

He pulls up the location on Google maps and heaves a sigh. "They're smart. It's the middle of nowhere."

"I don't like relying on one option," Zane spits out, pacing back and forth behind us. "Did you finish searching the list of properties the other day?"

Sterling taps a few keys and brings up a document. "Most of these are local businesses he owns." The mouse pointer slides down the list. "His home. Two empty lots. And a warehouse."

Zane stops. "Is the warehouse one of the location dots?"

Sterling googles the warehouse address, right clicks on it, and grabs the coordinates. He converts the dots on the map to coordinates and compares the two. "Not a match, but maybe he didn't go to the final destination."

"I'll check out the warehouse," he replies. "Is there anything else?"

Thinking back to the last night, I try to recall what he said before they started my punishment. "Armando took the cartel leaders out to dinner last night. I don't know where. Nor do I know their names."

"Can you describe them to me?" Zane asks, grabbing a notepad. "I might have a contact that can reach out."

I describe them to him. "Sorry it's not more. I wasn't around long enough to get more information."

Zane's hand wraps around my shoulder and squeezes. "It's fine. Every little bit of intel helps. We have two starting points. It's enough." He grabs his gear. "Sterling, he spent quite a bit of time in the city. See if you can pick up some images from nearby cameras. It might help narrow down the list of cartel candidates for our friend."

Cartel. "If your contact doesn't know, could you reach out to Raider's brother… Paulo?" If his father was a cartel leader, and they took him out, somebody had to take over. It obviously wasn't Raider.

Shocked, they stare at me.

Defensively, I shrug. "He told me about Camila." When they continue to stare at me, I raise my hands. "What?"

Zane grabs an untraceable phone. "Call me if you find something. I'll call Paulo on the way to the warehouse." His grey eyes flick to me, speculation in their depths, but he says nothing before he leaves.

Margot glances across the room at Thomas. "I'm going to listen in on the attack plans." She heads over with a determined look on her face.

I wonder what that's all about?

"Raider never talks about his family," Sterling states softly. "It surprised us."

I frown. Are they upset because Raider and I became closer? Or is it because I slept with Cruz, and they're worried it might cause problems in the group? They haven't told me they know about us, but I'm sure they do.

"Keep me company while I search the footage." He carefully maneuvers me onto his lap.

Embarrassed, I try to get up, but his words stop me.

"I need to hold you for a bit. Reassure myself you're here and not a prisoner somewhere," he admits, without looking away from the screen.

With a sigh, I relax into his arms. "Would you be my driver tomorrow night?"

Unlike Cruz, who uses unscented products to avoid detection, Sterling smells mouth-wateringly good. The scent of bergamot, an undertone of fruit, and a musk. A few other notes I can't identify. It makes me want to bury my nose in his neck.

His nose wrinkles in distaste. "A driver? I'm a lord, you know."

I roll my eyes. "Fine, I'm sure one of the men here would be happy to do it."

"Not happening, beautiful, but good try," he inserts with a chuckle. "Since I'm the only one who employs a driver, I would be the logical choice. At least I know the duties." His mock consideration makes me laugh. "Plus, you'll be able to see how good I look in a suit."

"I saw you in a suit the first night. At that restaurant," I remind him. "You looked very dashing, if I recall."

"Of course, I did," he says smugly. "Now, what are you going to wear?"

I blanch.

Sterling sees the panic on my face and immediately takes charge. "Right. Once Cruz and Zane get back, we'll see about getting you a dress."

"And high-heels. Unfortunately, boots or tennis shoes would be frowned upon," I murmur.

Visions of striding confidently into Armando's domain are slowly being replaced by a teetering version of me in an ill-fitted dress. Sucking my lip in, I nibble on the skin.

A lean finger taps my lip. "Stop chewing your lip. We'll make sure you have everything you need." He sweeps an arm toward the room. "If we can pull together almost a hundred men in two days, we can find you a beautiful dress and shoes."

His green eyes are steady and reassuring, and the panic subsides a bit.

The search for video footage of Armando in the city last night brings up a lot of hits. We start scanning them one by one. It's tedious work.

Sterling's hand slides up my back to my neck and strokes back and forth.

Heat flares inside me, but when I look over, he's fully engrossed in the search. He must not even be aware of what he's doing. I silently count backwards to distract myself from his hands, and the heat finally settles to a simmer. He stops stroking and pulls me in tighter.

Within the security of his arms, my lids droop. The pain kept me awake last night. Well, that and Raider. The thought of him jolts me out of my sleepiness. I shift to sit up straight.

Sterling puts a hand on my leg. "As much as I love the feel of you sliding against me, if you don't stop moving, you're going to feel a lot more of me than you do now."

My eyes dart to his, and I freeze. "Sorry."

"I'm not, but maybe it's not the best time and place," he murmurs, looking pointedly at the room full of people.

I nod and go back to looking at the footage, careful to keep myself still.

We're still scanning videos when Zane returns an hour later. "Warehouse is empty. Heard anything from Cruz?"

"Not yet," Sterling replies. "And we haven't found anyone with Armando yet. Did you speak to his brother?"

Zane shakes his head. "No, I left a voice mail asking him to call me." He motions to the other group. "I'm going to check on the revised plans for tomorrow night." With an impassive glance at me, he pivots and heads straight toward Thomas.

"Is he upset because I'm sitting on your lap?" I blurt out.

Green eyes meet mine, and he hesitates. "Maybe, I'm not sure."

"Is it because I'm getting close to more than one of you?" I ask hesitantly.

He shifts his focus to me and leans back. "Yes. Zane wants you to be a part of the team, but he's concerned about the repercussions a more… intimate relationship will have on us, especially if it's with more than one person."

"I've only slept with Cruz," I murmur, not wanting the whole room to hear my statement. "But I've kissed you, Raider, and Cruz. No promises were made, though."

His eyes lock onto mine. "Do you want more with me or Raider? Or do you only want Cruz?"

Beads of sweat roll down my back. "I hadn't thought about it." I hold his gaze, even though I want to look away from the lie hanging between us.

Disappointment flashes across his face. "I thought you would be more honest with me, but maybe it's too soon." He reaches up and swipes his thumb across my lips. "You should know, though. As much as I enjoy kissing you, I want more. I haven't said anything because I know this isn't the time."

His thumb glides down my neck to rest at the base. "Your heart is beating so fast." He taps up and down with the beats. "Given Raider's willingness to tell you about Camila and his family, I'm sure he feels the same way."

The low murmur of his voice and the warmth of his hand make me want to fall into his lips and arms.

I jerk away and slide off his lap. "I can't think about this right now. Let's concentrate on rescuing Raider and the rest of it."

I'm sorry, I silently tell him.

The closeness of a moment ago shatters, but I don't look back when I walk away.

30

QUINN

Cruz calls in three hours later. When Hugo went home for lunch, he grabbed him and took him to the abandoned restaurant Sterling found for him.

"I've worked on him for the past hour. Nothing yet," he relays. "He's old school. I can break him, but it's going to take time."

Frustration bleeds from every word.

Zane grunts. "Put me on speaker."

A second later, Cruz comes back. "Are you there?"

Zane looks at us and lays a finger against his lips.

"Remind Hugo that he's got a wife and kids at home. Maybe he'll give you the answers we need. But if you don't think it's going to happen in time, silence him and get back here. That's an order," Zane states loudly, wanting him to hear the alternative.

"Copy," Cruz replies quietly. "Call you back in two hours. One way or the other." He hangs up.

"Good play," I tell Zane.

He shrugs his big shoulders. "It may or may not work. Time will tell."

Sterling walks up, rubbing his eyes. "Still looking through the footage. Have you heard anything from Raider's brother?"

Zane shakes his head. "No, I called the main number, but maybe he's already dumped it. I'll try a couple of others." He raises his voice. "If anyone needs me, I'll be outside."

Sterling turns to me. "You need to go get a dress."

I cross my arms over my chest. "I'm not leaving until we find Raider."

"Are you prepared to show up to the event naked? Or in fatigues?" he asks, his mouth set in a flat line.

"What if we can't find Raider?"

"One man isn't worth all those lives," Sterling says hoarsely. "Even if it was my father, I wouldn't trade one life for all. Raider would agree. The attack can't be pushed back any further. This many men will be noticed soon. Any advantage we have will be lost."

Zane strides up. "I left a few messages." The tension between Sterling and me is taut with unspoken words. "What's going on?"

Sterling turns to him. "The event tomorrow is formal. She needs the proper attire."

I narrow my eyes at them both. "I'm not going shopping while Raider is being held hostage. If it comes down to it, I won't..." I pause.

Would I really throw away this opportunity to save Raider? I think about it for a minute. If I don't go, I'll have to find another way to get to Armando because he doesn't give second chances. It would be harder to grab him, but I have his address now.

"I won't go." Nausea makes sweat break out on my forehead, but I plant a stoic look on my face and wipe it off.

For some reason, Sterling and Zane look satisfied with my answer. Just a minute ago, they were stressing the importance of the event.

"The attack must happen tomorrow night. We'll either have Raider out or we won't, but if you take out Armando, it won't matter. Nobody will call the guards to give them kill orders," Zane surmises. "The event gives us the perfect opportunity to strike both the facility and his home. We know where our target will be at a specific time. He'll also be pre-occupied for several hours and won't realize what's happening until it's too late. It's too big to pass up." Zane calmly lists the reasons behind his strategy.

"What are you going to do if we rescue Raider at the eleventh hour? If you don't have a dress, you won't be able to go. If you're prepared, you can get ready quickly," Sterling interjects, his eyebrow raised high.

I heave a sigh, knowing he's right. If only I could clone myself.

A feminine laugh breaks through the clutter in my mind. I dart a glance in the corner and find Leo talking animatedly to Margot.

I walk over. "Excuse me. Can I borrow Margot?"

She immediately stands. "I'll catch you later." Tossing her hair over her shoulder, she follows me to the window. "What is it?"

Sophia used to get everything she wanted from me by using her sweet voice and pretty brown eyes. "You're free to stay here, but I hope you won't because I desperately need your help to find a formal dress and shoes for Armando's event tomorrow night," I say, my tone pleading. I throw in some puppy dog eyes, too.

Blue eyes assess me closely. "This isn't an attempt to give me something meaningless to do, is it? I'd rather chew nails than shop."

"I need a formal dress that will make me look fierce and have the ability to conceal a knife and a garrote—and they will be patting me down. Is that challenge enough for you?" I dangle the carrot in front of her, silently praying she says yes.

She shrugs, but I can see the interest in her eyes.

"Fine. Do you have any money?"

"Lots. Criminal activity pays well, don't you know?" I reply, only half-joking. It's the one thing I've gained over the past couple of years. More than I can spend in a lifetime. Lose your soul, become rich. "I'll buy you some clothes, too. Fatigues for the attack tomorrow and some everyday items."

"You think they'll let me go with them tomorrow?" she asks with a snort.

"If you want to go, don't let them stop you. Can you shoot?" I ask. When she nods, I shrug. "They want someone confident at their back. Keep being your usual self. I'll make sure you go with them."

She straightens her posture. "Deal. Give me your card."

Snatching my backpack off the floor, I dig into the bottom of it. "I'd feel better if you took someone with you," I reply, handing her my card.

She scans the room. "Leo, darling man, would you mind coming with me on a short errand?"

I stifle the laugh threatening to escape. Short errand.

A second later, I close the door behind them and return to Zane and Sterling. "Margot is going to do a little shopping for the both of us."

Zane gives me an admiring look. "Delegating. Good answer." He raises his hand and begins to count the people in the room. "We'll probably need to order dinner in another hour. It takes a while to get food for twenty people."

Dinner comes and goes. The phone is silent. Margot hasn't returned yet, either. My head is pounding from worrying about everyone, but it's keeping my mind off tomorrow night.

I'm going into this event blindfolded. With his brother, Julio, I planned every detail, from his kidnapping to his last breath. While I have picked out a location for Armando, I have no idea how I'm going to take him down and get him there. It makes my stomach cramp, but I refuse to let it dissuade me.

Zane's phone rings.

Sterling and I look up.

He listens for a few minutes, then hangs up.

"Cruz is on his way back. Hugo wouldn't talk," Zane states wearily. He drops into a chair.

I walk over to the window. Thoughts of last night swirl in my brain. Out of all the men in this group, Raider's calm acceptance of me and what I have to do centered me more than anything. Or maybe it was just the man himself. I sigh. Can I do this knowing his life is at stake? My hand creeps up to rub my chest. I long for the simple days before they got here, when my only emotions were rage and cold-blooded determination. I lay my head against the cool glass and stare down at the street.

Movement below catches my eye. Leo's walking rapidly across the parking lot, his arms full of packages and a huge scowl on his face. Margot's practically skipping beside him, her smile radiant in comparison. And satisfied. I assume she accomplished the task I gave her.

Minutes later, they walk in. Leo dumps the packages on the bed in the corner. With a grimace, he stalks off.

"Thank you for all of your help today, Leo," Margot states graciously, but the smirk on her face tells me it's facetious.

I wonder what happened between those two. "Looks like you had a successful day," I muse. "Did you find everything?"

"He's just grumpy because he didn't get his way," she says with a dismissive shrug. "Are you ready to see the dress I got for you? And the shoes? It's perfect. I surpassed myself."

I laugh. "Bold words. Let's see it."

We head downstairs, where a three-sided mirror stands. After dusting it off, I exchange my jeans and t-shirt for the dress.

"No bra," she instructs me.

Swallowing hard, I nod. I'm not sure why but going without a bra in front of my enemy feels like I'm giving up my armor.

I unzip the bag and pull out a concoction of tulle and lace. Dismay fills me. Maybe I shouldn't have let Margot get me a dress. I sigh. Too late to change my mind. I step into the dress and pull it up. It fits. One hurdle down.

There's a raised dais in front of the mirror, so I stand on top and twirl. The champagne-colored dress flares out, then floats softly down. Surprised at the image in the mirror, I stop twirling and stare. It's beautiful and perfect. The top is all boning, covered with the sheerest tulle. Tiny cups made of delicate lace mold to my breasts, leaving very little to the imagination. Tiers of tulle cascade down in a modern, layered effect, making it look almost like feathers. A slim rhinestone belt wraps around my waist.

My eyes meet Margot's in the mirror. "With some make-up to cover the bruises, it will be absolutely perfect. The knife will fit along the inside seam under my arm." I run a finger down the large boning on the side. "The belt is thick enough to hold the garrote."

Her eyes gleam. "And the bastard won't be able to take his eyes off you." She hesitates for a second. "Are you sure this is what you want? The Luciano family would gladly make a statement out of him."

She'd heard some of the story from one of the others. "Everywhere I turn, I see her. Laughing, crying, the moments of her life. She haunts me. I need to give her peace." Maybe find some for peace for me, too.

She nods slowly. "It's what I would do if I had a sister." With a flick of her wrist, she opens the shoe box. "Now, the shoes."

Nestled in the box is a pair of glittery sandals with a block heel. Surprised, I flick her a look.

"The block will be better if you need to fight or run," she pertly informs me. "And it allows us to insert a tracker in the heel."

Impressed with her thinking, I smile. "You're pretty remarkable, you know that? Thank you. They're perfect." Using her shoulder for leverage, I let her slip them on my feet and buckle them up.

Flipping my foot to the side, I let the light catch the sparkly rhinestones. It plays off the belt. Everything is deliberate and well thought out.

I grab my knife from my pants and hold it up to the side of the dress. The boning will easily conceal it, even in a pat down.

It's hard to stop the wicked smile from spreading across my face. Beauty is its own weapon, but it can always use a few accessories.

31

QUINN

After packing everything back in its bags and boxes, we head upstairs. Cruz' brown eyes meet mine the minute I'm in the door. Shadows darken their depths.

Remembering my promise, I turn to Margot. "Did you get some fatigues?" When she nods, I drag her over to Thomas and Zane.

"Which group is Margot joining tomorrow?"

Zane's grey eyes slide to Margot. "Is there one you prefer?"

She straightens her shoulders. "I'd like to be in the group entering the women's quarters. They know me. Once they see my face, they'll do whatever you need quickly and quietly."

Her foresight is impressive. It makes me wish I'd raised Sophia a little differently.

Zane considers her answer and flashes a four at Thomas, who nods. He flicks a look at her. "You can shoot and hit your target, right?"

"Absolutely. My father demands perfection in all things," she reassures him.

He frowns. "You've got good instincts. Rely on them, not your father's opinions. Thomas will outfit you with some weapons. You'll be joining group four."

With a firm nod, she follows Thomas over to the armory table. It's filled with an assortment of weapons, from knives and guns to batons and garottes.

"We have a dress and shoes," I announce to the three men standing in front of me. "Do we have any news on Raider?"

"No, but Cruz left a message with his brother's right-hand man," Zane returns with a weary sigh. "Did you find schematics for the house?"

Sterling yawns, and brings up a 3D model of a large, gated home. "We'll come in here, at the front gates, up the circular drive. There are two other visible entry points—here and here." He points to the side- and rear- gates. "The layout of the house has been sent to all of your phones, but we can do a quick walk-through."

"Entry is two-story with a double-sided staircase and a balcony looking down into the foyer," he begins, tapping the model to turn it. "Study here, formal two-story living room, dining room, kitchen is toward the back, primary down. Upstairs has several bedrooms, bathrooms, and lounge areas."

Blood money. All I want to do is burn it down. Hypocritical of me, I know, but I don't care. I want to stand on its ashes.

Cruz' phone rings, and we tense. He glances at the number and dips his chin. "Paulo, we have a situation here. Normally we wouldn't call, but we believe you might want to help." Not wanting anyone else to hear, he steps outside to talk to him.

When he returns, surprise is written all over his face. "He's here, in Monterrey, and you'll never guess who he had dinner with last night."

I frown. "He's one of the leaders who visited the facility?" The image of the three pop in my mind. There were only two men—the one with a paunch and a cold, dark-haired man. I doubt Raider's brother has a belly.

Cruz shakes his head. "He might have an idea of where Raider's being held. Armando talked incessantly about the beautiful horses he's breeding on his ranch last night. Paulo's going to call him and ask to see the horses, possibly to breed them with his. He'll call us back."

I drop into a chair to wait, wincing at the twinges of pain.

Sterling mutters something and stalks away. When he reappears, he's holding a jar of the miracle cream. "Raider gave us each one. Put it on."

Cruz' eyes flick between Sterling and me. Wanting to keep my secrets, I grab the jar and stalk to the bathroom. After thoroughly applying the cream to my front, I realize I can't reach my back. I'll have to ask Margot for help.

When I open the door, Sterling is standing there waiting for me. "I'd like to help you put it on your back."

Damn him.

Without waiting for my reply, he steps forward until I back up and let him in.

"Fine," I snap, turning my back to him and raising my shirt. When he doesn't immediately start, I huff and look over my shoulder.

This is the man I saw fighting in the tunnel. Gone is the warm, golden, sexy man. In its place is a hardened soldier.

His eyes meet mine. "Cruz told me you let Armando do this to you because you wanted him to believe he has power over you." The accent is barely noticeable right now. His hand clenches into a fist. "Once. That's all you get. Never again. Do you hear me? Truly hear me? This is never happening again."

I flinch. "It won't." The decisions I made the last two years haven't been made with me in mind, which has led to some pretty bad incidents, but this is probably one of the top five worst ones. Yet, even knowing the outcome, I would do it again.

"It better not," he murmurs almost menacingly.

I turn around to face the wall and avoid the censure on his face. "Are you going to apply the cream, or do I need to get Margot to do it?"

A ragged breath escapes. "I'll do it," he snarls.

I tense.

Seconds later, warm hands stroke softly across my back. "Don't worry. I would never hit you. Even if you push me to the brink of insanity with your decisions."

It's bound to happen again before this is all over. "Good to know. I would hate to have to add you to my kill list."

"So fierce and strong, like a falcon on the hunt," he murmurs, stepping closer to me. His lips graze the side of my ear. "All done."

A shiver runs down my spine, but I don't turn to face him. If I do, all my intentions will go out the proverbial window.

"Thank you," I manage to choke out.

The door opens, and he steps out.

A quick peek ensures he's gone. I pull my shirt down and lean against the wall. The damn man is lethal. One side is sexy, hot flirting, and the other is hard and domineering. Sweet and savory. Catnip and a spanking. I shudder, wanting both.

Peeling myself away from the wall, I grab the jar and saunter out of the bathroom. He doesn't get to know I'm the least bit bothered by him. I hand him the jar and keep walking until I find a seat, away from all three men.

Margot smirks. "Your expression is smooth waters, but I'm sensing a tidal wave of emotion under the surface. Want to talk about it?"

"Want to tell me what happened with you and Leo today?" I drawl, my voice coated in honey.

Her eyes dart to the man in the corner who's been studiously ignoring her all night. "Nope. I'm good."

We look at each other and laugh. The only two women in a room full of testosterone. It's a miracle we haven't killed them.

The phone rings, and I pivot to face them.

"Paulo acquired an address for the ranch. I don't know if it came from Armando or someone else. It's not the same as the house. We're going to check it out," Zane informs me, eyes filled with relief.

"I'm going with you," I state firmly.

"You can't," Zane refuses. "Paulo doesn't like strangers. If he sees someone with us, he could go on his own."

Frustrated, I raise my hands. "Fine. But call as soon as you have him."

"Sterling is staying here with you," Zane remarks quietly. "We'll keep you both updated." He gives Sterling a reassuring look.

I wince. I'd forgotten how hard this situation is for Sterling, too.

"Thanks," I murmur.

When they're gone, I grab the dress from the closet and start working on adding the garotte to the belt. It must be easy to pull off, but completely hidden from view. I find the groove at the bottom. It feels big enough to fit the wire. Carefully picking apart each seam, I slide the wire in between, then add a loose stitch to keep it in place.

"What are you doing?" a smoky voice asks beside me.

I turn to find Giovanni watching my hands.

"I'm adding a garotte to the belt," I explain, showing him how I intend to do it. "I've done it with almost all of my belts, and it's come in handy."

"Do you mind if I watch? I'd like to give my tailor instructions to do the same to my belts," he asks.

I contemplate the man beside me. "I'll let you watch me add weapons to my dress, if you'll tell me how Samantha and Aria are doing."

His mouth twitches. "A hard bargain, but it's a deal." He blinks. "Did you say weapons? What else are you adding?"

"Don't tell me you don't remember my knife?" I joke, reminding him about the one I used to threaten him.

He smiles, and it transforms his face. "You're a very interesting woman, Quinn."

I pick up the needle and thread, then pause. "Well?"

While he tells me about their homecoming, his voice is filled with anger and relief for Aria, but something else entirely for Samantha. A protective energy that feels so familiar. I peek over at Sterling and find his eyes locked on me.

"He's not going to come over and kill me, is he?" Giovanni's amused voice murmurs.

"Maybe, but not before the attack. We need every single man and woman tomorrow," I retort.

He laughs.

Dante sends him a sharp look.

He shrugs.

I finish the garotte and begin on the knife.

Giovanni stays to watch me. "I should have this done for Aria and Samantha."

"It's always good for a woman to have more than one weapon at her disposal," I point out.

He nods his head in agreement.

With one last snip, the sheath for the knife is finished. Testing it out, I make sure it fits snugly and is hidden by the boning. It's perfect. I smile in satisfaction.

Giovanni softly claps his hands. "Thank you for letting me watch." He smiles and stands. "I'm going to grab some sleep."

After hanging the dress, I wander over to Sterling.

"Hello, beautiful. Still mad at me?" He flashes a worried smile.

I smooth his thick, gorgeous blond hair back. "They've been gone a couple of hours."

The door opens, and Zane walks in alone. I grab Sterling's hand.

"Where are Raider and Cruz?" I demand, unable to think the worst.

With a sigh, he drops into a nearby chair. "Raider is fine.

They're treating him well. He figured a way out but was waiting until after the evening and morning check-in calls with Armando. He didn't want him to suspect anything. Cruz wanted him to leave immediately. Raider's brother, Paulo, is furious. Not about Raider, but because the horses have been mistreated and starved. He wanted to burn the place down immediately."

He pinches the bridge of his nose. "The three of them have settled on middle ground. There are about twenty men at the ranch. They've decided to stay and take them down tomorrow night when the attacks start."

I blink. The three of them are going to take on twenty men? "Should we send them some back-up?"

Zane laughs. "They would only get in the way or get hurt. Those three don't play by the rules. I hope they get it done quickly."

"When we get back, I'm going to find a way to make our trackers smaller and less detectable. Maybe Mateo and Henley can help," Sterling mutters, obviously angry at Raider for worrying him.

"Good idea," Zane replies, squeezing Sterling's shoulder. "Get some rest. We start early tomorrow." He looks at me. "You, too. I want you rested and ready to take on that bastard."

"What about you?" I blurt out. "You've been up planning for days." I frown at Zane.

Sterling chokes on his water. "I'll show you to our accommodations, Quinn." He stands and holds out his elbow.

Threading my arm through, I murmur goodnight to Zane and let Sterling lead me over to the other corner of this tiny studio. I eye the mattress on the floor. What I wouldn't give for a good, comfy couch.

Sterling waves a hand at my duffel on the floor.

"We've been sleeping over here to let Margot have some privacy," he explains. "Plus, we've added Thomas and the man he brought with him. And the Luciano crew."

With a tired nod, I grab my stuff and head to the bathroom to brush my teeth and pull on some leggings and a t-shirt. Minutes later, I'm lying on the mattress staring at the ceiling. The tiredness disappears, replaced by the questions swirling in my head.

What will I find in Armando's house? Who is this family he wants me to meet? Is this the beginning of the end?

Sterling eases down beside me. "Can't sleep?"

I shake my head.

"Me either," he says with a sigh.

I look deep into his eyes. Even though he knows Raider is safe, the worry is still there. "Tell me about your dad."

He shifts onto his back to stare at the ceiling. "Everyone kept telling me he died on his last mission, but I refused to believe it. He was too tough and smart. So, I kept searching for him. Everyone told me to give up. When I finally found proof he was alive, I wasn't surprised. It took us two months and a lot of money to rescue him and the other hostage," he explains, anguish in his voice. "When I saw him for the first time in two years, he didn't even look the same. All his vitality and strength were gone. They stripped him to the bone."

I entwine my fingers with his. "And yet, he never gave up. He fought hard to make it through and come home." I pause. "What was he like before?"

"The man was bigger than life. Not just physically. He lived every moment to its fullest. He laughed loudly. Fought with equal vigor. He loved my mom fiercely and showed her all the time. He prided himself on his integrity and dedication to his country. And even though I wasn't his biological child, he swore to always be my dad." Sterling's voice trails to silence.

Fingers grip mine. "I thought everything would be better once he returned, but the nightmares and pain were continuous. It drove him mad. He committed suicide a few weeks later. I felt so helpless because I couldn't save him."

"You did save him," I state firmly. "He fought to return to you and your mom. To his country and home. If you had accepted everyone else's opinion, he would have never gotten that chance. It's a miracle, honestly. His body and mind were broken, but you got him home."

"I never thought of it that way," he rasps. "I thought I failed him."

I give him a sad smile. "I understand. I feel the same way about Sophia. I was on the police force for eight years, a Texas Ranger for four years, and I failed to find my sister until it was too late. It was incomprehensible to me. I felt powerless. I think I would have gone mad if I hadn't shifted my attention to finding her killers."

He looks at me. The lines of tension on his face are gone. "You're remarkable, you know that? Thank you." Firm lips find mine for a thorough goodnight kiss, and for a minute, I can't help but fall into it.

"Good night, Sterling," I murmur, my lips tingling with desire when I pull away. Carefully rolling over, I stare at the wall across from me, watching the shadows dance on the wall. If something happens to me, are these men going to feel like they failed? Disturbed by the thought, it takes me forever to get to sleep.

32

ZANE

My gaze lingers on the beautiful woman lying beside me. Even asleep, peace eludes her. When I saw her tossing and turning, my arms ached to pull her in tight, but instead, I scooted in as close as possible until she could subconsciously feel my presence. For a little while, it helped.

Her eyes open and stare at me in confusion.

"Good morning," I say hoarsely, my voice shot from speaking so much yesterday. Coffee will help bring it back.

When I stretch, her eyes widen. Whether it's from the realization that we slept next to each other last night or the sight of my large body in the morning, I can't tell. With a chuckle, I rise and head to the bathroom.

When I walk out, she hands me a cup of coffee. "Good morning." A blush steals across her cheeks when she notices I'm not wearing a shirt.

I should put a shirt on, but when her eyes linger on me, it feels too good. "Thank you. You didn't have to get up," I tell her.

"I don't sleep much," she admits with a shrug. "Plus, there's a lot going on today."

I run a lazy hand down my chest, lightly scratching, and watch her eyes follow the movement. Does she like what she sees, or am I too old for her?

She slams the coffee cup on the counter. "I need a shower." Spinning on her bare heel, she grabs the pile of clothes behind her and slides past me into the bathroom.

With a grin of my own, I pour myself another cup of coffee and finish getting dressed. It's going to be a hell of a long day. I crack my neck to get the kinks out from another night of sleeping on a hard mattress.

One more run through, I think.

An hour later, I step back and admire the plan. "Thomas, I'm not sure I could have done this without you. You're a hell of a tactician. It makes me wish I hadn't recommended you to Thiago."

He chuckles. "If I get bored, I'll let you know." He taps the plans in front of him. "We just need to decide who's going to lead the charge at the house."

Me, I think.

"Dante, maybe? Cruz won't be back in time. Sterling will be inside, posing as Quinn's driver."

My eyes drift to the corner of the room to find Quinn. She's sitting on a chair while Margot styles her hair for tonight.

"Hmm," he replies nonchalantly.

"What? Do you have someone else in mind?"

He leans over the table to look me in the eye. "I'm quite capable of running the operation at the facility. Why don't you lead the one at the house?"

"It's not about capability, but responsibility. I brought everyone here to run an operation. If anything happened, I'd feel damn guilty."

He taps a finger on his chin. "I could lead the charge on the house, but my focus has been the facility. I'm not sure there's enough time to get me up to speed on a new location and plan of attack." With a quick shuffle, he stacks the plans together. "If you trust the Lucianos to lead, I'm sure it will be fine."

My teeth grind together. I don't have someone I can trust. Not with them or with her. When they storm the house, will they remember Sterling and Quinn are inside? Still, I can't bring myself to switch.

Irritated, I call Cruz. "Status," I bark, dropping all pleasantries.

Cruz says nothing. Not a word. Damn it.

"Sorry. With you and Raider gone, I have to assign someone to run the op on the house." I run my hand down my face.

Cruz hums. "What about Sterling?"

"Quinn asked him to be her driver, which puts him in the house. I want him inside and close to her. Any suggestions?" Cruz has run a thousand ops, so maybe he can pick up on something I'm missing.

"I only trust her safety to the four of us."

His statement is crystal clear. It's me or someone we don't trust. "How's Raider?"

"Eating a damn fine breakfast," he says derisively. "Bastard knows we're watching, too. His eye is twitching… repeatedly."

It takes everything in me to smother my laugh. Raider must be in good spirits if he's winking at them. "Keep me updated. Don't take unnecessary chances." I hang up.

"Is Raider still in his cell?" Quinn asks, concern gleaming in her eyes.

I lean down to whisper in her ear. "They served him a big breakfast. He's even winking at Cruz and Paulo, knowing they're watching him, although he'll regret that later." It's true. The danger comes when they attack, but I don't want her to worry about those three today. She'll need every bit of focus for herself.

She huffs and walks off.

The day is interminably long. Serious faces review plans or sit in silence, waiting for the moment we pull the trigger.

When the clock finally ticks closer to go time, Margot and the men stuff weapons in every conceivable spot on their body.

I'm already armed to the teeth, so I run through both plans to keep my mind sharp.

Sterling has the 3D models up and running for anyone who wants to take a last look. He's stuffing computer gear in a back-pack to take with him in case we need anything during the op. It will stay in the shiny black car waiting downstairs.

His tailored black suit fits his role perfectly, although it's considerably more expensive than the typical chauffer could afford. The black leather driving gloves are a touch over the top, but he insists they are necessary.

We pass earpieces out to everyone, then hand the rest to Thomas to give to the others.

"Ten minutes," I announce.

It's redundant. Every man and woman in this room is aware of the time.

Where the hell is Quinn?

The sea of men by the door parts when Quinn appears.

I swallow. Fuck me. She looks naked. It's not just the nude color, but the dress is held together with sheer fabric and lace. My jaw locks. This changes everything.

"Margot is never allowed to pick out a dress for Quinn again," Sterling snarls beside me.

"I'll be leading the operation at the house," I announce, catching Thomas' eye. When he grins, I subtly flip him off. There's no way in hell I'm allowing anyone to take charge of her safety.

Margot flashes her two thumbs up, and I suddenly have the urge to throw the young woman out the window. This dress is pure enticement. How the hell is Armando going to react?

"Stunning," Sterling declares with gritted teeth.

I glower at her. "Beautiful."

A knife appears in her hand like magic. "Deadly, too."

Intrigued, I look closer at the dress. "Where the hell did that come from?"

She taps the side of her barely covered breast. With a flip of her hand, the knife slides into its sheath, disappearing from sight.

"May I?" I ask, holding up my hands. Can it pass a pat down?

She holds her arms out to the side.

I slide my hands down her sides, but all I feel is dress and her sweet curves. When I get to her tiny waist, I go back up just to make sure.

"Nothing," I declare. Thank fuck.

She heaves a sigh of relief. "Margot did a fantastic job. I might have to get her to pick out all my dresses in the future."

Sterling mutters something unintelligible beside me. When she looks at him, he thrusts an earpiece toward her. "Do you have somewhere to hide this?" His tone is doubtful when he looks up and down the dress.

She slips it into her cleavage.

A strangled noise comes from his throat.

"Move out," Thomas yells.

The crew going to the facility starts filing out of the tailor's shop. He'll be taking ninety-seven people with him, leaving me with the remaining fifteen. Most of the men will be picked up by a bus along the way. Ten men to a bus.

When the operation is finished, we'll use the same buses to transport the rescues out of the facility to Miami where Thiago and Henley are waiting to give them new identities.

"Dante, I'll lead the attack on the house. You take the grounds. Your men will follow you better than they will me," I inform him.

By the satisfied look on his face, he agrees.

Sterling takes my phone and adds an app to it. "This will allow you to hear the conversation in the house. You will not be able to respond, but it's a back-up in case we can't use our earpieces."

I look at my watch. "It's time. Go."

Sterling holds out his elbow for Quinn to take. "Ready for this?"

She jerks her head. "More than ready."

I grab her hand. "Be careful. If it doesn't feel right, get out. You can always get him later."

Her brow furrows, and I can tell she's already dismissing my words. Determination isn't reserved solely for her, though. I intend to make sure she has every advantage we can give her, starting with the annihilation of Armando's men.

She squeezes my hand. "You too."

33

When I take a deep breath, the smell of Sterling's cologne wraps around me, alluring in its sexy confidence. Green eyes meet mine in the rearview mirror.

"How are you doing?" he murmurs. Gloved hands turn the steering wheel to the right, bringing us closer to my enemy.

My stomach flutters. "Nervous. Like Zane, I prefer to plan and control my attacks. Surprises aren't my forte."

I slide my phone out of the small rhinestone clutch. Swiping through the images I've already committed to heart, my nerves steady and a coldness steals over me. He did this to her. I don't need his confession, just his blood and pain. And when I'm ready, his death.

The car pulls through the gate and up the driveway. Armed men are everywhere. When the car in front of us drives off, we pull up to the entrance.

This is it.

"This is it," Sterling states softly. "I'll come around and open your door. After parking the car, I'll text you my location, likely the garage or kitchen."

We've gone over this several times, but I know he needs to say it again.

The door opens, and I step out. A nearby guard looks at me and turns his head to speak into a mic, likely alerting Armando of my arrival.

I shake out my dress and thread my arm through Sterling's elbow. "Thank you, Sterling." My tone is formal to match his role, but my grip on his arm is anything but.

"There she is," Armando exclaims loudly from the door, causing several people to turn around and stare at me. "My guest of honor." Now, they're beyond curious to know who I am.

Long strides bring him directly in front of me. "May I?" His elbow is out and waiting.

I slip my arm from Sterling's to Armando's. From good to evil. The thought brings a smirk to my face.

His hand squeezes mine hard. "Smile, Quinn darling. We want the press to print our best side."

I bare my teeth, and the photographer captures it. That's one set of pictures I won't be buying.

When we get into the house, the formal living room has been transformed into a glittering ballroom. Wearing their best suits and gowns, guests line the dance floor, sipping on beautiful cocktails or chilled champagne. A few brave souls are dancing to the surprisingly good band.

We glide through the crowd like a king and queen, cold and haughty, looking upon the masses. When we pass the ballroom without stopping, my stomach clenches with equal parts anticipation and uneasiness.

He escorts me into a study. Several armed men line the perimeter of the room.

"Relax. I brought you in here to pat you down. Unless you

disobeyed my orders and brought weapons with you, this will go quick," he reassures me. "Hold your arms out."

Warm palms glide up my bare legs to the silky strip of thong between my thighs, the first inclination of his intent. Gripping my control with both hands, I flash him a cold look.

"Icy glares turn me on," he confides, cupping me under the dress.

I raise an eyebrow in response.

Large hands glide from my thighs to my hips and eventually, to my breasts. Shaping them with his hands, he chuckles. "These are certainly a weapon, but not one you can use against me."

He glides one hand up until it's circling my throat. Jerking me close, he inhales. "Delicious. It would be so easy to snap your neck, but death shouldn't be easy, should it?"

His won't be.

I smile in agreement.

His hands cup my breasts, then slide to the sides. Emotionless eyes watch me while he finishes patting me down. What he is hoping to see, I have no idea, but I give him nothing. Once he's finished with my body, he runs his fingers through my hair.

A speculative gaze lands on me. "I'm impressed. No weapons. Did the party give you a false impression of safety?" His eyes dart to the window.

Paranoid asshole. Needing to allay his suspicions, I give him an answer sure to flatter him. "Leverage, remember? It was certainly an incentive."

He preens. "Ah, yes. I almost forgot about my little plan. Although I wasn't sure if it would work. You care so much for this man—Raider, is it?"

I snort. "Hardly. He has powerful friends, and I have enough enemies without adding more to the mix."

Fingers sweep the line of my jaw. "Enemies are truly the spice of life. Take you, for instance. When I first heard that a beautiful, petite woman had come to Monterrey in search of new work, I laughed and threw you scraps. To my surprise, you took the jobs, did them well, and returned for more."

He signals his men. One by one, they file out of the room.

Every muscle in my body goes rigid. This is the true beginning of tonight's festivities. His level of excitement is off the charts.

When they're gone, he leans against the mahogany desk in front of me. "Would you be successful with more challenging work? So, I gave you more, you succeeded. Surprisingly, you asked for nothing in return." He picks up a gold coin from the desk and runs it through his fingers. "Everyone wants or needs something. It made me suspicious. Rodrigo is a good spy. For months, he watched you and reported back to me."

Zane was right. I glare at him. "No wonder he became obsessed with me."

He tilts his head. "It's baffling, to be honest. All you did was work and go to sad little cantinas. Who lives such a pathetic life?" Broad shoulders rise and drop. "After thinking about it, I came up with two possibilities—either you were sent by the cartel to test me, or you were working for one of my enemies. There was not enough information to indicate one or the other, so our monotonous game continued."

He steps closer. "See this coin? It belonged to my brother. He found it in the street when we were children. A simple gold coin. We took it to a pawnshop, and when the owner's eyes lit up, we knew it was valuable. I wanted to sell it to buy food and shelter, but Julio refused. Always the dreamer. He saw it as a sign of our future. One day, we would be so wealthy, the idea of selling it would be laughable."

He murmurs, "He was right."

Dark eyes study mine intently. "Needing to break the stalemate between you and I, I decided to test you. The van full of young women. Rodrigo's idea, actually, although I hate to admit it. You failed, of course, but it led me to believe you worked for one of my enemies. Rodrigo investigated but found nothing. You were a ghost." His voice rises in excitement. "A ghost! Finally, something interesting."

A patronizing smile graces his lips. "It was also your biggest mistake. I became obsessed with finding your past. When nothing turned up, I wondered if you were sent by the Lucianos or some other important family, but you didn't seem to care about the girls. Stumped, I was ready to concede defeat. But Rodrigo saved the day again. He decided to pay you a visit before he left town. You pulled a knife on him." He looks at me, expectation on his face, like I'm supposed to understand what this means.

"He was acting psycho," I retort.

"Your knife is very distinct," he says, walking around his desk to open a drawer. "In fact, I have one identical to it. Do you want to know where I got it from?"

I swallow. Raider warned me about habits. Why did I stick with the same knife?

"Tell me," I taunt him, unable to help myself. He knows it was me who slaughtered his brother and his brother's men. And I'm glad. It feels good to have him look at me and know I did it. Nobody else.

"From my brother's body. It was buried to the hilt in his chest," he reveals, his voice full of fury.

On the verge of pulling my own knife, something interesting catches my eye. "There's fury in your voice, but admiration in your eyes. You like the way he died, don't you?"

He ignores my question. "My first thought was retaliation. But the more I studied you, the more I realized how perfectly we match. Your fierce dedication to vengeance is quite remarkable. And you're stronger than your sister and my brother combined. Steel encased in ice. Which brings us to tonight's celebration. Shall we?"

His mood pivots so quickly, it takes me a few seconds to catch on.

My body goes rigid with tension. It takes a lot of effort to put my arm through the elbow in front of me, but somehow, I manage it. He struts out of the study with me on his arm and heads to the small stage where the band is playing.

"Are you going to kill me in front of all these lovely people?"

His eyes light up. "It would make this a truly memorable event, but no. I've got an important announcement to make," he says, flashing me an intimate smile.

I fucking hate surprises.

He steps up and pulls me into his side. "Ladies and gentlemen, may I have your attention, please?"

When the crowd settles down, he raises his hand and signals to the back. A woman and child start walking toward us.

My gut starts cramping.

When they reach the stage, they stop.

Confused, I look at Armando.

"As you all know, my brother died tragically a little over a year ago. Que esté con Dios." He pauses and makes the sign of the cross. Several people in the crowd repeat his action and words. "It was an incredibly sad time, but luckily, I had someone very special to help me get through the pain. My nephew, Gabriel." He motions for the woman to give him the child.

Sweat beads on my forehead while I stare at the crowd in front of me. Their faces are full of sympathy and speculation.

Light blue eyes catch mine for the briefest of seconds before disappearing again. Raider? Can't be. He's at the ranch.

Brow furrowed; I swivel my head to look at the child. The boy.

"Gabriel is the joy in my life. He's everything to me," he says fervently. "I thought I was his only family. Imagine my surprise when I found out he had an aunt. Meet Quinn." He sweeps an arm towards me.

Everyone starts clapping wildly, but the sound fades to nothing. My eyes are glued to the little boy beside me. The autopsy confirmed my sister had a baby before she died. I assumed it had been sold on the black market or had died.

He would be three years old. He looks old enough, but is he really hers? I search his miniature features. It's been a long time since I saw a baby picture of Sophia, but her eyes were distinct—mahogany brown with a glint of gold in them. The same eyes staring at me right now.

34

QUINN

Aunt Quinn. I'm an aunt. The little boy waves hi, and I automatically raise my hand to wave back. He giggles. Armando watches our interaction closely. "Do you want to hold him?"

In a fog, I hold my hands out to take Gabriel from him. For a second, he looks a little uncertain, but I hold his eyes with mine and patiently wait for him to make up his mind. In a sudden move, he launches himself forward.

Oof, he's heavier than I thought he would be. My arms close around him tightly. His smile is sweet as he stares at me. With her eyes. Sophia's eyes. But unlike the ones I see in my nightmares, these are full of life.

Once upon a time, I held her in my arms. A gangly thirteen year enamored with her beautiful three-year-old sister. It was like having a living baby doll to carry around, and I never got tired of it. My mother used to tell me I was spoiling her. I'd laugh and retort, "who cares?" Sophia would mimic me and laugh, too. My mother would throw up her hands and join us silly girls.

When Armando guides us off the stage, the crowd surges forward, jolting me out of the past and into the present. I swing to place my body between Gabriel and his guests.

A fiercely proud expression crosses Armando's face.

Blocking him out, I absentmindedly accept congratulations from those around us, but my mind is a whirlwind. Thoughts slide by like smoke on the wind, but all I have are questions. No answers.

How did they meet? Did Julio kidnap her or was she in a van with others? Why her? Did my sister care for Julio, or did he force himself on her? If he cared for her, why did Armando kill her?

The autopsy reports showed older bruises under those given to her when she died. Her life here wasn't peaceful, but was it Julio or Armando abusing her? Or both?

My phone pings, but I can't get to it with Gabriel in my arms. Is that the signal for the attack? How long have I been here? Panic engulfs me.

Sweat beads on my forehead, and my neck starts to feel clammy. I scan the room rapidly, looking for a way out. My eyes skim the fireplace, then stop and return to the ornate gold clock sitting on the mantel. Is that the time? Relief makes my knees weak. Thank God. I've only been here forty-five minutes, which means the attack is an hour away. My arms close protectively around Gabriel.

Seeing the motion, Armando snaps his fingers. Men surround us.

He holds his hands up to the crowd. "If you'll excuse us, it's time to put Gabriel to bed. Please enjoy yourselves. We'll be back in a little while."

Striding toward the corner of the room, he leads us out of the party.

Along the way, the woman from earlier joins us. She tries to take Gabriel from me, but I shake my head.

We head upstairs and down a long hallway. The noise and music fade into a murmur. The men surrounding us slowly drop off until it's just the four of us— Armando, the woman, Gabriel, and me.

The woman scurries ahead and opens a door. I follow Armando into the room and stop.

Gabriel's room is decorated in various shades of green and filled with jungle animals. Toys and books lie scattered in the corner. A brown toddler bed in the shape of a tree sits on the floor to the right.

It's the idyllic setting for a little boy.

The woman reaches for Gabriel, and I narrow my eyes.

"Maria is Gabriel's nanny. She'll take good care of him," Armando informs me. "It's time for bed." He holds out his arms, and Gabriel falls into them. After a couple of airplane swoops, Armando gives him a kiss and hands him to Maria.

He giggles when she makes faces at him.

She holds out two pairs of pajamas.

Gabriel points to the one he wants to wear.

"Come, let's leave them to finish," Armando urges. Gripping my elbow, he steers me into the hallway and closes the door.

I jerk my arm from his. "I want answers."

He sighs. "Julio met your sister in Austin. He'd gone to the university to investigate the best spots to 'find' girls for our new operation. He must have looked lost because your sister asked if he needed directions."

How many times have I told her not to talk to strangers?

"They started dating. Every time my brother went to Austin to find girls, they went out. His visits became more frequent. When I questioned him, he told me about Sophia." His eyes hold mine as he tells me their story.

I think back to the time before Sophia's disappearance. We used to meet for lunch every two weeks, but we hadn't met for over two months before she disappeared. Every time I asked, she cited school or work, but it was him. She didn't want me to know. And I would have. Sophia couldn't keep a secret from me.

He waves a hand. "Long story short. She went to San Antonio, to the River Walk, with girlfriends one night and saw him pick up a girl. Furious, she confronted him. He panicked and grabbed her, too."

I close my eyes.

His fists clench. "I ordered him to take her back, but he told me she wanted to be here. I couldn't tell if he was right. They would fight, make up, fight again. It was tumultuous. Soon after she got here, she became pregnant. Things settled down for a while, but after Gabriel was born, she wanted to take him home to… introduce him to her sister."

I smile.

"I didn't think much of it, even encouraged it, until Julio told me the full story." Even now, the fury he felt is apparent in his voice. "I didn't know about the statewide hunt for Sophia, or the fact that her sister was a Texas Ranger. They kept it quiet."

Dread fills me. I raise my hands in front of me as if I can stop the words from coming.

"I made a few phone calls. One of your superiors confirmed my concerns. Zoe Fairchild would never give up searching for her sister. To make matters worse, you were beginning to uncover the officials we so carefully cultivated to assist our operations," he says in a blasé tone.

Bitterness eats at me. "You mean bribe? I knew they were dirty, and I tried to prove it, but they made it sound like I was out of mind because of Sophia."

There's some truth to his words, which makes them bite all the harder. Why didn't she call me? If I'd known she was okay, I would have dropped the search. Was I that rigid back then?

The bastard laughs. "Well, you made them pay for it. Literally. The drugs and money you stole when you left was meant to line their pockets."

I can't stop the satisfaction I feel when I hear those words, but it pales to the words I need to hear.

"Tell me about her death."

He grimaces and runs a hand through his dark hair. "I went to offer her a deal. I'd let her visit you, but she must convince you to drop the investigation. She eagerly agreed… until I explained Gabriel would stay here."

"She laughed. Told me Julio and Gabriel were going with her. She said he'd told her how much he hated me and the cartel. As soon as he returned, they were leaving. I could hear the truth in her words, and it made me crazy. My brother's been beside me all my life. I knew he wouldn't leave if she wasn't here to fill his head with those thoughts." He stops talking to judge my reaction.

I take a deep, shuddering breath. "You didn't just kill her, though, did you? You beat her, raped her, took her organs." My voice rises, and I move closer to him. "Then, you left her naked body in the desert for the vultures. That's not a crime of passion. A sudden loss of control. You hated her. Why?"

When he says nothing, I slap him hard across the face.

"Answer me, you bastard," I scream, slapping him again. "Why?"

"Because she was taking my brother, my family from me!" he roars and backhands me. "That slut thought she could take my family and I wouldn't retaliate?"

Cupping my cheek, I stare up at him, hatred bleeding out of my pores. "You took the one person I loved most in this world and ENDED her. All because you couldn't stand to be alone?" Tears run down my cheeks, and I swipe them away. "At least your brother would have been alive. How much of him was left when you found him in the desert staked out for the vultures?"

He slams me into the wall. "Shut up."

"Or what? You're going to kill me, too?"

The click of a hammer being pulled back is like a crack of lightning in the quiet hallway. "No, I'll kill Gabriel."

"I saw the way you looked at him," I scoff. "You love him. And he loves you. His Tió."

"You're right. I couldn't kill him," he states softly. "But Rodrigo would be happy to get back in my good graces."

I still. Staring into his eyes, I see the vein of madness running in them, and the seriousness of his threat. It would kill him, but he'd do it. No sacrifice is too great to get what he wants.

"What do you want from me?"

"I want my own Gabriel," he murmurs, a fervent light in his eyes. The gun glides up to my lips. "Look at what your sister and my brother produced. A beautiful, happy little boy. He's perfect, but he's not really mine. He doesn't call me Papá."

I rear back and shake my head in denial.

The barrel slides across the tops of my breasts. "A piece of Julio and a piece of me, growing up together, just like we did. It's more than that, though. Your loyalty to your sister is remarkable. The sheer determination and strength you've shown as you've hunted me is impressive. Your sister couldn't hold a candle to you. Our child will be magnificent. A true heir to take over my empire."

Shock renders me speechless. He's certifiably insane. "Legacy."

He nods. "Our legacy. You'll have to give up your vengeance, but look at everything you gain in return. Family. A piece of your sister. Wealth. Your own child." The gun glides down to my stomach.

I subtly slide my hand up to my chest, closer to my knife.

A soldier steps into the hallway. "Sir, we've detected movement in the garden."

It hasn't even been close to an hour. Something must have happened.

Armando puts the gun to my temple. "What have you done?"

I look at him in confusion. "Nothing, why?" When he doesn't

answer, I roll my eyes. "You know I work alone. I'm sure it's just a cat or something."

He snorts. "Lock her in Gabriel's room. If anything happens, shoot them both." His head dips, and he presses a kiss to my lips. "Think about my proposal. When I come back, I expect an answer." He turns on his heel and strides down the hallway.

I scrub my hand across my lips to remove the feel of him.

The guard motions me into the room and locks the door.

Maria is fast asleep in the rocker. Gabriel's sleeping in his bed.

I hurry over to him.

"Quinn."

Whirling around, I see Cruz standing in the corner.

I quickly look at Maria.

"She's sleeping. Temporarily," he says, holding up a familiar silver box.

It's the same one Zane had that day.

I leap forward and throw my arms around him. Holding on tightly, I desperately pull his quiet strength into me.

His hand cups the back of my head. "Do you want to leave?"

"No," I whisper. "I just need a second." Armando's words are reverberating in my head.

"Take whatever you need," he murmurs, pulling me in tighter.

"How is Raider? And Paulo? Did everything go okay?"

"We took out the men at the ranch. Paulo is supervising the removal of the horses. He'll transport them to his ranch in Brazil. Raider's here. Didn't you see him earlier?"

It had been him. "I thought I was seeing things."

"She's going to be waking up soon. I can stay if you need me?" he offers.

I shake my head. "No, but can you ask Sterling to come up here as soon as possible?"

He taps his ear. "He can hear you. We've been speaking to you, but you haven't responded. Where's your earpiece?"

I dip my fingers into my cleavage. "I'd forgotten I had it." Quickly slipping it in my ear, the murmurs of men getting into position reach me. "The attack is happening now, isn't it?"

"A guard noticed one of the buses at the facility, so we had to move up the timeline," he explains.

Wood creaks behind me, and I turn to glance at Maria. She's moving restlessly.

"Hold out your hand, palm up," he orders.

I hold it out.

He scrapes the side of his thumb until a clear ragged edge appears, then pulls off the fingerprint cover. Grabbing my hand, he places it over my thumb and smooths it down. Then he does the same with my pointer finger.

"Gelatin?" I ask, admiring the smoothness of the material.

He nods and hands me the silver box. "Make sure you only use these two fingers when you handle the cloth inside."

"Cruz, we're in position," Zane murmurs.

Hard lips capture mine and time stops for a second.

"Almost there," Sterling's voice comes through my ear.

He releases me and disappears.

I hurry over to the bed.

"Sterling, I need you to stay close," I murmur.

"I'm down the hall," he returns.

I smooth Gabriel's hair back. He's a beautiful little boy. Sophia's son. A piece of her still exists in this world. Legacy is a powerful thing. Gabriel is the only family I have now.

I'm so lost in my thoughts, I miss the door opening behind me.

A gun appears in my peripheral vision. Startled, I look up to find the guard staring down at Gabriel.

Maria screams and rushes the guard.

The gun goes off.

She stumbles back, her hand clutched to her chest, blood trickling through her fingers. "Gabriel."

The guard stares at her in shock, then raises his gun again.

I move to the right, but the guard's eyes never leave Gabriel. With a quick step back, I put myself between them. "What are you doing? He's just a little boy."

The guard spits on me. "He took my son, and now, I'll take his." The gun comes up level with my chest.

It fires.

The guard crumples to the ground.

Sterling stands behind him with his gun raised. "Bloody hell, that was close." He holsters his gun. "Armando is on his way back."

I pull the sleeping child up into my arms. Grabbing the animal in his bed, I hand both of them to Sterling. Then I reach back and grab his blanket.

Surprise flits across Sterling's face.

I grip his hand tightly. "Promise me you'll get him to safety. And if something happens…"

"Quinn," Sterling interjects, his voice hoarse with emotion.

"Listen to me. If something happens, make sure he has a good home with the best parents," I plead. "I'm entrusting him with you because your parents were wonderful. Those are the type of parents I want for him. Do you hear me?"

"Five minutes," a voice says in my ear.

"Promise me," I repeat, staring at him.

"I promise. The best of parents." Sterling's arms close tightly around the sleeping boy.

I stretch up and kiss them both. "Go. And whatever happens, tell the others Armando is mine. If he kills me, then they can have him."

Silence reigns for a minute. "Copy, Quinn."

Knowing the attack will distract me, I slip the earpiece out and tuck it into my clutch. Maria's blank eyes stare at me from the floor, and I kneel to close them.

"What did you do? Where's Gabriel?"

With my back to him, I flip the silver box open and pull out the cloth. "I didn't do this." I kick the man lying on the floor.

"He said something about you taking his son and pointed a gun at Gabriel. Maria rushed him and he shot her."

He blanches. "Where's Gabriel?"

"Gone. I sent him to safety," I reply. "But he won't be coming back."

He bellows, an anguished sound full of pain and rage, then rushes over to me.

When he gets within two feet, I step forward and claw his cheek with one hand, while I swipe the cloth across the other.

Fingers spear themselves into my hair. "You'll give him back to me, do you hear?" He yanks me up to my tiptoes.

Pain streaks across my head. I drop the cloth and reach for him. "Never." With my other hand, I pull the knife from its hiding spot and slash his wrist.

He laughs. "Not sure where the hell that came from, but you'll have to do better than that when you stab me." With a twist of his hand, he flips me onto my back and starts walking toward the door, dragging me behind him. "I grew up on the poorest streets in Monterrey. Knife fights were a daily occurrence."

I scramble to get my feet under me, but the damn dress keeps getting in the way. Realizing the futility of it, I twist to my side until I can see him. He's too far away to reach with the knife in my right hand. I transfer it to my left and slash wildly at his legs.

He curses me loudly but doesn't stop.

I start stabbing straight backwards. The tip slides into one of his legs, and he stops.

A large hand grabs for the knife, but I avoid it. The hand changes course. Grabbing a handful of my dress, he picks me up and throws me against the wall. Pain radiates down my spine, and I drop face first to the floor, plaster and dust raining down on top of me.

The plush carpet softens the landing, but it's still jarring. His feet appear. I shove a hand under my chest and push myself up. Only to find a familiar blade pointed at me.

35

QUINN

He twirls my knife in his hand. "This is fitting, don't you think? Nice knife. Good balance, but how does it cut?" The razor-sharp knife slices across my cheek.

Blood wells up and drips down my face. At first, it barely stings, but when the skin fully separates, it's excruciating. Fuuu-uuuck! A whimper escapes. I clench my jaw against the pain.

A piercing whistle fills the air. "No wonder you favor this one. I'd never seen one like it, so I looked it up. Its purpose is to fillet meat. I suppose you knew that when you picked it out."

His hand whips out and slices down one arm.

Bastard.

A river of pain follows. In, out. In, out. Panting helps ride out the tidal wave of pain washing over me.

My fingers pluck wildly at my belt, while I do my best to piss him off.

"I did. One for Julio and one for you. It's only fitting that twins share the same death, don't you think?" I spit out.

Enraged, he raises his hand.

Taking advantage of it, I loop the garotte around his wrist and yank the two ends. It slides through the skin and muscle surrounding like a hot knife through butter, but unfortunately, it stops at the bone.

Screaming in agony, he drops the knife and stumbles away, cradling his hand.

Quickly snatching it from the ground, I dance forward to hit him again. Cuts on his arms and legs don't seem to faze him, but hopefully, his face is different. I slash from his hair to his chin. A line of blood appears. He freezes.

Hurts like a bitch, doesn't it?

With a roar, he swivels toward me, a gun glinting in his hand.

Can he shoot with his left? Not willing to risk it, I drop to the floor. The gun goes off above me.

I army crawl forward and stab the knife into one of his calves, hoping to bring him down.

He laughs. Drawing his foot back, he punts hard.

Pain explodes across my entire face. It's agonizing. I roll into a ball, clutching my face. My mind is screaming for me to get up, but it's impossible. The pain is overwhelming. He kicks out again, and it glances off the side of my head. When the third kick misses its target, I move my arms and look up.

He's staring at the wall behind me.

I scramble back to figure out my next move.

He sways and goes down on one knee.

"Drugging me? That's beneath you, isn't it?" He sneers.

I eye the gun in his hand. "Talk is cheap when you bring a gun to a knife fight."

Silence. He's out.

I slump to the carpet.

"Fuck me, that was brutal," I whisper, tears flowing down my cheeks as a river of adrenaline releases all at once.

His body twitches. How long did Zane say he would stay asleep? Ten or fifteen minutes? Not long enough. Bones creaking,

I make it to my feet and look down at the man I've been hunting since the day I found Sophia in the desert.

He looks like he lost a round with a meat grinder. One hand is dangling by the bone. The cut on his face is flayed open. Blood seeps from every part of his body.

I smile to see the amount of damage I did.

Now, how the hell am I going to get him downstairs?

A shiny red wagon full of stuffed toys sits proudly by the toy box. I consider it for a second, then sigh. Nope. He's too fucking big.

Not willing to take chances, I swipe him a few more times to keep him asleep, before tucking the cloth back into the silver box I found on the floor beside it.

I cut off the bottom part of the skirt, then straighten the top until I'm fully covered again. The bloody garotte lies a foot away. I snatch it up and loop it around my belt, then sheath my knife.

Pain wracks my body, but there isn't any time. My face feels the worst, stiff and painful. I slide a finger across my cheek and dried blood flakes off in my hand. He put up a hell of a fight, but I expected nothing less from a man like him.

Bending, I pick up his feet and drag him inch by inch into the hallway. Sweat beads and falls to the floor. I drop his feet. He's too heavy. Maybe I should just kill him here. A house this big has to have a basement.

"Need some help?" Zane stands at the end of the hallway like an avenging superhero. Gun out, dirt and blood covering his face and arms, but damn, he looks really, really good. His long legs eat up the distance between us.

Uncertain, I bite my lip and consider his offer. "Are you going to stop me from doing what I need to do?"

"Raider's getting the car. He and Cruz are going with you," he replies in a hard, non-negotiable voice. When I continue to stare at him, he raises his hands. "Would I be happy if you weren't going to do this? Hell yes. Will I stop you? No. I heard everything he said earlier. He deserves to die. Arguing over the semantics is moot." He moves forward, picks him straight off the floor, and throws him over his shoulder.

"That's impressive," I remark, my eyes glued to the muscles bulging in his arms. He'd be a beast to fight. "Thank you."

Zane is straightforward and blunt. I might not like what he has to say, but he wouldn't lie to me.

I lead us down the stairs and out of the house.

The Luciano men are standing in the driveway when we come out. Dante dips his arrogant chin in some sign of respect. Giovanni's cold eyes barely stray from the man draped over Zane's shoulder. Leonardo is leaning against the wall holding his bloody arm, watching everything.

Zane drops him into the trunk and slams it shut. "How long until you get to your destination?"

"An hour. How did the rescue go?"

"Everyone's out. Guards either ran at the first sight of trouble or they're dead. Buses are on the way to Miami with all the rescues. Sterling and I are following," he states gruffly. Large hands gently lift me off the ground and into a bear hug. "Do what you have to do and come back to us. We'll be waiting for you in Miami. Gabriel, too."

I grip his head in my hands and do the one thing I've been wanting to do for days—I press my lips to his and hold them there until his soften. When they do, I slowly suck in his bottom lip before pulling away.

Shocked grey eyes stare at me while he slowly sets me back down. He swallows and opens his mouth, but nothing comes out.

I slip the silver box into his hand. "This weapon sucks. Tell your friend to find a better and faster solution. Too much can happen in the five to seven minutes it needs to start working."

Pivoting, I look at Raider, who's standing by the driver side door. "Let's go."

Raider looks across the hood at Cruz, a silent message passing between them. I slide into the back seat and wait.

"Where are we going?" Raider asks when he gets in the car.

I text him the coordinates to the little house in the desert I bought a year ago. There are no neighbors within ten miles of the place.

THANKS TO THE MARVEL OF REMOTE ELECTRONICS, THE HOUSE IS LIT and warm when we arrive. The desert can be cold once the sun goes down. The adobe house is small, only about nine hundred square feet. Two bedrooms and one bath. But it has a very special feature—a fully enclosed basement that's completely hidden. I don't know what the previous owners used it for, but it wasn't good.

Cruz and Raider carry an unconscious Armando into the house. Somewhere outside of Monterrey, Cruz injected him with something guaranteed to keep him asleep, and he'd been out ever since.

"Where do you want him?" Raider asks, looking around the small house.

I lead them to the kitchen, step inside the small pantry, and hit a latch. "This way."

Eyebrows raised, they follow me down.

I point to the far wall. "If you wouldn't mind standing him up, I'll get him into the shackles."

A couple of minutes later, I step back to survey the man manacled to the wall. He fits the macabre room with the dark stains that coat every available surface. I scan the table and floor. The good news is that there aren't any fresh stains since I was here last.

Raider and Cruz exchange a tense glance.

"None of this is from me," I assure them. "Julio died in another location."

"You bought a place with a basement covered in blood?"

Cruz asks in disbelief. "What if the owner comes back? Or if there are bodies buried here?"

When he flicks his eyes at me, I shrug. "I only visited a couple of times, never spent the night, and the purchase wasn't completed in my name."

"I'll leave the door unlocked and the keys on the counter when I'm done. Whoever is brave enough to defend it is welcome to keep it. It was bought with blood money, anyway. Seems appropriate."

Raider laughs. "There's so much DNA on the floor, it will be hard to separate Armando's from the rest."

"Exactly," I concur. "If you'll excuse me, I need a shower, clothes, and ibuprofen." Maybe some stitches, too.

Upstairs, I drop my bag onto the toilet seat and stare at the bloody mess in the mirror. Reaching under the cabinet, I grab a washcloth. When I first bought the house, I made sure to stock it with some essentials. Although, to be honest, there's no way in hell I'd sleep here by myself.

Carefully washing off the dried blood, I probe the cut on my face. When no blood appears, I dig into my bag to find the butterfly stitches. Carefully pinching the edges of the cut together, I place the first one. Seven stitches later, my face is done. Now for my arm.

Once the bandages are in place, I hop into the shower. What I wouldn't do for hot water, but lukewarm and trickling will have to do. My skin is crawling with the feel of Armando, and even though the water stings like a bitch, I wash every inch of my body.

Once out, I slip on some soft joggers, a t-shirt… and my socks and shoes. I'm not walking around this house in bare feet.

Cruz is standing at the front door, looking out into the night, when I return. He motions me over. "Let me see."

I stand in front of him.

He slides a finger down the cut on my face. "Good job. Any scar you have will be faint."

"Like the ones on your body?" I ask, lightly running my hand down his chest. "Are those from your father or work?"

"Mmm, both."

How could his father use real knives to train him?

I didn't realize I'd asked the question out loud until he answers.

"Ghosts are often captured and tortured. I needed to be trained to handle pain so I could rise above it. The kind of secrets I carried couldn't see the light of day," he explains softly, his low voice tinged with a slight southern accent, telling me his emotions are close to the surface. He holds his arms out to me, and I slide into them.

I snuggle in tight wanting him to feel me close. "Where's Raider?"

"We needed food, ice for your face, and gas."

"Ice would be heaven," I mumble against his chest. "Did anyone else get hurt?"

"You saw Zane," he reminds me. "Sterling and Gabriel made it out without harm. Thomas took a bullet meant for Margot, but thankfully, he was hit in the shoulder—through and through. A few other wounded, but nobody died. A successful operation."

I lift my head to stare into his intense eyes. "Thank you for… this. All of it."

He bends down and tenderly places kisses on my lips and the left side of my face. "We've got you."

"What's the plan?"

Anger and adrenaline are still pumping wildly in my veins. "I need to rest and decompress first. Get rid of the anger." The only way I can do what I need to do is with icy control.

Taking a few steps back, he guides me over to the couch.

My eyes take in the sleeping bags draped over every inch. The exhaustion I'd been pushing aside since we got here rolls over me like a Mack truck. I swallow the lump in my throat. "Watch over me?"

"I'll be right here."

36

Shivering, I burrow into the body lying next to me. Warm arms wrap around my shoulders, and the cold disappears. Blinking, I peel open my eyes and find Cruz staring down at me. My face is numb, but the rest of my body is throbbing. The fight comes back to me in full technicolor detail.

"Why am I so cold?" I murmur.

He raises a bag of ice. "We've been applying it every thirty minutes to keep your eye from swelling shut."

"Raise up," Raider softly orders. When I sit up, he slips an oversize hoodie over me. "We didn't want to wake you earlier."

I glance outside, but it's still dark. "How long have I been asleep?"

"About an hour," Cruz replies, looking at his watch. "Are you hungry?"

The thought of food makes me wrinkle my nose.

Raider holds a tortilla up to my mouth. "Just take a bite."

The warm tortilla is lightly filled with refried beans. "It's good." And mild enough to not upset my stomach right now.

He hands me half. "You eat half, and I'll finish the rest."

"They're pretty good. Where did you get them?"

"These are store bought. Homemade are the best. My mother used to make fresh refried beans and tortillas from scratch for me when I was young. It's what I eat whenever I need some comfort food," he admits, but I see the way his eyes smile when he takes a bite. This simple food means a lot to him.

I look over at Cruz, who's eating his own. "What's your favorite comfort food?"

"As a southerner, I should say something like shrimp and grits or cornbread, but it's spaghetti. Not the fancy kind, either. Prego from a jar. Add ground beef and it's my childhood on a plate. But I haven't had it in years," he says with a bittersweet smile.

"Did your mom pass away?" I ask, familiar with the look on his face.

He nods. "Heart attack. Five years ago. She went quickly."

I slide my hand into his and squeeze. "I'm sorry. It doesn't matter if you're ten or thirty, losing a parent sucks." I grab Raider's hand too. "What was she like?"

He chuckles. "Sweet, with a backbone of steel. As a nurse, she worked a lot, but on her days off, she'd always plan something fun for us to do. Hike a new trail, see a movie, take a day trip… you name it. Her favorite thing to do was to turn up the radio and dance." His thumb rubs the top of my hand. "But she was strict when it came to following her rules. If you didn't, her punishments could be just as inventive as her rewards."

The look on his face makes me laugh. "Tell us." Swiveling, I lean into Raider to watch Cruz while he recounts the story.

Raider's arms wrap around me.

"It was my job to mow the lawn every two weeks. The summer I turned fifteen, I learned how to skateboard and quickly became obsessed. I'd spend hours practicing at the local skate park. Needless to say, two weeks stretched into almost four. The lawn looked like shit. Every day, my mom would remind me to cut the lawn when she left for work, and I'd promise her it would be done, but I never got around to it," he says in an incredulous tone.

He flashes a wry smile. "I came home one day from the park to find her mowing the lawn. When I tried to take the lawn mower from her to finish the job, she wouldn't let me. For two hours, I sweated and paced, knowing my punishment was going to be worse because she had to do my job. Finally, the mower cut off, but instead of wheeling it to the garage, she parked it in the driveway and put a gas can beside it."

"I went outside to put it away, but she stopped me. 'Mrs. Barclay asked if you wouldn't mind mowing her lawn. She offered to pay you, but I told her it wasn't necessary. Her bridge club is coming over tomorrow, so she needs it done now.' Figuring this was my punishment, I went over and mowed Mrs. Barclay's lawn."

He's shaking his head. "When I came home, my mother gave me a list with five more neighbors on it. I ended up mowing six lawns to earn my allowance. Needless to say, our lawn was mowed every two weeks the rest of the summer."

Both Raider and I laugh.

"Sneaky. I love it. Kind of fits, you know?" I wink at him.

He looks surprised. "Didn't think about it, but you're right. She was sort of sneaky and very creative."

Raider pulls me closer and leans back. "She sounds wonderful." His voice is wistful. "It's hard to remember my mother sometimes. I was so young when she died. Tell us another."

Cruz pulls my feet into his lap. "Rest a little longer. We'll keep watch."

Softly rubbing my legs, he recounts another story, and I slowly fade away.

37

QUINN

When I wake, Raider's standing by the door with his gun.

"What's going on?"

"We heard something. Cruz went out to check," he murmurs.

I quickly stand. "What kind of noise?"

He frowns. "It sounded like laughter."

"Could it have been a hyena or coyote?"

"Maybe," he offers, although I hear the doubt in his tone.

Tense, we wait in the dark, listening to the sounds of the night.

Cruz appears beside me, and I clamp a hand over my mouth to muffle my scream.

"I didn't see anyone, but someone is out there. I feel him. We'll have to wait and see if he makes any moves." He keeps his voice low as he steps over to the window. "Somewhere in that direction, I think, but he could have moved by now."

"If he makes a move, come get me. My mind is clear and calm. It's time I finished this," I state firmly.

I leave them standing guard and head to the bathroom to get ready.

When I enter that room, the only thing I want to think about is what I need to do. The fewer distractions, the better. I scrape my hair back and secure it in a bun, then pull on the clothes I picked out. Blood can be distracting. Black hides it well.

The last thing I do is swipe through the pictures on my phone. The sight of her destroys me. Knowing why only makes it worse. I breathe in and out, concentrating on each detail.

My body becomes colder and colder, as if death himself is possessing me.

It's time to pay your dues, Armando.

WHEN I ENTER THE BASEMENT, I'M NOT SURPRISED TO SEE HIM awake.

"Welcome to my house. It's not quite as grand as yours, but you should embrace it. This is the last place you'll ever see."

He looks around and raises an eyebrow. "It's better than the house I was born in." The blood stains on the floor captures his attention. "Is this where you killed Julio?"

"No." I roll out the tools I'd chosen specifically for the two brothers. An array of scalpels, knives, hooks, a cautery pen, and a few other items. I plug the pen up to the machine to charge.

"Well, where did you kill him?"

"Where did you kill my sister?"

He contemplates answering for a brief second. "In my house. My study. The one you were in last night."

I freeze. The last time she had been alive was in that room.

He sighs dramatically. "It made such a mess I had to remodel the entire room." A malicious smile crosses his face.

"Well, we don't have to worry about making a mess here. As you can see, several people have met their end in this basement. It makes you wonder who previously lived here, doesn't it?" A note of curiosity in my voice.

I pick up the scissors and cut off his clothes.

Once naked, he tenses for a microsecond. "I won't beg you for forgiveness… or mercy, no matter what you do to me." He eyes the tools. "Where are you going to start?"

"You can tell me where you started with Sophia, or I can pick based on the pictures I have of her body. Which do you prefer?"

I pick up my phone and hold it up as I swipe through the pictures. Each image is more brutal than the last.

His brother cried when he saw the pictures. Knowing what I know now, I can see Julio cared for Sophia. Maybe he even loved her. I hope so. She deserved to know love before she died.

Armando's laugh brings me back to the present. "Some of my best work." His eyes glint with anger. "It's hard for me to remember. Did I start off hitting or fucking her?"

I carefully put the phone down on the table and pull on black latex gloves. "I'll take it easy on you. We'll start with the hitting first." My fingers walk along the line of tools until I come to the miniature bat. I grab it.

When he sees the bat, the muscles in his body automatically tighten. "I didn't have to use a weapon. My fists did the job quite well."

"Yes, I'm sure they did. Big meaty fists like yours against my tiny sister. They probably felt a lot like this," I say, striking hard across his face with the bat. Blood sprays out of his mouth. "You're right-handed, correct? The coroner reported severe bruising here, here, and here." I strike hard along the left side of his body across those same spots. "Oh, and a few on this side."

He grunts each time the bat lands but manages to laugh at the end. "A walk in the park."

"You're right. This isn't too bad. I'm sure it wasn't for her, either. She was tougher than you think. She would have survived the beating. If only you had stopped there," I lament.

"I would have if she'd have shown me the proper respect," he reveals in a rush. "Instead, she taunted me with the fact that Julio had found someone to love. And with Gabriel's birth, their little family was complete. He didn't need me like I needed him. And when he got home, she was going to tell him what I'd done."

My eyes drop to the appendage hanging between his legs. "Is that why you raped her? To show her that you were in charge, not Julio. Or was it to show Julio that you could take what was his?"

A flicker of satisfaction in his eyes tells me the truth.

"I thought so." I walk over and pick up the scalpel and the tongs. "You're never going to rape someone else again."

The stoicism disappears, replaced with cursing and yelling.

"It would be less painful to use the garotte or my knife, but the punishment needs to equal the crime," I explain.

Grabbing the flaccid dick with the tongs, I methodically cut until it's completely severed from his body. I toss it in the corner.

When I look up, tears are rolling down his face, and his eyes are blown wide with shock. But he doesn't beg for forgiveness or mercy.

"Tell me, when was the last time you cried?" I ask, curious to see if he'll give me a real answer instead of a sarcastic quip.

His eyes are full of rage and madness, but he answers. "When I saw my brother's mutilated body."

Truth.

"Something we have in common," I muse. "What did you think when you looked at your brother's body? You said my sister's death was your finest work. Did you see art when you looked at him? The wounds are identical, after all."

A light dawns. "He didn't have anything to do with her death," he rasps. Guilt shines brightly in his eyes. But only for his brother, not Sophia.

"If only someone had come forward and confessed," I mockingly say. "He's not exactly innocent in all this, but I didn't know what role he played until you and I had our chat last night. When I killed him, I didn't understand everything he was telling me. He kept blubbering about Sophia, and his love, and someone named Gabriel."

Armando closes his eyes. "I guess we're both responsible for their deaths."

My brow wrinkles in confusion.

"Your sister could have gone home at any time, and yet, she didn't. Was she afraid of you?" he taunts, his voice tight with pain.

The statement is delivered matter of fact, but it's a perfect hit. My heart cracks in two.

"No," I retort, reluctant to share a piece of her with him. The smug look on his face settles it. "Sophia didn't like confrontation. Ever. If there was a problem, she ran away until it was over."

He scoffs. "She was pretty confrontational with me. If she hadn't been, she would likely still be here." He clicks his tongue. "I think she was scared you would hate her for falling in love with my brother. A member of the cartel. She told Julio the law and your career meant everything to you."

Rage threatens to break through the iciness surround me. Why am I listening to him? "I could never hate Sophia. It's not even a possibility. Let's get back to the point of this exercise—her death. And yours."

I slam the utensils down on the table and take several deep breaths until I can feel the coldness taking over. The cautery pen glows beside me. I pick it up and walk over.

He flinches when the pen gets close. "What is that?"

"It cauterizes wounds. It will help stop the bleeding," I explain.

"Let me bleed! Let me bleed!"

I cluck my tongue. "We have a long way to go. If you bleed

out now, I won't be able to finish." The smell of burning flesh drifts into the air.

He screams and screams until the only thing coming out of his throat is strained air.

When the bleeding stops, I pull the pen away. "You have a remarkable tolerance for pain. Your brother passed out when I cauterized him."

His whole body is shaking with adrenaline. Hanging his head, he fights to overcome his body's reaction.

Dismissing him, I step over and place the pen by the machine. Two rounds down. Final round coming up. A part of me is impressed by his continued fight. The other part of me wants to hear him break.

The sound of retching draws my eyes back to him. Vomit covers him and the floor beneath him. With a sigh, I grab the bucket and douse him and the floor with water.

I grip his chin and pull his head up. "Are you ready for the finale?"

White teeth flash in an attempt to smile, but the pain is slowly taking over his entire body.

"According to the coroner's report, you took her kidneys, liver, and heart. I hear the heart can go for over a million dollars on the black market. All total, you probably cleared about two million?" I speculate, keeping the rage stuffed down deep.

His laugh is hoarse. "Over two million. Her age and health were a prime factor. If I'd had more time, I could have harvested all her organs."

"What did you tell me you wanted last night? That's right. Legacy. Congratulations. It might not be the legacy you wanted, but little pieces of you will live on in this world. I'm donating your organs to the hospital on my way out of town," I inform him, walking back to the table to get the scalpel. "We'll leave the heart for last, okay?"

"I'm a member of the cartel. An important one. They'll

avenge my death, you know. There's nowhere you can hide where they won't find you," he snarls.

"Not anymore," I interject. "You promised them millions from your trafficking operation, but unfortunately, you won't be able to deliver."

"What are you talking about?"

"How many women were in that room? One hundred and seventeen. That's right. Now, there are zero. Do you really think the cartel will avenge your death? You're a failure," I state matter-of-factly.

Physically, he's taken hit after hit today and has come back swinging. But these words break him. He howls in rage, madness stealing across his face.

"In one night, we destroyed your entire world. Your operations, the ranch, your home, and all your men. There is nothing left, and soon, you'll be gone, too. Ashes and dirt. Food for the vultures. Just like Julio."

He jerks against the manacles, straining his body toward me, but I'm out of his reach. The insults and threats start again.

Growling in frustration, I yank my arm out of my shirt, cut the sleeve off, and stuff it in his mouth.

The next few hours are tedious but quiet. He passes out for most of it. Once most of the organs are in special canisters and coolers, I take the cloth out and inject him with enough drugs to wake him up. They also dull the pain, but it can't be helped.

I use my arm to wipe the sweat from my forehead and pick up the bone saw. Sometimes, late at night, when the world is still and dark, I wonder about the person who received my sister's heart. She always had so much love and joy to give to others. Will they be able to feel her inside them?

With his strength gone, his body sags against the manacles.

I tap his cheek. "We've come to the end of our journey together. The only thing left for me to do is take your heart and leave you in the desert. Is there anything you'd like to say before you die?"

His voice is barely a whisper. "You and I are two sides of the same coin. In taking your vengeance, you've made yourself into my twin." A hoarse laugh escapes. "Hell, you made yourself into me. Julio was always the better man. Looks like Sophia might of have been the best of you both. We're the reason they're no longer here. They were innocent, caught up in love and the machinations you and I orchestrated. This is a fitting punishment for me. How will you punish yourself?"

I say nothing.

"Tell Gabriel, his tío loves him. I still think our child would have been magnificent," he rasps. "See you in hell, Quinn." With one last shallow breath, he passes.

My mind tries to latch onto his words, but I refocus my attention on the task in front of me—extracting his heart.

38

<u>RAIDER</u>

Cruz slides into the house like a shadow. "There must be hiding spots all around this house. Every time I get close, he disappears." He cocks his head to the side. "It's quiet."

"All noise ceased about thirty minutes ago," I inform him. Cruz and I had been periodically checking on Quinn to make sure she was okay. "Do you want to check on her?"

He nods and heads to the kitchen.

The morning sun glints on a piece of glass. Somebody is watching us. The question is who? The owner of this fine establishment? A neighbor? One of Armando's men? The possibilities are endless.

Cruz appears with several coolers. "She's coming up now."

I study the coolers. "Are those what I think they are?"

He gives me a look and an affirmative nod. "We need to drop off a donation at the hospital on our way out of town."

"That's generous of her. Personally, I'd have incinerated the bastard, but it's her decision. Speaking of Armando, what's the plan?" I ask Cruz.

"The last step is to leave him in the desert. In the same position as Sophia," she says behind me. Her Texas accent is almost non-existent right now.

When I turn to face her, it becomes apparent why. Cold blank eyes meet mine.

"Okay. Why don't you get a shower, and we'll leave?"

She hesitates.

I flick my wrist to look at the time. "It's almost noon. Plenty of daylight. Plus, I don't think you want to walk into the hospital with blood and guts on you." Not to mention, she looks like she went a few rounds in the ring with a heavyweight champ. Maybe I can get her to stay in the car.

She looks down in distaste. "Right."

Cruz swivels around. "Are we good to place him in the trunk?"

"Yes," her voice drifts off as she walks away.

"Now begins the hard part," Cruz murmurs.

"Climbing out of the dark," I confirm.

It takes us an hour to get everything loaded and ready to go, including the body in the back.

Quinn drops the keys on the kitchen counter and walks out the door. Not once does she look back.

In the car, my phone pings with coordinates, and I flick my eyes to the backseat. She's looking forward, eyes steady, but blank. Without a word, I put the car in gear and follow the phone's directions.

Thirty-seven minutes north of the house, we reach a desolate patch in the middle of nowhere. A stake sticks out of the ground with a black ribbon around it. We haul Armando out of the trunk to the designated spot.

She maneuvers him until he lies spread-eagle on the ground.

"Is this what he did to Sophia?" I ask softly, keeping the

rising anger from entering my voice. The last thing I want to do is trigger her.

She stands back to assess the position of his body. "When I found her, I couldn't fathom why someone would do that to her. She was already dead. Why display her?" Her lips compress. "I know now that he wanted to send a message to his brother. And he needed a public way for the body to be found, so I'd call off the search. Two birds, one body."

A satisfied sigh leaves her. "I'm almost done. We just need to drop off the coolers." She walks back to the car and gets in, leaving Cruz and me standing by the body.

My eyes catalog the damage done to the man in front of me. "Her work is precise and clean, almost looks like a surgeon did it." I can't help but be impressed.

A gleam of admiration shines in Cruz' eyes as well.

Two vultures land nearby.

Cruz takes several pictures of the body. I spit on it and walk away, back to the car and Quinn.

Instead of pulling up to the hospital entrance, I follow her directions to the back parking lot nearest the morgue. We convince Quinn to let Cruz slip in quietly and deliver the coolers.

"Where do you want to go now?" I ask her while we wait for him to return.

When she doesn't respond, I turn around to face her.

She's staring at the pictures of Sophia on her phone. "Do you think she'll be able to rest in peace now?"

"Her death is avenged, and her son is safe."

At the mention of Sophia's son, Quinn flinches.

The door opens before I can ask her about it. Cruz gets in. "All good?"

Cruz gives me a nod and turns to look at Quinn. "I made sure the surgeon on duty found them. He immediately rounded everyone up and got them moving to type the organs and contact Mexico's transplant agency CENATRA."

"Thank you. Maybe he can do some good in this world and save some lives instead of just destroying them," she murmurs, her mouth twisted in thought.

Cruz darts a look at me. "Did we decide where we're going next?"

I shake my head. "Not yet. Quinn, is there anything we need to do here?"

"No." Her voice is small.

"Are you good if we head to Miami?"

She unzips the duffle beside her and pulls out my hoodie, the one I slipped over her last night. With a shiver, she puts it on.

I frown. It's at least eighty degrees outside.

"Miami is fine," she replies.

"We need to change cars first," Cruz reminds me. "Sterling left us one by the tailor's shop."

When we pull into the lot, a dark grey Nissan Altima is parked right in front. "It's three hours to Laredo, Texas, where we'll cross the border. Let's use the restroom and grab some provisions here. With the attacks last night, everyone's on alert, and I want to get out of Monterrey."

"Second that," Cruz states firmly.

After gathering food and drinks, and using the restroom, we're ready to head out.

Quinn stops to stare at a picture on the wall. "I can't go."

My eyes dart to Cruz, then back to her. "Why not?"

She taps the glass. "Eduardo. I promised Eduardo I'd get Rodrigo for him. I can't believe I forgot about that psycho."

"Rodrigo's gone," Cruz tells her. "I've got feelers out looking for him, but he's not in Monterrey. Sterling also has facial recognition software running. If he goes through any transportation center, like an airport, we'll find him. When we do, we'll figure out a way to get to him."

For a brief second, emotion flickers across her face. "Thank you."

He runs his hands down her arms. "Believe me, we want the bastard just as much as you do. We'll find him."

She eases out of his hold and heads down the stairs.

Cruz' mouth turns down. "This is going to be harder than I thought. I hate seeing her like this—so withdrawn."

"She's actually doing better than I expected. When Paulo and I finished getting our vengeance, we stayed drunk for three weeks." I pause. "You know it's going to get worse before it gets better."

"I know," he confirms. "Let's get out of here."

39

QUINN

The darkness surrounding me is never-ending. Is it a trap of my own making or the punishment Armando told me I deserved? His voice whispers to me constantly, full of truths and half-truths. I want so desperately to deny his words, but I can't.

The loudest whisper is truth. She could have come home at any time.

Even thinking those words tears me up inside. Eleven months of sleepless nights, searching video footage, and questioning suspects. Eleven months spent tracking down every lead. Eleven months of imagining the worst. All I thought about was her.

I wish he'd never told me.

It doesn't change what he did to her. Or what I did to him in return.

But it stirs up anger and guilt where there was none.

When she disappeared, I pulled every string I could reach.

The Texas Rangers, my friends at my old precinct, the FBI, press contacts, you name it. I made it a huge deal. I thought the awareness would help us get leads, but if she'd been watching, the pressure would have been immense, making her terrified to come forward.

And she knew if Julio came to talk to me, I'd shoot first and ask questions later.

Inflexible. Driven by my own rigid sense of right and wrong. The law had been everything to me. It started off as something my dad and I shared, but after he died, it became my guide to life.

If she had told me about him, I would have forbidden her from seeing him. Or had him stopped at the border. My baby sister dating the cartel? Never.

Armando said they were in love, but there were indications of older bruises on her body. Did Julio abuse her? So many questions.

"Quinn, we're stopping for gas and a restroom break," Raider calls from the front seat.

The words filter through the fog in my brain, but it takes a minute for them to register.

"Okay," I mumble.

Do I need to go to the restroom? It feels like we've been traveling for days. It's probably a good idea.

Minutes later, I stand in the bathroom, staring at the mirror while I wash my hands. If the old me stood next to this one, they would barely resemble each other.

I'd just turned thirty when Sophia was abducted. The whole world was at my feet. After two years as a Texas Ranger, I'd found my groove. My superiors were giving me bigger cases. I was dating a couple of different men. Nothing serious, of course. My career was everything. And with Sophia in her sophomore year at university, life was good.

Three-and-a-half years later, I barely recognize the person in the mirror, and not just because of the bruising and stitches. My face is full of lines from the life I've lived since she disappeared. And the real irony? The law failed me. My moral compass now resembles the very people I used to loathe.

I thought I'd be free when I found out who killed Sophia and I did the same to them, but I'm still caught in a web of the unknown. I have answers, but also more questions. Where I had zero doubt, I'm now overflowing with it.

Where to start? Maybe if I saw them together, I could get some insight into their relationship. If they dated in Austin, there has to be footage of them. Sophia had her favorite haunts. I can start there.

I walk out and find them waiting for me.

Why is it so cold out here?

Raider steps forward and wraps his arms around me. The warmth radiating from his body draws me in closer.

His hand sweeps the hair back from my face. "We've been driving for about nine hours. It's almost two a.m. None of us got much sleep last night. We're going to get a hotel room for the rest of the night, okay?"

Exhaustion weighs me down, but every time I close my eyes, Armando's voice gets louder. Maybe if they stay with me, it will help.

"One room for all of us." I'm not sure whether I'm pleading or demanding it, but I can't sleep alone.

He squints at Cruz and sighs. "At least he's quiet."

I meet Cruz' stare with my own, but the intensity makes me uncomfortable. He sees too much. Things I want to keep hidden. And I turn away and get into the car.

Raider pulls out of the gas station and follows Cruz' directions to a nearby hotel.

Cruz made the reservation and checked us in on the way so we can head straight to our room. When we get there, an app on his phone unlocks the door. I'm so thankful I didn't have to see anyone, given the state of my face.

Kicking off my shoes, I immediately climb into bed. It feels amazing. When was the last time I slept in one? Feels like years.

Raider eyes the hoodie I'm wearing. "Aren't you going to get hot in that thing?"

All I feel is cold. "It feels good."

A possessive glint enters his eye. "You look good wearing my clothes." He slides off his jeans, leaving only his boxer briefs. Black, of course.

The bed dips behind me as Cruz slides in and curves his body around mine. Heat radiates from him to me, and I sigh. The cold surrounding me begins to melt.

Raider cuts the lights and slides into bed, facing me. The curtains are partially open, and there's enough light coming in through the window for me to see him staring at me.

"Close your eyes," he murmurs. "We've got you." His lips brush mine a few times with a tenderness that makes me want to cry.

Knowing he won't sleep if I'm still awake, I close my eyes. The whispers immediately start up, but I count to drown them out. Four thousand. Three thousand and ninety-nine. Three thousand and ninety-eight. Three thousand and ninety-seven. When sleep tries to claim me, I stop counting and open my eyes.

Raider's steady breathing tells me he's out. Unable to help myself, I shift my gaze to his chest. His upper body makes my breath catch. Broad and well-defined, my hands tingle in memory of how hard his muscles felt beneath them. I lick my suddenly dry lips. He's so incredibly good-looking, but I sort of forget about it when we're together. I'm too caught up in him and what he's saying or doing to think about it.

Here in the quiet hotel room, I look my fill. The tattoos I'm curious to know more about are easily visible in the dim light. There's an elaborate cross with beads trailing off… a rosary. Camila's name and a flower. It doesn't look like a rose, but it's similar. It's hard to tell without more light. Both are interwoven with vines.

There's another female name. Maybe his mother or a past love?

My eyes trace an unusual, but very interesting, design on his left pec. Three circles intertwined, a number in each, surround a jaguar wearing a crown. The design is stylized and hard to see with other tattoos overlapping it, but it's clear the symbols go together.

I'll have to ask him about it. Warm for the first time today, I struggle to stay awake, but my body finally gives up and I drift to sleep.

"Thanks, Rob," I say warmly to the man standing by the car. "I appreciate it." My smile feels like a grimace, but it's the best I can do right now.

"I've got one at home myself. Just as stubborn," he replies with a shake of his head. "Take it easy."

"Let's go, Sophia," I order, furious at her behavior. "What have I told you about drinking and driving? I've been your age. I know you're going to drink, but driving endangers others, not just yourself. How do you think Papa would feel to lose you, too?"

Red creeps over her face. She flashes a strained smile at her friends. "I'm so sorry." They look in disbelief as she gets up and walks away.

She stomps toward me. "I hate you," she whispers furiously. "You ruin everything." She looks back at her friends, but they're flashing her dirty looks and whispering amongst themselves. "Why couldn't you just let me go to jail?"

"Because Papa can't afford it, and neither can you, not if you want to go to Austin and the University of Texas in the fall. You're lucky I'm able to get you out of this. Now, let's go."

"Lucky," she snorts. "I can't wait to go to university where you won't be able to watch my every move. I'll be able to make my own decisions without you around to question everything. You're not my mother, and I'm sick of it. I'm sick of you!"

. . .

With a jolt, I wake. Her screaming voice reverberating in my head. At the time, I'd dismissed her comments, but maybe there was more to it than I realized. Things were better when she went to school. I'd tried to give her space and not ask her about her grades too much.

My only rule was our lunch date every two weeks. And I'd even let that slide a few times if she was busy or cited school-work, which happened a lot before she was kidnapped. When she disappeared, I kicked myself repeatedly for not insisting she meet me for lunch.

She knew I was looking for her. Distraught. I'd been on the news, asking for everyone's help. Was she really too scared of me to come forward?

If she had returned after a month, I would have been furious, but so very, very thankful. Eleven months later would have been... a miracle... and tough. But I have to believe we'd have gotten through it. She was family.

40

QUINN

Lost in my thoughts, I didn't realize Raider was awake until his finger traces the line between my brows.

"Good morning, mon petit oiseau," he murmurs. His tone is light, but his eyes are sharp. "What has you frowning so much?"

I stare at him, unable to say the words. The fear that I might have played a part in her death… "Your tattoo. I've been trying to figure out the meaning of it." My finger reaches out to trace the individual symbols and numbers. "At first, they look random and separate, but the way they've been drawn, the individual lines curling into each other… It's one tattoo, isn't it?"

Surprised, he tenses. "You can see that?"

"At first, no. The tattoos around it overlap the edges, but if you stare at it long enough, it becomes clear," I explain. "What does it mean?"

He stares at me for a second. "You know my father was a

drug lord, right? The jaguar with the crown was his mark. It was tattooed on us when we reached sixteen. When my brother took over, he added the circles to represent Camila, me, and him. He and I chose our numbers, but most of the members are assigned numbers based on a variety of factors."

"Does this mean you're in the cartel?"

"In the beginning, I had to be. Paulo needed support to take over my father's role. But the life wasn't for me. It was too restrictive," he says. "Once he was firmly established, I left."

"Where did you go? France?" I ask, thinking of his penchant for speaking the language.

He chuckles. "An organization in the US offered me a job overthrowing governments, and it sounded a hell of a lot better than going to university, so I accepted."

Shocked, I stare at him in surprise. "The same organization Cruz worked for?"

A wry smile appears. "No, mine didn't officially exist. Still doesn't. Its sole purpose is to manipulate power in the world. To that end, we were sent all over the globe to make sure our preferred candidate was placed on the throne, so to speak. Turns out, the cartel is fantastic experience for that line of work."

"Did you like it?" I ask, although the spark in his eye seems to indicate he did.

"For a long time, I did. Over time, the widespread devastation brought about by the changes in power got to be too much. When I found myself faced with the decision of rescuing a group of people or fanning the flames of the revolution, I realized I couldn't do it anymore. I saved those people, then Zane and Marcos saved me," he says with a shrug, but I can see the toll it took on him. He taps my nose. "Whenever I wasn't on a job, I lived in France."

I think about how his brother came to his rescue. "Are you and Paulo close? Now that you're past the days of fighting on the playground," I tease.

To my surprise, he has to think about it. "What we went through together created a bond between us that will be there for the rest of our lives. But we're not close. Being the head of the cartel is a lonely job, but he seems to prefer it that way." A trace of sadness lingers on his face.

"Well, if it hadn't been for him, we wouldn't have found you before everything went down. I know you probably would have escaped by then, but twenty-to-one, odds were not in your favor," I gently remind him. "Paulo dropped everything and came without his guards. Pretty risky behavior for someone in his position."

His brow furrows in thought.

"Although I'm the last one who should be giving sibling advice," I say bitterly. The darkness threatens to pull me under, but I keep my focus on the moment and the men around me.

An arm snakes around my stomach and pulls me backward. "It's too early to have deep conversations, especially without coffee," Cruz grumbles from behind me. "Although waking up to you by my side certainly makes the day better."

I stroke the arm around my stomach. "Sorry, I didn't mean to wake you."

Raider stretches and eases out of bed. "We have sixteen hours of driving ahead of us. I'm going to grab a shower."

Cruz snuggles into my back. "Good. Wake me when you get out."

After Raider leaves, we lie there quietly together. With Cruz, I don't feel the need to fill the silence.

His hand slides back and forth across my stomach lazily stirring the desire simmering under the surface.

Raider walks back into the room wearing just a towel.

I inhale sharply. With the hard body behind me and the one in front, the temptation is too real and sharp.

"I'm next." Scrambling out of bed, I beeline for the bathroom and shut the door. Thoughts of the two of them and me and the large king bed swirls around in my brain. I turn on the cold water.

Sixteen hours gives me plenty of time to dissect everything. The fights Sophia and I had when she was growing up. My determination to keep her on the straight and narrow. Her rebellion against me.

My mind jumps to Julio. At the time, I'd dismissed the words coming out of his mouth, even blocked most of them, but now I'd give anything to remember everything he'd said about Sophia. The one thing I do know—he never mentioned his brother. Not once did he tell me Armando killed her, not him.

We're passing Tallahassee when a thought occurs. Rachel, Sophia's best friend, had to have known. She never said a word when I spoke to her after Sophia disappeared, but those two were tight.

There's only one tiny issue. Like the rest of the world, she thinks I'm dead.

Digging around in the duffle, I find my special phone. It's one of the most secure phones on the market and the encryption is military grade. Tracing it requires access to military satellites and decryption software unavailable to most law enforcement.

Me: Rachel, it's Sophia's sister. When you have a second, can you text me back? I have a question.

It's an hour before I get a reply.

Rachel: Zoe is dead. Who is this?

Me: Did she tell you about Julio?

Rachel: This isn't funny. Both Zoe and Sophia are dead. Who is this?

Me: Do you remember the time I caught you girls drinking Papa's beer in the field? I never told your mother because I didn't want you to get in trouble.

Rachel: …

Five minutes go by.

Me: Rachel. Please, please tell me about Julio.

Rachel: Sorry, I can't stop crying. God, I miss you two.

Me: …

Me: I'm sorry. You can't tell anyone. Ever.

Rachel: I know. I won't.

Me: Julio?

Rachel: She made me promise not to tell you. I wish I had. When she disappeared, I wanted to say something. I almost did, but I got a text from an unknown number telling me not to tell you. If I did, he would get really mad at her. And he wasn't someone I wanted to mess with. I didn't know what to do.

The pain of that statement makes it hard to breathe.

Me: It's okay.

Rachel: After you found her dead, I was so angry at her for making me keep my promise. And angry at myself. What do you want to know?

Me: Everything.

Rachel: They met at the university. He was lost and good-looking. Instead of giving him directions, she walked him to the bar he was asking about. She said they talked for hours. He asked her out. They dated for two months, I think, before she disappeared.

Me: Did you meet him?

Rachel: I met him a couple of times. When they started dating. She wanted my opinion. He seemed nice and good-looking. Funny. Rich. I told her she hit the jackpot. But things were weird the second time.

Me: What happened?

Rachel: I hadn't seen her in a month because she'd been so tied up with him. We were having a girls' night. Catching up. The whole time she was with me, he kept texting her. She would immediately text him back. Every single time. I got mad. Told her I was leaving. She promised not to text him. But it killed her. Every time she got a text, she would look at the phone and start stressing.

Rachel: He started calling her when she wouldn't text him back. Over and over. She answered. Told him where we were. He stormed in fifteen minutes later. Grabbed her arm. Told me she was leaving. I shoved him off her. He raised his hand to hit me, but there were some guys in the bar who stepped in. He apologized. Gave her some sob story. She left with him.

Rachel: I called her the next day. Told her something was wrong with him. She laughed. Told me he was just jealous and possessive. Worried about the guys hitting on her at the bar. It made him a little crazy. Nothing I said changed her mind.

Rachel: When she first disappeared, I thought she just ran off with him. Then I got that text from her. I didn't know what to do. I'm so sorry. Maybe if I'd told you, she'd still be alive.

Me: You were a good friend. We all made mistakes with Sophia. Maybe me most of all. Was Sophia scared of me? You're not going to hurt my feelings. I'm just trying to understand why she didn't want to tell me.

Rachel: Sophia loved you. But she knew you would investigate him. At first, she told me she just wanted to keep him to herself for a little while longer. But I don't know. After our girls' night... I wonder if it wasn't him.

Rachel: Do you think he killed her?

Me: He didn't.

Rachel: You're not just saying that?

Me: The person who did will never hurt anyone else again. Take care, Rachel. Thank you for being her friend and loving her the way I did.

Rachel: Thank you. It's hung over me for so long. I just can't...

Rachel: Thank you. I promise I won't tell.
Bye Zoe.

Whether she will or won't, I'm not sure. It's a lot to ask. It doesn't worry me. Very few would believe her, but even if they did, they wouldn't be able to find me. And I don't plan on coming back from the dead.

Sophia hadn't been scared of me, but she had been afraid to tell me. After all the times I told her I would always be on her side no matter what she did... It didn't matter. She didn't have enough confidence in my reaction.

The incident in the bar disturbs me. Was his jealousy a one-off? Or did he have a dark side? He was Armando's twin, and they grew up in a rough neighborhood, fighting for scraps. That had to have an impact on him.

I need to see footage of them together.

41

QUINN

In the early morning hours, we pull into the driveway of a house in Miami. Stunned, I get out of the car to stare at the large modern-looking house. The outside is made of stucco, I think. It's white with large sections of brown siding or wood. There are lights everywhere, shining up the walls and showcasing the landscaping. The huge front doors are glass with bronze framing and light from the inside is spilling out onto the driveway. Surely this isn't their home?

"Do you like it?" Raider asks beside me.

"Whose is it?"

His eyebrow raises in confusion. "It's our house. Zane, Sterling, Cruz, and me. We all live here." He darts a look at Cruz and a silent message passes between them. "Are you ready to go in?"

I hesitantly nod.

Trailing behind Cruz and Raider, I have time to look around the stunning house. When they said they all lived together, it didn't occur to me that it would be this nice. Maybe it should have. After all, they're four grown men in their thirties—I glance at Zane—and forties, who had careers before they came together. Plus, apparently, Sterling is loaded.

It's just so far removed from the small ranch houses and apartments I'd known. I walk past the foyer and stop. The living room is massive, with a U-shaped couch taking up most of the room. The brown leather sofa sits in front of a two-story fireplace and an excessively large television. I think the size is what boggles my mind the most. The room is probably larger than the kitchen, dining, *and* living room of the house I grew up in.

Zane and Sterling are sitting on the couch waiting for us when we walk into the house. Now, all four men are staring at me.

"Your house is… big. It makes sense with all of you living here. And none of you are exactly small people. Like me." I stop blabbering. I suddenly realize big isn't a compliment. "It's nice. Very nice."

"Damned with faint praise," Sterling says with a chuckle. "Let's give you a tour around our 'very nice' house, shall we?" He walks over and looks down at me. A broad, warm smile graces his face, but there's a concerned look in his eye. His gaze sweeps over the bruises on my face and the long cut across my cheek.

When he puts his elbow out for me to take, I recoil, unable to stop from remembering Armando doing the same thing.

"Sorry, I just… can't."

Smile in place, he changes gears and holds out his hand. "What about holding hands?"

I slip my hand into his and grip it tightly.

"Obviously, this is the living room with Zane's monstrosity of a television." He begins the tour, his hand waving at the wall above the fireplace. He swivels around and points to surprisingly comfortable dining room. "This is where we eat together."

The table is casual-looking, with a vibe that matches the leather couch behind us. A bronze statue sits on the buffet, and a large abstract painting hangs on the wall. It's minimal but fits them.

He pulls me over to the kitchen. It's an open floor plan with a huge island.

It includes the usual appliances and stuff that's contained in a kitchen. Although everything seems higher end with more buttons to push. I note where the refrigerator and microwave are located.

Zane eyes me. "Do you cook?" When I shake my head no, he looks relieved.

The other three laugh.

"Zane's the cook and doesn't like anyone messing up his kitchen." Sterling pretends to whisper, even though we can all hear him. "Ok. Laundry room." He points to a room beside the kitchen. "Powder room is behind the kitchen."

"Let's see." His eyes scan the room and land on the glass doors. "The best part. Come on."

Cruz and Raider slide by us and they each grab a door. Instead of pulling, they slide the doors along a track, folding each section like an accordion, until the wall of glass is gone.

There's an entire outdoor living room and kitchen right outside the doors on the covered patio. Beyond that, a large yard with a pool.

A sandbox and several trucks catch my eye, along with a big wheel. I stare at them.

"Gabriel loves playing outside," Sterling tells me with a huge grin on his face. "We try to spend a little time out here in the evenings before bed."

"Where is Gabriel?" I ask with a frown.

"We put him in the room next to mine," Sterling informs me. "I'll show you when we go upstairs."

"How's he doing? Does he mention Armando?"

Sterling's smile drops. "He misses home, including his tío and Maria. He understands English, but he's a bit confused on why everyone around him is speaking it, too. I think he used to go to preschool or something because he talks about school and his friends."

He squeezes my hand. "It's going to take time. Gabriel's a smart, wonderful little boy. He was treated well, spoiled even, but he'll be fine once he settles in some more."

The emotion in his eyes makes me wonder if I should find him a new home sooner rather than later. "Thanks, Sterling. I appreciate you taking such wonderful care of him."

His bright green eyes are watching me carefully. "Let's continue." Walking back inside, he pivots to a hallway on the left, which leads to a large bedroom suite. "Zane's room."

Decorated in blues and greys, the room is sparse but includes a large comfortable-looking chair in the corner with an ottoman. A giant bed sits along one wall, along with two nightstands. And another big television, of course.

"That's not a king, is it?"

"California King," Zane states behind me.

With his size, I bet it's hard to find furniture that doesn't feel miniscule. "You really like your televisions, don't you?" I tease him.

His brows lower in a mock scowl. "Don't start. I'm from Texas, remember? I need football like I need air."

How could I have forgotten about how obsessive Texas football fans can be? It reminds me how far away the real world has been for the last couple of years.

"Of course. You're an A&M fan, right? Go Aggies!" I throw up my fist and shout my team spirit.

Large arms fold across his chest. "Not even close. University of Texas. Go Longhorns." His voice isn't quite as full of spirit as mine, but it's not his style.

"I see. Maybe we'll have to place a few wagers," I joke.

It's been ages since I watched football. Even when I was going to school, I'd been pretty driven to get into the police force to start my eight years of service. My ultimate goal was always the Texas Rangers, like my dad, and they require a minimum of eight years of prior service to apply.

An evil grin takes over his face. "I'll take your bets, but I warn you. I'm not going to be asking for money."

Shocked at his flirting, I contemplate the man in front of me. When his smile starts to slip, I realize I hadn't said anything.

"You're on," I confirm with a wink before nervously pulling Sterling out of the room.

"Right, let's go," Sterling reiterates. "Upstairs. A quick tour, then bed. For you. And me. Alone. In each of our rooms."

Somewhere along the way to Zane's room, we lost Raider and Cruz. Sterling points to each of their doors when we get upstairs. He briefly opens the door to his room, but I'm curious to see it, so I make him stop.

Where Zane's room was utilitarian, this room is masculine and rich. The back wall is painted the deepest of greens, including the molding. The furnishings and materials are of high quality and in varying shades of grey. There's a study off to the side with a ton of computer stuff and monitors. He's even got a fireplace in his bedroom. It's also immaculate. Not one thing in the room is out of place.

I raise my eyebrows at the extravagance.

He follows my gaze. "In England, a lot of bedrooms have fireplaces. While it's much warmer here, it reminds me of home."

"It's a lot nicer than a television," I assure him. Sexy, too.

We leave his room and take four steps to the one next to it. He holds up a finger to his lips and opens the door. I peek in and see a race car toddler bed with a dark-haired little boy tucked into it, clutching his stuffed animal. On the floor next to the bed is an oval rug with a race car track on it. A toy box sits against the wall next to a glider.

My heart aches when I look at him. He's an orphan. I don't know what Armando told him about his parents. I'll have to find a way to ask, but Gabriel did call him tío and not papá.

As much as it would kill me, maybe it would be better for him to have a home where they have no knowledge of his tumultuous background and can give him a normal life.

I draw back to the hallway. "My room?"

Sterling takes me down a short hallway to a guest bedroom.

I walk into the room and look around. "This is wonderful. Thank you. Not just for me, but for everything you bought for Gabriel, too." I peek around the corner and find a bathroom. Another door leads to a walk-in closet.

He's leaning against the doorframe, watching me. "We can decorate it however you want."

"There's no need," I say, bewildered by the frown on his face. "It's a beautiful room." Does he think I don't like it? The walls are painted a light grey. White curtains and a fluffy white comforter give it a fresh feeling. Everything is neutral and calm.

For some reason, he seems upset. "When you're ready, we'll talk about it. Raider put your stuff in the closet." He bends down and kisses me. "Get some sleep, Quinn. I'm glad you're here with us." The door closes behind him.

Like the previous night, I slip off my shoes and fall into bed. The sigh that escapes is long and heartfelt. I thought the bed last night was comfortable, but this one is like lying on a cloud.

Surely after sixteen hours in the car, I'll be able to sleep. Four thousand, three thousand nine hundred and ninety-nine, three thousand nine hundred and ninety-eight... Sleep pulls me under, but when the whispering starts, my gritty eyes fly open.

Maybe a hot shower will help.

The rain head in the shower is a nice surprise, and I stand under it for a while, letting the water cascade over me. Feeling a ton better, I step out and reach for one of the ridiculously fluffy towels hanging on the rack.

I don't bother wiping off the mirror. The sight of my face is something to be avoided because it will only stir up things I want to forget. There's a comb in the drawer, but it's not made for thick hair like mine, so it takes a while to get the tangles out.

Once it's gliding through smoothly, I hitch up the towel and open the door.

Sterling said Raider put my bag in the closet. A movement in the corner startles me. Swiveling, I see a man sitting in a chair, and my heart drops out of my chest. My right hand instinctively reaches for the knife that's no longer there.

"Cruz! You scared the hell out of me," I exclaim, when his face becomes clear. "What are you doing in here?" No wonder he was so successful in his missions. He could have killed me without anyone being the wiser, including me.

"Wondering why you're up and showering at almost three a.m."

"I couldn't sleep. Decided to take a shower." I hitch the towel up and watch his eyes follow the movement.

That would be one way to exhaust my body, I muse.

He glides silently over to me. "Would you like me to stay with you?"

"To sleep?"

His eyes fill with heat. "Your choice."

It takes a millisecond for me to drop the towel. "Stay."

We both reach for each other at the same time. Wanting to even the odds, I grab his t-shirt and pull it up and over his head. My hands map the contours of his body, while my lips trail across his chest, placing kisses all over.

"I've wanted to do this every day since the last time we were together." I can admit now that I'm not worried about dying.

He grunts. Lean hands hover over my body. "You're covered in so many bruises, I'm afraid to touch you." The rasp in his voice tells me he's bothered by all the damage he sees.

I grab his hands in mine and place them on my breasts, then reach up and drag his head down to reach mine. "Kiss me. I won't break."

Firm lips take possession of mine, devouring them in a kiss I feel down to my core. A hand sweeps behind my neck to hold my head, while his other softly caresses my body. I groan. The butterfly touches are driving me crazy. I don't care about the bruises. I need more.

My fingers unsnap his jeans, then push pants and briefs down to the floor. I walk him backwards until he's sitting on the bed. He kicks off the rest of his clothes and reaches for me.

With a sigh, I sit on his lap and smooth back his long hair. His brown eyes are watching me with more than his usual intensity, and it drives me crazy. Hooking his hair behind his ears, I lean forward to lick and trace along the lines of his neck and along his jaw, needing to show the strong man in front of me how much his support has meant.

Beneath me, he hardens even further, and I arch back, fusing our bodies together.

"I love the way you feel against me," I murmur, as the ache builds inside me. My body instinctively rubs against his, and my breath catches.

The hand on my back brings me forward until he can latch on to my breast, but instead of his usual dominance, he carefully licks and nibbles them.

I wrap my arms around his head and pull him tight. "Harder," I breathe. "You're not going to hurt me."

The pressure increases, but no matter what I do, he refuses to let loose. Frustrated, I push him down to the bed. "Lie back."

He chuckles. "Frustration makes you bossy." With an impressive ab move, he lowers inch by inch until he's lying in front of me.

His laugh changes my frustration to determination. I slide off his lap and bend over to kiss those abs I just admired. Tracing the lines with my tongue, I slide over each one until I'm right above the thing I desire the most—him. Taking him into my mouth, I pull out every trick I know to make him lose his control.

He groans, and I look up. His eyes are wide and gleaming with heat, while his hands grip the bed beside him. I lick around the rim and watch his breath rush out. He tastes so good. It makes me want to linger until I push him over the edge.

"Quinn, I need to be inside you," he rasps.

When I continue to ignore him, he spears a hand into my hair and tugs me forward until I release him. "Please."

Placing a knee on each side, I position him beneath me and sink down onto him. Our groan is almost simultaneous. For a second, I don't move, content to look at him, but my body begins to make demands I can't ignore. Rolling my hips, I get into rhythm, slow at first, but my need for him is like a fire rushing toward the only oxygen in the room, and I speed up.

His hands grip my hips and keep us aligned, allowing me to concentrate on our pace and the feel of him inside me as we race toward the edge. His hips start thrusting up when I come down, and the change in friction sends me over the edge. My muscles clench, and a wave of heat spreads from the center outward until even my toes tingle.

In one smooth move, he flips us, putting me on my back, to get the pace he needs to finish. His hips move quickly, and I moan at the feel of him pounding into me.

This is what I needed, to feel his possession, the edge of roughness in his desire. My body quickens again, and I reach down to touch myself.

His eyes follow the movement, and I feel him harden even more inside me. "I love to see you touch yourself."

My body's so sensitive, it doesn't take much before I'm coming again. When he feels me tighten, he thrusts a few more times until his release hits. He shudders and drops down to his elbows.

When our breath eases and our racing hearts calm, he slides out.

"Damn it," he murmurs. "I didn't put on a condom."

I lift a shoulder. "I'm clean. You're the only man I've been with in years."

With my statement, a strange look crosses his face. "I'm clean. Let me get you a washcloth."

I expected him to ask me about birth control, but maybe my statement freaked him out. It's the truth. Even before my sister disappeared, I was dating a few guys, but sleeping with none of them. Men weren't a priority, only my career.

After washing off and using the restroom, I slide back into bed beside him.

He gently pulls me into his arms and runs his hand down my hair.

With a sigh, I drop into sleep. The whispers held at bay by the man at my side.

42

QUINN

Sophia is standing in front of me, pleading for me to help her, but I can't. Hands are locked around my arms. I kick and fight but can never get to her. She disappears, and I look back. It's Julio.

Waking in a sweat, I look out the window and see the first hint of sun. Relieved, I check the phone. Six-thirty a.m. Three hours of sleep. A little less than average. When I move to get up, Cruz instantly wakes.

"I'm going for a quick run. Go back to sleep," I tell him.

He frowns and rubs a hand down his face. "What time is it?"

"Six-thirty," I reply.

After a few stretches to work out the kinks from the car ride, I get dressed in my running gear and bend down to give him a kiss.

"Stay," he urges.

I slip from his grasp and head out. It's been almost a week since my last run.

My body aches in places I didn't know had muscles, and the first mile is painful. Eventually, my body loosens, and my feet hit their rhythmic stride. Several people give me strange looks when I pass them, but I ignore it.

A few blocks from their house, I hit a gate. Backing up, I take a side road and keep running. I didn't realize we were in a secluded neighborhood, but as I look around at the houses, they all seem pretty luxurious.

It didn't take me long to transition from Texas to Mexico. Both felt almost the same to me. This neighborhood feels completely foreign and out of my element.

My usual five-mile run is cut short by the pain. Three-point-six miles. It's all I had in me today. I tap on my phone to find the pin I dropped and walk back to their house.

Three surly men greet me when I return.

"What happened?" I ask Zane.

He glares at Sterling. "Someone forgot to give you the code to the alarm. It went off when you left."

I wince. "Sorry. I'm going to grab some water, then get a shower. Why don't you text me the code?"

In the kitchen, I quietly open and close cabinets until I find the glasses and get some water from the built-in dispenser on the refrigerator door. After chugging it down, I head up to my room.

Once upstairs, I get a shower and dress. With my laptop in hand, I head back downstairs. It's empty except for Sterling… and Gabriel, who's watching cartoons and eating a kids' cereal bar.

"What do you want him to call you?" Sterling murmurs.

"Quinn," I reply, my eyes glued to the little boy.

"Not aunt or tía?" he asks, carefully studying me. "Why not?"

"Because he's old enough to remember me. What's going to happen if I find him a good home and he remembers his aunt gave him up?" I ask him.

Anger sparks in his green eyes. "Why would you even

consider giving him up? He's the only blood family you have left."

My own anger rises. "Are you going to explain to him how his beloved t-i-o killed his m-a-m-a? And his aunt killed his p-a-p-a and t-i-o? I don't want him to carry that burden. It's not right."

Sterling opens his mouth to say something else, but Gabriel interrupts him.

He points his little finger at me. "Hurt."

Sterling pulls him into his side. "Yes, she's hurt. Do you want to kiss it better?"

Gabriel walks over to me, and I bend to get his wet kiss on my hurt cheek.

"Thank you," I tell him softly.

"Better," he confirms with a nod. "Caroline coming?"

"Who's Caroline?" I ask him, a smile on my face.

Beautiful brown eyes study me intensely. "Babysitter."

I glance over at Sterling, who silently confirms it. "I see. Do you like Caroline?"

"She's fun," he replies. "Your name?"

"I'm Quinn," I say, introducing myself. "And what's your name?"

He points to himself. "Gabriel." With a squeal, he runs over and grabs his cup. "Juice."

I take the spill-proof cup from him and eye Sterling. "You thought of everything."

His face is inscrutable. "Not everything. Can you watch him while I go let Caroline in?" He holds up his phone to show a video of an older woman walking up to the door.

The doorbell rings.

I flash the little boy a smile. "Let's go get you some juice, Gabriel." He reaches up and grabs my hand, and we walk over to the kitchen to get a refill.

When Sterling returns, an older woman, in her late fifties or early sixties, is standing next to him laughing. "Caroline, this is Quinn. She's staying here with us."

She holds out her hand. "Nice to meet you." Her eyes take in my bruised and cut face. "Goodness, were you in an accident?"

Her light blue eyes are full of concern. "Nice to meet you, too. Yes, a few days ago."

Gabriel lets go of my hand and runs over to Caroline.

"Good morning, Gabriel," she says, crouching down to give him a hug. "What are we playing today?"

He thinks about it for a second. "Dinosaurs."

"Rowr," she roars, her hands up in the air.

He laughs and squeals.

"Okay, let's get dressed, then we'll play dinosaurs," she says firmly, holding out her hand.

When they're out of sight, I turn to Sterling. "Can I get the password to the Wi-Fi? I've got some things I need to take care of."

He grabs a pen and notepad from the side table and writes it down, then hands me the paper. "Almost all of the women from the facility came to Miami. We've been able to get IDs and official documents for roughly thirty of them, but we have a long way to go. If you want to join us when you get done, just let me know. I'll send a car to pick you up."

"Thanks, if I finish, I'll text you," I say, eager to start searching for the footage of Sophia and Julio. Before I go upstairs, I pause. "Caroline seems really nice, and Gabriel likes her a lot. Thank you for taking such good care of him and making sure he has everything he needs."

He stiffens. "You don't have to thank me for taking care of Gabriel. He's a wonderful little boy. I'll see you later."

Deciding to tackle this like an investigation, I block off the time period—two months before her disappearance—and write a list of her favorite places in Austin. It's not a long list. A coffee shop, bookstore, three restaurants, and two bars. We never looked at these places in the investigation. She disappeared from the River Walk and all our focus remained there when nothing unusual turned up at school or work.

By ten a.m., I have the footage for the coffee shop. Sophia never drank coffee after noon. It hurt her stomach. So, I concentrate on the mornings. The first time her face flashes on the screen, it shocks me. I quickly freeze the video to stare at her. She's alone. Wearing leggings and a sweatshirt, and carrying her backpack, she's obviously on her way to class. The barista says something to her, and she laughs.

I rewind the scene at least ten times. The laugh kills me. She looks so happy. When water hits my hand, I glance down in confusion. It takes me a minute to figure out it's coming from me. I'm crying. Something I hadn't done since her funeral. God, she was amazing.

Finally tearing myself away from that clip, I save it and keep searching. The following week, she comes in around eleven a.m. Instead of leggings and a sweatshirt, she's wearing a cute summer dress. I sit up straighter. Sophia only wore dresses when she was on a date.

The man behind her is tall. So tall, she only comes up to his chest. His hands are on her shoulders and she's laughing up at him. They step forward, and I pause the video. It's Julio. He's looking down at Sophia with a bemused smile on his face.

I hit play again and watch while she orders them both a coffee and pays for it. Together, they move to the side to wait for their order. Not once do their eyes leave each other, and they stand close, barely an inch between them. She's animated, talking and laughing with her hands, and he's hanging on her every word. Even in the video, the chemistry is explosive.

Her heads swivels to the counter, and they move forward to

pick up their drinks. Her friend, the barista, says something to her, and she laughs and pats Julio's chest. They move away, but I catch something unusual at the end. Rewinding it, I play it again, but slower. Julio is scowling at the barista behind Sophia's back.

There are several more clips from the coffee shop. All following a similar pattern. But towards the end of the second month, they change.

The next time they enter, the vibe is completely different. Like before, she stands in front of him, but his arm is wrapped completely in front of her. After ordering, they move to the side. She's looking up at him with a strained smile on her face. He must say something about it because I see her shoulders lift in a shrug. Her smile widens, and she stretches up to kiss him. A minute later, her head swivels in the direction of the counter, but instead of her getting the coffee, he walks up to get it. He ushers her out, a hand resting on her lower back.

Intense. They could have been having a fight, but the control aspect is new in this video compared to the previous ones. What changed?

The last clip is startling. She enters one day by herself. Instead of laughing and smiling, she's staring down at her phone and biting her lip. Her shoulders are hunched. When someone accidentally bumps her, she immediately moves to a more isolated spot. While waiting for her coffee, she texts repeatedly on her phone. The barista must notice something is wrong because he reaches out and lays his hand on top of hers. She jerks it away and leaves the store—without her coffee.

In the videos, she isn't even acting like her usual self anymore. Did something cause their relationship to change that quickly?

Searching the bookstore footage takes a lot longer. I'm through the first month and starting on the second, when there's a knock on my door. I shut the laptop.

"Come in."

Cruz sticks his head in the door. "We missed you today. Sterling thought you were coming down to the warehouse to help." His dark brown eyes scan my face, before he comes in and sits down beside me on the bed. "You look like you've been crying. Want to talk about it?"

"I watched a video of Sophia and the emotions hit me," I say lightly, brushing off his concerns. "Sorry about the warehouse. I got caught up in other things." I hold my breath and his stare until he seems satisfied with my answer. "What time is it?"

He continues to watch me. "Time for dinner. Do you want to freshen up first?"

"Definitely. Thanks." I move off the bed toward the bathroom. "You don't have to wait for me."

His fingers are typing rapidly on his phone. "It's fine. I need to follow up with Henley on a few details from earlier today."

I glance uneasily from the laptop to Cruz. When it's apparent he's focused entirely on his phone, I silently berate myself for becoming so paranoid.

Three minutes later, I walk out of the bathroom. The laptop is where I left it, and Cruz is leaning against the bedroom door waiting for me.

Downstairs, the atmosphere is tense. The men are exchanging looks with each other using their own silent language. Forcing a smile, I sit between Zane and Cruz. Gabriel sits down across from me with Sterling and Raider on each side of him. Sterling reaches over and cuts up the little boy's chicken and veggies.

Gabriel is a chatterbox, telling everyone about his day. Playing dinosaurs must be one of his favorite things to do. When I ask him which one is his favorite, he starts naming them in order, along with a description, the food they like to eat, and a million other facts.

"Not hungry?" Zane interjects when Gabriel pauses to take a breath. I look to see who he's talking to, only to find him looking down at me.

Blinking, I slide my gaze to my plate. I've taken a few bites of the chicken and the salad. "It hurts to chew right now. It's good, though."

Remorse fills his grey eyes. "Sorry, Quinn. I should have made a pasta or something softer for you. I'll remember tomorrow."

Liar, liar, my inner voice taunts me.

It's not entirely a lie. It does hurt to chew, but not as much as he might believe. I just didn't want to explain my lack of appetite.

Raider's staring at me, eyes narrowed, like he knows I'm not being entirely truthful.

Gabriel suddenly shouts. "Quinn!"

Startled, I look at the little boy. "Yes, Gabriel?"

Now that he has my attention again, he immediately launches into his next favorite dinosaur.

Relieved, I focus entirely on him until dinner's over.

With all the looks I'm getting, I know if I disappear upstairs, they'll worry something is wrong. So, I sit on the floor in the living room with Gabriel, oohing and aahing over his dinosaur collection for the next hour until it's time for his bath and bed.

Sterling picks him up and flies him over to kiss each one of the guys. The sight reminds me of when Armando did something similar, and I turn away.

"Want to go up with us?" Sterling asks, a hopeful look in his eyes.

If I go up now, I can head to my room afterward. "Yes, thank you."

His warm broad smile stretches over his face. "I have to warn you… Bath time is an adventure. You might get soaking wet."

I roll my eyes and tickle Gabriel's tummy. "You better not splash me, or the tickle monster will get you."

He squeals and pushes my hand away. "No."

We wave bye to the others and head up.

In the bath, Gabriel loves to dive bomb his toys, splashing water everywhere. The whole time I'm trying to wash him, he's either wiggling around to find new toys to show me or dive bombing them into the water.

Sterling watches the entire thing from the doorway, laughing.

In retaliation, I pick up a wet sponge in the shape of a car and toss it at him. It splatters against his shirt and slides down to the floor.

Gabriel finds this outrageously funny and begins to throw more toy sponges at him.

Sterling mockingly roars like a dinosaur.

Gabriel squeals and picks up a plastic toy to throw.

I try to grab it out of his hand, but he jerks it away and lands a pretty good punch on my sore cheek. Shards of pain streak across my cheek.

"Okay, that's enough," Sterling says in a serious voice. "Let's get out and dry off." He reaches over me and plucks Gabriel out of the bath. "Are you okay?"

Gabriel's watching me, his lip quivering, and I smile. "It's fine. Just an accident."

He leans over and places wet lips on my cheek. "Sorry, Quinn."

I pat his back. "It's okay, sweetheart. Get your jammies on."

While Sterling puts him to bed, I let out the bath water and clean up. Boys are certainly rougher than girls. Sophia's baths were full of bubbles and princess tiaras.

Sterling's reading a book to him when I come out. Something about a racing dog. Gabriel's listening with sleepy eyes.

That delicious British accent sends shivers down my spine, and I lean against the door to listen to the story.

Sterling looks over at me and stops mid-sentence. His eyes slide to my shirt and back up, heat stirring in their depths.

Confused, I look down and close my eyes when I see my t-shirt molded to my breasts, nipples saluting the world. Heat rips across my cheeks, and I duck out, leaving him to finish the story.

In my room, I toss the wet clothes over the shower rod and slip on pajama shorts and a tank for bed.

When I come out, Sterling's waiting for me. His eyes widen, and he groans. "I'm not sure which one I like more, gorgeous."

I cross my arms over my chest. "Did Gabriel get to sleep?"

He steps in front of me. "He did. I came over to check on your face. He clocked you pretty good." Fingers lift my face to the light so he can examine my cheek. "Looks like the stitches are intact. I'll get you some ice to help with the swelling."

I wrap my fingers around his wrist. "It's fine. I put a cold washcloth on it for a few minutes."

He leans over and places a tender kiss on my lips. "I guess I'll have to wait a little longer to kiss you like I want. But that's okay. I'm a patient man." He drops a kiss on the place between my neck and shoulder. "A few tastes of your delectable body will tie me over."

Fingers slide the strap of my cami down to my elbow. Green eyes glittering like emeralds watch my face, but I offer no resistance to whatever he's planning to do.

With his hand bracing himself on the wall behind me, he slides his mouth from my neck down my cleavage to my breasts. "Ever since I saw you in that dress, I haven't been able to get your beautiful breasts out of my mind." His tongue swirls along the outer edge of my nipples. "And then to see you in a wet t-shirt..." He chuckles. "I wanted to drag you down to the floor and worship every inch of your body."

Heat spreads across my face and chest.

"But the reality is so much more than I expected," he murmurs. "You're so damn beautiful." With one last nibble, he groans and pulls up my strap. "Please get better soon."

I laugh at the heartfelt plea.

With a broad grin, he places his mouth near my ear. "Good night, Quinn." The timbre of his voice in my ear makes me shiver.

"Good... night, Sterling," I reply in a breathless voice.

When he's gone, I lean back against the cool wall and catch my breath.

43

QUINN

The clock reads two a.m. when I shut the laptop. To my disappointment, the bookstore yielded nothing. It's kind of surprising, too. Sophia loved reading and spent more time in the library and bookstore than in any other place. Her favorites were romance. She'd get starry-eyed after reading a particularly good book.

My eyes droop, and I scoot down until I'm flat.

Sophia's standing in front of the mirror, adjusting the small tiara on her head. "How does this look? Is it too much?"

"You look like the princess you always wanted to be," I reassure her. "Now, if he tries to take you to a hotel room, call me. I'll come get you. No questions asked, I promise. Boys seem to think prom is a license for sex."

She rolls her eyes. "Please. Peter Allen knows he's not getting anything from me. I have no interest in boys. One day, I'm going to meet a man who will sweep me off my feet. He'll be handsome and rich, of course, but most importantly, he'll love me more than anyone."

I snort. "Well, you'd better make sure you get a degree and career in case your Prince Charming doesn't show up until later."

She sniffs. "I'm looking for a king, not a prince."

She twirls and laughs. The image of her laughing rewinds and plays again. She laughs. Rewind. She laughs.

I wake with her laughter ringing in my ears. The room isn't dark, but the sun isn't up, either. My phone's clock displays five thirty a.m. Three and a half hours of sleep. Less than I like to get, but knowing I won't get any more, I dress and head downstairs. This time, I punch in the code after opening the door.

The run clears the lingering dreams from my head. With a satisfied grunt, I slow to a walk. Four miles is the most my body will do, but it's better than yesterday.

When I walk in the house, it's the same as yesterday. Four grumpy men are staring at me from the couch.

I raise my hands. "What? I punched in the alarm code."

Raider stands and stretches. The black shorts he's wearing hang dangerously low on his hips. "It's our fault. We're light sleepers and not used to hearing anyone in the house. We'll get used to it."

He walks over and studies my face. "I don't like the dark circles under your eyes. If you can't sleep, ask one of us to stay with you. I can assure you, every one of us would jump at the chance to hold you all night."

Stunned, I watch him walk up the stairs.

"Damn bastard's too smooth," Cruz murmurs in my ear. "He's also right. It's killing us to see you try to go through this alone. We have all been there, and we know how hard it is to find your way. Don't shut us out, Quinn." Lips graze the top of my head before he follows Raider.

Sterling opens his mouth, but Gabriel's voice comes over the baby monitor and interrupts whatever he was going to say. With a wry smile, he slips past.

Zane eyes me from the couch. "Want some breakfast?"

My stomach rumbles on cue, making me laugh. "I think so."

He immediately brightens and claps his hands together. "Eggs, pancakes, French toast?"

"Pancakes," a small voice behind me says.

I look at Gabriel's hopeful face. "Definitely pancakes."

He gives me a serious nod and wiggles his feet.

Sterling sets him down, and he runs over and grabs my legs. When I look down, it's the past meeting the present. Instead of Gabriel, I see Sophia standing there, her beautiful brown eyes pleading with me to pick her up. I shake my head and back up a step.

"I'm going to grab a shower," I tell him. "Why don't you go play with your toys, and when I come back, we'll eat pancakes, okay?"

"Zane," Sterling's voice snaps out.

In the kitchen, Zane puts down the whisk and comes into the living room. After a glance at Sterling, he moves over to Gabriel and asks him about the cartoon characters on the TV.

Sterling grabs my hand, pulls me out of the living room, and up the stairs. "Tell me what just went through your mind downstairs. Please. I want to understand. One minute you're warm and laughing with him, and the next, you're backing away."

I jerk my hand out of his and start walking toward my bedroom. "I don't owe you any explanations. He's my nephew."

He steps in front of me. "Actually, you do. You put him in my arms and told me to take care of him. I don't want to see him hurt. Just tell me what it is. What are you afraid of?"

I sigh. "I want what's best for him. And that might not be me. He should be in a good home with parents who didn't murder his family."

His head shakes back and forth for a minute. "That's not all of it, is it? There's something else. When you look at him, you get a pained expression on your face." Like a light bulb going off, his big brain figures it out. He steps forward and takes my hands in his. "Say it, Quinn."

My entire body starts trembling. "I can't."

"You have to," he states implacably. "You need to say it." Green eyes drill into me until I finally cave.

"Oh, God. I… I see her when he looks at me. Her eyes. And it kills me. It's not fair—I know it's not—but sometimes the pain is too much. It's worse when the memory of the past collides with the present. Like today, when he stared up at me, pleading with me to pick him up. She used to do the same thing," I say hoarsely, pushing the words past the lump in my throat.

"And yes, there's the guilt. Because of me and Armando, he's an orphan. I know you don't want to hear it, but the best thing for him might be a whole new life. A clean slate with no hint of the past. Think about it. Please," I urge him. "I can see you're getting attached to him. And the last thing I want to do is hurt you."

He heaves a sigh and pulls me in tight. "I may not like the idea, but I'll think about it. And I want you to really think about what it means for him. Just don't make up your mind yet, okay? Promise me."

The pain in his voice makes my heart ache. "I promise." I wrap my arms around him and squeeze tight.

He wraps his body around me, cocooning me from the world. "Do you have a picture of Sophia at that age?"

"Yes."

"Would you send it to me? I'd like to see the resemblance," he asks hesitantly.

"I'll text it to you," I promise him. Easing back, I look up and see the troubled expression lingering on his face. "I'm going to take a shower."

As soon as I enter my room, I strip off my clothes and step

into the shower. Tears cascade down my face. The thought of hurting either of them is tearing me up inside, but so is the thought of Gabriel learning his history. And, if I'm being honest, I don't know if I can bear to be around him because of her. The decision doesn't have to made today, but the longer it takes, the harder it's going to be for everyone.

I drag myself out of the shower, dry off, and wipe my face. Before I go downstairs to get pancakes, I text several pictures to Sterling.

Gabriel's sitting at the island eating when I come down. His mouth full, he grins. "Panmfscakes."

"Pancakes," I repeat his muffled word. "It looks yummy. Zane, can I have some delicious pancakes?"

All four men are gathered around Sterling's phone, looking at the pictures I sent and comparing Sophia to Gabriel. A look of astonishment on their faces.

Zane walks over and hugs me. "Pancakes, coming up."

Gabriel howls. "Kiss! Kiss!"

Zane's face reddens. "Gabriel had to give me a kiss for his pancakes."

The whole kitchen stops moving, as if the very house is holding its breath.

I tilt my head. "I see. A kiss, huh?" I look at Gabriel, who gives me a serious nod. "Where did you kiss him?"

Gabriel laughs and puckers up his lips.

I crook my finger toward Zane to get him to bend down. "One kiss for pancakes." Capturing his lips with mine, I kiss him slowly, giving him time to pull away.

His entire body is rigid except for his lips. For a second, his lips soften and cling to mine, but they become firm again, and I know the kiss is over.

"Pancakes coming up."

Gabriel claps, and the world starts spinning again.

Zane sets a plate of pancakes in front of me, and a few minutes later, Caroline arrives.

When they ask me to go to the warehouse with them, I shake my head. The disappointment in their eyes is almost more than I can take, but I refuse to let it sway me. I'm determined to see all the footage.

44

ZANE

Sterling's staring at his phone with a troubled look on his face. When he suddenly smiles, and I know he's switched his attention from Quinn to Gabriel. My gut clenches to see Sterling with Gabriel, knowing things are still up in the air for all of us. I worry he's getting too close to the little boy. Hell, we're all getting too close to him.

I peer over his shoulder. "Did she leave the house today?"

"She didn't leave her room," he snarls. "I know Raider and Cruz said to give her time, but since she's been here, she hasn't shown any interest in a life outside that room. I wish I knew what she was doing in there all day. We know she isn't sleeping."

Pulling on my best poker face, I try to calm him down. "She's been here a week. If she doesn't come with us tomorrow, I have an idea on how to get her out of the house. Okay?" When he nods, I wave a hand towards the kitchen. "I'm going to start dinner. Why don't you grab Gabriel and let Raider get Quinn?"

When he's gone, I let my own anger and frustration show. We all know she needs time, but I don't have the first fucking clue on how to help her through it. As leader of the team, I am the glue that holds everything together, including us. And I'm failing her, and it's driving me fucking crazy. She seems to be falling deeper into a hole and sleeping less. Her morning run started at four thirty a.m. today.

An idea came to me earlier when I was speaking to Henley about Gabriel. It's worth a try. While my mind plots out all the details, my hands are busy pulling together grilled chicken tacos for tonight. Cooking helps me decompress from the day, and it's a good way to get in some nutrition. The places we go to don't always have healthy alternatives.

Gabriel's singing a song when they grab a seat at the table. I can't help but smile when he misses a few lines and begins singing the chorus at the top of his lungs. I believe Raider taught him that song. It's his favorite. Sterling's not the only one who's becoming attached to Gabriel.

Quinn strolls into the room with Raider behind her. He's laser focused on Quinn and frowning. It's not a good sign. When I silently ask him about it, he flips his thumb down.

"Cruz is checking on a possible Rodrigo sighting," I briskly inform Quinn, trying to snap her out of her apathy. "He'll call us shortly to let us know if it's valid."

Her spine straightens, and she nods.

"Rodrigo bad," Gabriel states solemnly. "Tío not like." Anxious, his small fingers knead the napkin beside his plate.

Quinn's eyes dart to Gabriel, and she lays a hand over his. "We will keep you safe, I promise."

He studies her, as if judging her sincerity. "Promise?"

She makes an x over her chest. "Cross my heart. I promise."

His little brow furrows, and he raises his hand to his chest.

She takes his finger and draws one line across his heart, then the other. "Cross my heart."

When he successfully repeats it, she bends down and gives

him a kiss. "Good job." Her eyes shine with pride instead of sadness.

Delighted with learning something new, he does it several more times over dinner. We chuckle at his antics, and he preens with all the attention.

These two deserve so much more than they've been dealt. If only she would let us in.

THE ALARM CHIMES ON MY PHONE AT FOUR A.M. BLEARY-EYED, I watch Quinn punch in the code and head out for a run.

I quickly send out a text to Sterling and Raider. "Let's give her some space this morning. Our emotions are too hot to keep things neutral."

Raider and Sterling text back their agreement.

When Raider went to grab her for dinner, he could hear her crying, but when he entered, the laptop was closed.

Quinn didn't join Sterling and Gabriel for bath time last night. For the first time since she arrived, she skipped it.

Cruz sent an encrypted message last night on our private channel. The tip is valid. He's tailing Rodrigo through Texas right now.

With a grunt, I get up and head to the gym. Might as well get an early start.

The gym is the one place I can let all my aggression loose. There's no politics or agenda. It's pure physical energy. Releasing it here helps me stay even-keeled the rest of the time.

I check the regimented schedule for today's workout. Arm day. I pick up the dumbbells and start with the triceps. The repetitions get increasingly harder, but I continue until I hit fatigue. Then I start with a different exercise and muscle. Then another. An hour later, I wipe my face and set the weight in my hand on the floor.

I'm mixing a smoothie in the kitchen when Raider comes down.

"Quinn's not back," he informs me.

I set the glass on the counter and pick up my phone. There's been no activity since she reset the alarm at four.

"Text Sterling and let him know. I'll grab my keys," I yell, sprinting down the hall to my bedroom. Once I have my wallet and keys, I head straight to the garage, knowing Raider's already there waiting.

The garage is open, and he's sitting impatiently in the SUV.

"Do you know what route she takes?" I ask, backing out of the garage.

"She said she usually runs to the gate, then takes a side road farther into the neighborhood," he says, his eyes peeled for Quinn.

"The gate's coming up. Right or left?"

He closes his eyes. "Right."

Raider strongly believes in following your gut. His is usually right, too.

The sun is cresting the horizon when we spot her sitting on the side of the road massaging her calf.

We pull up beside her and get out. "What happened?"

She makes a face. "Cramping. I pushed too hard. Here, help me up."

Ignoring her comment, I squat down and pick her up. My arms quiver for a second, making her squeak. "If I'd have known you'd need rescuing today, I would have skipped arm day. Don't worry, I've got you. Muscles are just a little fatigued."

Raider opens the back door, and I slide her inside. He gets in after her and props her leg up on his lap.

When we get back, I carry her inside and sit her on the couch. "I'll get the salt and Gatorade."

"Salt?" she repeats.

I walk into the kitchen to grab the items for her. "Usually, a dime size amount will make the cramps disappear, but you might need a little more this morning. It's a trick my father taught me before I went into basic training. I'd grab salt packs from McDonald's and other fast-food restaurants and carry them in my pockets. The other guys thought it was hilarious until they tried it."

She winces. "I'll try anything to get the cramps to stop."

I hand her the Gatorade. "Hold out your hand, palm up. Cup it a little more. That's it. We'll start with a dime and see how it goes." The white crystals pile into her hand.

She raises her hand, but I stop it.

"Probably best to lick your finger and dip it into the salt. The taste isn't the best, but the Gatorade should help." Licking my finger, I demonstrate my instructions.

She licks the salt off her finger and grimaces. "I see what you mean."

Raider yawns and stretches. "You left pretty early this morning. How many miles did you do?" His tone is nonchalant, but I can see the simmer in his eyes.

"Seven," she answers. "Too many, I know. I was lost in thought."

He says nothing, but I can see he's come to the same conclusion as me. We need to do something to jolt her out of this hole.

"Why don't you come to the warehouse today? We're only halfway through the rescues, and we could use more help. We'll take you on a tour of Miami and grab some dinner out," I say, adding an incentive to sweeten the deal.

She stiffens. "Maybe tomorrow. I'm still working on a few things."

"Tomorrow, okay," I agree. Today, too, if my plan works. "How's your leg?"

Her eyebrows raise. "The cramps are gone. It's amazing." She carefully puts her feet on the floor and stands. When nothing happens, she walks across to the TV and back. "Thank you. I'll have to put some salt in my pockets."

Raider stands up. "You need to stop pushing yourself. It's not going to help. This isn't going to go away until you deal with it. Accept it."

The blankness on her face tells me she doesn't understand what he's saying. "You don't understand."

He looks at her incredulously. "I don't understand? Me? If there's anyone here who knows what you're going through, it's me."

"You don't know the whole story," she cries.

"Tell us. Let us help. I can't stand seeing you like this, mon petit oiseau. Please," he rasps.

Gabriel's singing ends the conversation.

She takes advantage of his arrival to flee.

Curse words flow in French from Raider's mouth, and he storms out of the room in the opposite direction.

"Morning," Gabriel says, his arms extended toward me.

I reach over and hug him. "Morning. How's my favorite boy today?"

"Good. Eggs?" he asks.

"We can have eggs this morning. Let's go whip some up," I agree cheerfully. "It's going to be a great day."

"Yeah," Gabriel agrees, and I laugh.

Gabriel takes the last bite of egg. "Done," he announces with pride.

"Great job. High five," I praise him, and raise my hand for him to smack. "Now, why don't you go into the living room and wait for Caroline? I'll put Paw Patrol on for you."

He grins and scrambles down from his chair.

Sterling watches until he sits down in front of the TV. "What's up?"

"I've got a plan to get Quinn down to the warehouse today. Henley's agreed to change Gabriel's birth certificate, so she can copy it and plant his new ID in the civil registration office in Monterrey. It will allow us to request an official copy. It's the best way to establish a solid background for Gabriel. I wanted you to know, though. It's a risk. If she wants to proceed with adopting

Gabriel out, it will give her official documentation to do so." I watch him swallow hard at the news.

With a pained expression, he spears his fingers through his hair. "She needs to take a step forward, move beyond the past, and if this is what helps, I'm all for it."

45

<u>QUINN</u>

I'm scanning the video footage of the last restaurant on my list. Over the last week, I'd found more footage of them together. It's almost all the same. The first month they were together, everything was roses and love. But it slowly started to evolve into a controlling relationship—for both of them.

There's no doubt Julio was a jealous man. But Sophia would also do things, like flirt with a guy in front of him, to provoke that response. It's like they fed off each other.

In one video, they would be fighting. In another, making out and laughing.

I'm losing my mind. If everything Armando said is the truth, he's right. I'm just like him. I deserve to be punished. Not for his death. He deserved it. But for Julio's death.

The phone buzzes, and I pick it up.

Zane: Henley's searching for an identity for Gabriel. Do you want him to have both Mexican and American nationality?

Me: I'm not sure. Haven't really thought about it. Does she need to know today?

Zane: It can take days to create a solid identity. Henley doesn't just create fake IDs. She backs them up with backgrounds that can withstand government scrutiny.

Me: I want him to have the best ID. And we should honor his heritage. Dual nationality.

Zane: I'll let her know. Thanks.

I'm in the middle of the first month's footage when the phone buzzes again. With a sigh, I pick it up.

Zane: She says the easiest thing will be to doctor his current birth certificate, then place an electronic copy in the civil registration office in Monterrey. It sticks close to the truth and gives him a plausible background. We can then request an official copy of his new ID.

Me: I don't know where it is.

Zane: Let me ask Sterling. He requested an official copy from Mexico in case we needed it for medical purposes.

Zane: It's in Sterling's study. In his bedroom. Top drawer on the right.

Me: Can't you take it tomorrow?

Zane: Henley's not always here, and she's the best at this kind of stuff. Do you mind grabbing it and bringing it down to the warehouse? We're only twenty minutes away. I'll send a car for you.

Me: ...

With a frustrated sigh, I close the laptop and walk over to Sterling's room. The air is thick with the smell of him, and I inhale deeply. It smells so good. Sexy and sophisticated.

I move into the study and over to his desk. Everything is in precise order and immaculate, which doesn't surprise me. What does surprise me is the photo of him and Gabriel he framed and placed on his desk. It's obviously a selfie. The two of them are laughing at the camera. I slide my finger down both their faces. They look good together. Happy. I can't help wishing he was his father. With one last look, I put it down, open the top drawer, and grab the birth certificate.

Me: I found it. Send the car.

I hurry into the bathroom to brush my teeth and swipe a little mascara across my lashes. Grimacing at the joggers and old t-shirt I'm wearing, I quickly exchange them for jeans and a sleeveless blouse.

My phone beeps, and I see the driver is waiting for me outside.

The driver drops me off at a huge warehouse. When I step inside the cool interior, I'm shocked. It's full of miniature stations. The floor is taped with a walk line to visually guide people from one station to the next. It's extremely efficient. People can pick up clothes, groceries, and other necessities. Register for their IDs, school, or find a place to live.

I spot Zane in the corner and head towards him. He's on the phone, so I wait for him to finish.

"Hang on just a second," he says into the phone. "Quinn! Sorry, I'm on a call. Can you take it over to Henley? She's in that far corner. Pink hair. Thanks. Okay, I'm back."

With an exasperated sigh, I turn on my heel and heads over towards the corner. A young woman with shockingly pink hair stands up when I get closer.

She holds out her hand. "You must be Quinn. I'm Henley."

Her handshake is firm. "Thanks for doing all of this, especially for Gabriel." I hand her the certificate.

A look of satisfaction crosses her face when she sees the document. "It's perfect. Have a seat." She takes a picture of the document.

"Oh, I was just going to head back to the house," I reply, but she's not even listening, so I sit down beside her.

Her hands fly across the keyboard. I'm not sure I've ever seen someone type that fast. It's like an extension of her fingers. Screens open and close on the computer.

"Okay. What do you want Gabriel's last name to be?" Her fingers hover over the keys, waiting for me to answer her.

For some reason, I look over at Sterling. He's sitting nearby. "I'm not sure. Can we skip that part?"

She hesitates for a second. "We can fill out the rest of the information, but to complete the document, we'll need a last name."

I nod to show her I understand.

Leaning forward, she continues to the next piece of information. "I assume you want to keep his first name. What about his middle name?"

I turn my head to look at the screen. "What middle name?"

She squints. "Roberto."

My stepfather. This proves Sophia loved Gabriel. "Yes, let's keep it. Also, let's put his last name as Lopez."

"If someone looks for him, it's better if you change the last name," she states softly.

"What name is on the certificate?" I ask with a frown.

"Lopez. Gabriel Roberto Lopez," she reads. "Didn't you know?"

Gabriel had Sophia's last name, too. "Not Morales? You're sure?"

"I'm sure," she replies. "Are you okay?"

I lift a shoulder. "I don't know."

"Why don't we put this one aside and work on yours?" she

states firmly. "Zane told me you were dead. That's great. It's like having a blank slate."

Uneasy, I glance at her. What did Zane tell her? Did he give her my life story?

Her hand reaches over and grabs mine. "It's okay. I probably should have told you a little about myself before jumping into all of this. Knowing might make you feel more at ease."

"My real name is Henley. Henley Night. My last name used to be something else, but after a crazy stalker tracked me down, I had to die. Or at least the old Henley had to die," she begins with a laugh.

Her story reels me in immediately. I find myself completely fascinated by this seemingly innocent-looking woman who's actually a hacker genius, who went after a murderer, and ended up gaining the freedom to live her life again. Minus the crazy stalker.

"And where are these men who helped you?" I murmur.

She swivels and points to three exceptionally handsome men behind us. One is tall and fierce looking, obviously the Thiago in her story. Next to him is a lean man with tousled hair. She described Mateo as a sexy professor, so that's undoubtedly him. Which leaves the impeccably dressed man as Grayson.

"Which one did you end up with?" Curious to see if I guessed right.

She blushes. "All of them."

"Sorry, did you say all of them? You're dating all of them? Lucky woman!" I exclaim.

"No, it's forever. Permanent. They're stuck with me," she says cheerfully. She laughs at the expression on my face. "I love all three of them, and they love me. We live and work together. Although we have separate companies." She shrugs. "It works because we want it to work."

"I'm surprised, but that's amazing. It's pretty brave of you, all of you, to throw traditional convention out the window," I remark.

For the first time, her smile disappears. "I didn't choose to be a hacker. I was forced into it by my stalker. The police weren't any help. If I hadn't found Marcos, I'm not sure I'd be here today. My skills provided me with food, shelter, and a life. Traditional convention labels hackers as criminals and yet, not once did the world wonder how I became one, nor did it help me. Marcos did. He founded this rescue foundation. Why? Because his brother-in-law, an accountant for the cartel, murdered the rest of his family. Marcos saved his remaining family by using his own skills, some of which weren't legal. I'm not going to hide because the world thinks what I did or do is wrong. It's why I continue to use my skills to help these rescues even when I own a multi-million-dollar business.

"Screw traditional convention. I choose to live the life I want. To be happy. I fucking deserve it," she says fervently. "I don't know all of your story, but if you had to die to get to this point, it means something got royally screwed up. People don't go to extremes unless they feel they have no other choice."

"I certainly went to extremes," I remark with a sad smile.

She shrugs as if it doesn't matter. "You know, if you ever want someone to talk to, give me a call," she says, writing down her number on a sticky. "And don't beat yourself up. You can only make decisions for the road you see in front of you, not the one behind or the ones up ahead."

I squeeze her hand. "Thank you. I appreciate it. I know I want to keep my first name as Quinn. It's important to me, but I'll have to let you know on the rest of the names for both me and Gabriel." I look over at the wall. "Maybe next time, you can introduce me to your men."

She smiles and hands me Gabriel's certificate. "It's a deal. Here. I have a copy in the system now."

Taking it from her, I stride over to where Sterling's sitting.

With a sad smile on his face, he leans back in his chair. "What did you change his name to?"

"I didn't," I reply, watching his eyes light up with relief.

"Why didn't you tell me his last name was Lopez?" My finger taps the name on the certificate.

He tilts his head. "I got it in the mail and threw it in the drawer. It didn't occur to me that it was different."

I shove the certificate towards him. "His name is Gabriel Roberto Lopez—after my stepfather. He also has Roberto and Sophia's last name. She loved Gabriel."

"That's good, right?" he asks, with a bewildered look.

"Yes. I…"

"Were you seriously going to come to the warehouse and not come by and say hi to me?" a snide voice asks from behind me.

"Margot?" I stand up and turn around to find her standing there with her hands on her hips, glaring at me.

46

QUINN

She pulls me to her and gives me a hug. "I heard you gutted that psycho, Armando. That's good. He needed to be taken out."

I smile weakly. "He did."

She tilts her head. "Don't tell me you're feeling sorry about it."

"Not about Armando," I say slowly. "Maybe some guilt around killing Julio." For some reason, maybe because she used the word gutted, I find myself telling her all of it—about Gabriel, what I found out about Sophia and Julio, and the words Armando said to me before he died. "To top it off, I don't know what to do about Gabriel. If I keep him, what the hell do I tell him about killing his father and beloved uncle?"

She heaves a huge sigh. "Wow, that's a lot to unpack. And I think somewhere along the way, you lost the plot."

"What do you mean?" I ask, biting my lip.

"First, let's talk about Sophia and Julio. It sucks she didn't tell you, but honestly, I wouldn't have told you either." When I rear back, she throws back her hair. "I'm attracted to bad boys and psychos. If there's one on the East coast, I'll find him. Just ask my father. He's had to get rid of more of them than he'd like to admit." She raises a shoulder and laughs. Clearly not the least bit concerned about her father getting rid of her boyfriends.

I raise an eyebrow. "Sounds like an appropriate response to me."

"He doesn't kill them, or at least not all of them. He either pays them off or gives them a job. Both of which instantly makes me lose interest in them," she says, with an airy wave. "Your sister was around the same age as me, right?"

"Same age, but less worldly," I remark. If Sophia had been the powerhouse Margot is, I might not have worried quite as much.

She gives me a wry smile. "I've got you fooled. I'm capable and smart because I've had to be. The world I grew up in isn't pretty. But if you think I know everything I'm doing, you're wrong. If I did, I wouldn't have fallen for a guy who trafficked me to Mexico!" She holds up a finger. "My father did kill that one."

She easily reads the confusion on my face. "The fact is… I trusted and fell for the wrong guy. It happens. Your sister did the same thing."

"I've seen them together. He genuinely seemed to love her," I protest. "But then, he does something crazy, and I feel like maybe he was just manipulating her."

"I think you might be the less worldly one," she murmurs. "Look. Just because he loved her doesn't mean he wasn't manipulating her, or he wasn't a psycho. Believe me, the stuff my illustrious father dug up on the two brothers would make you sick. You did the world a favor when you got rid of them."

When I still look uncertain, she puts an arm around me and turns me in a circle. "These are good men. Anyone who would put their own life aside to help these rescues is a good person. Use them as your marker, not Julio."

"I understand what you're saying, but I just don't know. For some reason, my mind is stuck," I say, trying to explain what's going on in my head.

Her eyes narrow in thought. "Maybe because it's the last person your sister loved? In fact, she loved him so much, she let you lose your mind rather than leave him and her child. Maybe you're not feeling guilty about Julio's death. Maybe you're angry with Sophia for choosing that psycho over you," she offers. "I don't know. Maybe it doesn't matter."

When I look at her in disbelief, she shrugs. "Do you honestly think growing up with Julio would have been the best thing for your nephew? He wasn't a good man. His only redeeming grace might have been that he loved your sister. Me? I think it's better that he's dead and Gabriel doesn't remember him."

Her words hit hard. It gives me hope that Gabriel and I could stay together, and that he would understand when he got older why I killed them.

She grabs my phone and puts in her number. And Henley's too when she sees the paper I'm clutching. "Go. I can tell you need to think. Call me if you want to talk."

In a daze, I leave.

47

<u>STERLING</u>

Margot throws her arm around Quinn, and they turn in a circle to view the warehouse. When they start to face my way, I quickly type nonsense on the keyboard. Five minutes later, I turn sideways to check on her and she's gone.

Damn it.

Shoving my laptop into my backpack, I scramble to catch up with her. Her conversation with Margot looked serious, and I hadn't wanted to interrupt. It made me feel better to see her talk to someone. Maybe Zane's plan worked.

"Quinn!" I shout, seeing her down the street. When she doesn't turn, I hurry over to my car and get in. The street leading to the warehouse is long, and it only takes me two minutes to reach her. Rolling up beside her, I stop the car and get out, but she doesn't even look at me.

In a few strides, I reach the sidewalk and grab her elbow. She comes out of her daze swinging. Blocking the fist heading toward my eye, I grab her wrist and wrap it around her body, locking her back to my front.

"Bloody hell, Quinn. Stop fighting. It's Sterling," I relay over and over until she hears me.

With a shudder, she stops fighting. "Damn it, you scared the hell out of me," she curses.

I lay my chin on the top of her head. "I called your name several times. You must have been thinking pretty hard."

Her body sags against mine. "I was… am. My mind's been trapped in this whirlwind for a week, and I haven't been able to see my way out."

"I know. We've been so worried about you, but we didn't know how to help. You wouldn't let us in." I can't stop the frustration from leaking into my voice.

"I don't know how," she says in a small voice.

It hurts me to hear her so unsure of herself, but I refuse to let her hide anymore. "Or you're scared to." I turn her around to face me. "To say we care about you sounds so… insipid. It doesn't explain what we feel for you. We've never found someone who fits with all of us. There's always been an odd man out. You fit so bloody well, it scares the hell out of us, too."

Her beautiful, deep green eyes look down as if she's afraid to hear what I'm saying.

I pull her chin up. "We'll wait however long you need, but we need to know you want to move forward. And if you don't, we'll help you get where you want to go."

A horn blares nearby. This is not the best place to have this conversation. With a hand at her back, I guide her to the car and shut the door. Rounding the back, I stop for a minute to breathe in and out. I hadn't meant to say all that to her. What if it's too much?

She says nothing on the way home, and I grip the steering wheel with white knuckles, certain I've fucked this up before it's really began. And there's still one thing I need to say, and it can't wait.

I pull into the driveway and park. "Quinn, I want you to know that I've thought about all the benefits Gabriel would have with a new family. They don't compare with what he could have with you and us."

"I know what it's like to have my family ripped away," I tell her, my voice full of pain from that time in my life. "It hurt more than I can express. Everyone told me I'd benefit from the world I was entering. Without a doubt, it was privileged. As the son of a lord, I received the best education money and title can buy. Doors that would have been closed were open to me. It was completely foreign to me and tough, but I did benefit from the change."

I pull out my wallet and show her a picture of the man I thought of as my father. "I would have given it all away to be his real son and stay with him. He loved me more than life. My biological father gave me every material thing in the world, but he never loved me. You hope the people who adopt Gabriel will love him, but you can't know for sure. What if he's adopted and four years later, his parents die? Life is unpredictable at best. With us, he would have four strong men to help guide him and a fierce aunt. And most importantly, love."

"I know you're still thinking about everything, but I needed you to know how I felt," I say, looking into her eyes. "I didn't mean to dump all this on you, but like you, it's all I've been thinking about since you arrived, and I couldn't hold it in any longer."

"I'm glad you did," she whispers. "I promise to think about everything." Sliding out of the car, she heads into the house.

With one last look at the picture, I put it back in my wallet and punch the steering wheel. Unable to concentrate, I decide against returning to the warehouse. Maybe a drive will help.

Two hours outside of Miami, in Marathon, FL, I stop to get a beer. This place is a favorite of mine. The sight and sound of the ocean lapping the tiny beach in the back feels like a place out of time. Today, it doesn't soothe me in the slightest.

I shouldn't have pushed her. It was the same with my father when he came back from Africa. I felt this need to fix things. Make it all better for him. And I couldn't. He would smile and pat me on my shoulder and tell me how happy he was to be home, but I couldn't accept it. When he committed suicide, I fell off the deep end. Thankfully, Zane was there for me. He didn't try to help. Simply gave me a job and told me to get to work.

The phone rings, and I pull it out of my pocket. It's Zane. I reluctantly answer. "I know what you're going to say…"

"Is Quinn with you?"

I immediately drop some money on the table and head out to the parking lot. "No. I dropped her off two hours ago." Dread settles in my stomach. "I said some things to her. Pushed her. This is my fault."

"We'll discuss it later. One of the cars is missing. Can you track it from your location?"

I tap the speaker button. "Which one?"

"Cruz' Mustang."

"Hold on," I say, tapping into the app for the vehicles. I'd installed trackers on all of them. Sometimes I wish I could inject everyone with trackers, or at least my family. "The car's at South Pointe Park Pier. I'm two hours out."

"Go home," he insists. "I'll find her."

With a heavy heart, I hit the road.

48

____

<u>ZANE</u>

She's sitting on the beach, staring out over the water. Her knees drawn up with her arms around them, she looks tiny. Vulnerable. The opposite of the tiny force I'm used to seeing. Is this because of whatever has been bothering or something Sterling said earlier?

With a heavy sigh, I sit down beside her.

She tenses when she sees me. "Zane."

I cock my head to the side. "What made you choose Cruz' car?"

"It's the only one I recognized," she says dryly.

"Raider loves European sports cars," I agree with a laugh.

"Did everything go okay with the birth certificate today?"

Her face crumples. "No. I didn't know how much she loved Gabriel until today."

With those words, it all comes spilling out. The words Armando said to her when he was dying. Her search for video footage of Sophia and Julio. Her confusion about their relationship. The overwhelming guilt of having killed Julio and leaving Gabriel without a father. The terror of how he's going to feel about her when he grows up.

Tears are flowing steadily down her face. She goes through her conversation with Margot. "She's right. I'm angry with Sophia. And that makes me feel like shit. I don't want to be angry at her."

I look out at sunset breaking on the water. "So, don't. At nineteen, I didn't know my head from my ass half the time. I'm not sure I knew what it meant to be an adult until I was thirty. And yet, the US government gave me a uniform, weapon, and a rank." I shake my head, thinking back to the gangly, brash kid of my past. "She was nineteen and in love for the first time."

"What do you think about Julio?" she asks, biting her lip.

I look her in the eye and give her the truth. "Even if he wasn't directly responsible for Sophia's death, he knew what would happen if he brought her into his world. And when Armando brutally killed the woman he loved so much, he did nothing. At the very least, he could have taken Gabriel and left. He had money and resources."

The lines between her brow smooths. "Margot said Gabriel was better off without him as a father. Coming from her background, it's certainly a bold statement." She flashes a wry smile. "But I don't know how to tell him about the past. I'm afraid he'll hate me. It's why I've been so afraid to keep him."

"All you can do is tell him your version," I tell her. "I'm not sure you're ever going to know everything about your sister. That was her story. But you can tell Gabriel the stories you do know."

"How do you feel about Gabriel?" she asks, studying my face.

I can't hold back the smile that spreads across my face. "He's remarkable. Smart, funny, a terrible singer, and loving. He adapts quickly, easily accepting people and situations. And the sheer joy he brings to four bachelors has been remarkable."

"How do you feel about me? I know how the other three feel, but you never give me the slightest clue whether you even like me," she asks, a blush stealing across her cheeks.

Swallowing hard, I realize she's not the only one who has to take a step forward. "I feel things I shouldn't feel. I'll be forty-three years old next month. Almost ten years older than you. I'm at a different stage in life, and I don't want to get involved with someone who isn't serious about a relationship.

"When I met you, I could see the impact you were having on my team, almost from the start. And yet, you and I were completely at odds. I told myself we were too different from each other," I admit, grimacing at how hard it is to open up.

"You reminded me of my old self," she admits with a sigh. "It dredged up a lot of painful inner reflection. Things I thought I'd come to terms with long ago."

"I could see flashes of the real you when you weren't focused on Armando. It drew me in, made me want to know more," I reflect. "And the closer we came to the end, the more I realized how much you meant to all of us, including me. Instead of being happy about it, I worried what might happen to my team... my family, if you didn't make it out.

"Since you've been here, I've been waiting for you to show me that you want to stay with us. And I've been holding back because I wasn't sure if you were just teasing or if you think you could want more with an old man like me," I say, only half-joking about the age part.

"Oh, Zane," she says with a laugh. "You don't act or look like most men in their forties. In regards to age, I don't think of you any differently than the others. Hell, I feel old. Some days, it feels like I've aged two decades since all this began."

"Do you want to stay with us? Build a life here with Gabriel?" I'm almost holding my breath when I ask her.

"I spoke to Henley today," she says, making me blink at the change in subject. "She told me about her relationship with

Thiago, Mateo, and Grayson. When you ask me to stay, are you saying you want something similar?"

This is it. "Yes, we are. All of us. I know you have feelings for the others, and you and I are at the beginning, but I'm not in a hurry. I only need to know it's a possibility."

"Maybe you should give me a real kiss and find out," she taunts me.

Picking her up, I haul her into my arms. My lips find hers, and it's the sweetest thing I've ever tasted. I take my time, learning everything there is to know about kissing this woman. The shape of her lips, the stroke of her tongue, and the little things that make her catch her breath.

The kiss heats up, becoming urgent, with the sharp edge of desire. Shifting her closer, I give her a taste of the passion simmering under the surface, waiting for her. Her kiss becomes wilder and deeper, while her body shifts restlessly in my arms.

Needing to know what she's thinking, I slow the kiss and release her lips.

She stares up at me, her face flush with need, and drawls, "That was one hell of a kiss."

"So, you'll stay with us?" I ask again with more confidence.

"I want to hear it from each person," she insists, waiting until I nod in agreement. "But yes, we'll stay. Gabriel and me."

49

QUINN

When I pull into the garage, Raider is waiting for me. I sit there for a moment, trying to wrap my head around the day and Zane's kiss.

"Hi," I greet him, getting out of the car. "Zane will be home soon. He's picking up Chinese."

He pulls me into his arms and kisses me hard on the lips. "I couldn't care less about food. I'm just glad you're back." His eyes hold mine while he delves into all my secrets. "Something's changed. You look lighter."

"I feel lighter," I reply. "I let myself get sucked up into this whirlwind of emotions around Sophia and Julio, and I couldn't let it go."

"And now?"

"Talking to Margot and Zane helped me work through a lot of it. It's going to take a while to come to terms with some things, and maybe I never will, but I won't shut you out," I promise him.

He nods in satisfaction. "Good. I don't like to see you in pain. It makes me want to kill someone."

Wanting to test out the truth of Zane's words, I lean forward and place a soft kiss on Raider's lips. "You say the sweetest things." Out of all the men here, Raider is the most romantic. It could be his Latin heritage or the time he spent in France, maybe both.

He narrows his eyes. "What are you up to?"

Just testing out a theory. "Fine, I won't compliment you," I reply with a roll of my eyes.

"Where's Sterling?" I ask, needing to tell him about my decision to adopt Gabriel.

Raider tilts his head. "He's upstairs with Gabriel, giving him a bath. He's worried he might have scared you off." He gives me a speculative look.

I frown. "He didn't. And I'm sorry I made him feel that way. I'll fix it." I hand him the keys to Cruz' car and head upstairs.

Gabriel's squeals and laughter fill the hallway. I quietly tiptoe through his room to stand in the doorway and watch the two of them.

Water covers the bathroom floor, and Sterling is soaked. Gabriel's hair is standing up in a mohawk. Both are laughing. From here, it looks like they're having a squirting contest or battle. It's hard to tell.

"QUINN!" Gabriel shouts at the top of his lungs.

Relief flashes across Sterling's face. "All right. Time to get out." He dries him off and puts on his dinosaur jammies.

"Go, put him to bed," I murmur. "I'll clean this up, then we'll talk."

It takes fifteen minutes to put the bathroom back together. Sterling's still reading Gabriel a story when I walk into the bedroom.

"I'm going to grab a shower. Why don't I meet you in your room afterward?"

He gives me a terse nod.

My muscles are tight from the tension of the day. I can't help but contrast the despair I felt earlier with the hope I'm feeling now. Maybe there is a path forward. A way to put the past behind me and be proud of myself again.

The thought of being here with all of them sounds too good to be true. But I'm willing to find out if it can work out. Each of these men fulfill a different part of me, both the old and new me. Can I really do the same for them? Will they be happy with me as I am—full of broken pieces and shadows?

Sterling's door is open, and he's pacing in front of the fireplace.

"Hi," I say softly, not wanting to startle him. "May I come in?"

He waves a hand. "Please."

I sit on the edge of the chair by the fireplace. "You told me I fit with all of you earlier today. Did you mean it?"

Surprised, he nods. "I did—do. You share Cruz' willingness to leap into the unknown, Raider's darkness and determination to fight for those he loves, Zane's strong sense of personal code and integrity, and even though you've lost everything, you still have the ability to laugh, something I find remarkable."

"I'm sorry about earlier," I tell him. "There was so much swirling around in my head, I felt like I was going in circles. It took a lot of courage for you to put yourself out there first. And I'm sorry I didn't say anything in return."

I take a deep breath. "When you laugh, it warms all the cold bits inside me. I've never met anyone with such a joy for life. Even with everything you've been through, you have the capacity to love deeply and fiercely, like your father. I want more with you." My voice trails off when I see his eyes close.

They open and fix me with a hopeful stare. "And Gabriel?"

"He's staying here, with me. I'm going to adopt him," I announce, with tears in my eyes.

He falls to his knees in front of me and grabs my hands in his. "Thank God. I'm always trying to fix things, and I thought I'd screwed up royally this afternoon. You were falling deeper and deeper into this black hole. And it terrified me. It felt like the situation with my father all over again."

His thumb slides along my cheek. "When you didn't change Gabriel's name, I knew I had a small window to tell you how I felt. The timing sucked, but I needed you to hear my words."

"You love him, don't you?" I remark.

He places my hand on his heart. "Something happened the moment you gave him to me. I felt like I'd been waiting for him all my life. I can't explain it. I think I loved him instantly."

The doubt lingering in my mind disappears. "Do you love him enough to adopt him with me? Whether things work out with us or not, I want him to have you in his life. A strong man to show him the way like my fathers did for me." Both my dad and stepfather had been a huge presence in my life, and I want that for Gabriel.

A broad smile spreads across his face from ear to ear. "Seriously? Yes, yes, yes." He pulls me up from the chair. "Stay with me tonight?"

I push aside the top of my robe to show him a hint of the lace cami underneath. "I was hoping you'd ask."

He slowly peels off my robe.

The lace cami and shorts are one of the few things I kept from my old life. The set makes me feel incredibly sexy. Something every woman needs.

Fingers trail down the side of my neck and shoulder to the strap. Sliding it to the side, he bends down and follows the same path with his mouth.

Arching my neck to the side, I offer him whatever he wants.

Hands slide up the inside of my cami to my breasts. His thumbs glide back and forth across my nipples, making me gasp.

The dampness of his shirt against my skin makes me shiver. Needing to see and feel only him, I slowly reach up and unbutton it. My hands glide up his chest to his shoulders and slip it off.

Hands grip my waist as he picks me up and lays me on the bed.

"Our first kiss blew me away. It felt like the most natural thing in my life, like I'd kissed you a million times before and could kiss you a million times more. I wanted to kiss you for days," he says huskily, sliding up beside me on the bed. "In fact, some days, all I can think about is kissing you."

His lips descend, incrementally, and place the lightest of kisses over the hurt places on my face. Skating along my jaw, he slowly makes his way to my lips. When his lips finally land on mine, the kiss is languid and deep, as if he has all the time in the world.

A bubble descends, and time ceases to exist. I can't tell if his kiss lasts thirty minutes or thirty days.

His lips finally leave mine, but only so they can continue their journey, paying homage to all the delicious areas of my neck and shoulders.

A hand beneath my back lifts me up, and I raise my arms to help him take off the cami.

"So beautiful," he murmurs, looking down at me. He lowers his head and buries it between my breasts. His mouth lavishes attention on the one, and when it's aching and heavy, he moves to the other.

Arching my back, I hold him to me, while the other hand skates along his body, reveling in the feel of him in my arms.

He shifts restlessly, and I widen my legs to accommodate him.

I gasp as his mouth hits a particularly sensitive spot and pull his hips into mine, wanting to feel his hardness against me. "You have too many clothes on."

He reluctantly leaves my breasts and leans up. "You have the most gorgeous breasts I've ever seen. I could bury my face in them for the rest of my life."

With a quick twist, I switch our positions until I'm on top. "Maybe I want a turn and a taste or two." My mouth and hands seek out his sensitive spots, the ones that make his body tighten. Needing more, I remove the rest of his clothes, and mine, so I can explore the rest of his body.

Licking and touching every tantalizing inch, we drive each other crazy until neither of us can stand it anymore.

He pulls himself up to lean against the headboard, and I follow, taking him inside me. Looking deep into his gorgeous green eyes, I rise and fall, lost in the world we've created. Our lips meet in breathless kisses, while our hands grip each other tightly.

Our emotions amplify each tiny moment, each one building on the previous, causing the slow build to the pinnacle to be a tsunami rolling over us when it hits.

I shudder and lay my head on his chest, panting heavily. Sweat glistens across my skin and his.

Held within his arms, he lightly strokes my hair and back. "That was amazing, love."

50

QUINN

Armando's dark eyes shine with glee despite the blood pouring out of them. "We're two sides of the same coin, Quinn. We share in the responsibility for their deaths. How will you punish yourself?" His voice is a whisper, drowning out every other thought in my head. "See you in hell."

It's so hot. I open my eyes and find Sterling wrapped around me. As soon as I move, he wakes. "Going for a run? Want some company?"

The word no forms on my lips, but I need to start letting them in and not just when we're in bed together. "Yes, and yes. I'm going to get dressed. Meet you downstairs in ten minutes?"

His smile is extra wide. "In ten, gorgeous."

I leave his room and head to mine. After brushing my teeth and throwing my hair into a ponytail, I get dressed in leggings and a tank. While I'm tying my shoes, I stare at the sleek silver laptop lying innocently on the bed. The temptation to pick it up and finish reviewing the footage from the restaurant is strong. I reach out and grab it.

If I open it, I can see her. Alive, laughing, crying, living her life. My hand trembles. Opening the dresser beside me, I quickly toss it in and shut the drawer.

Sterling's stretching his hamstrings when I enter the foyer. "Ready to go?"

With a nod, we head out into the still dark morning. Our rhythm syncs quickly and by mile two, we're going strong.

"That's not the face I want to see on the woman who just spent the night in my bed," he jokes. "Was it that bad?"

"Well, we are up early…" I tease him.

"Killer blow," he retorts, his hand clutching his heart.

Last mile.

"Now that I've found that footage, all I can think about is finding more so I can see her again." The words spill out onto the pavement.

He's quiet for a minute. "Is that what you've been doing in your room every day?"

I tell him about Sophia and Julio. "Talking to Margot and Zane helped me wrap my head around most of it. But I still feel this overwhelming need to see more of her."

"It makes sense to me," he says, slowing to a stop when his watch beeps at the five-mile mark. "For the last three and a half years, you've thought of nothing but Sophia. Her disappearance, the investigation, her death, finding her killers, and delivering vengeance."

When I nod in agreement, he continues, "You need to retrain your mind. Find something to focus on. Preferably something that will engage your brain in the same way. Zane always needs help fielding rescue requests. We don't accept every mission. There's a strict filtering process."

A cramp kicks up in my calf, and I dig into my pocket for the baggie of salt.

"Zane?" he asks with an amused grin.

"It works," I reply with a shrug.

The house comes into view.

"You're not just Lord Charming, are you?" I tease.

A mischievous glint enters his eye. "Race you to the house? Winner makes breakfast." Without waiting for a reply, he takes off.

I kick it into high gear behind him, knowing his long legs will beat my short sticks in a straight race every day of the week. I laugh. Little does he know… I can't cook worth a damn.

He turns in a circle, arms raised high in the air, cheering his win. I plow into him, but he barely even stumbles.

"You win," I announce, with a fake pout.

"With the proper incentive, I could be persuaded to forget about the win," he offers, his voice husky. "A shower perhaps?"

Unable to resist, I stretch up and claim his mouth with mine.

"We do have neighbors, you know," a familiar voice says behind me.

I immediately tense and pull away from Sterling. "Cruz! I…" What do I even say? I'd always dated several guys at once but drew the line at sleeping with more than one. Do I tell him… Zane told me I didn't have to choose?

Sterling and Cruz exchange glances, a message passing between them. "I'm sure Gabriel is up by now. I'll see you at breakfast." He bends down and gives me a quick kiss, then strides into the house.

Cruz runs a hand through his hair. "I heard you took my Mustang out for a ride yesterday. How did it handle?"

I wince. "Sorry, I should have asked. Everything was crashing down on top of me, and I needed to get out of here. The Mustang is the only car I thought I could drive."

He grabs my shoulders. "Whoa, it's fine, Quinn. You can have anything of mine you want. There's very little that means much to me. The men in that house, our work together, you, and Gabriel. That's it. Everything else is just… stuff."

I blow out a breath. "Zane said… I'm staying. Gabriel, too. I want all of this. You." Words are escaping me. "I want more with all four of you."

He exhales and drops his forehead onto mine for a second. "You had me worried for a while. Every day, I thought you were going to run and leave us behind. I've been trying to give you support and space, but it's been tough as hell. When I left to find Rodrigo, you were so distant. I didn't know if you'd be here when I got back."

Shock renders me speechless. "I never had any idea."

He raises his head and cups my jaw with his hands. "In Monterrey, you made your priorities very clear, and I had a lot of respect for your decision. Since you've been here, I couldn't tell what you needed or wanted."

"I'm sorry," I murmur.

"What I want—we want—from you isn't going to be easy. It's going to be damn complicated and hard. Are you absolutely sure this is what you want?" he says, his keenly observant eyes watching for the slightest nuance of uncertainty.

"A hundred percent. I even asked Sterling if he would adopt Gabriel," I assure him.

He bends down and takes possession of my lips. Every stroke reminds me of him. Demanding and confident. Possessive. Sexy.

When the kiss ends, my doubts are gone.

"What's this about breakfast?" he grumbles.

I wrinkle my nose. "Sterling dictated the prize. I highly recommend getting your own breakfast or having Zane cook you something."

He glances at me in surprise. "You can't cook?"

"Not a lick," I reply.

When we enter the house, Zane is placing a plate in front of Gabriel. He scowls when he sees me. "Sterling said you were cooking breakfast?"

"For him, yes," I return, walking into the kitchen. "Do you have a toaster?"

Raider enters the room and slaps Cruz on the back. "Welcome home." He looks around at everyone's face. "What's going on?"

Sterling sits down at the island beside Gabriel. "We raced back to the house. I won, which means Quinn has to fix me breakfast. I'd like some eggs and bacon with toast, please. And juice."

Zane puts the toaster on the counter and crosses his muscular arms.

I wink at him, and his mouth twitches.

"Skillet?"

He points to the bottom cabinet nearest to him.

I squat down and grab a skillet. My other hand glides up his leg as I stand.

His head tilts, and a spark of interest flares.

I set the skillet on the stove and brush past Zane to get the butter and eggs. My whole body slides against his. "Excuse me."

"Playing with fire this morning, aren't we?"

"Little bit," I murmur, darting a look at him.

Cracking an egg into a bowl, I add a little butter and use the fork to whisk it. I set it aside. Turning the gas on, I debate whether to add anything to the skillet and decide a little olive oil couldn't hurt.

There's a glass container of it by the stove. I grab it and swirl it into the pan. Then, I throw the bacon in and turn it on.

While that's going, I turn to Zane. "Bread?"

His large hand is covering his mouth, so all that comes out is 'pantry.'

I look around, and he points to a door to the right of the kitchen. When I open it, I find shelves full of various foods and drinks. I grab the loaf of bread and close the door.

I put two slices of bread in the toaster. And turn back to the bacon. It's popping loudly now. I grab two forks and flip each piece over. They still look a little fatty, so I turn the heat up.

The bread pops up, and I put it on the plate with a slice of butter. The bacon is starting to look sort of done, so I punch in thirty seconds on the microwave. The timer goes off. I take the bowl of eggs out, but they still look runny, so I put them back in for another thirty seconds.

The bacon is dark, so I turn off the stove and add the bacon to the plate. The microwave dings. The eggs look done. I add those to the plate and put it in front of Sterling.

The entire kitchen is silent. I look around and find Cruz silently communicating with both Zane and Raider. Sterling's looking at his plate with trepidation.

Zane comes up behind me and puts an arm around my shoulders. "Aren't you going to taste it?" he taunts Sterling.

"Eat and grow strong," Gabriel chimes in.

We all laugh because it's the same thing Zane says to Gabriel every morning.

Sterling takes a bite of the toast. "It could use a little more toasting. What was the setting?"

I look at Zane. "There's a setting?"

He chuckles. "I'll show you for next time."

Sterling plunges his fork into the eggs and takes a big bite. He chews for a second, then swallows. "A little rubbery."

"What about the bacon?" I ask, leaning over to grab a piece. I take a bite. It's got a weird taste to it and it's sort of burnt. "Not good."

"You can't cook, can you?" Sterling asks wryly.

"Nope. Never had the patience for it," I reply, shrugging. "I did try, though. A bet's a bet."

Zane wraps both arms around me and bends down to kiss my lips. "Never come into my kitchen again. Got it?" When I agree, he looks at the rest of them. "No more cooking bets."

They all look at the plate in front of Sterling and laugh.

51

QUINN

After breakfast, Cruz brings us up to date on Rodrigo. "I lost him somewhere around Baton Rouge. He's headed this way, though. How he knows we're here, I'm not sure."

The four of them communicate silently.

Zane leans forward with his elbows propped on his knees. "Sterling, set up surveillance on any blank areas around the house and warehouse. He'll watch before he strikes." He turns to Cruz. "My guess is he knew you were there. I want you to be visible from now on. It's not your preference, but I want him to get comfortable, cocky even."

Cruz glowers but agrees.

"Raider, I want you to do your thing. Blend with the warehouse staff, become the most uninteresting person in the world. Plain sight. To the point he dismisses you," Zane orders.

They all swivel to me.

"You haven't carried a weapon since you got here. Why?" Zane's voice is hard when he questions me.

I think of the weapon I left buried in Armando's empty chest. "I left the gun at the apartment above the tailor's shop when I went to the event. It wasn't there when I returned." My hand clenches. "The knife became less of weapon and more of a symbol of my vengeance. I'm not sure I want to carry one anymore."

"We grabbed all the weapons when we left. I'm sure it's in the weapons room," Zane informs me. "A gun is more noticeable, but we'd feel better if you had something on you."

Me too. "I'll find one."

Raider narrows his eyes. "I'll help Quinn figure out a weapon."

Zane lifts his chin in acknowledgement. "I'm going to increase my exposure. Give him a target to focus on. I want him to think I'm the only obstacle he has to get through to get to Quinn."

"That won't be enough," I state.

"Why not?" Zane retorts.

"He wants me. If he doesn't see me, he'll sneak around until he finds me. It's better if I'm visible. Almost attainable," I point out.

The arguing starts immediately. All four men throwing in different alternatives and scenarios. I say nothing, knowing they need to come to their own conclusions.

"What about a compromise?" Zane suggests. "If you and I are frequently seen together, he'll still be able to covet you, but he'll target me first."

An idea sparks. "We may be able to speed things up." I look at the man across from me. "If he thinks we're dating, it will incentivize him to hit sooner rather than later."

Zane breaks out a rare smile. "That can be arranged."

The other three scowl.

"If he doesn't get here soon, I'm going hunting," Raider mutters.

Cruz and Sterling shoot Raider a look that clearly states their wholehearted agreement.

Zane stands. "I'm headed to the warehouse in an hour."

"I'm coming with you," I confirm, much to his surprise. "If I stay here, I'll drag my laptop out of the dresser and lose myself. Sterling thinks my brain needs to be retrained by shifting my focus to something besides Sophia. The warehouse seems like a good place to start."

Zane darts a glance at Sterling, then clears his throat. "Sounds good."

Zane explains on the way to the warehouse how it was necessary to group everyone when they got here. It allowed them to move them through the system more efficiently, based on whether they needed to be transported home or given new identities.

Those who just needed transportation home were placed in Group One. Once they were gone, they grouped individuals according to where they wanted to live after they left here. The foundation's resources are strongest in the United States, but with technology, there isn't a place they can't reach.

When we get there, the stations are already busy. People are filing through each one to get what they need. Zane introduces me to the first few stations and lets them know I'll be working with each station today to learn what they do and help them out.

He drops me off at the first station and heads back to his desk.

I hold my hand out to the woman manning the station. "Hi, I'm Quinn. What can I do to help?"

She clasps my hand briefly and hands me a stack of cards.

"Martha. Hand one of these to each person and ask them to write down their clothing sizes. I'll need you to add a note or two on height to help us figure out which clothing will be best for them. Clear?"

For the first hour, I help everyone get clothes. By the time I move to the second station, which is shoes, most of the group is already through that one, along with the one for necessities. I move to the fourth station.

I introduce myself to Bill, who explains that this station takes down personal information—hair and eye color, height, weight, date of birth, country of origin, languages spoken, and preferred exit country.

"Everyone grabs a ticket. You call them up one by one."

"Exit country?" I ask.

"Where they want to go from here," he explains. "We'll call up the first few together until you get the hang of it, then I'll set you up on your own, okay?"

With a smile, I sit down, and he calls the first number.

The young woman who comes up answers each question quickly. I write them on Bill's form but stop when she gives me a couple of answers that aren't correct.

"I'm sorry. I believe you gave me the wrong height," I tell her, showing her the answer she gave to me. "You said five feet ten inches."

"Yes, that's correct," she replies.

"At best, you're five feet eight inches," I inform her.

"I know how tall I am," she states angrily.

Bill leans over. "What's going on?"

I explain the situation.

"A couple of inches doesn't matter," he says, bewildered by my insistence.

"It does if you're using this information to create a passport and driver's license. A mistake like that will prompt customs or law enforcement to look deeper," I coolly inform them both. "Do you want a cop to start questioning you?"

She shakes her head vigorously.

"Then you need to give us the correct information. I'll put five feet eight inches for your height. Now, about your birth date."

She changes her birth date to the correct one.

Bill stomps off to speak to Zane, while I continue to take down information. Most of the people give me the correct info. There's only a couple who try to fudge something or outright lie in the case of one girl who didn't want to tell me her country of origin because she was afraid we would send her back.

Zane comes over with a wry smile on his face. "Bill quit, which means you're manning this station the rest of the day."

"At least you'll know the information is correct," I remark with a wink.

He bends down to whisper in my ear. "I'm looking forward to our date tomorrow night."

I can't help but smile. "Me too."

After he walks off, I finish the last two people, then sit there waiting for the second group.

Henley comes over and plops down beside me. "You were a cop, weren't you?" She props her elbow on the table and waits for me to answer.

I debate telling her, but since she trusted me enough to share her story, I feel I can do the same. "Eight years a cop. Almost four years as a Texas Ranger."

"Thought so. Nobody but law enforcement cares about details. I've been correcting Bill's information for two weeks. The documents have to be correct, or they aren't worth the fake paper they're printed on," she states, with a roll of her eyes.

I laugh. "Exactly. How are you doing today?"

She yawns. "Tired. I've been working on a new prototype at night, and I'm working here during the day. It's taking a toll."

"What kind of prototype?"

She looks around to see if anyone is nearby. "It's a new cyber-security app that will turn any smartphone into a secure phone.

With one tap, text messages and calls will go out encrypted, and all ancillary functions or open doors like Bluetooth will shut down. Some of this is available now, but only if you buy an expensive secure phone. I want to make this available to everyone who needs security."

"A bit dangerous to the public, but most of the world's master criminals have a secure phone. Will making it more attainable help the smaller criminals be more successful? Doubtful," I tell her. "In my experience, they usually get caught for lack of common sense, not because law enforcement tapped into their phone." I smile wryly. "Do you mind if I ask you something personal?"

"Within reason," she replies.

"How do you make your relationship work? I mean, is there a trick to it or some kind of agreement?" She's the only person I know who's in the type of relationship I'm entering.

She laughs. "I see. Good for you. Zane and the rest are good men. Even Raider, although he's also a bit scary. Transparency and communication are your best tools. You can't be shy about talking about... things like threesomes or whatever. It's hard to find time for everyone and yourself, but it's important to make sure nobody gets left out." She yawns. "Sorry."

When she yawns for the third time, the three men from yesterday come over. She swings around and introduces each of them to me.

"Nice to meet you," I state firmly.

All three are polite, but their focus is entirely on the pink-haired woman in front of me.

Thiago crosses his arms. "Henley, you're going home to rest."

When she protests, Mateo steps forward. "I'm quite capable of inputting data. You can finish the documents to your standards later."

Grayson smoothly reaches down and helps her stand. "Come on. I could use a nap, too." He gives her a conspiratorial wink, and she blushes.

"Sorry, Quinn. We'll talk more another time, I promise. And you can always text me with questions," she says pointedly.

Thiago narrows his eyes at her. "But not today. Today, you're going to rest."

A spark of defiance enters her eyes, but then another yawn hits her. "Fine. Take me home and put me to bed. Good night, Quinn."

Mateo walks over to work Henley's station. The other two leave with her.

The second group arrives, and we all get busy again.

I'm down to the last four people. Calling out the next number, I wait for the young woman to approach. When she does, she spits in my face.

"Murderer!" she screams.

I wipe my face off with my sleeve and stand to face her. That's when I realize it's the dark-haired girl from the van. Shocked, I stare at her.

"Working for a man like Armando, trafficking girls for him, you're just as responsible for her death as he is," she spits out angrily. She steps back and points to me. "Murderer. She helped traffic me for Armando."

Whispers come from the group of women nearby. Several faces fill with hate and anger. Coming closer, they start surrounding us.

Sterling and Zane push through the crowd and stand between the two of us. "What's going on?"

"She doesn't deserve to be here," she screams. "Because of her, my friend is dead." Her eyes swivel to me. "You remember the pretty blond next to me? Who held my hand and told me to be brave. Tell me—do you remember her?!"

I lift my chin. "I do. What happened?"

"One of Armando's men came and got us. He took us off the plane, then found the trackers you put behind our ears and injected into us. Armando questioned us. When he didn't like our answers, he snapped Mel's neck and put me in with the group at the facility," she answers in a voice full of hate. "One day, I'm going to kill him. And you!"

Both Zane and Sterling step forward to take control, but Cruz steps directly in front of the young woman.

He silently observes her for a minute. "She was working undercover. If she had saved your friend, all of these other people, including you, wouldn't be here. It's a tough call, and it sucks. Your friend, or yourself and a hundred and sixteen other women?"

I grip the back of Cruz' t-shirt to hold myself together.

The girl stares at Cruz, trying to decide if he's telling the truth.

With a sigh, he pulls out his phone. "You must promise never to tell anyone about this, do you hear me? If you do, your life will end. I guarantee it." His voice is soft, but the threat comes across clear. He hands her his phone.

"You did this?" she asks him.

"No, she did," Cruz replies softly.

She pushes past him and shows me the picture. "Swear on your life that you did this to him."

I look down at the picture of Armando spread-eagle in the desert with a knife staked through him and smile. "I swear, I did that to him."

With tears in her eyes, she hands the phone back to Cruz and looks at me. "I will hate you until the day I die, but with him gone, maybe I can sleep in peace."

Sterling ushers her over to the station to get her information.

Zane signals to Cruz, who takes one lingering look at me, then disappears again.

"Come on, I'll take you home," Zane says gruffly, taking my hand and tugging me away from all the people who are staring at me with contempt.

I barely hear him over Armando's whispers of punishment and hell.

52

___

QUINN

Heading straight to my room, I dig through the duffle until I find the secure phone and shoot off a text. While I wait for it to come through, I pace back and forth from one end of the bed to the other, berating myself. I should have confirmed they'd been saved a long time ago. Now, all I can think about is how her family must feel.

> Wolf: Three confirmed saves. Two missing. Still searching.

> Me: Found the fourth. Fifth dead.

> Wolf: Damn it. Perp?

> Me: Dead. Operation dismantled.

> Wolf: Good work. Later.

I can't stop thinking about the beautiful blond girl clutching her friend's hand to give her strength. An innocent girl.

Going into this, I knew I'd lose parts of me that I'd never get back, but this fucking *hurts*. Another family who will never get their daughter… sister… friend back. Who will forever wonder what happened to her and never get the answers they deserve.

This is my punishment. To know I had a hand in the trafficking and death of a young woman. Pain spears through my chest like lightning.

A door slams, and I hear someone yelling my name.

Staggering into the bathroom, I shut the door and strip off my clothes. Tears pour down my cheeks. A sob escapes, but I clamp a hand over my mouth to stifle it. I turn the shower on and get in.

The cold water stings like needles when it hits my skin. I sink to my knees and cry for Sophia, for 'Mel', and for all the young women who are kidnapped or trafficked and never make it home. Violent shivers rack my body, but I can't seem to get up. My legs won't move. I drop my head on my knees.

Strong arms reach down and pick me up. "I've got you."

The water switches from cold to warm and gradually to hot. His hands briskly rub my arms and legs until the feeling starts to come back.

When I open my eyes, there's no escaping Raider's ice-blue eyes or his fury. "You have to accept who you are now."

"I do," I insist, but my voice lacks conviction.

"Tell me. If Sophia disappeared tomorrow, would you take the same path? Knowing the outcome, would you do it all over again?" he spits out.

Would I? The image of Sophia's body splayed out in the desert flashes in my mind, and the fury I felt then rises inside. I would. She never deserved the death she received at his hands.

"Yes."

He grips my chin, refusing to let me look away. "What did you feel when you looked at the image of Armando today?"

I close my eyes.

"Look at me," Raider orders, his voice hard. "Tell me. You

liked the image, didn't you? The dark places inside you rejoiced to see him spread-eagle, on the dirt, with your knife in his chest. His dick cut off. His organs gone."

I compress my lips, refusing to let the words out.

He slams the tile beside me. "Tell me how it made you feel!"

"I fucking loved it. If I could do it all over again, I would!" I scream back at him, unable to hold back the words. "Oh God. What is wrong with me?" I drop my head back against the tile.

He jerks me up against him. "You invited the darkness in and used its strength to deliver your vengeance. There is no going back. It will never leave you. Embrace it. Feed it. Own it."

The shadows inside pulse in response to his words.

His eyes flash hot and cold. "What did you see in me when we first met?"

"Darkness. A killer," I murmur.

"Did it scare you?" he asks, jerking his briefs down.

Remembering how drawn I felt to him, I shake my head. "It was enticing. The darkness inside me recognized the darkness in you, and all I felt was need. Voracious need."

He picks me up and slams his mouth down on mine.

The kiss is rough and hard, and I can't get enough of it. I moan and wrap my legs around him. My teeth scrape along his bottom lip, and his cock jerks between us. I grip it tightly. Mine.

Lips and tongues dance and clash frantically, the battle intense, while each of us tries to make the other surrender.

A finger slides inside my body, out to rub the bundle of nerves at the top, then inside again. He ends our kiss to stare down at me. I watch the blankness that comes over him as the darkness in him takes over.

My body clenches with need, both my desire and the darkness rising up to meet his.

"That's it. Feel the darkness filling you up inside?" he asks, his voice laced with shadows. He slides another finger inside me.

"Yes," I answer, my body matching the rhythm he sets.

"How does it make you feel?" he whispers.

"Strong," I murmur.

"Louder," he orders, his hand pausing.

Needing to come, I move my hips, but he refuses me.

"Strong," I state clearly. "Please."

"Louder," he grits out, refusing to give in to my plea.

"Strong! Fearless!" I shout, and with a cold smile, he takes me over the edge. My body pulses as the pleasure rushes through my body. My chest rises and falls rapidly until I catch my breath again.

He stands there holding me until it subsides, then turns off the water. Tightening his grip, he stalks out of the shower to the bedroom and lays me across the bed. Without a word, he slides inside.

I moan at the feel of him, thick and hard, inside me.

His ice-blue eyes flicker between light and dark. He thrusts in and out, hard and fast. There's nothing soft about his possession.

"Deeper," I plead, needing more of him.

He pulls my legs to his shoulders, and I moan to feel him filling me up so completely.

"You're so fucking perfect for me," he rasps. "From the moment I met you, I was intrigued. A beautiful woman who carried the same darkness and capacity to kill? You were meant to be in my life."

"I've hungered for you, waited for you to find yourself again. To revel in the darkness that matches mine," he breathes out. "Stop trying to reconcile the old and the new. You're all of it. It's why you fit so well with us. With me."

He's relentless. I reach my hand up for his. When they meet, I entwine our fingers together and grip hard. "I need you. So much. And the darkness. I am stronger with both."

He closes his eyes. When he opens them, all the rage is gone. There's nothing but heat and desire. He sinks into me over and over until the pieces of us merge into one.

This time, I fall over the edge and take him with me.

Breathing hard, he pulls out and stands staring down at me with satisfaction. "You're so damn beautiful."

After cleaning up, we lie naked under the fan, trying to cool off.

"How did you know?" I ask him.

"We could all see it was a breaking point, but I told Zane to take you home and drop you off. I knew it was time. You needed me to remind you that the darkness inside makes you strong, not weak," he explains.

He rolls off the bed and picks up my robe. "Up, we need to go pick out a weapon."

"Now?" I give him an incredulous look.

"Nobody's home. I want to see you naked in the weapons room," he states with a shrug. "So, yes, now."

Bemused, I slide my arms into the robe he's holding. "What about you? Plan on going naked?"

With a smirk, he reaches into the bottom drawer of the dresser and grabs a pair of boxer briefs.

Surprised, I raise my eyebrows. "Confident, weren't you?"

"No, I was terrified you would run from the darkness and lose yourself," he says gruffly. "This was pure hope." He links his fingers in mine and pulls me out of the room.

When we get to the basement, I'm amazed. The safe is one big room filled with weapons. Beside it is an enclosed shooting range, and an area to practice throwing knives.

I whistle. "This is quite the setup."

"We tend to make enemies, so we need to be prepared," he replies. Waving his hand around the room, he urges me to check out the weapons.

I pick up and put down several guns until I eventually decide on the SIG Sauer P365. Spotting a garotte on the wall, I add it to my pile, along with a few of the Kubaton weapons.

Raider adds a switchblade to the pile, and I frown.

"You need to stop being so predictable and carry more

weapons," he informs me, before picking up another knife and handing it to me.

As soon as this one hits my palm, I wrap my hand around it. "It feels good," I tell him. "What is it?"

"Benchmade Fixed Adamas," he replies, running his finger down the blade. "I have one. Good balance. Lightweight."

I add it to the pile and drop my robe.

Heat flares between us. Picking me up, he lays me back on the table next to the weapons and slides down my body. When his mouth closes over me, I arch up and lose myself to his fantasy.

53

Ending the day early, Sterling, Cruz, and I rush home to find out how Quinn is doing. The look on her face when I dropped her off had me debating whether to kill Raider or not, but he'd asked me to trust him, so I let her go in without me.

When we walk in the house, Raider and Quinn are watching Gabriel sing "Bye Bye Bye" by NSYNC, and she's cracking up. Stunned, we stop and stare at them.

"Who taught him this song?" Quinn asks, her cheeks flushed from laughing so hard.

All of us point to Cruz.

I silently ask Raider if everything's truly okay, and he nods. Damn, is that a smile on his face? Close enough. A twinge of jealousy hits me, but I know it's going to take time for her and me to get there. But I do get to have the first date.

Cursing the string around my neck, I toss it down on the bed with the other two. If the dress code didn't require it, there's no way I'd put on one of the damn things. I don't know why Sterling loves them.

A smothered laugh draws my eyes to the door.

"You can stop laughing and help any time, Slick," I grumble at Sterling.

Using his forefinger and thumb, he picks up one of the ties from the bed and dangles it in front of me. "This is a mangled mess of a perfectly good tie. Good thing I came prepared."

Sliding a finger in the tie around his neck, he loosens and removes it. The grey silk drops around my neck. "There. Now all you have to do is tighten it but let me do it. Just in case."

I stand straight while he gets the tie perfect. "I don't know why I'm so damn nervous. It's not like I haven't been on a date."

"In the last year?" Sterling asks dryly.

I glare at him. "Yes, I'm not that bad," I reply stiffly.

He sighs. "She's different. Not only is she a beautiful woman, but you respect her. And you're afraid you'll fuck it up for all of us." A huge smile spreads across his face. "She asked me to adopt Gabriel with her."

I clap him on the back. "That's wonderful. He's already starting to look at you like you're his dad."

If she's asked this of Sterling, she's serious about staying with us. Some of the pressure eases.

Sterling taps his wrist on the way out. "ETA—two minutes."

Standing straight, I stare at the man in the mirror. Tall, shaved head, muscular. The black suit looks good on me. Not bad, old man. Except for the glint of silver on my shaved head that I swear wasn't there last year. Forty-three will be here in just a few weeks. Am I really starting a relationship at my age?

I stride into the living room. All three men give me a thumbs up.

"Are we ready?" I ask softly, not wanting her to hear.

"Ready," they reply in chorus.

Gabriel comes bouncing down the stairs. "Quinn is coming." He jumps up on the sofa between Cruz and Raider.

Raider leans down. "How does she look?"

"Beautiful," he whispers with a giggle.

The tap of her heels makes me straighten the sleeves and smooth the jacket one more time.

She rounds the corner, and my jaw drops.

Thank you, big guy, I say silently to the man upstairs.

She's beautiful in a green silk dress that looks like it wraps around every curve on her body. The only thing holding it up are two tiny little straps. Her legs are bare all the way down to the strappy shoes on her feet.

Clearing my throat to make sure it still works, I step forward. "You look beautiful. The green really brings out your eyes."

She brightens. "Thank you! Margot said it would look incredible on me."

"Margot helped you pick it out?" I ask. Now I'm conflicted because I still haven't forgiven Margot for the last dress she picked out.

"She sent it by courier earlier today. I tried to pay her, but she wouldn't accept it," she says with a glint in her eyes that tells me she'll find a way to pay Margot. "Honestly, I thought it was a little… short, but she assured me it wasn't. What do you think?"

She turns around in a circle, and we all groan. It stops short enough to make your palm itch to slide over her sweet curves.

Her lip is between her teeth. "It's too short, isn't it?"

"No, it's damn near perfect," I assure her. "Our reservations are in thirty minutes. Are you ready?"

She pats the small diamond pin on one strap. "Dress. Tracker. Weapon. Ready."

Hearing her say tracker and weapon eases some of my worry, but now I can't help but focus on where she could have possibly hidden a weapon under that dress.

Gabriel jumps off the couch and runs over to her. "Kiss!"

She bends over to kiss the little boy's cheek, and I see Raider slap a hand over Cruz' eyes in jest.

I usher her out of the house to the SUV sitting in the driveway. Opening the door, I lift her into the front seat. "Probably easier for me to help you in and out tonight."

"Good idea. Don't want to flash everyone," she says with a grin.

"Nope. I would have to knock someone around. It would get ugly. You would get mad. I probably wouldn't get a kiss. Better if you just stay modest and let me help," I say, only half-joking.

The first ten minutes of the drive is silent.

I sigh, worried this might have been too soon, but then I remember the whole purpose was to let Rodrigo see us. Raider and Sterling had already caught him watching us at the warehouse.

"I haven't been on a date in years," she blurts out suddenly. "It's been at least three, probably closer to four. I'm kind of nervous."

"Sterling asked me tonight if I'd been on a date in the last year. I told him yes, but I honestly couldn't remember," I admit with a chuckle.

She turns her body towards me. "There are a million things I want to know about you. Some of them are serious and some are the usual get-to-know-you questions."

"Really?"

"You're not exactly an open book. When you take a break from working, which isn't that often, you focus on someone or something around you instead of yourself," she says with a roll of her eyes. "I know you like to cook, work out, and work. And work. Did I mention work?" She chuckles when I scowl. "You're protective of everyone around you, but mostly of those in your house. You genuinely care about the world and the people who need your help. And you're an incredible kisser."

Stunned, I don't know what to say.

"See, exactly my point," she crows.

Intrigued to know what she finds important; I pick up a thread. "What is one of the more serious questions on your mind?"

She taps a finger on her mouth. "Your parents. Do you talk to them? Are you close?"

"I call my mother every week. She's a spitfire. Likes to shake things up," I say, flashing a wry look at her. "Her name is Rose, and she'll tell you herself—she has thorns."

"She sounds lovely," she replies wistfully. "And your father?" Her face is carefully neutral when she asks about him.

I tilt my head. "We don't speak."

"I'm sorry," she offers. "Do you have any siblings?"

"No, only child," I tell her.

She snorts. "Probably why you're so bossy."

"Maybe," I remark. "What else?"

"Have you ever been in love? Married?" Her eyes flick to mine.

"Yes, a long time ago. In my twenties. We were engaged, but she hated the military, and I wouldn't leave," I say softly. "What about you?"

"Hmm, never," she replies with a sad look on her face. "Love would have interfered with my career. I vowed I wouldn't fall in love or have babies until my mid-thirties. I dated a ton, but nothing serious."

"Do you want children? Besides Gabriel."

She looks surprised. "I don't know. Haven't even thought about it. What about you?"

A picture of her, belly extended, crosses my mind, and need rips through my gut. "I'm open to it. Gabriel's wonderful."

Easing my grip on the steering wheel, I pull into the parking lot of the restaurant.

When I come around to help her out, she stops me. "Did you pick this place out?"

I freeze. "No, Sterling did, why?"

She looks around at the cars and people. "Would you mind if we went somewhere else? Do you have a favorite place by the beach—something more casual?"

"Is there a reason you don't want to eat here?"

With a sigh, she waves her hand. "You're already formal most of the time. Not in the way you dress, but in the way you conduct yourself. If we go in there, you're going to adopt that demeanor. I'd rather keep this relaxed vibe going." Her eyes search mine, trying to see if I'm offended or not.

I smile. "Do you like seafood?"

"Love it."

She scoots back in and buckles her seatbelt.

About ten minutes down the road, I pull into another busy parking lot. "It's called The Admiral. An old Navy vet bought it thirty years ago. He's retired, and it's now run by his son. The best seafood around, and you can put your toes in the sand after dinner."

"Perfect."

I send a quick text to the team to let them know we changed venues just in case the trackers aren't working.

When I come around to get her, she stops me. "Maybe take off your jacket. But leave the tie. It looks good."

I slip it off and toss it in the back, then roll up my sleeves. Gripping her by the waist, I lift her out.

The joint is hopping with regulars. Most of them military men, like me. It's a place we can hang out and talk about the service without anyone overhearing or butting in with their opinion.

Joe, behind the bar, calls out a greeting and waves me to the tables. I point to the outside patio, and he gives me a thumbs up.

"Which one?" I ask her.

"They all have fabulous views of the ocean. This one." She decides and moves to one of my favorite tables in the corner.

I pull back her chair before taking the seat across from her.

Joe comes around and asks us what we want to drink. To my surprise, she orders a beer. I do the same.

"Didn't know you were a beer drinker. What are some of your favorites?"

"Mmm, I'll drink a few sips of anything, but I really love the darker beers. Brown ales, especially."

We toss a few of our favorites back and forth until Joe returns. "Here you go. A Hooter Brown for the lady, and a Crazy Lady for Zane. Now, what can I get you for dinner?"

She looks at me. "What's good here?"

"Everything. I'll take the fresh catch," I tell him, handing the menu back.

"Same," Quinn repeats.

When he walks away, she stares out at the ocean in the moonlight. "The contrast between a few weeks ago and this moment is stark. If a psychic had predicted I'd be sitting at a beachside patio, with a handsome man, on a romantic date, I probably would have shot them for being a fraud."

Romantic date. It takes everything in me not to grin. "I know we're not in the same place as you are with the others. Do you mind?" I tip my beer back while I wait for her to answer.

"To be honest, everything has been so fast. I'm loving the idea of dating and everything that goes along with it. Getting to know each other, talking about the serious stuff, flirting, and making out, of course," she says with a smile.

"Hmm, it does sound better, especially the flirting and making out part," I say, wiggling my eyebrows.

My phone buzzes with a text. "Showtime," I murmur, discreetly slipping the earpiece into my ear.

She frowns. "What is it?"

"Rodrigo," I whisper. "We took precautions just in case."

A shutter comes down over her face. "I forgot the reason we were on a date."

The earpiece makes me hesitate for a brief second. Screw it. "Quinn, everything about this date is real. The way I feel about you, my answers to your questions, my favorite place to eat. All of it. You look so damn beautiful tonight. It makes me want to shoot him on sight."

She searches my face for the truth, and I hold my breath. Pushing her chair back, she stands and walks over to my side of the table. "Thank you." Her lips brush mine several times. "If you'll excuse me, I'm going to the ladies."

"Damn, I need to step up my game," Raider says with a whistle the minute she walks away.

I chuckle. "Get in line, boys."

Sterling breaks in. "Is she back yet?"

I immediately stand. "No. I'll go check." The door to the ladies bathroom is wide open. Panic tries to take hold, but I stomp it out. A flash of green at the bar stops me in my tracks. She's at the bar laughing with the old man next to her.

I come along her side and place my arm around her waist. "Admiral." I greet the old geezer with a respectful nod.

He glares at me. "Zane. Damn it, I was hoping this pretty young thing was available. How did you swing her?"

I look down at her green eyes shining with laughter. "Hell, if I know. She didn't like me much at first. Guess I wore her down."

He laughs and slaps the bar. "Good for you."

Joe sets two beers down in front of her, but I reach out and take them.

"Thanks, Joe. Admiral."

"Is he really an Admiral?" she whispers when we walk away.

"He was. War hero, too," I inform her.

Our food comes shortly after we sit back down.

"This grouper is delicious, but the hushpuppies are chef's

kiss!" she exclaims. "You know we're going to have to come back here often, don't you?"

The words settle into my bones, erasing any lingering doubts about her feelings for me.

54

QUINN

Using his arm to balance, I slip off my shoes and walk out onto the cool night sand, with Zane behind me. The inky midnight water is smooth as glass tonight, with little waves lapping onto the shore. We walk for about a half mile, then stop. I breathe in deeply and turn to flash Zane a smile. Even with the threat of Rodrigo hanging over us, this has been an incredible date.

He wraps an arm around my shoulders and pulls me back against him. "So, where are we going on our second date?"

My mouth twitches. "A cooking class?"

He chuckles. "Absolutely not. What about a jazz club?

I shrug. "I'm not sure I've ever really been to one."

"There's a great indoor—outdoor jazz place here. Perfect for dancing," he tells me.

"Dancing, huh? You really are pulling out all the stops," I tease him. "I'd love to."

He bends down and whispers, "He's here. Behind me. Are you ready?"

I slide a hand to the inside of my thigh and pull out the knife Raider picked for me. "Ready."

He chuckles. "I want you to tell me later how you managed to hide that big knife under that tiny dress. Wait for it. Now."

Zane and I turn. Rodrigo rushes toward us. Cruz appears suddenly, to the right of Rodrigo, forcing him to come to a stop.

"We've been waiting for you, Rodrigo. Tell me, what did you hope to accomplish? Or was the need driving you? You know, the one that escapes from you now and again," I taunt him. "The one that made you kill Lupe."

"You're mine. Armando promised you to me when I told him you killed Julio," he hisses.

"Funny, Armando told me he wanted me for himself," I say in a droll voice. "Which is it?"

Rage eclipses the cunning in his eyes. "He had some crazy idea to raise Gabriel with you. It didn't mean anything." He waves a knife in the air. "Remember this? I found it buried in Armando's chest."

Confused, I tilt my head. "The only way you could have found it is if you followed us. How?"

"Did you enjoy playing in my house?" He cackles wildly. "I couldn't believe it. You chose my house to gut that coward, Armando. When I arrived to lick my wounds, I saw him"—he points to Cruz—"standing in the doorway. Curious, I stuck around to figure out what was going on."

He takes out his phone and waves it around. "I have pictures of you, and those other two, staking Armando's body in the desert. When I show them to the cartel, they won't blame me for his death. Of course, your dead body will be in my trunk. It will be my invite back to the party."

"You're outnumbered," I tell him, waving at the three of us.

"You don't think I'd show up without leverage, do you?" he says with a snarl.

The darkness sitting beneath the surface blinks at him. "Tell me, what do you have that I could possibly want?"

"Gabriel," he says smugly. "Armando put a tracker in him. He was always paranoid something would happen to his sobrino. I went back to the house and found the information in his study. Tracked Gabriel to their house." He points to Zane. "He was fast asleep in his little race car bed. It was incredibly easy to pick him up and carry him out the front door."

My blood turns to ice. "Where is he?"

"Not too far away. Will you trade yourself for him?" His beady eyes are full of glee.

Does he not think I'll kill him when Gabriel's safely away? What makes him think he can make the exchange without that happening?

I step forward. Cruz and Zane follow.

"You two step back," he warns them. "Or I'll blow up the car with the boy in it." He holds up a small black object.

I contemplate whether the device is real or not, but it doesn't matter. I'm not willing to chance it. "How do you want this to work?"

"You and I will walk to the car. Once you're inside with the bomb, I'll release Gabriel," he says.

"Fine, let's go," I say impatiently, tired of fucking around with this little toad.

"Not so fast. I need to make sure you're not carrying more weapons. Give the big guy your knife," he orders me. Once I give it to Zane, Rodrigo motions me closer. "Turn around, arms out."

His disgusting hands pat every inch of me down.

The only way I get through it without losing my shit is to look at Zane, who holds my gaze the entire time.

"It's not rocket science. Are you almost done?" I ask with a chuckle.

He punches the back of my head.

Cruz steps forward, but Zane grabs him.

He grabs my elbow and pulls me along, making sure to keep me between him and Cruz.

When I get to the car, I look in the backseat and see Gabriel sleeping. The icy cold rage I thought had died with Armando flares to life. Raider's right. There will always be a part of me that lives in darkness.

"What did you do to him?"

"Just a little injection to make sure he stayed asleep. He'll wake in a few hours," he says, rolling his eyes. "Get in."

When I'm in, he jabs my arm and shuts the door.

I turn around and watch while he picks up Gabriel and carries him over to Cruz, who angrily questions him about why Gabriel's not awake.

It makes me glad I'm not wearing an earpiece. Sterling must be losing his mind right now. My thoughts are drowsy. Raider's face pops up by the driver's side passenger window, but when I blink, he's gone.

Rodrigo gets in and looks over at me. He slaps my cheek a few times. I try to slap him back, but my hand waves uselessly in front of me.

It's the last thing I remember.

When I wake, I'm hanging by a rope, my toes barely scraping the floor below me. The tightness in my wrists tells me I haven't been hanging long. I scan the rest of me and sigh in relief to see my dress intact.

The smell of farm animals and manure permeates my senses. Lifting my head a tiny bit, I see straw nearby. A barn?

A snuffling sound from my left confirms it. Without a doubt, that's a pig.

"Oh, look who's awake," Rodrigo says cheerfully.

The snuffling sound comes again. "A pig barn, huh? How appropriate."

He backhands me, and pain explodes across my face.

Damn it. I had almost healed.

When the pain recedes, I raise my chin and spit at him. He

stalks forward, but this time, I lift my leg in a roundhouse and kick him across the face.

Cursing, he stumbles back, cradling his cheek for a few minutes. With a grin, he spits blood on the floor and pulls out my knife.

He cackles. "For the first time, I don't have to worry about Armando finding out about me. He kept me on a tight leash. Always threatening to go to the cartel and tell him about my little playthings." His hand caresses the knife. "For months, all I dreamed about was you, but he refused to give you to me. But now, you're mine. I've been waiting for you for so long."

The crazy look in his eyes is worrisome. He might just kill me before the others can track me down. I start swinging my legs to get momentum, preparing to give him the fight of his life.

The coldest blue eyes I've ever seen comes up behind him. Raider quickly slices across Rodrigo's wrist several times.

Howling, he drops my knife and turns to face his attacker.

"Where did you come from?"

"The same place you're going... hell," Raider says, striking in three new places. "Pick up the knife. Go ahead, I'll wait."

Rodrigo picks up the knife, and Raider slashes across his face.

"Good one," Rodrigo says, slashing out with the knife in his hand.

Zane, Cruz, and Sterling enter the barn.

Rodrigo panics, but Raider steps in front of him. "It's just you and me. They're here for her." He slices him three more times.

Rodrigo slashes out wildly with the knife. When he can't hit Raider, he pivots and rushes toward me. Zane steps up and smashes his fist into his face.

Rodrigo falls to the ground, nose bleeding profusely, but quickly scrambles back up. He searches for the nearest exit, but it's blocked by Cruz. Squaring up, he runs toward him, knife raised, but Cruz grabs his wrist and twists until the knife is pointing at Rodrigo. Cruz uses sheer strength to make Rodrigo push the knife into his own stomach inch by inch. Rodrigo starts screaming, but with Cruz' hand wrapped around his, he can't let go.

The murderous look in Cruz' brown eyes is utterly captivating.

Cruz shoves Rodrigo back to Raider.

Sterling gets the rope untied from the wall and lowers me down into Zane's arms. Who then gives me a kiss and sets me down on my feet.

When Rodrigo sees me standing nearby, he scrambles in my direction, a plea for mercy on his lips. Sterling steps in front of me and brutally lays into him, hands and feet flying, until he's crumpled on the ground.

Rodrigo laughs. "Looks like I'm going to hell tonight."

I walk over to the sick bastard. "Get up."

He shakes his head no.

Raider grabs him by the hair and jerks him into a standing position.

Without another word, I move to Raider's side and take his hand. Together, we slice across Rodrigo's throat. Blood sprays everywhere, and he's dead before he hits the ground.

The pride gleaming in Raider's eyes makes me smile.

I turn to Sterling. "Gabriel? Caroline?"

"He woke up an hour ago. Our doctor is checking him out," he assures me. "But he thinks Gabriel will be fine." Green eyes meet mine in relief. "Caroline's got a concussion. She's spitting mad that he grabbed Gabriel, but she'll fine too."

Thankful, I close my eyes for a brief second.

The phone. "We need to get Rodrigo's phone and delete those pictures."

Cruz holds it up. "Done." He takes the SIM card out and puts it in his pocket. He strides over and kisses me hard on the mouth. "Let's go home."

55

QUINN

Neither of us were willing to let Gabriel out of our sight last night, so Sterling and I put him between us. I sit up and glance at the clock. Nine-thirty a.m. Gabriel's staring at me with wide eyes. He swivels his head to look at Sterling, who's also wide awake and staring at the two of us with a fierce expression on his face. It will take him a while to get over this.

"Is everyone awake but me?"

"Now everyone is awake," Cruz grumbles from the floor.

I lean over the bed and find three mattresses scattered around the bed. Raider, Cruz, and Zane are all looking up at me.

"Well, I don't know how you're going to top that date night," I tease Zane.

He grunts. "I'll take something a little less exciting for eight hundred, please." His grey eyes scan my face. "How are you feeling?"

My lips twitch at his Jeopardy! quote.

"Sore, relieved Gabriel's okay, happy he's gone," I state, looking at Raider with a smile. "How did you get there so quickly?"

"Raider slid into the backseat at the restaurant. He couldn't do anything with you drugged in the front seat. We knew you had the tracker, but it's not foolproof. When you arrived at the barn, he couldn't get cell reception to alert us to your location, so he had to climb to the roof. When he climbed down, he saw you kick Rodrigo in the face," Zane explains, anger in his voice.

I wink at Raider.

"Can we remove the tracker from him?" I pointedly nod at Gabriel.

"We need some pretty sophisticated equipment to even locate it. Thankfully, Henley has something that will work at her office. Once we find the chip, we'll pull it to the surface and cut it out. It's incredibly tiny, so he won't require more than a dinosaur band-aid," he says, wrapping Gabriel in his arms.

"And no more talk of tagging us?" I eye him, knowing that he's been thinking about it.

"No," he shudders.

Standing, I stretch. The long t-shirt I'm wearing rides up to the tops of my thighs, and Cruz' brown eyes smolder.

I pull it down and walk around him to get to the door. One second, I'm standing, and the next, I'm lying beside Raider with a knife in my face. "Don't forget your knife."

I wrap my hands around the hilt and lean up to give him a kiss. "Thank you." Scrambling to my feet, I make my way out of the room.

After showering and doctoring my face, I head downstairs to search for Zane. He's talking to Gabriel while he eats his breakfast. The sight of this huge man talking to this tiny little boy makes my heart melt.

I slide my arm around his waist. "When you're done here, want to call Eduardo with me?"

His eyes light up. "Yes, definitely."

Fifteen minutes later, I'm sitting in Zane's lap, calling the number Eduardo gave to me.

He picks up on the first ring. "Hola."

"Eduardo, it's Quinn. We got him. Él está muerto."

"Gracias, thank you," he says over and over with the sound of tears in his voice.

I hand the phone to Zane, who talks to him about using his tailor's shop for future missions. He'll pay him to rent it.

He hangs up a few minutes later.

Lying back in Zane's arms, I run my hand over the silky smoothness of his head and down the back of his thick neck.

Zane's eyes are slate gray when he looks down at me. "You feel good in my arms."

"You know, there was only one thing wrong with our date," I muse.

He raises a single eyebrow. "Only one?"

"I didn't get a kiss," I reflect. "Such a shame. I really, really wanted one."

Pouty lips capture mine. Shifting in his lap, I pull him in tighter, wanting to feel his big body wrapped around mine. Arms come around me and hold me tight while the kiss obliterates every thought in my brain.

He pulls back and ends the kiss. When I reach for him, he captures my hands. "We have all the time in the world. I'm enjoying this slow burn."

"Me too." I wink. "I think."

He stands straight up with me in his arms. "Besides, we're all feeling a little anxious today, especially when you're out of our sight. Let's go find the others."

I've been feeling the same way about them and Gabriel, so I nod.

When we get to the living room, everyone's lounging around. Zane sets me down between Raider and Cruz and grabs the recliner.

I look from Cruz to Raider, and I hear Henley telling me to be transparent and communicate. Even when it's delicate situations like threesomes. The thought of spending the night with these two men has me squirming.

My eyes wander to Sterling and Zane. I wonder if all four of them would be up for a group night.

Maybe after we've been together a while, I muse. Zane and I aren't even to that stage yet.

The fact that I can even think about the future is a miracle. I never expected to walk away from Mexico. Yet, here I am, with an adorable nephew and four incredible men who will fight for our future. My family. The one I've been missing for such a long time. I'm slowly finding my own peace and coming to terms with the person I am now. Light and dark. Someone who matches them in every way.

Almost four years ago, my sister disappeared. For a long time, I couldn't picture her at peace, but I feel it now. I think she found peace when I found Gabriel. Maybe she wasn't sticking around because of her death, but to help me find the son she loved so much.

EPILOGUE

QUINN

Six months later…

With a groan of exhaustion, I shut the door to the warehouse. All one hundred and seventeen women have found a way forward, either by returning home or finding a new one.

The young girl from the van, Ana, went home to her family. Still angry and confused, but alive.

Over the last couple of months, I've started to work with Zane to learn how to filter the requests that come in from all over the world. People pleading with the foundation to rescue them. It's been tough work, sifting through the information, picking out different details that raise a red flag or present a potential danger to our team.

Our team. It feels so good to say it. A month ago, we rescued a young scientist who had found a new cure for a specific type of blood cancer. His government wanted to sell it to the highest bidder, but he wanted to give it to the world.

Not only were we able to get him out, but Henley helped him develop the solution by putting him in touch with the right people and sponsoring the development with her company. The complete remission numbers are significantly higher than previous treatments, indicating a higher number of cured people in the future.

Zane padlocks the door and tugs me into his side. "It will be nice not to have to come to the warehouse every day."

"It will give us more time to spend on the foundation and together. All of us. It seems like we've all been spread thin the last few weeks," I remark.

A yawn catches me off guard.

Zane frowns at me and holds the back of his hand to my forehead. "You're not getting sick, are you? You've been tired all day."

"It's been a late couple of nights," I murmur. "After a shower, I might grab a nap. Care to join me?"

While Cruz will often take a nap with me, the others are usually too full of energy to relax.

To my surprise, Zane agrees. He must be worried about me.

Nobody's home when we get there, and I head straight to Zane's room. Dropping clothes into the basket, I get in the shower and let the hot water cascade over my sore muscles. It took us a while to stack all the tables and chairs.

Large hands knead my shoulders, easing the tension and erasing the knots, until I'm almost putty in his hands. "Mmm, that feels good."

He grabs the soap and slowly washes my body from head to toe. With every stroke of his hands, my body hums with desire.

Breathing heavily, I turn to face him. "My turn."

He shakes his head and sinks to his knees. "Let me take care of you." He raises my leg over his shoulder, and his mouth works its magic. Need thrums in my veins, and I push my hips forward, wanting more. When he sucks me into his mouth, I explode.

He stands, picks me up in his arms, and slides into me.

His cock is thick and feels so good. His pace is slow at first, building the heat between us, but it picks up. Moaning, I throw my arms around him and hold on tight while he thrusts rapidly. I reach between us and stroke myself, until I come again. My body milks his as I ride out the waves racing through my body.

Hearing my release, he thrusts a few more times until he follows with his own. Breathing hard, he slowly lets my legs drop, then sets me down.

After washing off again, the tiredness hits me like a wave crashing down on me. In one of his large t-shirts, I crawl up the bed and lie down. He slides in behind me, holding me in his arms, and I fall asleep in seconds.

"Sweetheart, it's almost seven. Do you want to get up and have some dinner?" he asks, smoothing back the damp hair from my face.

I stretch. "Sounds good."

"Will you please go to the doctor and get checked out?" he pleads.

I smile at the worry on his face. "I already went."

"And?" His brows are lowered while he waits for me to answer.

I'd already fallen in love with the others and told them so, but Zane and I moved at a different pace. He wanted to go out on dates and romance me. Secretly, I'd loved it, although I was thoroughly frustrated by the time we actually had sex. The man is seriously patient.

"Zane, I love you. I know I haven't told you yet, but I've been in love with you for a while."

He sits up. "You're scaring me."

Smiling, I lay my hand on his cheek. "I'm pregnant."

He stares down at me in shock. "The doctor confirmed it?"

I nod. "What do you think about becoming a dad at forty-three?"

His eyes fill with tears. "On our first date, you asked me if I wanted children. I'd never thought about it, but suddenly, I could see you swollen with our child." He shudders. "I love you so much. And I can't wait to be a dad." He lays his hand on my flat belly.

A loud squeal comes from the living room. "Come on," I say, pulling him to his feet.

When I enter the room, Gabriel runs over and launches himself into my arms. "Aunt Quinn!"

While I love Gabriel like a son, I wanted him to know Sophia. I told him he can call me whatever he wants. Right now, he calls me Aunt Quinn.

"What did you do with Caroline today?"

He's telling me all about their puppet show when Sterling, Raider, and Cruz walk in. In a flash, he abandons me for them.

I go into the kitchen and try to help Zane set the table, but he refuses to let me.

"Quinn, I've got this. Please go sit down," he snaps at me.

I throw up my hands and grab a seat at the table.

"What's going on?" Cruz says, giving me a kiss.

"Nothing," I say, glaring at Zane.

The three men exchange worried glances. "I give up. I wanted to wait to tell you after dinner, but keeping a secret around here is impossible. We're having a baby."

Cruz glances over at me and runs a hand through his hair. "You're pregnant? How? I mean, I thought we were using something."

"I was late getting my shot renewed," I reply, my eyes narrowed in anger.

"I'll make an appointment for you to go to the doctor first thing in the morning," Sterling states firmly, picking up his phone.

Turning to Sterling, I shake my head. "My doctor's appointment was on Monday. Everything is good."

Raider still hasn't said a word.

Gabriel comes over and sits down next to me. He's quietly watching it all. His lip quivers. "Are you sick?"

"No, sweetheart. I'm not sick," I reassure him. "We're going to have a baby. Do you think you'll like having someone to play with and protect?"

He thinks about it for a second. "No."

Sputtering, I laugh. "We'll see."

Sterling comes over and lifts me out of the chair. "Another one. I feel like you're spoiling me, giving me all these children. I can't wait." His kiss is tender and sweet.

Cruz comes over, an apology on his lips. "I'm sorry. That shouldn't have been my first question. It was such a shock. I never thought about having one of my own." He looks down at my stomach with a worried expression on his face. "Do you think I'll be a good father?"

"Yes," I say, cupping his face. "Look how good you are with Gabriel. Just give him the important stuff you missed out on with your dad."

He buries his head in my shoulder and lifts me up. "I love you."

"I love you, too," I murmur, kissing him fiercely this time. It amazes me how good he is with Gabriel when you consider his experience with his father.

He sets me down and I look around for Raider, finally finding him outside.

"Are you unhappy about the baby?"

He turns to me, and a tear slips down his face. "I can't wait to be a father, but I warn you, I want more than one."

I slip into his arms. "That can be arranged."

His kiss is demanding, and deep, almost like he's already thinking of more.

"I missed you," I tell him. "How did your visit go with your brother?"

"He's naturally suspicious, but I assured him we could start with a conversation on the phone every once in a while and figure it out from there." Leaning down, he captures my lips in a heartfelt kiss. "Thank you for pushing me."

"Family's important," I remind him.

He lays his palm on my stomach. "It is."

Zane sticks his head out and scowls at Raider. "She needs to eat."

When we get inside, all four of them start discussing me and the baby as if I'm not even here. How much sleep I'll need, what foods I can eat, the things we'll need for it, and so much more. Instead of getting irritated, I bask in it. In the beginning, I wondered if I deserved to be happy, but I don't anymore. They're mine and I'm theirs. For us, it's that simple.

THANK YOU!

Thank you for reading! I wanted Cruz, Raider, Sterling, and Zane to have their HEA, but I couldn't picture them with Henley from The Savages Series. (Although I certainly flirted with the idea.)

I'd love to hear your thoughts. Whether it's "give me more," or "I want to see a book with…" reviews help me write the next story. Please consider leaving one for this book.

*If you find an error, feel free to email me at Stellabrie@stellabrie.com.

To get a free eBook copy of my first book, My Salvation, just subscribe to my newsletter.

Website: https://www.stellabrie.com/my-salvation

AWESOME PEOPLE

Huge thanks to everyone who make my books possible!

To my readers, friends, and fans! Thanks for all the wonderful words of encouragement, friendship, and love for my books! And for participating in my shenanigans and all the other weird things I post. You guys rock! I couldn't do it without you!!!

My beta readers, who catch so many big and little things, help me with names, show me such amazing friendship, encouragement, and excitement, even when you can't share it with anyone! I know my books are a thousand times better because of your feedback. Thank you, Nia, Bianca, Iliana, Melissa, Rachel, Sandi, and Debbie for everything!

My ARC teams who gives me so much support and enthusiasm even though I drop things on them at the last minute. Ooh, look, cover reveal! Book's launching in a week! Seriously, I appreciate all of you!! Love all the generous reviews and gorgeous content you create for TT and IG. You guys are truly awesome for taking the time to give my books and me some love and showcase your incredible creative talent! Thank you!

My biggest supporters—my husband and mom. I'm so lucky to have you both! Love you!

And always… a special thanks to all the wonderful authors in the why choose community who support each other day in and out. Writing would be a lonely and weird world without you. It would be me and my characters sitting around chatting (drinking) while we plot the next book. Your friendship and support mean a lot to me!

ABOUT THE AUTHOR

Stella Brie lives outside of Nashville, TN, with her husband. After mentioning her desire to write a book a million times to her husband, he challenged her to sit down one day and write a paragraph. Instead, she wrote her first book, *My Salvation*.

She traded in her career in digital marketing, working on big brands, for this wildly creative one. Armed with a notebook crammed full of ideas, she's constantly thinking about bold heroines, sexy men, and HEAs. Whether it's a paranormal book full of creatures and magic or a contemporary romance full of heat and drama, she's always thinking about how she can bring her books to life.

Latest News and Updates:
Facebook Group: Stella's Stalkers
Instagram: @stellabrie_author
TikTok: @stellabrie_author
Join my Newsletter: StellaBrie.com - Exclusive sneak peeks, cover reveals, giveaways, and more!